Second Chances

A **ROMANCE WRITERS OF AMERICA**® COLLECTION

RWA

Romance Writers of America®
14615 Benfer Road
Houston, TX 77069

This anthology is a work of fiction. The names, characters, places, and incidents are products of the writers' imaginations, have been used fictitiously, and are not to be construed as real. Any resemblance to persons living or dead, actual events, locale, or organizations is entirely coincidental.

SECOND CHANCES: A ROMANCE WRITERS
OF AMERICA® COLLECTION

Table of Contents

THE FISHER MEN: LEVI'S STORY
A WILD SEASONS SHORT

Christina Lauren

Levi

IT'S A STRANGE FEELING to have every tiny moment of my life documented.

Granted, I *should* be used to it by now: last fall a camera crew boarded the larger of our two boats—the *Linda*—and, aside from the few precious moments we're in the bathroom each day, have barely left our sides since.

There's not much else that's off limits. *The Fishermen* airs on The Adventure Channel every Thursday during primetime and chronicles the lives of my two older brothers and me as we fish up and down the Pacific Northwest, spend our downtime at the local bars, and generally try not to make complete asses of ourselves on national television.

The constant presence of cameramen and boom mics is why, as I step through the tiny pocket door from the bathroom and into the sleeping quarters I share with Finn and Colton, I've put on a towel. Dave stands, tinkering with the settings on his camera for dim light. Ellis is watching him, waiting for the go-ahead.

Colton is mumbling something as he fully comes to, cranky. It's three in the morning, and Dave woke us all up a half hour early when he knocked his equipment box down the narrow steps into the belly of the boat. Of course, Colt can't complain about that on camera so he's staring at the floor, face a tight portrait of *Irritation*.

I try to maneuver around the crew as I gather my clothes and head into the bathroom to dress. When they're not filming, we're on the boat for twelve, maybe fifteen hours, and then back to land and home to our own beds. Much preferred by all. But our producer, Matt Stephenson-John, likes the "dynamic of the brothers on the boat," which I really think means he likes when we get at each other's throats. So, when the film crews are here, the three of us stay for an entire week in the *Linda's* cramped sleeping quarters. Colton complains about every damn thing, and Finn wants to murder us after two nights.

The worst part is right now we're not even out on open water; we're still docked at the slip, awaiting a shipment of lumber we need to fix a couple of interior walls. The life of a fisherman often includes more maintenance than actual fishing.

Like today. While we do the repairs, Hollywood will be shooting filler footage—the stuff that's coupled with dramatic music or narration to set up a subplot about the rough life we have out here or to lead into some much-deserved down time with "locals" (aka models flown in from Vancouver). If there's one thing I've learned so far, it's that shirtless filler footage seems to trump everything else. I'd like to pretend the focus of the show is the plight of the modern-day fisherman, the changing environment, and our constant struggle to keep up with it all, but as my sister-in-law, Harlow, repeatedly points out, the show is really just about the man candy.

And by *points out* I mean she sends us Tumblr memes, GIFs, and, once, notice of the hashtag #noshirtthursday trending on Twitter.

It drives Finn crazy but, to be fair, I'm not really bothered by it. The show is the reason we still have a boat and the reason we're even still on the water. Without it, we would have lost everything, and the life I've always known—along with the company my grandfather started—would have been gone for good. Fishing these waters isn't the same as it was when my great-great-grandfather was doing it. There's more competition and fewer fish. The odds are against all of us. So if I get to be out on the water, who cares if there's a camera in my face?

The air is cold as I make the short climb to the deck. I hear Finn before I see him, already shouting orders to Colton as they attempt to untangle a net that snagged on some debris.

"Walked up here to find him like this," Colton says, unruly hair covered by a wool cap. I can still see the pillow lines on his face as he squints down at the wire he's splicing. "Thought I'd at least give him someone to yell at."

I look past them to the pallets of wood on the weathered dock. "Everything here?"

"Yeah, delivered about an hour ago." Colton looks up. "Rain coming in. Probably need to get it all on board and covered before it starts."

I follow his gaze to where the sun should be, but there's nothing but gray sky and angry clouds in the distance. "Let's get to work."

I stand on the deck, watching as the crane operator lifts the banded material and the machine creeps toward me.

"Easy," I shout, motioning for him to come forward, keeping an eye on the bottom of the cradle as it swings in the air. It's even darker now; the incoming storm is reflected in the gunmetal waves as they lap with increasing force against the hull. The temperature continues to drop and the air smells of pine and salt as the wind picks up, whipping at our clothes and jostling the *Linda* against the dock.

"A little higher." I lean farther over, needing the load to clear the side. "A little more …"

Out of the corner of my eye I can see the camera rolling and, for a split second, I take my eyes off the crane. And that's when it happens. The operator swings a hair too wide as the wind whips through the harbor, and the entire thing tips. Two boards slip from the center of the bundle and hit the deck with a thundering crack, a section of one shearing off with the impact and ricocheting against the wood and then up, straight toward me.

I'm thrown back from the force of it.

I hear Finn and Colton's voices—they're yelling, they're running—before I realize what's happened. Warmth seeps along my leg, and when I push myself to sit, I see a two-foot-long shard of wood going through my pants and straight into the center of my thigh.

Chapter Two

WHEN I OPEN MY eyes again, my head feels fuzzy.

"There you are," Colton says. His fingers are cold against my arm. "Should have known you'd try to get out of work."

"Holy hell." My throat is dry and my voice cracks. When I try to sit up, I find that I'm tethered to the bed with about a dozen tubes and cords. My leg feels like it's on fire. I just *hurt*.

Finn leaves the group of men he's been talking with and moves to stand on my other side. "If you needed a nap, you could have asked."

The doctor is at my side almost immediately. "How're you doing there, Levi?"

My voice is broken glass and sandpaper. "I've been better."

"You've got a pretty nasty puncture. We were able to get most of the splinters out, but because of the nature of the wound and the chemicals used in the pressure-treated lumber, we're not going to stitch it up yet."

I blink at the group of men in the corner, including Matt and the other producer, Giles Manchego. Panic clenches in my gut. Although the first season has started to gain steam, and we've just begun filming the second, I know the contract allows for termination at any time if we're unable to perform our regular duties.

Like, one might think, *fishing*.

Finn correctly reads my expression and squeezes my arm. "It's okay, Lee," he says quietly. "I don't think they'll admit it, but they fucking *love* this. They got it all on camera." He motions to my bandages. "Something tells me they're going to milk the shit out of it."

I ignore him.

"What do I need to do to get back on the boat?" My voice is stronger now, and I push up onto an elbow.

Finn and Colton share a look before being joined by the producers. "I had a feeling you were going to say that," Giles says, pleased. "We've come up with a compromise. If you agree to it, of course."

"Okay," I say, wary. Finn's jaw is tight, and I know him well enough to know—whatever the idea is—he doesn't love it, but isn't going to say no, either. Colton, on the other hand, looks like he's about to laugh.

"We're going to let you return to the boat next week, on the condition that you allow a nurse on board," Matt says, and manages to deliver this news without giggling gleefully.

A nurse on the *Linda*, tending to my injuries while we shoot filler footage of Finn and Colton throwing nets and rewiring the fuse boxes?

The hell?

"A nurse?" I repeat.

Matt nods. Finally, Colton can't contain his laughter, and a giddy bark breaks free of him before he covers his mouth with a fist, coughing out, "Sponge baths, man."

"I still think this is a bad idea," Finn growls. "I mean, come the fuck on."

"We realize it's not ideal, but we've already scheduled the water crew for on-deck shoots for the next couple weeks," Matt tells him. "We can't change the shot list without a lot of juggling, guys."

"And once we push off, Levi won't want to stay at home, off the boat," Giles reasons.

I nod. "It's true, but—"

Matt puts his hand on my arm. "There is no *but*. Without medical personnel monitoring the injury, the studio lawyers won't let you step foot off the dock. This solution satisfies everyone."

"And helps ratings," Finn says, looking over at them. "I mean, let's at least call it what it is."

"You're right," Matt says, nodding. "It's television. This is a bump in the road, but let's at least use it to our advantage. The audience is going to want Levi there. Because, yeah, if I'm honest, capturing his frustration is good TV." He looks at me, apologetically. "All right? We'll keep her on the crew ship. She'll only come on the *Linda* to check you out."

None of us can argue with that.

Finn lifts his chin. "Why do I have a feeling you already have someone picked out?"

Matt's mouth twitches. "We're looking into some options. We'll keep you posted."

Chapter Three

THERE ARE ABOUT A hundred ways to be killed on a fishing boat on any given day. Things swing overhead, lines and nets are all over the place, we're being constantly jostled by the ocean, and—even while trolling—we're moving at a speed of up to eight knots at any given time.

Add in a bum leg, painkillers, and a set of crutches, and it's a recipe for disaster. But obviously, the producers of the show realize that this is an angle they can manipulate—the danger of life at sea—and only six days after the accident, I'm at the harbor, following my brothers and the crew to the slip.

"You sure you're okay to do this?" Finn asks for about the tenth time since he picked me up.

As the kid brother, I'm not surprised that Finn is hovering, but I'd still like to push him off the side of the dock.

"Would you stop?" I growl, and he shoots me a stony, protective look.

Beth, our location manager, stops us before we climb on board and looks at her clipboard. "Today we're getting—" she flips the top page up and then drops it down, "ten shots."

The boom operator comes to me, adjusting the wireless mic hidden in my parka.

"We're pushing off as soon as we can get everyone loaded and micced," Beth says, nodding to Ashleigh, the PA, to go ahead and get aboard the *Lenny Lou*, the ship the crew is based on and which houses all of the sound, filming, and mixing equipment. They're supposed to remain as unobtrusive as possible, but really, they're not very good at it.

Looking to Finn, Beth says, "Emmy will ride with you guys today."

"Emmy?" Finn says and then turns to look behind me. The protective big brother hat slips for a moment, and a sharp laugh bursts past his lips. "Well, would you fucking look at that."

How had I possibly forgotten about the nurse? We turn to see a woman in the distance, confidently making her way toward us. I'm relieved to see she's wearing jeans, boots, and a heavy ski jacket rather than a tiny white dress and nurse's cap.

But fuck me if my chest doesn't grow tight at the sight of her. Emmy Lewis.

A familiar pang settles in my chest when I think back on how fucking in love with her I was. It was sweet at twelve, desperate at fifteen, and nearly painful when we turned seventeen and I still hadn't got up the courage to tell her how I felt.

Fucking Matt, fucking Giles.

I blink over to Matt, my pulse racing. "Is this a joke? She's not really a nurse, is she?"

"Of course she is." He rocks on his heels. "Registered nurse. We borrowed her from Mount St. Mary's over in Victoria." I can see the glimmer of delight in his eyes. He's hit the jackpot. "Let's hop on board and keep the cameras rolling."

So they can capture her climbing onto the boat.

Because right now, they're capturing *my* reaction and I'm too stunned to school it.

I turn, letting Colton help me up the stairs.

"Did you know?" I ask him under my breath.

"Nope."

I growl. "How the hell'd they find out about her? I never told anyone."

"I suspect the same way they knew Elise would want a revenge fuck over things that happened ten years ago, and that Tiff would fly off the handle on camera in a jealous rage."

This nearly makes me laugh. Colton's drama with all the women he juggles keeps our ratings at the top of our time slot.

"But to be fair, Lee, you were never all that subtle about it," he adds. "Pretty sure even Dad knew."

"But *you* didn't tell them?" I ask.

"Hell no."

I look over at his face, seeing the truth in his expression.

"This gonna be okay?" he asks me quietly.

"Is it gonna be okay that I have to pull my pants down and let Emmy Lewis check out my thigh two inches from my cock every goddamn day for a week?"

"Probably more than once a day, too." He laughs, shaking his head and helping me get both crutches beneath my arms when we're on deck. "I don't fucking know, Levi. This whole thing is a goddamn rollercoaster."

We line up on deck, cameras rolling as we pretend to be going over what we need to do before we can push off.

Emmy climbs aboard—so fucking pretty, still. Her eyes are too wide, a little wild, and I wonder if she feels the same way I did the first time I was around so many people and their cameras and mics I'd been instructed to ignore.

"Hey, guys," she says.

We all say our greetings—with various degrees of enthusiasm (Colton) and wariness (Finn). I land somewhere in the middle, but inside I feel the tight hum of anxiety.

I can see it now, how the episode plays it, putting her name up on the screen—*Emmy L.*—and, below it, a little bit about her. *Nurse at Mount St. Mary's Hospital, Victoria.* Will they even need to add, *And the girl who starred in a majority of Levi's teenage fantasies*, or will the expression on my face suffice?

Because I know for sure it's written all over me. Her hair is longer than it was in school, pulled into a smooth ponytail that hangs midway down her back. Her brown eyes are round with jitters, her cheeks pink in the wind. Fuck, that mouth. I know that mouth better than my own, I'd bet. She's wearing more makeup than I've ever seen on her, but I suspect that's thanks to the producers, and not anything she'd do on her own. Emmy was never that girl.

She was always quiet, but unlike me—gangly and geeky from day one—Emmy's beauty made it easy for her to pick and choose how much she wanted to join in on the school's small social scene and not take any heat for it. I'd reckon every guy in school was in love with her. But other than Jackson McDaniel for most of junior year, I never saw her with anyone. Her dad was the principal of our high school; her mom ran a local flower shop in Bamfield. Her two older sisters moved away as soon as they graduated, but something about Emmy told me she'd always stay nearby. I always guessed she liked the calm of Bamfield, the peace of Barkley Sound.

And I'd been right, because here she is.

"Hey," she says to me, coming over. The wind whips her ponytail across her face, and I nearly reach out to help her disentangle it from her lip gloss. I'm positive the camera catches the tiny jerk of my arm, the focus of my eyes on her mouth. She grimaces, pulling it free. "Ack."

"Hey, Emmy," I say, shaking her hand. My legs feel weak, but it's got nothing to do with the stitches running down my thigh.

She blinks, her cheeks flushing pinker. "You remembered my name."

"Course I do." Can the mic pick up the heavy pulse of my heartbeat? "So you're here to look after me, then?"

She smiles, revealing the tiny dimple in her left cheek. "Hope that's okay."

Is she fucking kidding me?

"Yeah, I think I can manage." Even if I *can't* manage to wipe the grin off my face.

Finn clears his throat. "Maybe you two should …" He waves to the cabin, where the bunks are, letting his words trail off.

"*What?*" I ask.

Narrowing his eyes at me, he clarifies, "Let her check out your leg before we push off, dumbass. We need the all clear from your nurse."

"Oh," I say, mouth dry. "Right."

"For fuck's sake," Finn growls, and then turns, heading to the stern to untie the ropes.

Turning to Emmy, I feel the heat of the camera's attention on us, feel the dark shadow of the boom mic inches from her face. "Maybe we can head into the galley, and you can take a look?"

She swallows, nodding quickly. "Sure."

Emmy waits while I maneuver my way down the stairs.

I look at her over my shoulder. "Where do you want to go?"

She thinks. "A bedroom maybe? A bathroom?" Lowering her voice as if it won't be caught on camera anyway, she whispers, "We could go to the kitchen, but I don't know if you want to go where they can follow us in? Since you'll have to … uh …" She motions vaguely to my pants, and I understand what she means: *I'll have to take my pants off.*

In truth, it won't matter where we go. There are cameras everywhere.

I give her a smile that's meant to be reassuring. "It's all right, let's just head in here."

She follows me into the galley, around through the bedroom, and into the lavatory. The bathroom is small on its own, but with the two of us inside, and the camera crowding the doorway, it feels minuscule. But surprisingly, the light is good, it's clean, and there's running water, which is clearly all Emmy needs because she motions for me to sit, washes her hands, and begins unpacking her medical bag on the counter.

"You still live around here?" I say, lowering myself carefully to the toilet.

"I moved away for school but came back closer, to Victoria, when my dad got sick. I'll need you to …"

I follow her gaze and realize what she means. "Oh right," I say, and begin unfastening my belt.

"Here, let me help you."

When she reaches for my pants, I shake my head, mindful of the bandage as I ease the fabric down my hips.

"Your dad got sick?" I ask, feeling the heat in my neck, on my face, as I sit in front of her in boxers, my pants at my ankles while the cameras roll over her shoulder.

She pulls on a pair of rubber gloves, and—in a move that absolutely isn't making this any easier—kneels in front of me.

"Cancer," she says. "In his liver. I came back when he got sick." She pulls the seal off a bottle of antiseptic and opens a new roll of bandages. "Mom moved him closer to me in Victoria for a while.

I was working nights in the ER so I could care of him during the day. He died about a year ago."

I think back to a year ago. In all honesty, it feels like a lifetime ago. It was around the time things were really bad. The money was gone and everything on the boat that could break down did. Finn was back and forth to San Diego, and Colton and I barely had time to leave the boat. "I'm so sorry, Emmy. I hadn't heard."

"It's okay."

"He was a good man," I add.

"Thanks, he was," she says quietly. "But yeah, he was sick. He's better off now. Does that sound terrible?"

I shake my head, staring at her face. I've never been this physically close to her.

"Does this hurt?" she asks, fingers pressing into the skin around the bandage.

I can barely breathe. "No."

She nods, whispering, "Good," as she tests other spots closer to the wound, getting a sense of whether there's sensitivity, I guess.

"My mom died of breast cancer when I was four," I say after a beat of silence. "I don't remember any of it. I think it was easier on me than my brothers or my dad. I'm sure it's hard to lose someone you've known your whole life."

"Yeah," she says, and looks up at me with a shy, grateful smile. "Thanks. You know, I've seen you a few times. Filming."

"You have?"

She begins to unwind the bandage, and I force myself not to think about how she looks kneeling in front of me or how many times I've imagined just being near her like this. Hand-to-heaven, I'd change positions with her in a heartbeat.

She unwraps the tape and begins to gently peel the bandage away. "Out at Dockside with your brothers. And once on the boat, when Mom heard you guys were docked."

"Why didn't you say hi?" I ask. We're breaking the rules talking about the show—that sort of circular awareness that we're on television is a little too meta for the producers and, invariably, they cut it. But I love the idea that she's sought me out.

All of this—every second—feels surreal.

"I don't know," she admits, "I guess I wasn't sure you'd even remember who I was."

"You think *I* wouldn't remember *you?*" I say, hoping she doesn't notice the embarrassing emphasis to my words.

She nods, pulling the gauze from the puncture wound, and I hiss in a breath.

"Sorry," she says, wincing. "I know it's sore. I've got to clean this out and irrigate it."

"It's all right," I tell her. "Do what you need to do."

I watch as she flushes out the wound, keeping my eyes on her face and not on the grotesque hole in my leg. The injury doesn't seem to faze her in the slightest; she works with gentle but meticulous focus.

Seventeen episodes in and I know the producers want to see something of my off-hours—something personal. Finn and Harlow juggle their marriage in two places, and the audience loves their heat and humor. Colton sleeps with—and inevitably breaks up with—every pretty girl who crosses his path, and viewers eat it up. Matt and Giles have sent models out to talk to me and tried to get some of the cuter girls in town to hang around Dockside when we're filming, but, much to their disappointment, nothing ever happens. The few girls I've been attracted to seemed less interested in me and more interested in when the cameras might be around.

I stare at Emmy only inches away, studying the curve of her mouth, the smooth slope of her cheekbones. Her face is so familiar and twangs some aching, vulnerable string inside me. My brothers think I'm a twenty-four-year-old virgin, and while it isn't true, I don't have a ton of notches on my bedpost, either.

I don't play the game as well, I guess.

But then it hits me. Is this as fake as the rest of it? How much are they paying Emmy to be here? What have they promised her?

She blinks up as she finishes the final piece of tape and smiles proudly. "You're all set."

"Thanks."

She helps me stand, and, in the small space, it feels even more intimate. Always on the tall side, I shot up even more after high school. Emmy isn't small by any stretch, but she only comes up to just below my chin, and now she's standing with barely any space between us. I can feel the heat of her body, can smell her shampoo.

"You okay?" she asks.

I swallow. "Yeah."

"Is there something—?" she says with a small giggle and touches the side of her face. "You're staring."

I blink away. I can't get out of the bathroom until the camera moves, and then Emmy leaves, so I'm trapped. But fuck, the last thing I want to do is make her uncomfortable. "I'm sorry."

Her fingers brush mine. "It's okay. I wasn't complaining."

We're so close and she's right *here*. My brain goes fuzzy.

The words are out before I can think better of it: "I was in love with you."

Her eyes go wide, genuinely surprised. "You—what?"

"Yeah. I …" I look down, embarrassed. "I spent my entire life imagining what it would feel like to say that. I never imagined there'd be cameras around when I did."

I try to smile to take the bite out of what comes next. "So, if you're here for money, Emmy, or to mess with me somehow … just, go easy, all right?"

I lift my chin to the cameraman, Dave, silently telling him we're done here.

Chapter Four

FINN CATCHES MY EYE when I come aboveboard, and I read the question in his face: *All good?*

It's rhetorical; he knows me well enough to know I'm not thrilled with this entire situation. I've become hyperaware of every interaction I've had since the show started: locals who are suddenly my new best friends, girls from around town who never noticed me and now do, phone calls from distant relatives we haven't heard from in years. These all felt pretty obvious; I knew that kind of shit would happen.

But this Emmy situation feels like a low blow: bringing in someone I had genuine feelings for and playing it for ratings?

I move past Finn on my crutches, growling inwardly at the realization that nothing would feel better than some hard, physical labor right now. Instead, my options are limited to some rewiring we could do on the fuse box or sitting on the deck with a book while my brothers bust their asses for the camera.

Nodding to one of the crew members that I need my tools, I move inside to the control room and pull up a stool. Guess for the time being I'm the ship's electrician.

Finn and Colt give me a wide berth. I know we'll talk later. I don't know when Emmy comes upstairs to head over to the crew ship, but by the time we push off and into the open water, she's on the *Lenny Lou* behind us with the crew.

Downstairs that night, it's a good forty-five minutes of eating our dinners in grunting silence before anyone brings it up.

I can tell it's killing Colton, but for once he's keeping his shit together and leaving me alone. Finally, Finn wipes his mouth, puts his napkin on the table, and leans back, looking at me.

"How'd it go?"

I nod, eating another bite of canned green beans before answering. The crew has been waiting all day for this conversation.

"Fine," I say.

Finn nods, too, working to find the best way to do this without putting me on the spot too much. "She's been working at Mount St. Mary's?"

I take a swig of my beer. "Yeah."

"Weird to see her, I bet," he says, and when I look up at him, his eyes are tight. Fuck. I know that face. He's been instructed to talk it out and hates it nearly as much as I do.

Most of the things we've had to do for this show have been a breeze. Fix up the ship on their dime? No problem! Get more days off and get paid more out on the water? Sure thing! But these social things—the heart of the show, and we know it—really do suck sometimes. Viewers have watched our dad struggle with the health ramifications of a stroke he had over ten years ago; they've watched Harlow and Finn try to find their footing amidst distance and all this insanity. They want the danger and excitement of life out on the ocean, but they want the real parts, too. Unfortunately, the Roberts men aren't really known for being chatty.

"Yeah, it was weird," I say, and fuck it. Might as well lay it all out there. It's not like she'll be around when it airs, anyway. "She's the only girl I ever liked that way, you know? But it's different now when people talk to us."

"Yeah," Finn says.

"And it's one thing if it's Mellie at the bar or Dustin calling to chat after we haven't seen him in seven years." I take another long pull of my beer before finishing my thought. "But to have someone I liked my whole life show up ... just makes it hard to trust."

"Well," Colton says, leaning in, "look at it this way: if she's only around when the cameras are here, then you know."

He's got a point.

"Just let her do her job," Finn says quietly. "The way you look at each other is enough to have Matt and Giles dancing. You don't need to do any more."

Dave grunts, irritated, from behind his camera. That'll have to be cut. But fuck it. I feel about a million times better just having talked it out a little.

Emmy comes aboard the following morning with her little bag and a tentative smile. Goddamnit, she's sweet. I want to be irritated with her being here, but it's just not possible. It's not her fault that we did this show and it's left me paranoid about people's intentions.

Even though I know, yeah, she may be here for the novelty of it, I'm still wary of being alone with her after my huge confession yesterday. So I pull my pants down inside the control room, in plain sight of everyone.

Colt whistles, leaning on the lever that pulls up our biggest net. "Getting indecent up in here."

Emmy blushes but gets to work.

"Still doesn't hurt?" she asks again, feeling around the edge of the bandage.

"No."

"It's not red, so that's a good sign," she says. I can only nod, not sure what more to say.

Her hands are both careful and competent. And while she unwraps the bandage and takes care of me, she fills the space, asking about my brothers and about fishing, never once bringing up what I said.

A week. A whole week with Emmy, every day. At first, it's a little stilted, but how can it be helped? Emmy is there a couple times a day, cleaning me up and then disappearing so the cameras can get all the shirtless filler footage and Levi-Hates-Sitting-Still footage they can handle. When a seine net is dumped on board and some of the fish escape the hold, Colton has one of the extra hands step in and take my place. A line snags on the way in, and I'm not quick enough to get to it before it breaks. But when Finn trips over one of my crutches and insists that *surely* it's time for Emmy to check my leg again, I lose my temper and throw a roll of electrical tape overboard—much to the delight of our producers who catch it all on film.

She stays away otherwise, careful to give me space, but I start to look forward to our time together. I ask her about school in Oregon, and she tells me about joining the women's rowing team there. And I see it now, in the strength of her shoulders, her back. She asks me about my dad, and I tell her that he's stronger now but not as strong as he used to be.

She fills the silence with quiet words; she doesn't boast, but she's never self-deprecating, either. Cynically, I try to read her to see whether she's watching for the camera or turning her body to face this way or that, but she never seems to.

I don't want to like her, but it's getting harder and harder to remember why.

Six days after Emmy first came aboard, we're finally back at port. Finn, Colton, and a bunch of the crew are off for a night out, which means beer, peanuts, and rude jokes at Dockside.

I'm just coming out of the shower, my leg wrapped in plastic below my hip, when I hear someone walking aboveboard. It's after eight; everyone who would normally be here should have left an hour ago. When I check my phone, I don't see any missed calls.

We have crew members guarding the boats in a sort of half-assed way all the time. Mainly because there's always someone tinkering with the equipment on the *Lenny Lou* or sleeping on the boat when we're docked. But even though there isn't anything all that valuable to take off the *Linda*, it doesn't always stop the local kids from climbing aboard and taking pictures they can share with their friends or post online.

Pulling on a pair of sweats, I limp up the steps, calling out, "Who's up there?"

When no one answers, my pulse picks up, and I grab the bat we always keep tucked just inside the door to the control galley.

"It's not a good idea to climb up here, guys," I say, moving along the railing toward the stern, where the rear deck spreads out wide and flat. "Tons of stuff to get tangled in if you don't know what you're doing."

"Levi?"

I whip around at the sound of my name and then drop the bat, horrified.

"I'm sorry!" She approaches, her face partially obscured in the darkness. "I didn't mean to startle you. I left my bag here and need it for my shift."

"Holy hell, Emmy, you nearly got clocked in the head. You should have called."

She shakes her head. "I don't have your number. Only Matt's. I thought you'd be out with everyone else."

Glancing around, I see no cameras, no crew, no fuzzy mics hovering just out of view. "I know they want us all there, but a night at home sounded better to me."

"Makes sense." She smiles, and *this* I can see in the darkness.

I expect her to leave, to find her way to the dock, and head into town with everyone else, but she lingers instead, sliding her hand over the railing at her side.

"Can I ask you something?"

I nod, realizing we're truly alone for the first time. "Sure."

"What happened the other day?" she asks, looking up at me after she says this. "You said you ... liked me, and then ..."

I pause for a moment, not sure what to say. "I got wary, that's all," I admit finally. "All kinds of people are coming out of the woodwork since the show started. I don't mind it, usually, but when you showed up ..." I shake my head. "I didn't know what to think."

She takes a step closer. "I can understand that." I feel her hand come over my forearm and slide higher, and it's only now that I realize I never put on a shirt.

"I get it, how it would be hard to trust people." Her gaze is fixed on my face as she says, "It's not about the show for me. They asked around the hospital and when I heard it was you … well. I guess I didn't like the idea of it being some sexy model-turned-nurse from Vancouver." She gives me a tiny, guilty smile. "I needed a break from the ER. And … I *like* you. I always liked your family."

I nod. There's a thunder rolling in my chest. It causes a riot inside me; my blood feels too hot. "Well," I say, struggling for breath, for words, "I …"

"But I do get it," she says, a little quieter now. "Why you'd be wary. If you liked me before, you probably think they're using me to get a reaction out of you."

I laugh. "I'm *sure* they're using you to get a reaction out of me."

"Well, I wanted you to know that *I* wasn't part of it," she says. "There was no subplot pitched to me. They asked for a nurse, and I agreed. I get it now, but I'm not here to play you."

I nod, unsure what else to say. Having her so near me is almost painful. Of any of us Roberts boys, I have the least experience with women, but really, I'm not all that surprised when she takes another step closer, and then another, so she's up against me.

Her hands come to my chest—cold from the night air, maybe cold from nerves, too—and then she stretches, pressing her mouth against the pulse in my throat and whispering, "I wish you'd have said something when we were seventeen."

I feel dizzy, and it has nothing to do with the movement of the boat. "What're we doing?" I ask, but my hands come around her waist, settling at that sweet curve between back and ass, and I hold her to me. Fuck, it's heady. How many times have I imagined this? She's warm and firm, and I could see how it might feel to pull her over me, when no one's around like this, and take my time making her feel good.

"I don't know," she admits, and her voice shakes a little. "I just wanted to see you again. But then you said that thing about liking me, and being here all week … watching you work out here …"

I chase her mouth, swallowing her words with my kiss, and it feels every bit as good as I dreamed it would. She makes these noises that seem to hit me as tiny pricks of heat, exploding all along my skin. I want to be slow, to go easy and notice every little touch, but it's hard when she's there, pushing me against the wall to the galley, her hands moving up and all over me.

She likes my skin—I know because she tells me—and her fingers slide over every inch of my torso while her mouth is busy on mine. Pretty soon it's like her wildness gives me permission to do more than just stand there stunned by her, and I pull her onto the deck, undoing that little sweater so I can get my mouth on her, tasting the pulse in her neck. I want my hands on her, touching that sweet place between her legs that makes her gasp and bite me and beg.

It's headed somewhere—fast—and I don't have anything.

I pull away, groaning, because she's shoved my pants to my knees and has a grip on me, and it would be so goddamn easy to go right where we both want me.

"Wait," I say, trying to distance myself from how good she feels on my fingers, how much better it would feel to … "Do you have anything?"

Her eyes meet mine in the dark, and I see the moment she understands.

"Oh." She swallows, breaths choppy. "I—no. I didn't expect …"

We look at each other, surely each of us weighing the hundreds of reasons why we shouldn't, with the single, urgent reason why we should. I *want* her. But she doesn't deserve the complexities that come with that sort of rash decision. And no matter how good she smells or tastes and how much time we've wasted, we can wait one more day.

So I stroke her until she's shaking, until she's begging, until she's falling back in relief, and then pull her right up to me. While she catches her breath, I talk about anything that comes to mind—the boat, the fish, my family—and then ask her to tell me more about being out on the water, rowing. Hearing someone you're fond of talk about loving something you love, but loving it differently, is like hearing poetry. Her voice is even, and smooth. A little scratchy, too. And with her curled up on top of me, I think it might be heaven.

A foot creaks just beyond, in the shadows, and as we both go still, and slowly sit up, we know.

My heart drops, my skin pebbles with gooseflesh. "There's someone here."

Footsteps retreat, and I hear the person climbing down the ladder. I'm hoping for the best-case scenario—that it was one of my brothers stumbling upon us by accident or someone from the crew looking for a forgotten sweatshirt or coffee mug—and not someone with a camera, capturing this on film.

Emmy is rushing to pull on her clothes, but I can't see her expression in the dark. Did she know?

"Was there a camera here?" I say, putting a finger under her chin and tilting her face to mine.

She stares up at me, eyes wide. "*What?* I have no idea."

I stand, bending to cover myself until I can get my sweats on. "Goddamnit."

"Levi, I didn't set this up."

I want to believe her. I really do. I don't want a soap opera made out of Emmy and me.

She straightens her sweater, and I can't tell that moments ago she was curled up, nearly naked on me, talking about the water. Except her lips are swollen and her hair is wild, and she looks so fucking beautiful.

"You should go," I tell her.

Waves lap at the dock, bang against the sides of the boat, and I wonder if the ocean has always been as loud as it is while I wait for her to say something, anything.

"Yeah," she finally says, standing. "I should."

Chapter Five

I DIDN'T EVEN BOTHER going home. It was easier to clear the boat and head downstairs than it was to get someone to help me drive all the way to my place and help me along the muddy path to the front door.

I'm not generally a very pessimistic guy; if anything, I'm the one talking Finn and Colton down from the rafters when they get on a tear about something. But I'm also the first to admit that this lack of cynicism means I'm the one most likely to get messed with.

Maybe Emmy didn't know, maybe that much is true. But it feels like the safest path forward is to get better, work on the boat, get back on the fish, and leave the romance subplots to my brothers.

I'm already up by the time they come onboard the next morning, and I explain to them what happened.

Finn listens quietly and then lets out a curse when he looks up and sees Matt and Giles on the deck walking toward us. They're wearing the kind of clothes that are supposed to look old but fit way too well to be anything but overpriced. Giles steps up on the ladder in a pair of suede sneakers. Matt has on a white linen shirt.

"You two look ridiculous," I say.

Everyone turns to me. It's the kind of thing Finn would say, and definitely the kind of thing Colton would say. Something's gotten into me lately.

Matt grins at me when he's fully on deck. "Someone's in a mood."

"I don't like the Emmy game," I tell him, straight up. "It's shady."

He shakes his head at me. "We had to talk her into it, you know. Appearing on camera."

"All right," I say, skeptical. "But last night crossed a line."

"Last night?" Matt asks, confused.

Giles shifts on his feet.

"She agreed to help you, but it took some convincing to get her onscreen," Matt tells me, though my eyes are on Giles. "And she's not getting paid, if that helps. She told us we could pay her mom if we needed to put money somewhere. Think she's getting a new porch," he adds with a little shrug.

I stare at him. Finn has gone still, watching Giles, too.

"All right," Giles says, calm as can be even with all eyes on him. "Yeah, it was me yesterday. Someone saw Emmy head back to the boat and I sent Dave down. We did get some great footage on camera. He only caught you … well, after. We don't have to decide yet how to handle it. From a production standpoint, a new relationship—with Finn's marriage and Colton's constant bed bunnies—would be great for diversifying our personal angles. But from a dude perspective? Levi," he says, smiling, "don't fuck this one up."

I'm sure they know where I can find her—but I didn't stay long enough to ask. If Emmy returned to Victoria, that would definitely suck. But I also like to think that after watching her all these years I know her well enough to know she wouldn't leave town without one last word.

Turns out Matt was giving me a clue with the porch: construction has already started, and her mom is there, directing hulking men carrying pavers to the new walkway. I see Emmy in an upstairs window, and when I call out to her, she looks at me. Even at a distance I can tell she's determined as hell.

I've seen her make this face before anything from a math test to a relay race at our school's spring festival. My heart tightens in thrill and nerves.

Emmy comes outside and makes her way toward me. "I'm busy," she says. "You need me to find you a new nurse?"

I laugh. "The leg is fine. I'm here to talk."

"Come back later."

"Later, huh?"

She watches, fighting a smile. "Mom's going out. I'll be here."

I look past her at the house facing the water, the hulking gray stone building she grew up in. It's true that it's seen some wear over the years, lashed by salt spray and wind. The porch was probably collapsing, the windows need replacing, but the structure is good. That thing will last until the earth itself falls apart.

"When are you heading back to Victoria?" I ask.

"Not sure yet."

"You don't like it there?"

"I like it there fine," she says, her jaw set. "I like it here better."

"Not as many patients to tend to," I say.

"Plenty of patients, but they're all stubborn," she says, "or big man babies."

This makes me laugh, and I reach for her, pulling her close to me. "I know you didn't set us up last night."

"You know that *now*," she corrects.

"I'll always admit when I'm wrong," I tell her, kissing her neck. "I'm sorry, Emmy."

She shivers under my lips, and I feel her hands as they slide up my arms and over my shoulders. "Yeah?"

"Yeah."

When she opens the door that night, I nearly drop the bunch of flowers I've got clutched in my fist. Emmy is wearing a short dress and boots. Her hair is loose, spilling over her shoulders. She stares up at me like she knows me, like mine was the face she's been looking down the drive for, waiting on.

Emmy takes the flowers, thanking me with a peck on my cheek. We nearly had sex on the boat last night, but tonight she's a picture of sweetness, leading me into the kitchen, where it smells like bubbling tomato sauce, basil, and garlic bread baking in the oven.

"How was your day?" she asks.

"Good. Quiet."

She hums, nodding, and I watch as she puts the flowers into a vase and sets the whole thing on a windowsill.

Emmy turns, moving to the fridge and sliding her hand over my stomach as she passes. It's such a casual intimacy, and my heart is racing.

"Want a beer?" she asks.

I glance to the kitchen island and see she's got a glass of wine. "Sure, thanks."

The cap hisses as she pops it off with a bottle opener mounted to the fridge, and her fingers slide across mine when she hands me the bottle.

I wish I had more grace, but the question hammers at my thoughts until I can't keep it in anymore: "Are we gonna do this?" I ask her.

With a little smile, she looks up at me. "Do what?"

I don't even know the word for it. "Date? Stop wasting time?"

She shakes her head, smiling. "I don't want to *date*."

My brows pull together. "I didn't realize."

"Date, to me," she says, "means we're casual. It means we see other people, too."

I am far, far out of my element here. But Emmy doesn't seem to mind. I tell her, "I have no idea what it means since I haven't really done it, but … I'll put it out there, Em. I'd like to be with you, however you're willing."

She takes a step back, and then another, pushing herself on the kitchen island only a couple of feet away. "Then yeah, we're doing this," she says.

"There may be cameras sometimes," I remind her, following her on my crutches, and stepping between her legs when she reaches out with those boots, pulling me closer.

"We'll deal with it. But no cameras come into my bedroom."

I lick my lips on instinct, the way I might before taking a bite of fruit. "Do *I* come into your bedroom?"

She looks at my mouth, and her hands move to my chest, unbuttoning my shirt as she goes. "I think you can come anywhere you want."

I feel my face heat as the meaning of her words hits me like a whip. "Emmy, are you going to kiss me with that filthy mouth, or what?"

Her lips curve in a smile just before I capture them in a kiss. She's so soft, so sweet; kissing her reminds me of pressing honeysuckle to my lips as a kid, sucking out the nectar. Like this I pull sounds from her, realizing in a burst of heat that she's got this tiny dress on, with tiny lace underneath, and things like pasta sauce can just sit on the stove and be patient for a while.

Christina Lauren is the combined pen name of long-time writing partners/besties/soulmates Christina Hobbs and Lauren Billings. The number one international best-selling coauthor duo writes both young adult and adult fiction and together have produced fourteen *New York Times* best-selling novels. They are published in over thirty languages, have received multiple starred reviews from *Kirkus Reviews* and *Library Journal*, won both the Seal of Excellence and Book of the Year from *RT BookReviews*, and have been featured in publications such as *Forbes, The Washington Post, Time, Entertainment Weekly, O, The Oprah Magazine*, and more. Their third YA novel, *Autoboyography*, will be released in September, followed by a contemporary romance, *Roomies*, in December.

SCANDALOUS

Cassandra Dean

London, 1830

THE TOWNHOUSE WAS LIT like a bonfire, every sconce that could contain light ablaze. Laughter and music spilled through the air, the temptation of revelry too much to refuse an invitation to the Maddern ball, though it was a week before Christmas and as cold as the Arctic. Guests entered the foyer through the heavy oak doors, bitter cold brightening their cheeks as they shed their cloaks to reveal the finery beneath, and footmen scurried among them, burdened with discarded cloaks as they ushered the arrivals in the direction of the ballroom.

Shoulder against the wall, Edgington observed the activity. He'd accepted the invitation to this ball purely on a whim though he'd known it would be tedious, and nothing in the time since his arrival had disabused him of this notion. After an obligatory turn of the ballroom, he'd stationed himself in the entrance hall, gaining some faint amusement from the arrival of those so desperate for society they ventured out on a night like this. Ah, but then, what did it say about him that he was among their number?

A couple passed him, close enough he could almost discern their conversation. Tittering behind her gloved hand, the female glanced at him. Edgington met her eyes. The woman blanched, her gaze quickly skittering away as she urged her partner toward the ballroom.

He smiled faintly. His reputation was in full effect, it seemed.

Shifting his weight, he considered his options. Maybe he should make his way to his club or a gambling house or any one of a number of entertainments he'd previously patronized. While it held amusement to force his presence upon a society clearly unwilling to host him, there were vastly more interesting ways to spend an evening—not that he could think of any at this present moment. Of late, the life of a profligate had started to pall, and he found himself wondering about his estate in Ambleside. Of what might be involved in land management, and how the sun would feel against his skin as he stood in a field, the gentle bleat of sheep carried on the breeze.

With a twist of his lips, he dismissed such fancies. He must be getting old to become prone to maudlin thoughts. Besides, the earls of Edgington were bred for better things, or so his father had told him. However, his father had also told him he was a useless fool, and if his wife had managed to present him with a spare as was proper, he would not suffer his eldest son as heir.

Why his father despised him, Edgington didn't know, but he'd long reconciled himself to the knowledge that his father held no affection for him, and he'd found delight in living down to his opinion of him. A smirk twisted his lips. The greatest of his perversions could boast inception in his desire to enrage his father and, truth be told, he was a little lost as to his purpose now that the man was gone.

Once, though, he'd thought to have something more. His smirk died as memory curled about him. Once, he'd thought perhaps he was more than the sum of his parts, more than what his parents had made him. Once, someone had looked at him as if he could be better and, for a brief moment, he'd believed her.

However, that was ten years and a lifetime ago, and he'd gone in another direction. Maybe, though … maybe it was time to turn his path. Maybe, instead of his club, he would go home. Maybe tomorrow he'd strategize a new life, one that gave him purpose.

A laugh rang out over the throng. Something about it tugged at a half-remembered memory, something he'd convinced himself he'd forgotten. The hairs on his neck stood up, and he pulled himself straight, straining to look over the throng to find the owner of the laugh. Heart a fast beat in his chest; he skipped over each face and figure, certain he was wrong.

As if magic, the crowd parted. And he saw her.

His heart froze. For an endless moment, he stared. Then the world started again, his heart lurching to a wild rhythm he couldn't contain.

She'd only just arrived. Cheeks rosy, she removed a dark cloak to reveal she wore green, not the pale green of her youth but a deep emerald. A feather of the same hue set jauntily in her hair deepened the strawberry-blonde curls and no doubt brought out the green flecks in her hazel eyes. He couldn't see their color from here, but he remembered them, remembered their light as she beamed a smile. Remembered them wet, and then remembered them devoid of any emotion at all.

Face animated, she gestured at the crowd as she spoke to the dark-haired woman beside her. The woman said something and she laughed again, the sound of it skipping along his spine. Linking her arm with her companion, she made her way toward the ballroom, chatting all the while.

Edgington followed them. They entered the ballroom, and the whirl enveloped him, hundreds of people in a too small room, but the lure of the feather atop her head was too great.

The feather stopped. Pushing through the crowd, he saw her friend had greeted someone, temporarily leaving her to her own devices. A polite smile on her face, she looked about the ballroom, her smile brightening every now and then.

Hidden in the crowd, he watched her. Now, it was obvious why he'd come to the ball—for the slight chance he would see her.

He'd heard about her return. It had been in all the papers,

the triumphant return of Viscount Hargrove's sister. They'd been full of her exploits on the Continent, the countries she'd seen, the society she'd kept. Each article he'd devoured, unable to keep the distance he maintained with everyone else, but then, that was nothing new. He'd never been able to distance himself from her.

Ten years since he'd seen her, and she hadn't changed. Maybe she was a bit older, her hair a bit more gold, but she still looked as she did when he was a callow youth of twenty-one and more than a little infatuated. He remembered every curve of her face, the softness of her skin. The way her mouth moved under his.

Her gaze wandered to the dancing, and a wistful kind of smile occupied her face. His pulse a thunder in his ears, he wanted, quite stupidly, to ask her to dance.

Closing his eyes briefly, he shook himself. As if she would say yes. If he were to approach her, the smile would disappear from her features, as would all emotion. He knew. He'd seen it happen before.

Her gaze moved again and their eyes locked.

For a moment, a split second, her smile remained, and he had an insane hope that all had been forgiven, that, perhaps, he could approach her. Then, all expression bled from her face, and she regarded him coolly, her joy in the evening gone.

His heart sank. He'd known she'd react so, though a part of him had hoped he'd been wrong. A part of him had hoped he could approach her, could ask her to dance, could ask for her hand.

But, of course, he couldn't. She was Sofia Hargrove. The girl he'd ruined.

Chapter Two

SOFIE STARED AT VISCOUNT March. He had changed in the past ten years. His golden hair used to riot about his head in a tumble of curls, but now dark blond strands were clipped close to his head and slicked with pomade. His dress was sober, too, unrelieved black with a snowy white cravat, as if he knew such clothing would frame his pale skin, wide shoulders, and slim hips. His eyes would still be gray, not that she could see that from here, nor would she ever wish to confirm it. She'd be quite happy never to speak to him again, and thus forever be in ignorance if his eyes were the same shade of gray she, to her great disgust, still remembered.

The viscount—no. He must be the earl now. The Earl of Edgington. She'd read of his father's death in the English newspapers in Vienna ... or was it Prague? Wherever it had been, she'd skipped over news of him and very deliberately turned the page.

The earl stared at her. Sofie resisted the urge to check her hair and then cursed herself for even thinking it. She'd known she'd come across him eventually. The three weeks she'd been in London, she'd held her breath, certain she would turn a corner and there he'd be. Every time she'd attended a ball or a dance, the theater, even walking in the park she'd thought she'd see him. When she hadn't, she'd foolishly allowed herself to believe she would never see him, that maybe she would pass this time in London without encountering him again, visiting her family and friends before returning to the Continent and the life she had built for herself

More fool her.

"Sofie, what are you staring at?"

Diana's voice pulled Sofie from the earl to discover her friend regarding her, a crease between her brows.

Arranging a bright smile across her features, Sofie said, "Nothing. This ball is such a crush, isn't it?"

Diana was not so easily dissuaded, however, and Sofie knew the precise instant her friend discovered who had captured her attention. Anger soured Diana's expression as she glared at the earl. "What's *he* doing here?"

A wave of love swept her. The hostility in Diana's words spoke of her loyalty more than anything else could. "To be fair, it's the biggest ball of the season. I'd be surprised if he weren't here."

Diana scowled. "There is no fair about it." Her expression softened. "Sofie, are you well?"

Her smile turned bitter. "As well as can be. It was bound to happen sooner or later. I am only surprised it has not happened before now."

"I should scratch his eyes out."

Diana's fierce declaration startled a laugh from Sofie. "I should think you would have to join the queue."

"Well, point it out to me." Diana looked at her, her expression stricken. "He took you from me, Sof. You weren't even here for my wedding to Stephen. Why shouldn't I scratch his eyes out? Besides, he *hurt* you."

Sofie swallowed. He *had* hurt her. Ridiculous that she still felt the stab of it. "I survived, but I would not talk to him again, not for all the tea in China."

"You can't tell me you enjoyed the past ten years fully. You cannot tell me you didn't resent having to leave England under such a cloud."

"No, I don't, but I cannot regret those years either." It had started badly, it was true, but in the past ten years, she'd had more adventure and seen more wonders than she'd ever thought possible. "Where *is* Stephen?"

Diana waved her hand. "Somewhere. He can do well enough without me. I'm more concerned about you." Her eyes lit. "No, I will *get* him. It's time someone thrashed that man for what he did. Don't worry; Stephen will set things right."

Sofie concealed her smile as Diana hurried off, scowling at those daft enough to get in her way. Diana seemed to think Stephen could do anything, which was sweet in his context as Diana's husband but vastly disturbing when he was one's brother. *She* remembered quite clearly frogs in beds, dunkings in ponds, and roof-raising fights over who would get the blue croquet mallet.

The earl still stared at her. Smile dying, she looked elsewhere. She didn't want to think about that time ten years ago, but she could think of nothing else.

She'd been so thrilled when the scandalous Viscount March had paid her attention. She'd heard all the whispers about him, about his dissolute reputation, the wild escapades, the daring wagers. She and Diana had debated endlessly what it meant when the viscount had met her gaze across a ballroom. When he'd finally approached her at the refreshment table, she'd just about expired on the spot. They exchanged words, and then he'd touched her. Nothing overt, a single brush of his smallest finger against hers as their hands rested on the refreshment table, but it had been enough to tumble her headlong into infatuation.

When he'd asked her to meet him in the garden, she'd rushed to say yes. It had been foolhardy, but she'd been seventeen and giddy with her first season. Their first meeting, she'd thought he would grab her, do wicked things, but instead, he'd simply … talked.

Over the next months in the darkened gardens of society, she'd grown to know him. She'd discovered his wit and his humor, the emotion he hid under a mask. He shared himself with her, and she did the same with him. She told him of her desire to travel, her interest in architecture, how her mother drove her insane.

The whispers changed during those months, of how the scandalous Viscount March was suddenly not so scandalous, how he attended society functions and acted with, if not quite politeness, then at least civility. She'd been smug, knowing it was because of her, and she, foolish child that she'd been, had tumbled headlong into love.

Then had come the Silverton's ball, and everything had gone horribly wrong.

She hadn't meant to kiss him. They'd been in Silverton's garden, and he'd said something unbearably romantic about the stars. He'd been surprised at first, but then his hand tightened at her waist, he'd pulled her into him, and she'd melted. She had been kissed before, but never the way he had. Never with such passion, as if he'd die if he didn't taste her. As she'd die without him.

Of course, they were caught. For months they'd met without incident, but the one time, the *one time* they'd kissed, Lady Harrison, Lady Violat, and Mrs. Wilding, the worst gossips in society, had seen them.

It had spread like wildfire, that Viscount March and Miss Hargrove had been caught in a torrid embrace. She'd stubbornly clung to the hope that he would make everything right, that he loved her as she loved him, but when he hadn't arrived at her home, when he hadn't paid his addresses to her father, she'd realized she was wrong. Terribly, horribly wrong.

Six days after they'd been caught, she'd packed her trunk, taken her maid, and set sail for France. Stephen had been touring the Continent, wreaking havoc on the unsuspecting people of Paris. Her brother had been horrified at the arrival of his younger sister at his hotel, but once he'd finished his shouting, he'd taken her in. The fact that she'd promptly burst into tears upon the end of his tirade had probably gone a ways to convincing him. He'd been so flustered to see her upset he'd caved to any suggestion she made, including that she join him for the remainder of his tour.

At first, their parents had been furious she'd seen fit to decamp. They'd demanded she return home, but when weeks had stretched into months and then years, they'd relented. She'd stayed abroad longer than intended, well after Stephen had returned to England, but there'd been nothing for her in London. Those years on the Continent had been kind to her, and she couldn't regret it.

But she regretted him. The viscount. Bitterly.

"Miss Hargrove."

Her shoulders tensed. He *wouldn't*.

Slowly, with the fervent wish she'd misheard, she turned. Her stomach dropped, and her skin flushed as fury sped through her.

She hadn't misheard.

The Earl of Edgington stood before her. "Miss Hargrove," he said again, his rich, deep voice just as she remembered. "You have returned."

A wave of emotion hit her, so tangled she couldn't separate one from the hundreds. Did he truly expect her to respond?

No reaction crossed his features at her deliberately rude lack of response, but then he was an unfeeling automaton, wasn't he? *She* had been the imbecile who'd imagined emotion behind that impassive gaze. Well, no longer. She knew his measure now, and she had no desire to renew their acquaintance.

She noted, quite insanely, his eyes were the same gray.

A hush surrounded them, as society noticed the Earl of Edgington was addressing Miss Hargrove. Whispers began, and she could imagine what they said, as they repeated the scandal to those who didn't know, as they wondered if she would be so stupid as to believe his lies once more.

Cheeks burning, she lifted her chin. She wouldn't allow such whispers to affect her. Not again.

Finally, the earl spoke. "Miss Hargrove, would you honor me with a dance?"

Fury exploded. Trembling with it, she clenched her fists as she fought to control herself.

He stood there with his impassive face and tall body and thought he could treat her as if nothing had ever happened? As if she had not been forced to leave this country, her home, because of his actions? A voice whispered she was not wholly blameless, but she ignored it.

Drawing herself to her full height, she poured every bit of anger she felt into her response, the only response she could possibly give. "No."

Then she spun on her heel and left.

Chapter Three

LEFT STANDING IN THE middle of the ballroom, Edgington watched as Miss Hargrove—as Sofie—stormed off. She did not look back, quickly becoming lost in a crowd that tittered, gossiped, and stared.

Once he could no longer see the green feather adorning Sofie's hair, he turned his attention to the shocked, thrilled faces before him. They'd given the gossips much to discuss tonight, and no doubt by tomorrow the tale of how Miss Hargrove gave the Earl of Edgington the cut direct would be all over town.

Lifting his brows, he stared them down. Most dropped their gaze, and those that didn't appeared suitably cowed. Satisfied, he took his leave of the ballroom, finding an empty chamber so he could let the façade slip.

Running a hand over his face, he exhaled. God. Sofie.

She was even more beautiful now than she'd been ten years ago. Her hair looked as silky as he remembered it; his fingers itched to bury themselves in the strawberry-blonde tresses. The smattering of freckles across her nose was the same, and she no longer attempted to disguise them with powder, which he found unbearably erotic. She'd held herself proudly, as if daring him to do his worst, and then she had cut him and carried herself away like a queen.

He'd wanted nothing more than to haul her against him and cover her mouth with his.

It was the same as ten years ago, the same rush of emotion clamoring through him. She made him feel … The feelings were so big, he didn't know how to describe them. And he wanted her. Damn, how he wanted her.

That last night, he'd been desperate for her. They'd never kissed, never even so much as touched inappropriately, but he'd wanted to. Had been drowning in desire for her. Unused to restraint, he'd kept his baser instincts under ruthless control, terrified of scaring her with the strength of his passion. Then, she'd leaned over, her eyes sparkling, and her lips had brushed his so hesitantly. He couldn't have contained himself after that.

It had all gone spectacularly wrong. They'd been caught, and he should have convinced the gossips they saw nothing, should have used his privilege to ensure they spoke not at all. Instead, he'd been so caught up in Sofie he'd let them leave, and within moments Sofie's father had arrived to drag her away. From there, it had only been a matter of hours before it was the talk of the ton.

The next morning, he'd dressed to call upon her. He'd even gotten as far as her street before doubt crashed over him. What was he doing? He would ruin her, as he'd ruined everything else in his life. Panic had screamed through him, and he'd turned on his heel and left. He'd done her a favor, he told himself. She could not want him as a husband, not the disreputable Viscount March. When he'd heard she'd left for the Continent, he'd been certain he'd been correct. She was better off without him, and look how the years bore truth to his words.

Linking his hands behind his neck, he stared at nothing. He wasn't better without her. He'd always known that.

A sudden thought occurred. Why wouldn't she let him talk to her? It had been ten years. Surely, her anger should have faded by now, enough to listen to him at least. True, he'd been the wicked Viscount March and the blame for their disgrace could be laid upon him, but she'd agreed to meet him. She'd kept meeting him. *She'd* kissed *him*.

He needed to talk to her.

Turning, he left the room. She wasn't in the ballroom or any of the retiring rooms. She wasn't in the banquet hall or the foyer or anywhere else in the house.

Exhaling, he looked out the window of one of the dozens of rooms she wasn't in. Would she really go into the garden? It was freezing out there, the sky threatening snow ... but she'd always loved the gardens.

Procuring his coat and his gloves from a passing footman, he set out into the night. The cold hit him as soon as he passed through the door, slithering along the collar of his coat and pushing against his skin. Devoid of people, silence hung over the garden, a heavy expectation in the air ... or maybe it was his own thoughts that made it seem so.

Deep in the garden, deep enough the lights of the house had faded, he found her. Her back to him, Sofie gazed out over the Thornton's gardens, the emerald green of her gown a strip of color against the darkness of her cloak.

Stealing himself, Edgington approached her. "You always did like a garden at night."

Sofie's shoulders stiffened. She didn't reply.

Standing next to her, he laced his hands behind him. They stood silent, the faint strains of a waltz wrapping around them.

Finally, she spoke. "Why are you here?"

His heart sank at the derision in her tone. "I wished to speak with you."

"I do not wish to speak with you. Surely that was obvious."

"It was." How could he get through to her? "I wanted—"

She whirled around. "And your desires are more important than mine? Your wants? I do not *want* to speak with you. I *want* to be left alone. I am in England for two months, and I want that time to be pleasant."

Two months? She needed to let him speak with her. She needed—

With a sound of frustration, she made to turn on her heel. His brain shut down and, panic rushing through him, he grabbed her arm.

Immediately, her expression closed. "Remove your hand."

The coldness of her voice chilled him more than the winter night. Immediately, he let her go. "My apologies, Miss Hargrove. It was not my intention—"

She laughed without mirth. "It never is."

"It was not my intention," he continued, ignoring the thread of annoyance her dismissal caused, "to deprive you of autonomy. I only ask ..." He paused. How to say? "I should like to explain."

"I should think we are past the stage of explanation, Lord

March." As if realizing her error, she flushed. "I beg your pardon. Lord Edgington."

"Nonetheless," he said, persevering despite her glare. "I should like to explain. You did not allow me the opportunity before."

"I did not allow you?" she said. "I did not *allow* you? How, sir, was I to allow you when I was dragged off by my father, half-dressed and humiliated? Was I to allow you when you did *not* call upon me? When you did not, in fact, seek me out at all? Tell me, sir, when was I to allow you anything?" Her lips twisted bitterly. "I believe I allowed you enough."

"I am sorry," he said, unable to think of any other response.

She frowned. "What?"

He did not know how else to say it. "I am sorry. I should have handled it better. All of it."

"And that is to magically erase the past ten years of my life?"

"No. It is merely how I feel."

Still not looking at him, she picked up her skirt. "Well, I'm glad you've expressed how you feel. If you'll excuse me."

He couldn't let her go. "Miss Hargrove. I have still not explained."

"And I have said, I do not care for your explanation."

"Please, Miss Hargrove." He did not know how to make her stay, make her realize how much he needed to speak with her.

She hesitated.

An eternity passed while she decided. Finally, she inclined her head.

Relief rushed through him, and he held out his arm.

She looked at it and, quite deliberately, did not take it. Making her way to a stone bench, she seated herself. "Very well, my lord. I will listen."

Suppressing his admiration at her imperiousness, he said, "Miss Hargrove, perhaps we should go inside."

"No. You'll do this now, or not at all." Though her cheeks were flushed with cold, she sat on the bench as regal as a queen while she waited for him to begin speaking.

And, of course, now that he had her ear, he had no idea what to say.

Chapter Four

EVER IMPASSIVE, THE EARL stared at her. Moments passed, filled only with the faint strains of music and laughter.

Breaking their gaze, Sofie exhaled forcefully. Damnation, was he ever going to speak? He'd begged for her to listen, and now he said nothing at all. Folding her arms, she looked toward the ballroom. It would take less than nothing to leave him, alone in the dark with his unspoken explanations.

"I am thought to be dissolute, Miss Hargrove," Edgington said.

Surprise by the sudden words, Sofie glanced at him. Jaw tense, he looked somewhere left of her shoulder. Then, she realized what he'd said. Unable to help herself, she barked a laugh. "Do tell."

He didn't react to her sarcasm, but then when did he show anything approaching emotion? Immediately, a memory rose, of hot eyes, rasping breath, and urgent hands. Quickly, she quashed such foolishness to focus only on the present. Only on her hate.

"I am thought to be a wastrel, a useless thing," he continued. "I do not begrudge this reputation, you understand. Indeed, I do my best to adhere to it."

He was telling her things she already knew. "I do not—"

"I beg your indulgence." Something flickered in his expression, something that might have been discomfort or desperation. He cleared his throat. "It has always been so, since the time I can remember. My mother thought little of me, as did my father. I was raised by nurses and tutors, but that is an experience no different from any child of the aristocracy. I went to school. No one expected anything of me. It seemed my character had been determined, and no matter what I did, none would waver from it."

It did not matter. It did not matter his childhood was unhappy, that no one had ever believed in him. It. Did not. Matter.

Tightening her grip on her biceps, she hardened herself. "Again, I do not see how—"

"My apologies, Miss Hargrove, but it will become relevant." His features once more smooth, he again placed his hands behind his back. "I decided if I could not impress them, I would live down to their expectations. Indeed, I would exceed them. I became the worst sort of degenerate—wild, careless. I gambled. I made foolish wagers. I rode too fast, drank too much, I got myself into brawls with lads older and bigger than me. I set about to have my first woman and once I had done so, I sowed my oats indiscriminately." High color stained his cheekbones, as if he were embarrassed to be telling her this, and she knew her own cheeks blazed. Please God, he could not be embarrassed. She could not soften toward him. She could not.

Briefly, she closed her eyes. This. This is what she liked about him. He had always spoken thus, always told her everything, whether it had been fit for her ears or not. He'd delighted in making her blush, in flustering her, and she'd loved seeing his delight. Somehow, she'd known he'd had very little joy in his life, and she'd wanted to give it to him.

Foolish girl.

"When first I met you, I had six years of dissolute behavior behind me, and the knowledge that all who proclaimed I would come to a bad end were correct." He met her eyes. She inhaled sharply. He looked … he looked impassioned. Full of anguish, frustration, longing. An answering passion began a burn within her, and she tore her eyes from him. She remembered this, too. His gaze had always done such to her.

"I did not intend it to go as far as it did. I enjoyed my time with you. You … had no expectations. You simply liked me and thought to indulge that emotion. I was at fault for what happened. I should have known it would end badly. When we were caught, I should have done more to persuade them they had seen nothing."

She frowned. "You could not have—"

"I should have persuaded them," he said. "I was heir to the Earl of Edgington, with five hundred years of privilege behind me. If I decreed the sky to be green, people would hasten to agree. I should have been able to convince them they'd seen nothing. But I didn't. Then, I compounded my error by not offering for you."

His gaze never left her, and she found herself nervous under such intensity.

"You left, and I returned to my old ways," he said. "Indeed, I became worse than ever. I had ruined the one bright thing in my life, you see, so how could it be I was anything but a degenerate?"

She did not know what to say. How to feel. This was … He was making her … She would not forgive him. Nothing he could say would make right what he'd done. She hated him. She did.

He began to pace, his step agitated, the solitary sign that he felt something. Anything. "Tonight, I told myself I should stay far from you, but I could not help myself. I *cannot* help myself." He stopped abruptly, and gray eyes found hers. "I'd told myself to forget you. I thought I had. Then I saw you tonight, and I remembered. Too well, I remembered. Your wit. Your laugh. Your taste. The way you would argue with me just for the sake of arguing, the way you would tease me until I smiled. I remembered you loved lemon ices and the final light before twilight. I remembered you waxing lyrical on architecture, and how, though I cared not a whit for buildings, I was interested because you were. I remembered how I feel when I'm with you, how you make me feel, and I knew I could not stay away."

She felt herself waver. Damnation, he always did this to her, took what she knew to be true and skewed it.

Crossing her arms, she forced herself to remember. To remember he had been happy to abandon her, to take everything that had been special between them and make it seem tawdry and wrong. She had to remember her rage. "I don't care for your explanations or your contrition. I would much prefer you take yourself somewhere else." She ignored the voice that whispered *liar*.

A change came over his expression, one that forcefully reminded her of what he was. A dark, dangerous man, with licentiousness and dissolution to his name. "Why are you so angry?"

She licked her lips. "Wh-what?"

"Why are you still so angry?" He advanced, his eyes glittering in the dark. "Ten years have passed. You have traveled, have conquered the Continent by all accounts. Why do you care for a scandal over a decade old, which most have forgotten?"

"I—" She didn't know why she was so angry, why it had lingered. "They have not forgotten. They spoke of it in the ballroom tonight."

He ignored her, his body crowding hers. He was so close now, close enough to touch. "Why, Sofie?"

She closed her eyes, swallowed, at the sound of her name in his rich, dark voice.

Fingertips danced over her cheekbone, his thumb tracing her jaw. "Sofie," he whispered, and she lifted herself for his kiss.

He tasted the same, of brandy and smoke and that flavor that was his. The same emotions rioted within her, wild and free, and she wanted his hands on her, all over, as they had been before. Her hands tangled in his hair, the pomade strange to her touch.

His lips brushed her collarbone, and her fingers tightened in his hair. "Michael."

He paused, his breath ghosting along her skin.

Sofie closed her eyes. She'd said his name. She'd said his name, and damned herself as a fool. She remembered, just as well as he.

Michael pulled back, his chest heaving, as if he were as affected as her. Resting his forehead against hers, he cradled her face in his hands. "I never forgot you, Sofie. I tried, but I couldn't."

She hadn't forgotten him either. Every day she'd told herself she had, but she'd never succeeded. He was burned into her, so deep she couldn't remove him.

"Why did you not come after me?" It had hurt so much when he hadn't. She knew it had been irrational, knew it was foolish, but she'd been seventeen, and in love. She'd wanted him to be as much in love as she.

He smiled without mirth. "I'm a bastard. What can I say?"

Pain filled her. She made to pull apart, but he caught her to him. "Sofie, you cannot know how I regretted it. I was callow and foolish, and I wish so goddamn much that I *had* offered for you.

Do you know how proud I would be to have you as my wife? But I …" He swallowed. "I knew you would not be proud of me. How could you? I could not have given you all you have found for yourself. You are— Do you know how magnificent you are?"

Suddenly, in the midst of all this, humor found her. "Of course. I recite my magnificence to myself often."

A rueful sort of smile took his own expression. "You *are* magnificent. I always thought so, and I wanted you so much. I was twenty-one, and a fool." His thumb caressed her cheek. "Why did you run?"

A breath shuddered through her. "I … My parents were so disappointed. My father looked at me with disgust, and my mother wouldn't stop crying, so I, I left. I'd always wanted to travel, and Stephen was in France already, and …" She met his gaze. "I wasn't supposed to be ruined at seventeen, but if I hadn't been, I never would have become this person. I like her. I like me."

His lips twisted. "So I did you a favor?"

"Perhaps." She fell silent. "It wasn't pleasant."

"No."

"My parents were furious." His thumb stroked her shoulder. "Yes."

"Are you not going to apologize?" she said, frustrated.

The corner of his lip lifted. "Do you want me to?"

"I don't know! I don't know anymore. I don't know what to think, what to feel. For ten years, I've hated you, Michael. I can't … I don't …" Wild emotion rioted within her. She didn't know what to make of this, how she felt.

Oh God, she wanted to kiss him. She wanted to haul him close and feel his lips beneath hers. She gave a hiccupping laugh. How could she want such things? *How?* A mere half an hour ago she'd wanted never to see him again.

"Sof," he said softly. "Why are you still so angry?"

Uncertain, she stared at him. He waited, his gaze never leaving hers.

A harsh sob exploded from her, then another, and another. "Because I love you," she gasped. "Because I never stopped. Because for ten years, I compared every man to you and found them wanting. Because you left me, you *left* me, Michael, and I … I …"

He gathered her in his arms, whispering comfort and of how he was sorry, he was so damned sorry. "I should have come after you. I should have followed you to the Continent and *made* you listen. I should have done it any time these past ten years. I'm sorry I didn't. Sof, you've not a notion of how sorry I am."

"Fat lot of good sorry does me," she hiccuped, attempting a scowl but certain she failed miserably.

A smile. Finally. "Ah, Sof. How can I resist you when you say things like that?"

Hiding against his chest, she shook her head.

A gentle finger under her chin forced her gaze to his, and her breath caught at what she saw in his gray eyes. "Sof. You know I love you, don't you?"

She bit her lip.

"I do." He brushed her lips with his. "I love you." He kissed her cheekbone. "I love you." The hollow of her throat. "I love you."

She closed her eyes. She wanted to believe him. She did. "How can we feel this way? We've been … It's been ten years, Michael."

His lips feathered over her right brow. "Sof. You need time. We need time. Tomorrow, I will call upon you, and then I'll pay my address to your brother. I'll ask his permission to court you. No decision needs to be made. We'll take it as it comes."

"I don't know if—"

Pulling away, he took her by the shoulders. Jaw tense, he said, "Tomorrow, Sofie."

Words deserted her at his intensity, at her own foolish hope. She wanted that, so badly.

"Believe me, Sof. Believe us."

There was so much against them, so much. "Stephen will thrash you. He'll keep you from me."

Michael set his jaw. "He'll try."

A sudden, blinding happiness took her, surely too bright to last, but she would grab it while it burned. She brought his hand to her cheek, kissed the long, sensitive fingers. "Tomorrow."

Chapter Five

Three months later

THE BREEZE WRAPPED AROUND Sofie, warm in the darkness of the garden. Faint strains of music sounded from Diana's ball, and she could hear the laughter of others who had sought respite from the crush of the ballroom.

Exhaling, Sofie looked out over the garden. Though it was more than two months since her return to London, she had not returned to the Continent. How could she? Michael wasn't there.

Strong arms snaked around her waist, pulling her into a hard chest while soft lips brushed the spot beneath her ear. A deliciously deep voice said, "You always did like a garden."

Wickedness rushed through her as she turned in Michael's embrace. "They provide so much opportunity for mischief."

He raised a brow. "The Countess of Edgington has too much dignity to get into mischief."

Laughter bubbled in her, though she did her best to keep her expression solemn. "Well, it's a good thing I'm not yet the countess."

"Only for twelve more hours."

She lifted a shoulder. "It still counts."

As if he could no longer contain himself, a smile broke across his face, his eyes alight. "I won't win, will I?"

"No," she said, loving that he shared his humor with her. Loving him.

"Well," he said. "I shall have to cheat." And then he set his lips to hers.

His tongue danced along the seam of her lips, seeking entrance, and she opened to him, welcoming him into her as she dug her fingers into his back. He made a sound of pleasure, filling her, making her heated and empty. *Soon. Soon.*

"Miss Hargrove!"

Slowly, the shrill voice penetrated the haze he always created. Michael tensed against her, lifting his head to stare straight ahead as a tick started in his jaw.

Cautiously, Sofie peeped past his shoulder. Lady Darbyon stood before them, a horrified expression twisting her features.

Leaning her forehead against him, Sofie groaned. Dear God, not again.

"Miss Hargrove! I cannot *believe* this! And with the Earl of Edgington! Did you not learn your lesson the first time?"

Extracting herself from Michael's embrace, she squared her shoulders and entered the fray. "The earl is my fiancé. Surely we are allowed some leeway?"

"You still have a reputation to uphold. Come." With that imperious command, Lady Darbyon held out her hand.

"You saw nothing."

At the cold, hard words, Sofie glanced at Michael. He'd turned to face Lady Darbyon, and his expression … his expression was terrifying.

Clearly uncowed, Lady Darbyon tutted. "My lord, I saw—"

"Nothing. You will not speak of my countess. You will return to the ballroom, and you will forget you ever saw us."

"I hardly think—"

"Lady Darbyon," Michael said. "Do not test me."

The lady blanched, her eyes wide, then she hurried from them.

Sofie watched Lady Darbyon's retreating back until she couldn't see her anymore. "The sky is green."

Obviously distracted, Michael glanced at her. "Pardon?"

"You said you could convince people the sky is green."

His expression changed, becoming heavy-lidded. "I'd rather convince you to come deeper in the garden."

"Why, Michael," she said mildly, her heart racing. "How scandalous."

A smile lit his face. "We've only got twelve more hours. Come, Sof." He held out his hand. "Let's cause a scandal."

Cassandra Dean is a best-selling, multipublished author of historical and fantasy romance and was a 2016 finalist in the Romance Writers of Australia's coveted RUBY Award. Her latest novel, *Silk & Scholar*, is book four of her popular Silk series featuring law-loving peeps and their happily ever afters. Her next novel will be the final book in the Silk series, *Silk & Scarlet*, and she is working on a new series featuring husband-hunting sisters in Regency England, as well as a novel where a thief meets his match in a determined lady. Cassandra is proud to call South Australia her home, where she regularly cheers on her AFL football team and creates her next tale.

Visit Cassandra's website at http://cassandradean.com, and join Cassandra's mailing list at http://cassandradean.com/extras/newsletter-postcard-mailing-list. Follow Cassandra on Facebook at https://www.facebook.com/AuthorCassandraDean and on Twitter @authorCassDean

ONE HOT MESS

Tina Ferraro

"YOU'RE NOT SERIOUSLY GOING through with this, are you, Maddie?"

My best friend Linzee Holt's words felt warm on my neck as we inched our way down the stairwell. The final bell had sounded on the first Wednesday of the school year, and a cool thousand of us were making a break from Applewood High classrooms.

"You know I have to," I said over the tangle of dark hair on my shoulder. Even my clip couldn't keep that mess in place all day. "I promised."

"Sure, *that*." She paused at the first-floor landing, backing into an alcove to escape the press of students, leaving enough room for me. "But promises made under the influence of chlorine and sunblock are meant to be broken."

Linzee's gift of reasoning was among the things I adored about her. She could find a trap door, a silver lining, or something amusing in just about anything. She was my other half—my better half—and I appreciated her sparkle all the more these days, what with my in-the-toilet love life and the mounting tension at my house over bills.

Of course, that didn't mean Linzee was prophetic or always

right. Take the black dye that turned her blonde hair green. Or the smells in her house since convincing her parents to keep their cat's entire litter of kittens. But her biggest goof, as far as she was concerned, was something she *didn't* do: talk me out of my crazy scheme last June to throw myself at my baseball-playing, hot-stuff neighbor, Hayes Townsend.

I'd been crushing on him since he moved in across the street with his dad and stepmom. His competitive streak had instantly tangled with mine, and our neighborhood's once-casual swimming pool games, like diving for coins and Marco Polo, had arced to epic levels. I'd become all about winning, all about him. All about *winning him*.

It had taken a solid two years and one big lie for me to cross that threshold, and even then, we'd gone on to crash and burn. I adored Linzee for trying to take responsibility for missing the danger signs, but the whole of that hot mess was on me. I was the one who had to live with his accusation that I'd *used him for his body*.

"I'd love to get out of that ridiculous club, believe me," I said, shifting my backpack to the other shoulder. "But I'm stuck. Apparently, I am the president."

All this had been the doing of English teacher Mrs. Puglisi and my mom. The Puglisi backyard pool was *the* neighborhood hang spot on summer days, partly because the Puglisi family believed in "the more, the merrier," and partly because they were the only ones in our subdivision with an in-ground pool. The two ladies had been sipping iced teas and commenting on the new rage of appreciation clubs at the high school—Italian, LGBT, African Heritage, and the like. The clubs were open to all and had been gaining popularity by selling hot lunch alternatives on Fridays and other creative fundraisers. Mom and Mrs. Puglisi had decided our upstate New York town of Applewood needed its own club.

Next thing I knew, Mrs. Puglisi was filling out paperwork and calling me prez. Which, I was certain, was simply so I'd show up and, hopefully, to attract other members. Not that I was super popular or anything, but going into my senior year, I knew people. Nearly six-foot-tall girls had a tendency to get noticed.

Exactly *what* the club planned to highlight, however, was anyone's guess. That Main Street had as many pizzerias as traffic lights? That most of our local apples got squashed into applesauce? That our public library now had electronic books, too? I mean, our hometown was nice enough as far as these things go, but come on…

"That changes everything, Madame President." Linzee's eyes gleamed. "Down the road, when our own kids go to AHS, there'll probably be a plaque on a wall commemorating you as the club's trailblazer."

I shot her a look.

"Or not." She laughed. "Look, I gotta go or I'll miss dance. Call me later with all the awesome deets."

"I hate you," I deadpanned.

Moments later, I cruised through room 112's open door. Mrs. Puglisi stood by her desk, her face obscured by her signature oversized glasses, chatting up a guy with a shiny mouth of braces and a girl hiding inside her dark hoodie. I pegged the kids as freshmen and not likely on the fast track toward A-list popularity.

"Well, here she is," Mrs. Puglisi said, her voice resonating with warmth. "Meet Madeleine Elsey, our club president."

I tried to smile at the two kids. I mean, I might as well make the best of this nonsense.

"Let's get started," our fearless leader continued. "There may only be five of us now, but that's plenty."

Five? I glanced around until I spotted a long, lone figure gazing out the window.

Wait—

I knew that profile. Those broad shoulders. That wavy hair curling around the edges of the collar. More importantly, I recognized the way my blood was suddenly pumping and how hard it was to take a decent breath.

Holy crap!

What this club was hoping to accomplish was hardly an issue anymore. It was why a superjock with a real and legitimate life like Hayes Townsend would want to join. And how long he'd last … now he knew it meant putting up with *me*?

Chapter Two

"WHY, LINZEE, *WHY?*" I'D bemoaned exactly three months ago. Lying on my bed, we'd been flipping through a magazine, debating which celeb wore a designer outfit better. "Why is it the guys I don't want like me, and the ones I do want to be friends?"

"The age-old question. Probably what cave girls talked about while making boots out of mammoth hide. And cowgirls—"

"I get it." Sometimes it was best to cut her off before her brain wandered out of bounds. Besides, she and her college boyfriend, Emory, were making the long-distance relationship work so seamlessly I sometimes wondered if she was of this world. "It figures," I went on with a long sigh, "that Hayes is finally free of the wicked Willa, and yet *who* is texting me?"

"Alec," we grumbled in sync. Alec was a guy from school I'd hung out with a few times. I'd tried to like him back—really tried—but just couldn't get past his robot fixation and the silly way he ended most of his text messages with exclamation points!!!

Unlike Hayes, who had that intriguing habit of pausing before speaking, making me feel like he was carefully keeping the best parts of himself private. Making me want to get closer, to listen harder, to delve deeper…

But while sculling in the deep end earlier that day, I'd overheard him tell Mrs. Puglisi he was "taking a break" from dating to concentrate on his grades and his pitching in hopes of getting a college scholarship. I'd dunked my head underwater and screamed.

"Taking a break!" I lamented to Linzee. "Who *does* that?"

"I know, it's like your life is ass-backward, Mads. If only you could hang out in a pool with Alec and go to movies and make out with Hayes."

I opened my mouth to echo her "if only." When a crazy wonderful idea exploded in my brain. (Clearly, my bestie and her big thinking had rubbed off.)

Four evenings later, I got my chance. The neighbors had wandered home. Mrs. Puglisi was making dinner while her almost deaf mother—everyone called her Nana—snoozed in a lounge chair. So basically, Hayes and I were alone. I pulled myself up on the step, gave my bikini a little tug, and confessed that I had a problem.

Hayes, who was a nice guy, even though he had the looks and swagger to be a jerk if he'd wanted, turned to give me his full attention.

My heart beating so loud I was afraid he'd either hear it or seeing it thumping in my chest, I unveiled my rehearsed line. "You know Alec, right?"

Resting elbows on the pool's edge (making those baseball throwing muscles *bulge, baby, bulge*), he nodded.

"He and I have been hanging out lately. And, well, this is embarrassing, but it's just not working. The kissing, I mean. I'm not sure he knows what he's doing. Or maybe I don't."

Question marks flashed in his eyes. "And you're telling me this … why?"

No stopping now. "Because someone needs to show me how to kiss. So I can know if it's him. Or me. Or both of us together. So I know whether to move ahead with this thing or walk away."

His gaze swept the surface of the pool. "And you want that somebody to be me?"

More than my next breath. "Well, you're single again. And you know what you're doing. I mean, I saw you with Willa … I mean, everybody did at school."

"We were that bad?" he said in an uncharacteristically speedy comeback.

"You were that good!"

His dimples made a rare appearance. "Yeah, she was into PDA. Which was one of the reasons I wanted out."

Silence fell between us. Awkward and painful, especially since my heart thumped against my ribs.

"I don't know, Maddie." He pushed off the wall, sculling into deeper waters. "I want to help you out, but it's kinda weird, you know? And what would Alec think?"

I was ready for that. "He wouldn't know. It would be our secret. But even if he *did* somehow find out, well, he couldn't be mad. It's not like we're official or anything. And," I added, "I'm trying to do this for *us*." (Which wasn't a lie. Depending on which guy was implied in the *us*.)

Mrs. Puglisi strolled out to check on Nana, and that was that. But as I stood and wrapped myself in a towel, all I could think of was texting Linzee. Hayes might not have said yes, but he hadn't said no, either!

Chapter Three

"MADDIE IS PRESIDENT?" HAYES spoke to Mrs. Puglisi, taking long strides to the front of the classroom. "I thought this was the first meeting."

"It is," she responded, her voice a little strained.

"How'd I miss the election?"

This was crazy. Not only had he showed up for this ridiculous club, but he actually *cared* who was president? But then another thought struck me, more like an evil whisper in my head. Was he making this scene because he didn't want someone of my low moral quality to lead the club?

"He can have it," I blurted. "Hayes can be president. If he wants."

Mrs. Puglisi pushed her glasses higher on her nose. "The fair thing to do is vote, of course, I'm sorry, Maddie, but I guess I was too hasty. So anyone who'd like to be considered for club president or has anything to say on the matter, please state your case."

Both freshmen shook their heads.

I stood beside my desk, blowing off the loose strands that had escaped my clip. "I vote we elect Hayes," I forced out. Then I glanced his way. For the first time in months, our gazes connected. It was brief—but crackling.

"Hayes?" Mrs. Puglisi said.

"All right." His dimples made a fleeting appearance. "But maybe she'd like to be co-president?"

I shook my head.

"Then how about VP?"

What in the world was going on?

"All in favor of making Hayes the president and Maddie the vice president?" Mrs. Puglisi asked.

The whole room—well, the four of us students—sounded with "yea," marking the first official action of the Hometown of Applewood Club. Which was arguably the smallest, lamest, most pointless club on campus, but with Hayes included, was suddenly *a lot* more interesting.

I tried to stay focused during the meeting, to act as if I cared. Hayes's attention seemed to waver a bit, too, but who was I to judge?

When Mrs. Puglisi called adjournment, I shuffled out behind him. "Hayes," I said, falling into step. "Come clean with me. The Hometown of Applewood Club? *Really?* Why?"

After a pause so long I could have grown another inch, he cleared this throat. "I got talked into it."

Oh, of course. Mrs. Puglisi had twisted his arm, too. Although why she'd made me prez over him made no sense, since Hayes had far more of a social draw. "Yeah, what can you say to her but yes, when you spend the summer in her pool?"

"No, Mr. Last," he responded, referring to the guidance counselor. "He told me to get some diversity for my college apps, so I wasn't only about baseball. And being a senior, he figured I could land a leadership position, which would also look good." He shrugged. "But I didn't want to take anything from you, which is why I suggested co-presidents."

I would have loved it if he'd wanted to work with me because he thought me principled or clever or awesome, but I still appreciated that he thought of me *at all*. It was a world away from where we'd left things. "Thanks. College applications aren't an issue for me. I'm going to the CC."

He took a moment to digest that. "Right, your dad's business. How's that going?"

My body tensed. I hated talking about my dad's camera shop. But anyone with a cellphone camera and access to a laptop (and that would be everyone in Applewood these days, from first graders on up to Nana) knew his business was drying up. Not to mention that the last time Hayes and I talked about this—how I didn't know if we could afford to keep our house much longer, let alone swing college tuition—we had been in each other's arms. It was all too raw and personal now.

"No change," I simply said.

"You know Jenny O'Keefe? Scott's older sister?" His response would have come off as completely random if I hadn't spent those eleven nights getting to know how his brain worked. He wasn't big on smooth segues.

I nodded. Who didn't know the former head cheerleader and her baseball-playing brother?

"She just started at the CC and likes it. Especially the general ed classes," he added, slanting me a look.

He clearly remembered more about me than he'd been letting on. That's what I planned to take at the CC, while figuring out how to afford to finish at a university. I wasn't giving up on my dreams of becoming a magazine editor just because my family had fallen on hard times.

He pulled open the door to the parking lot, and then held it to let me through. Sweeping by him, I breathed in, getting treated to his clean, masculine scent. For that millisecond, I felt at one with him again. Almost in love with him again.

A car horn honked. Hayes waved to the driver idling in a near-by spot, and then slanted a look at me. "I'd offer you a ride, but we're not headed to my house any time soon."

I dismissed that with a wave of my hand. Again, I was grateful for the consideration.

It wasn't until he opened the passenger's side door that I saw the carefully plucked eyebrows and the slick blonde hair. Jenny O'Keefe herself.

I faked a big smile, praying it covered my raging jealousy.

"Good to see you, Maddie!" she called back.

Of course they weren't headed to his house any time soon. They had a lot better things to do first. The kinds of things he and I had once done. And I really, really wished we could do again.

I lifted my hand in a wave as they sped off. Even when life got immensely better, it could still suck.

Chapter Four

"I WAS THINKING ABOUT what you asked, Maddie," Hayes had said last June, sitting beside me on a top bleacher at the park's baseball field. His buddies had headed home from practice. The sun was setting, the field lights were off, and technically, the park was closing.

But no matter. He'd texted me and asked me to meet him. I would have gone to hell and back.

"About kissing." He settled in beside me. So close, our thighs almost touched. That in itself was enough to make my nerve endings come alive. "I guess I could help. I mean, I want to."

I'm pretty sure I gasped, but he kept right on talking.

"You're sure this is above board, right? Alec's not going to come after me?"

"*No* problem," I said with utmost sincerity. I wanted to tell him I hadn't seen Alec in a couple of weeks and had no intentions of being near his lips again. But that wouldn't be in my best interest.

"Okay." If I didn't know better, I would have thought he'd swallowed hard. "I know you've done this before, and there are no real rules. Mainly, you relax and do what comes naturally."

Nothing felt more natural than being with Hayes, but the relax part was out of the question. Every fiber of my being wanted to leap into his lap, run my fingers through his hair, acquaint myself with the stubble shadowing on his cheeks, inhale his masculine scent.

His hand pressed gently against my cheek. "Now close your eyes."

I did, and after some quivering anticipation, felt his lips over mine. Soft, at first. Then his hand moved to cup the back of my neck, and he re-angled, deepening the kiss. Our breaths mixing, our tongues dancing, our hands caressing; it seemed I could no longer tell where my body ended and his began.

"How does that compare?" he asked later, pulling apart. Somehow, we'd lost almost all light, except for the glow of full moon high in the sky.

"Compare?" I repeated dreamily. To what? Walking on air? Winning a lottery jackpot?

"*Kissing Alec*," he said, reining me in.

"Oh," I said and laughed—mostly at the fact his powerful kisses had robbed me of brain cells. "No comparison, really. He doesn't have anything near your moves or style."

Even in the dim light, I could see his smile.

For the next ten days, my life felt pretty perfect. Sure, my father went and sold the family van. Chlorine was doing a real number on my hair. And my conscience tapped a steady beat over my ongoing deception. But I was happy. And I was pretty sure Hayes was, too.

Rather quickly, we'd gone from teacher/student to essentially lab partners, learning and experimenting together. *Secret* lab partners. By day, we'd hang around the Puglisi's pool, trying to act same-old/same-old, not to give ourselves away. Although, somehow, I always ended up on *his* shoulders during the shallow-end chicken fight competitions, my thighs pressed tight against his neck, his hands solid on my legs.

Each night I'd drop by the park at the end of his practice. Increasingly, upon seeing me, his gaze grew stronger, his grin deeper. All mention of kissing lessons or Alec was history—just as Alec himself was history. I hadn't so much as texted with him in a couple of weeks. I totally had to 'fess up to Hayes about all that, but I was waiting for the right moment, something that showed he'd be up for a smooth transition to a legitimate couple.

But fate had other plans. Following a day spent helping my parents prepare for a garage sale, I'd arrived at the park later than usual. Hayes was pacing in hard circles on cement, a scowl etched in his brow.

"You fucking lied to me, Maddie!" No pause, no segue, just naked-ass truth. "Alec said you aren't even together."

My heart jumped to my throat. "You—you talked to him?"

"Yeah, I talked to him." He raked a hand through his hair. "He came by here earlier. To run the track, but I thought the worst. I went over to him, to try to smooth things over, only to have him act confused, then laugh, and be like, 'Dude, no worries. I'm *not* with her.'"

I opened my mouth to try to cover my tracks, but anything but the truth sounded ridiculous, even in my own head. "I'm sorry."

"He said he hasn't seen you since before school let out."

I grimaced.

"You're not denying this?"

"I really did have a couple bad dates with Alec a month or so ago, but I never cared about making things right with him." It felt a lot easier to look at the dusty cleats on his feet than at his face. "It was all about you. You and Willa had broken up. It was summer, and I was seeing you every day at the pool. Plus, I heard you telling Mrs. Puglisi that you were taking a break from dating, so I figured maybe you wouldn't mind passing the time with me."

"You tricked me." A flinty glare transformed his eyes. "Figuring what, I'd never find out?"

"I—I was going to tell you," I asserted, my voice quavering. "When?"

"When it felt right."

"Oh, and what would be the right time to tell a guy he got *used for his body*?"

My blood ran cold. "Wait a minute; I didn't make you do anything you didn't want to do."

"No, you didn't. And that's the worst part. I *let* you use me." A muscle jumped in his jaw. "Thing is, I felt for you, and what you were going through at home, and how you weren't sure if you were with the right person. I was trying to help. While you were using me, and probably laughing your ass off about it with Linzee."

"No." I stomped a flip-flop on the pavement for emphasis. "No! I was into you. I—I still am, more than ever."

He turned.

"Please, Hayes," I said, feeling I could neither breathe nor swallow. "Can't we talk about this some more? I'm really, really sorry. I mean, maybe we could just start over."

"Start over?" He pivoted toward me, his eyes on fire. "Sure, that we can do."

I drew a decent breath.

"Let's go all the way back to being strangers."

Chapter Five

TO MY HORROR AND shame—and probably some other things I was too horrified and shamed to name—Hayes kept to that resolution for the rest of the summer. He ignored me.

"I think he'd put Nana on his shoulders for a chicken fight before he'd choose me," I'd griped to Linzee during our back-to-school shopping trip. "Or Zelda," I added, referring to his very pregnant stepmother.

"It's as if he's developed the superpower of invisibility when it comes to you, Mads. Like, he can look right at you and not see you."

Almost. Except we both knew what Hayes *did* see when his eyes happened upon me. A liar and a user. I wasn't those things, of course—not really. What I'd been was stupid. Desperate. And in love. (Which I was coming to understand often went together.)

The evening after the first club meeting, I called Linzee as promised. She'd expected dull-as-dirt club talk, and I pretty much knocked her socks off with the updates on Hayes.

"Okay," she told me, "knowing he's with Jenny is the worst and the best thing that ever happened to you."

"Worst, yeah." I screwed up my face. "How is it the best?"

"Keeps you in the friend zone. Gives you the chance to show him what a good person you are. Then, down the line, when they break up ... well, who knows?"

Her words circled through my brain.

"And the cherry on top, Mads? You don't have to see them all over school, all over each other, like last time."

She was *so* right. At that moment, I could almost forget my pea-soup green envy over Jenny. "Oh, Linzee, have I told you recently how much I adore you?"

I could almost feel the warmth of her smile through the phone line.

Regaining Hayes's respect filled my head the next day at school. While cruising toward the cafeteria, I went with an impulsive decision to pop into the guidance office. Mr. Last was between appointments and agreed to see me.

"I know colleges are looking for diversity and leadership in their applicants," I began, practically repeating Hayes's words. "But say you were president of a small club. Would that be as impressive as being the president of an established one?"

Basically, should I use what influence I had to round up new club members to help Hayes look more important?

Mr. Last steepled his fingers on his desk. "You're absolutely right about diversity and leadership. Funny, I had a conversation like this yesterday, a senior who told me about a new club to honor our town and wanted to know how to best play his participation."

I felt my brow arch. He couldn't be talking about Hayes.

"I pointed out that being a founding member can be even more important than size or elected status. It highlights innovation and independence, two other traits highly favored by admissions committees."

Now my head was really spinning. "I'm in that new club, too, along with Hayes Townsend."

"So Hayes *did* join. Good. For both of you."

Moving like a sleepwalker in the halls, I didn't know what to think. I let my black ballet flats propel me down the hall. The door to room 112 was wide open.

"Hey there," she said when I poked my head in. Mrs. Puglisi was eating a salad at her desk. "Come on in."

I slumped in a first-row chair.

"Slow start with our club yesterday, Maddie. But it'll pick up, I'm sure." My face must have looked as shell-shocked because it sure sounded like Mrs. Puglisi was trying to reassure me. "I think we need to agree on an initial element to focus on first, something that will get people's attention." She mentioned a sports star who called Applewood his hometown and the resurgence of Main Street. "Why don't you and Hayes kick around some ideas to present at next week's meeting?"

I nodded as if that was going to happen. "Actually, I'm wondering if you could tell me how he knew about this club. Did you mention it to him like you did me?"

"My mother did."

I blinked several times, although it was my ears I was pretty sure that had failed me. "Nana?"

"One-on-one in a quiet environment is really the only way she communicates these days, and whenever he was the first to show up at the pool, he'd spend time chatting with her."

The idea of Hayes hanging with Nana sure rocked my boat. Score another point for him being an all-around good guy.

But that didn't change the fact he'd lied to me about Mr. Last. In fact, it proved it. What was I missing?

Chapter Six

FOR ONCE, LINZEE DIDN'T have any insights into Hayes's motivations. Talking on the phone that night, we focused on Emory's upcoming weekend home. But when a screaming siren announced the arrival of an ambulance out front, I promised Linzee a callback and hit the ground running. My parents were at a franchise fair, investigating options for their shop space, so I locked up on my way out.

A crowd was forming on the sidewalk across from the Puglisi house as I rushed through the cool night air. Ambulance doors had been flung open while paramedics wheeled an empty gurney up the walk.

Spying Hayes, I made a beeline for him. Nothing about us—past or present—mattered now.

"Is it Nana?"

Dressed in a tee, gym shorts, and a frown, he nodded. "Don't know if it's a heart attack or stroke or whatever."

I opened my mouth to try to say something supportive, but all that came out was a gasp.

His stepmom, Zelda, stopped before us, her belly huge inside a patchwork quilt. "I've gotta get off my feet. Keep me posted, Hayes." She shrugged the quilt off her shoulders and draped it around his.

Nodding, he grabbed hold of the quilt's edges, pulling one against his chest. Then he opened the other side and gazed invitingly at me.

My heart leaped to my throat. Admittedly, being barefoot in a knee-length sleep shirt was stupid in autumn night weather, but snuggling up with him wasn't a smart move for me, either. My new resolution with him was about boundaries, about respectability, about friendship, right?

"I know it's a little weird, Maddie, but no reason to stand there and shiver."

I shuffled from one foot to the other. And appreciating his stab at honesty, I went with my own. "What about Jenny? Would she be all right with it?"

His gaze narrowed.

"Well, she's your *girlfriend*, and I'm—"

"She's not my girlfriend. I don't *have* a girlfriend."

His words blowing through my brain, I struggled to find my own. "But yesterday, she picked you up."

"As a favor, on her way home from the CC. So I could work out with Scott in their backyard batting cage."

Wow, how I wished I could take my question back. He must think I had a real problem exaggerating/inventing relationships.

Hayes closed the gap between us in a couple of steps, and pulled me into his cocoon. My body was treated to the sensational heat of both the blanket and body variety. But I was pretty sure it was my cheeks that were flaming.

"Better?" he asked.

I let out a murmur of agreement, just as footsteps pounded from near the house. I looked up to see paramedics steering Nana out on the gurney, Mrs. Puglisi bringing up the rear.

"They say she'll be fine!" Mrs. Puglisi shouted to the neighbors. "They're just taking her in to be sure."

"Thank God," Hayes said, turning toward me. Our faces suddenly only a foot or so apart, the quilt around us tugged tighter. "I can't imagine losing her."

"Yeah, I know you visit Nana sometimes."

He smiled. "She's great, when you give her a chance. And you know, she was on to us this summer, the sneaking around. She heard us that day at the pool."

My brain circled. I was embarrassed to admit I'd discounted her as sleeping, and, well, hearing impaired. "Really?"

"She called it *romantic*." His brow quirked. "Then later, she kept after me to patch things up."

I saw no reason not to go for broke. "Is that when she told you about the new club I was joining?"

He did one of his long pauses. "She thought working together would get us back on track, even suggested the president/vice president thing."

"So it wasn't Mr. Last who came up with that."

He bit his lip, or maybe was biting away a smile? "I did talk to him about the club, but no, it was Nana who told me."

I drew a slow inhale, deliberately made him suffer through my long pause. "So let me get this straight, Hayes Townsend, when you said Mr. Last was behind all that, you *lied* to me?"

He seemed to flinch.

"You *tricked* me?"

A smile caught the edges of his mouth.

"You *used me?*"

"Wait, that one doesn't work here." His dimples flashed. "Unless you want to lodge a complaint about this quilt. Claim I'm using you for your body ... heat."

"Are you?" My pulse quickened.

"Maybe a little. But mostly it's seizing the moment to get close to you again, and try to explain why I acted like such an ass." He slid around next to me, leading me in slow steps toward our houses, while his hand gently cupped my waist.

"I never told you how things ended with Willa." He stared into space for a long moment. "She'd been cheating on me for months."

Aha, no wonder he'd wanted *to take a break from dating.*

"At the time you came to me with your idea, I was still pissed off—at her and myself. So I was torn. I mean, I definitely could see myself with you." He stole a look at me out of the corner of his eye. "But it was complicated. Eventually, I convinced myself it was a win-win, with you getting what you needed and me finding a safe way to move on. Not realizing how hard and fast I'd fall for you."

I went to remind him of the feelings I had for him, then thought better of it. For once, I needed to zip my lip and listen.

"When I saw Alec at the park, I assumed he was there to kick my ass. I got all pumped up, went over there ready—not just to defend myself, but against anything he said about you. So when he blew me off with a laugh, all I had left was the anger."

Stopping in front of my house, he gave his head a slow shake. "Which I, unfortunately, took out on at you. Yes, you'd made me feel stupid, but mostly I was furious at myself for not seeing the writing on the wall with a girl *again*. It took me a while to come to terms with all that, and to be in the right place to tell you how sorry I am."

My heart pounded. "I'm sorry, too. I should never have been dishonest with you. If I could take it back—"

"Forget it, Maddie. What I liked was your idea of starting over."

"Starting over?" Practically breathless, I stared deep into his eyes. "You mean, you're going to give me a second chance?"

"I was hoping you'd give *me* one."

Emotion swelled inside me as he sealed his lips over mine. I felt like the luckiest girl alive. Whatever I'd done, right or wrong, I couldn't be happier to be here, with Hayes, at this moment.

And when I got inside later, *omigod*, did I need to call Linzee.

Chapter Seven

THE HOMETOWN OF APPLEWOOD Club went from four members to forty in the next few weeks. Hayes and I came up with the idea to honor Applewood's emergency first responders as the club's launch project, which got a strong response. Mrs. Puglisi was very pleased and even brought Nana to a couple of the meetings. Sitting quietly in the rear, Nana tended to be forgotten, which I rationally understood but was a mistake I wouldn't make again.

In fact, Linzee and I had been dropping by on Saturday mornings to have coffee with Nana, to share details about our lives, and hear her takes—which could be even more out-of-the-box than Linzee's. We called Nana our life coach and our secret weapon, but never did she let us forget where her true royalty rested. She was Hayes's number one fan.

No problem there. I was all about making him happy, too—as happy as he was making me. For now, for our whole senior year … and well, as long as this wild ride took us.

Tina Ferraro is the author of numerous novels and novellas and is a two-time RITA finalist for Young Adult Romance. She can usually be found in front of a keyboard in the Los Angeles home she shares with her husband and their two cats, writing her butt off—or, let's be honest, adding more on.

She loves to connect with readers through her website (www.tinaferraro.com) and Facebook author page (Tina-Ferraros-Books).

SOMETHING OLD, SOMETHING NEW: A REALITY ROMANCE SHORT STORY

Lizzie Shane

"THE BEST MAN IS missing."

Victoria kept her don't-worry-everything-is-under-control smile firmly in place and turned toward the bride, who was currently wringing her hands as the rest of the party milled around in the sanctuary, waiting for the rehearsal to start.

Lolly, though genuinely sweet, was also young, sheltered, and wildly dramatic. She never missed an opportunity for exaggeration, so Tori hoped this was just another bridal overreaction.

"Define missing?"

"His flight was supposed to arrive *three hours ago*, but no one has heard a word from him, and all Kipp's calls are going straight to voicemail," Lolly moaned with the level of angst usually reserved for disaster movies about planet-wide annihilation.

"I'm sure he's on his way," Tori soothed. "His cellphone battery probably died because he overdid it playing Candy Crush on the plane."

"No, you don't understand. Taylor *never* plays. And he'd never forget to charge his phone. He's a machine."

Since Victoria had never met the Manhattan-based best man, she couldn't argue for his humanity—and the fallibility that came with it. Instead, since a wedding planner's primary job within twenty-four hours of "I dos" was to stave off bridal panic attacks, she amped up the reassurance in her smile and took Lolly's arm. "Don't worry. Leave it with me and I'll track him down. Right now, all you need to be thinking about is how perfect the ceremony is going to be tomorrow. Let's find Kipp and the two of you can speak with Pastor Jim about your vows while I get this wrinkle ironed out."

Lolly let Tori guide her toward the altar where her fiancé waited. "Do you think we made the right choice by writing our own vows? My grandmother's so traditional—"

"You love your vows. Your grandmother's going to love your vows. And when you walk down the aisle, all she's going to think about is how amazing you look and how happy you are."

Lolly's concern melted into relief. "You're so right. What would I do without you?"

Drive your mother insane by trying to do everything yourself. Victoria made a good living as a wedding planner, but she'd been told by many a mother of the bride that she was worth ten times her hefty fee, thanks to her ability to keep their precious darlings from turning into bridezillas.

Tori sent her charges off to speak with Pastor Jim—who had performed many a ceremony for her and knew his way around a bride and groom—and focused on the next item on the to-do list: Locate missing best man.

She strode to the rear of the church, flicking through screens on her tablet to bring up the files her business partner had left her on the Houghton-Gaines wedding. This happy event was supposed to be Sidney's headache, but her partner had gone on a reality dating show last year, fallen hard for the host, and had recently begun filming a spin-off show with him creating dream weddings for deserving couples.

Which was incredible exposure for their business, but meant

Sidney was virtually unreachable on filming days and left Victoria holding the bag for this wedding that had to be cursed.

Bridesmaids with allergies sneezing into their bouquets, a mother of the groom who insisted last minute that they had to have a separate four-tier wedding cake for gluten-free guests, and now a missing best man.

Tori had dosed the bridesmaids with antihistamines and cajoled the baker into making the second smallest tier of the original cake with almond flour. Now all she had to do was find the best man and pray nothing else went wrong.

Luckily, Sidney was as organized as she was. The best man's contact information and itinerary were all stored under a tab marked Taylor.

The itinerary file opened.

Victoria's heart stuttered.

She'd assumed Taylor was his first name. She'd never heard him referred to as anything else, but the name written large across the top of the itinerary and sending shockwaves through her perfectly ordered world was Nicholas. Nicholas Taylor.

It couldn't be her Nick.

It was a common name. There had to be hundreds of Nicholas Taylors in Manhattan. And probably dozens of those were California transplants.

There was no reason to suspect Nicholas Taylor, absentee best man, was the same Nick Taylor she'd loved with every atom of her teenage heart for three years of high school before college on different coasts had pulled them apart. The same Nick Taylor she'd reconnected with for an all-too-brief summer fling in the weeks after graduating from USC. The same Nick Taylor who had vanished back to the East Coast for law school and stopped responding to her calls and emails. Who had left her to fend for herself as she tried to figure out what the hell a twenty-two-year-old with a bachelor's degree in English and a mountain of student loans was supposed to do about the little blue line on the pregnancy test.

No. It couldn't be him. There were at least five million Nick Taylors in the world. This was a different one. It had to be.

Forcing herself to remain calm and poised, Tori pulled up the airline's flight status app—only to find the best man's flight had landed right on schedule three hours ago. Eden was a good hour north of LAX, but even in the most brutal traffic, he should have arrived by now.

Pastor Jim had things under control at the altar, so Victoria slipped out of the cavernous sanctuary and into the narrow entry hall to call the other Nick Taylor's cell.

It went straight to voicemail. Her blood chilled.

She shouldn't have recognized his voice. It had been eleven years since she'd heard it. She shouldn't have any memory of the sound, but her heart recognized it, even if her brain denied the possibility.

The tone was a shade deeper, somber, and businesslike as he went through the standard voicemail instructions. She was so shaken by hearing his voice, she heard the beep to leave her message before she knew it. She jerked the phone away from her ear and stabbed at her screen to end the call, heart racing.

Crap.

She was a professional. She had a reason to call him. And she was thirty-three freaking years old. She should be able to be mature about this.

But as the exterior door to the church flew open so hard it banged against the opposite wall and a man in a dark suit rushed inside, all thoughts of maturity vanished.

She was fifteen again, clapping eyes on Nick Taylor for the first time. Colors were brighter, emotions sharper. Everything was more intense when Nick was in the room. It had always been that way, the very air around him electrified by his presence.

The tangible force of his personality hadn't diminished in the past decade. If anything, it had intensified. But it was darker now, carrying a new hardness.

Was he happy?

And where had that thought come from? Why should she care if the man who had abandoned her was happy? She'd written him out of the story of her life. This was a blip. A momentary speed bump. By Monday he'd be in Manhattan, and she'd go back to forgetting him.

Nick rapidly scanned the entry and froze when his gaze landed on her. His jaw dropped, a crack appearing in his fierce focus. Those unforgettable amber eyes widened with shock.

Her daughter's eyes.

"*Victoria?*"

She could do this. "Hey, Nick. You're late."

Chapter Two

TORI JACKSON.

He couldn't process it. The love of his life was here. He'd known she was still in Eden, but he hadn't expected her to be inside the freaking church.

Her words were cool, but her face was flushed and her eyes were wide and … wary?

"You haven't changed a bit," he murmured, and the words held both truth and lies. She was as gorgeous as ever with her ivy green eyes and café-au-lait skin—but she looked different. More composed. Maturity, he supposed. She was a woman now, not the girl he'd remembered so many times over the years.

Victoria. His one regret.

Her eyes held his and a rusty thread of connection stretched taut between them, taking him back to a time when he lived to impress her. He hadn't felt this in years—this tightness in his chest, this shortness of breath. Funny how all the old feelings welled up as if they'd never left him, just waited until he clapped eyes on her again. Emotion still fresh after eleven years of hibernation.

He would have stared at her forever, but she waved him toward the sanctuary. "You should go in. We've already started."

"I know the drill. Stand next to Kipp. Hand him the rings. No rehearsal needed."

Her mouth pursed into a disapproving moue. "Nevertheless, rehearsals put everyone at ease. Go on. They've been wondering if you fell off a cliff."

"Tori." He didn't want to go. Didn't want to do anything that would take his eyes off her. Couldn't risk that he would lose her for another eleven years if he did. He'd considered looking her up while he was in town. Fantasized about it. But this wasn't how he'd pictured their reunion.

Focused intently on her tablet, a blush still rode her cheeks as she nodded toward the doors. "I should get inside."

"Then allow me." He held the door open for her. She moved quickly, avoiding brushing against him. Nick followed her inside, and a cheer went up from the groomsmen.

Duty called.

He tried to pay attention to the rehearsal, but it was impossible with Victoria moving between the pews.

The tablet. The teal sheath and tidy updo hairstyle. Her air of calm and authority. It all added up to one thing: wedding planner.

"Taylor? It's our turn."

Nick yanked his gaze off the wedding planner and focused on the maid of honor at his side.

"Right. Sorry." Belatedly realizing they were holding up the practice recessional, he extended his elbow to her, and they followed Lolly and Kipp up the aisle. The rest of the bridal party fell in line, but Nick was barely aware of them or the bridesmaid on his arm. His gaze had returned to the upswept midnight curls Victoria had somehow figured out how to tame in the past decade.

Once they had proven they could walk down the aisle without tripping over their own feet, the minister pronounced them ready, and the large group immediately broke into smaller clusters. Carpool plans to the rehearsal dinner flew, but Nick could only concentrate on Victoria as she disappeared through a small side door.

He detached himself from the party, moving toward that side door.

"Taylor! Wanna ride with me?"

Kipp's invitation was as loud as the Hawaiian shirt he wore. Normally, Nick would want nothing more than to catch up with his oldest friend, but this was *Victoria,* and that changed everything.

"Nah, I need to check on something, but I'll catch you at dinner, okay?"

Kipp hesitated, but Lolly tugged on his arm, and they headed out the front with the rest of the bridal party.

Kipp had never met Tori when they were dating. The Taylors and Houghtons had belonged to the same country club since he and Kipp were in diapers, but Kipp had gone to an East Coast boarding school for high school and had been living in Belize during that unforgettable summer after undergrad. He'd heard about her—there had been times Nick had talked of nothing else—but his friend had no reason to suspect the prim wedding planner Victoria was actually Nick's Tori.

The side door led to a small dressing room filled with clergy robes and natural light. Victoria had her back to him, one hand braced on the window frame when he entered. God, she was gorgeous. He'd forgotten the line of her neck, how sensitive she was there.

His fingers itched to touch and he closed the distance between them, giving in to the urge. "Hiding?"

At the first brush of his fingertips, she whirled away, putting half the small room between them. "What are you doing?"

"I don't know." Nick flexed his hand. "I just … I've missed you."

"You could have fooled me."

He deserved the bite in her words. "Things got complicated after I left," he said, reaching for the words to explain.

"You think?"

"With everything going on—" His father's fraud arrest … His mother's flight to a non-extradition country … And him struggling to keep his head above water in law school… "I thought a clean break was better."

"Better for whom?" She held up a hand. "Never mind. It doesn't matter. You'll be gone on Monday. Just stay away from me until then."

She stalked past him, but he caught her arm, sliding his hand down until he held her fingers. "Tori—"

A hidden door he hadn't seen in the north wall creaked open.

"Mom? Are we going soon? I'm done with my homework, and the wedding people are leaving."

The girl looked about ten. The skinny arms and legs sticking out of a school uniform were brown as a beechnut. Her hair was Victoria's wild midnight mop—and her eyes were the color of whiskey.

About ten.

Nick stared, his mouth going dry as realization slammed into his gut.

I have a kid.

Chapter Three

VICTORIA STARED AT NICK, willing him to keep his mouth shut. All it would take was one careless word for Lorelei to realize he was her absentee father. Lore had always wondered about her daddy. It was only natural. But Tori had kept her answers vague—*loved him very much but circumstances pulled us apart before we even knew you were on the way.*

Standing in the vestry of First Presbyterian wasn't how she wanted her daughter to learn her father was actually a self-centered asshole who'd abandoned them both.

"I'm almost done," she said to her daughter, amazed her voice didn't crack under the strain. "Why don't you wait for me in the entry? I'll be out in a minute."

She spoke to Lorelei, but her gaze stayed on Nick, silently pleading with him not to speak. Not to ask. Either her psychic powers were improving or he was silenced by shock, because he didn't say a word as Lorelei mumbled okay and trudged out with her bulging backpack slung over one shoulder.

His gaze followed Lorelei, staring after her long after the door clicked shut and her footsteps faded away.

When he swung to face Victoria, his eyes were hard. "How could you fail to tell me I had a child?"

She tugged her hand free. "I told you I was pregnant. A kid is the standard result."

His amber eyes flared like he was the injured party. "You never told me. It's not the kind of thing I'm likely to forget."

"Are you kidding? I called. I emailed. For five weeks, I did nothing *but* tell you."

He opened his mouth to retort, anger sharpening the lines of his face, but realization rolled over his face like a cloud, and he went still. "I deleted them," he whispered.

"What?"

"It was September. My father had been indicted, my mom skipped the country, and I was about to flunk out of my first semester of law school. I knew if I heard your voice or saw even a single word of sympathy from you, I'd give up and run back to California with nothing, so I deleted everything without opening them." He stepped away, falling onto a chair as if his legs would no longer hold him. "I never thought—Christ. It was for the best. I was so sure—"

"So you ignored me until I went away."

"I was twenty-two and my life was falling apart."

"Funny. So was mine."

"I didn't know you were pregnant."

"Would it have made a difference?"

"Of course it would have!" He surged to his feet, pacing in the tight space. "You know it would have. You know me."

"No, I don't. Not anymore." She tried to keep the words firm, but her voice was shaking. *She* was shaking.

She'd entertained the idea, over the years, that he might not have known about Lorelei—usually as part of some fantasy in which he'd been abducted by the Dread Pirate Roberts and fought tirelessly to get back to her side—but now hearing him claim he really hadn't known rocked the foundations of her carefully constructed world.

She'd built a life for Lorelei and for herself. What happened now? Would he want to know his daughter? What if he wanted more? What if he wanted joint custody and every other weekend in Manhattan?

She hadn't missed the designer cut of his suit or the glitzy watch that probably cost more than she made in three months. If he decided to make it a fight, he could pay for a more expensive lawyer in a custody battle. What if he tried to take Lorelei away?

She fought to take a full breath. She wasn't thinking clearly, hadn't been since Nick Taylor burst back into her life.

A reminder chime on her phone rang. The rehearsal dinner. She needed to get to the restaurant to make sure everything was going perfectly, but first, she had to drop Lorelei at her mother's to be spoiled rotten tonight and tomorrow while Tori ran the wedding.

She had a job to do. Already Nick had distracted her too much. Normally she would have been guiding the rehearsal, but she'd let Pastor Jim run the show because she was too flustered by Nick, standing beside the altar, looking like several million bucks and ten thousand regrets in his dark gray suit. She'd retreated to the vestry to get her composure back, but she couldn't seem to get herself together. Memories of the past were colliding with fears for the future and leaving her present an unholy mess.

"I can't deal with this right now. I have to work."

She didn't give him a chance to reply, rushing through the sanctuary without looking around. She collected her daughter and hustled her out to her car.

Lorelei flung her backpack into the backseat before flopping into the front. "Was that the groom?"

"Just the best man."

"Do you like him?"

Tori sucked in a breath as she pulled out of the lot, refusing to look in the rearview mirror. What must her daughter have thought when she walked in to see Nick holding her hand? Lore never saw her with men. Between taking care of her daughter, establishing her business and forgetting about Nick, Tori hadn't had the time or energy for relationships. She'd only been on a handful of dates in the past decade. "He's just someone I knew a long time ago."

Her daughter hummed knowingly—a mannerism she'd, unfortunately, picked up from her grandmother. "If you say so."

"I do," Tori insisted, and quickly changed the subject. Maybe it was cowardly, but she wasn't ready to discuss Nick Taylor with his daughter. Not until she could figure out exactly how she felt about seeing him again, because as much as she wanted to hate him, it sure felt like some part of her heart was still his.

Chapter Four

HE HAD A DAUGHTER.

The food at the rehearsal dinner was divine, but he barely tasted it. Activity flowed around him, but all he saw was a little girl with skinny arms, Victoria's hair, and his eyes.

He'd had a daughter for ten years, and he hadn't known.

He wanted to blame Tori, but she was right. He had cut her off when he'd left California to go to law school. When she'd tried to get in touch with him, he'd assumed she was calling to offer sympathy because his life was shit and he hadn't wanted to hear it. All that had mattered to his twenty-two-year-old mind had been carving out security so it could never be yanked out from under him.

Sure felt like the rug had been pulled out now.

That little girl changed everything—and he didn't even know her name.

"Taylor!" Kipp slung himself into the empty seat beside Nick, beaming like he'd won the lottery—and from the way Lolly looked at him, maybe he had. "You okay, man? You seem out of it."

"Just happy to be here." The last thing Kipp needed on the night before his wedding was to hear Nick's drama.

He was a good guy, Kipp Houghton. A loveable teddy bear of a trust-fund baby who had never had a blow that wasn't softened for him. But he was also the only person from Nick's old life who had stuck by him through all his family shit, even when Nick hadn't made it easy to do. And whenever Nick had asked him why, he would shrug and say Nick wasn't his parents.

And now he *was* a parent. Christ.

"You thought about the offer?" Kipp asked, dragging him out of his thoughts. "I know I said I wouldn't bug you until we got back from the honeymoon, but Lolly says it doesn't hurt to ask and ya gotta listen to your wife-to-be, right?"

The offer. One look at Victoria and all thoughts of business had flown. But he was supposed to be using this weekend to make up his mind about Kipp's offer to join his expanding company as chief legal officer.

He'd been fence sitting, uncertain about returning to California even though his life in Manhattan was all work and no life. He didn't date—except when he needed someone on his arm for a work function. His sole focus for the past decade had been building something solid and real, as far from his father's sleight-of-hand brand of success as possible. But now …

The little girl with skinny brown arms and his own whiskey eyes flashed in his mind. "I'll take it."

Kipp's jaw dropped. "Wait? Are you serious?"

"Yeah. It's time I moved back." A lightness filled his chest at the thought—not just of seeing his daughter and Tori again—but at the idea of leaving New York. Coming home again.

"Dude. I can't believe it." Kipp teared up, slapping him roughly on the back. "You don't know what this means to me. Best freaking wedding present ever."

"It's not a gift." Nick caught a flash of a midnight updo at the opposite end of the room. "You're great at what you do," he said, and it wasn't a lie. Kipp might be a loveable teddy bear, but he was a teddy bear with a Midas touch who had turned his gaming hobby into a cutting-edge game design company. "I'm honored you want me to be part of expanding GottaPlay. And I need a change." The teal dress tugged at his attention. "But right now I see someone I need to talk to. Congrats on the wedding, buddy."

"Thanks, man." Kipp grinned. "I gotta tell Lolly."

He galloped off, bouncing with enthusiasm to tell his bride. Nick wasn't sure he'd ever been that excited to share his life with another person. Even before that awful first year of law school, when he'd constructed granite walls around himself to keep out the whispers and stares, he'd never let another person that close to him. Even Tori. She'd been an amazing girlfriend, but she'd been a part of his life, not his whole world. And he'd cut that part out when it felt like an anchor dragging him back to a past it felt like weakness to remember.

He owed the mother of his child the mother of all apologies.

Nick threaded through the crowd, stalking that curvy figure in the teal dress.

She was being hunted.

Tori was hyperaware of Nick, so she knew the very second he rose from his chair and began weaving toward her. She'd dropped off Lorelei at her mom's place and rushed to the restaurant only to find everything was going perfectly. Venue? Lovely. Food? Delicious. In another half hour the party would start breaking up, and she'd be able to escape.

She'd hoped to avoid talking to Nick tonight, but as he prowled in her wake, that hope died. At least she could control where they spoke. Her personal affairs would *not* be aired in the middle of a client's rehearsal dinner.

Victoria stepped off the private patio reserved for the rehearsal dinner and along the gravel path around the building. It was a pleasant night, but a chill breeze caught her as she rounded the corner of the building. She shivered, wrapping her arms around herself and wishing she hadn't left her blazer in her car. There was salt on the air, carried on the breeze from the beach to the hilltop restaurant. Victoria inhaled, taking comfort in the familiar scent, even as the crunch of footsteps on the gravel path behind her made every muscle in her body tense.

"Tori—"

She turned, cutting him off. "Are you going to try to take my daughter away?"

"What?" He stopped moving so fast his feet might have taken root. "How could you think that of me?"

"I don't know you anymore." She wrapped her arms tighter around her middle. "Lorelei doesn't know you at all."

He moved closer, shoes crunching the gravel. "Lorelei? You named our daughter after your favorite television character?"

She glared at him. "Forgive me if it seemed appropriate to name my baby after the *Gilmore Girls*. I was hormonal. You're lucky I didn't name her after the vodka we were drinking the night she was conceived."

"Lorelei is a beautiful name," he said, and it got harder to stay mad. "I want to know her, Tori. I'm moving back to California."

Her stomach plummeted. She'd been thinking he was only here for the weekend, believing if she could make it through to Monday, everything would be fine. Normal. Or as close to normal as a situation like this could be. But if he would be living here …

She could handle her feelings for him when he was the absentee father, but if he was there, living down the street, helping out with the carpool … she didn't know if she could do it.

And if he vanished on Lorelei like he had vanished on her …

"I'm not going to forbid you getting to know your daughter, but she's my world, Nick. She doesn't know much about you, but if you come into her life you have to stick. You can't make her care about you and then abandon her like you did me. I will hunt you down and gut you if you ever make her feel unwanted, do you understand me? You don't get to hurt her. Ever." Tori knew all too well what it felt like to have a father who walked away. She never wanted that for Lore.

"I won't. You know me better than to think I would."

"I thought I did, but then you ran away to Manhattan and stopped taking my calls. I don't know what kind of person you are these days."

His jaw worked as he nodded. "I deserve that. I'm sorry. I was barely keeping it together, and I thought you would talk me into moving back here—"

"I wanted to be with you. I didn't care where."

"You made it pretty damn clear you weren't leaving Eden."

"Because you never asked me to go with you!"

"Because you kept talking about how you could never live in New York!"

His voice echoed over the hill. Tori cast a nervous look toward the party. Very professional. The wedding planner causing a scene with the best man at the rehearsal dinner. "I can't talk about this here."

Pulling her arms tighter around her, she strode toward the parking lot.

"Victoria …"

It wasn't supposed to hurt like this, eleven years later. Time was supposed to dull everything, but where he was concerned, her feelings were as sharp as ever.

His feet crunched on the gravel, trailing her.

"Tori. Stop." His voice was close, just over her shoulder. A hand closed on her arm, pulling her around, his other hand cupping her opposite shoulder to hold her in front of him. He opened his mouth as if to speak, but then his gaze dropped to her lips.

His eyes darkened. His grip on her arms firmed. And she was fifteen again. About to be kissed by Nick Taylor for the first time.

The world simply fell away.

He lowered his head slowly, and by the time his lips brushed hers, so hesitant and sweet, she had forgotten everything she'd ever known except the taste and feel of him. He murmured something, too soft for her to hear, and deepened the kiss, angling, pressing, coaxing for more—and she gave him more.

She gave him the piece of her heart that had always had his name carved on it—the part she thought she'd excised years ago but that had been lying dormant, waiting for him to reappear to start beating again.

Suddenly she was too warm, the chill completely banished. This. This was what she had tried to forget. No one had ever kissed her like Nick. All that focused intensity. All that single-minded devotion. The attention that went into every stroke and touch.

He'd always been hell on her equilibrium. No wonder she'd wound up pregnant—

Tori jerked away.

Lorelei.

It wasn't just her anymore. She couldn't fall into his arms because she had always felt at home there. This wasn't just Nick, the boy she'd loved. This was Nick, the father of her child. And he wanted a relationship with Lorelei. For Victoria to get involved with him ... No. It was too complicated. Too many things could go wrong.

"I can't," she whispered and fled, thanking God he let her go, because she wasn't sure she would have been able to push him away a second time.

Chapter Five

"VICTORIA! I HAVE A mission for you. I need you to help me set up my maid of honor with the best man."

Tori froze with her hands wrist deep in lace. She kept her back to Lolly, pretending to be absorbed in rearranging the veil until she controlled her expression. "Taylor?"

Lolly, oblivious to her inner turmoil, pivoted in front of the mirror to study her fluffy princess dress from every angle. "He's such a catch, and now that he's moving back to California, it's perfect! Tammy needs to date someone good for a change. She has wretched taste in men. But that's all about to change. And you get to help me play matchmaker."

Victoria swallowed around the lump in her throat. "Are you sure he's … dependable?"

"Taylor?" Lolly said. "You heard about his family, I guess?" She practiced smiling in the mirror, batting her eyes. "That was sketchy, but trust me, Taylor's a keeper. He's like a brother to Kipp and if he's anything, he's a man of his word. He might not fall madly in love with Tammy, but he'll never lie to her and jerk her heart around, which is exactly what she needs. A good guy."

The bridesmaids rushed in from the connecting dressing room in a lavender swarm, saving Tori from having to reply. They plucked the veil from Victoria's hands and clustered around the bride in a giggling mass, cellphones waving for selfies with the bride.

Everything was running right on schedule. The chapel was filling, and in exactly seventeen minutes Lolita Carmen Gaines would walk down the aisle. The blushing bride was calm as a cucumber, hamming it up with her friends.

It was Tori who was quietly losing her mind.

She'd never been so nervous at a wedding before, and it had nothing to do with the event.

Was Nick really a good guy? She'd cast him as the villain who had abandoned her, but he'd never lied. He'd never promised her forever. Just the opposite. He'd been very clear that he was going away at the end of the summer.

Yes, she'd hoped he would come rushing back when he found out she was pregnant, but she'd never actually talked to him directly after she saw that little blue line. She'd played a part in the farce, too. She could have gone to New York to tell him in person, but she'd chickened out. Hurt by his silence, she'd chosen to believe the worst of him. It had been easy. After all, hadn't her father walked out on her? Why wouldn't the man she loved the most vanish on her, too?

She'd thought she had absolute faith in Nick, but it had been easy to shatter.

A scratch came at the door, setting off a chorus of squeals from the knot of bridesmaids. Victoria checked her watch. "We still have eight minutes. Just relax. I'll take care of whatever this is."

The bridesmaids resumed fluttering over Lolly and Victoria crossed to the door, grateful for the distraction.

But when she opened the door, it was Nick standing in the hallway outside the bride's dressing room.

"What are you doing here?" She ushered him away before he could enter the bride's inner sanctum, slipping through the door and closing it behind her. "You're supposed to be with Kipp."

Nick held up an envelope. "He wanted to send Lolly this."

Tori plucked it from his fingertips. "I'll see that she gets it. Now go back and keep the groom calm." She frowned at the envelope. "He can't be calling it off."

"Are you kidding? Kipp would walk through fire to marry Lolly. He said it was an inside joke, but my money is on a sappy love note."

"Good. Now go."

He didn't budge, standing there looking entirely too good for her equilibrium in a charcoal tuxedo and lavender silk tie. Her heart thudded heavily as his amber eyes took in every inch of her from the collar of her modest peach sheath to her most comfortable peep-toe heels.

"You look beautiful."

A flush hit her cheeks. "I have to blend with the guests."

"Is Lorelei here?"

The butterflies in her stomach turned to lead. "She's with my mom. She gets her grandma fix when I have a wedding."

Nick nodded. A strained silence fell.

"We'll have to, ah, talk about how you two should meet. When you've moved back."

He stepped closer. "Tori, about last night—"

Oh God no. They were not talking about The Kiss of Doom. "We'll need to be careful moving forward," she said hurriedly, speaking over him. "You can meet Lorelei, but you need to stop trying to kiss me." She hadn't realized she was going to say that until the words were out, but now there were more coming and she couldn't stop them. "I have to be looking out for Lorelei's interests, and I can't be as effective guarding her heart if I'm worrying about my own where you're concerned."

Disappointment flickered in his eyes. "You were never guarded with me before."

"You never broke my heart before." She swallowed, forcing herself to go on. "I know I played a part in the miscommunication, but the truth is when your life got hard, you cut me out of it. That isn't what you do to people you love. And I won't risk being hurt like that again. Goodbye, Nick." She lifted the envelope. "I'll see Lolly gets this."

Chapter Six

HE'D BROKEN HER HEART.

Nick smiled through the ceremony and the photos, saying all the right things and projecting happiness for all he was worth, but he couldn't stop thinking about Victoria and the simple words that had jarred him to his marrow.

He didn't know how to mend a broken heart.

But he wanted to. Not just because she was the mother of his child and he wanted to know his daughter with an ache in his soul he never would have suspected he could feel, but also because she was *Tori*. The one woman who made him feel like he was enough just by smiling at him. The one that got away.

But she hadn't *gotten* away. He'd thrown her away.

He'd never wanted to be like his parents—he'd struggled for most of his adult life to separate himself from their legacy and be seen as his own man—but he was more like them than he wanted to admit. Like his mother, he'd run away when things got tough. He'd hated her for it, and then he'd gone and done exactly the same thing.

He'd told himself it was better for Tori if she didn't have to deal with the circus his life had become, but was he trying to protect her? Or protect himself from the vulnerability that came from caring for someone?

Glasses clinked around the ballroom and the murmur of voices quieted as a microphone landed with a thunk in front of him on the table.

Kipp clapped him on the shoulder. "You're up, best man."

The toast. Shit.

Nick lurched to his feet. He'd had a speech prepared. Even now, he could feel the paper crinkling in his vest pocket. He'd planned to talk about his long friendship with Kipp and Kipp's unswerving loyalty, but now those words—though true—seemed somehow inadequate.

Victoria stood at the back of the room. In constant motion since the reception began, she now paused near a spray of flowers and watched him, waiting for him to speak—along with the rest of the silent room.

Nick cleared his throat, his grip on the microphone and his champagne glass suddenly sweat slicked.

"Kipp is my oldest friend, and we all know he's always good for a laugh. But he's also the bravest person I've ever met." He smiled at his friend and his bride. "It takes courage to give your heart completely to another person and even more to make the promise to always be there for them. Being trusted with someone's heart is a big responsibility. It takes a lot to love someone with all you have. I admire you, man."

Lolly smiled tearily, and Kipp sniffled—the big softie.

"Lolly, you couldn't have entrusted your heart to a more deserving guy. I know he'll be brave enough to keep it safe and never break it. He's a helluva lot braver than I am, but maybe it's not too late for me to learn." His gaze locked on the woman in the peach dress at the rear of the room as he lifted his glass. "To loving with your whole heart. To Kipp and Lolly."

Their names echoed through the room, chairs scraping as guests rose to their feet for the toast. Nick accepted Kipp's back-slapping hug and Lolly's teary embrace before sinking into his chair.

As the guests settled themselves and the father of the bride stood to say a few words, Nick's gaze boomeranged to the back of the room, but Victoria was gone.

Her heels thunked against the wooden planks of the small gazebo thrust out over the water on a floating dock. It was nearing dusk, and the yacht club was quiet except for the activity in the ballroom inside.

She should be part of that activity, but she needed a second to pull herself together. After Nick's speech, she didn't know what to feel.

She rested her hands on the white painted railing, lifting her face to the salty breeze.

"Tori?"

Of course, he'd come. She didn't take her eyes off the sunset, but she felt him behind her. He slipped off his jacket and tucked it around her shoulders, the familiar scent nearly buckling her knees.

"You always were good at pleading your case," she said, still facing the horizon.

"I never stopped loving you."

Her heart lurched and Victoria turned her face toward him. The setting sun gilded his familiar features.

"Even when I was an idiot," he went on, "I loved you. I told myself you'd moved on, were better off without me, but this weekend … seeing you again like this, doesn't it feel like fate giving us a chance to fix what we screwed up? I want to prove I'm not gonna run this time. I'd marry you this second if you'd have me."

"Marriage isn't proof." She'd seen enough weddings to know it took a lot more than a ceremony to make a happily ever after.

It took commitment and faith and trust and love. The kind of love that accepted someone as they were and made them a constant presence in your heart. Could she love him like that? Could he love her?

"Victoria?" He caught a stray curl and tucked it gently behind her ear.

He was so intent. So focused. It was easy to fall for a man who could look at you like the rest of the world didn't even exist, but she needed more than that. She needed his word.

She turned to face him fully. "Swear to me that whatever happens between us, you will never cut off communication again. Not to me and not to Lorelei."

"I swear."

He didn't make promises he couldn't keep. Her breath grew short. "Don't make me regret this, Nick," she whispered.

"Never." He moved a hand to reach for her, but hesitation held him in check. "Does that mean …?"

She caught his hand, lacing their fingers together. "You had an advantage. I never stopped loving you either. Even when I wished I could."

His heart in his amber eyes, he lifted his free hand to trace the curve of her cheek. "Is it okay if I try to kiss you now?"

"No."

He froze in the act of leaning toward her. She grinned and hooked a finger inside his vest, tugging him closer. Then *she* kissed *him*.

The familiar feel of his lips held the flavor of champagne and the hope for a thousand more kisses.

Epilogue

IT WAS, VICTORIA DECIDED, the best wedding she'd ever planned.

She stood in front of Pastor Jim with Lorelei and Sidney as her maid and matron of honor, respectively. Kipp acted as best man for Nick as they tied the knot under the gazebo at the yacht club.

It was a small ceremony—a larger group wouldn't have fit onto the floating dock—but it was perfect. They wrote their own vows, and Tori knew she'd have to ask Nick to repeat his later because after "I forgot how much I needed you, but fate brought me back to remind me" she started bawling and barely heard another word he said. And she wanted to remember those promises to love and honor because her husband never made a promise he didn't keep. Not to her and not to their daughter.

He'd said he would love them forever, and he was a man of his word.

Three-time RITA finalist and Golden Heart®-winning contemporary romance author Lizzie Shane was born and raised in Alaska and still lives in the frozen north when she isn't indulging her travel addiction. After college, she worked in the entertainment industry for about fifteen seconds before deciding she'd rather write about love in the wilds of Hollywood than live it. Now, she uses the long winter nights in Alaska to create more happily-ever-afters. Lizzie also writes paranormal romance under the name Vivi Andrews.

For more about Lizzie and her books, visit
http://www.lizzieshane.com.

RELOAD

Tara Wyatt

BRANDON CLARKE-DAVIES TOOK A long, slow sip of his pint of Guinness and laid an arm across the back of the red leather booth nestled into a quiet corner of the pub. His eyes dropped to the white folder on the table in front of him, the light blue MI5 insignia in the top left corner.

He tapped it with one finger. "Not that I'm complaining about the free pint, but what are we doing here?"

Harry leaned against the booth and glanced around the small pub. Despite the fact that it was just shy of two on a Thursday afternoon, The Red Lion was bustling with patrons.

"She should be here any minute." Harry drummed his fingers on top of the folder.

Brandon glanced out the windows on the opposite side of the pub, watching the traffic crawl by on Parliament Street. Weak summer sunshine filtered through the parting clouds, glinting off the puddles dotting the cobbled sidewalk. With an arched eyebrow, he shook his head at his boss's secrecy and picked up his pint. As a highly trained MI5 Intelligence Officer, he was used to discretion.

He'd just tipped the pint glass to his lips when the sharp click of heels against the scarred wooden floor got his attention and he froze, shock turning his blood to ice water in his veins. Chiding himself for his minuscule slip in composure, he set the glass down and leveled his gaze at the woman standing in front of their table. Wrapped in an elegant Burberry trench, her hands shoved casually in her pockets, she tipped her head and gave them each a small smile before sliding into the booth right beside Brandon.

"Gentlemen."

Her voice, just as low and husky and feminine as he remembered, hit him like a kick to the gut.

Harry shot Brandon a look. "Thought you might want to have the meeting here, as opposed to the office. In front of … you know. People. "

"You're a bloody saint, Harry," he said, his jaw wound so tight he was surprised he could speak. He forced his shoulders to relax, unclenched his fists, and didn't allow himself to reach for his pint. He dared a glance at the gorgeous woman sitting beside him, her legs crossed, her hands folded on the table as if sitting next to him were the most natural thing in the world.

But it wasn't, because he hadn't seen her in six years. Natasha Rowe. His ex-wife.

"Nice to see you, Brandon," she said, the hardened consonants of her American accent sharp against his ears. As a wave of nostalgic desire crashed into him, he looked at her with what he hoped was a bemused expression because he had no idea what the hell to say. He sucked in a deep breath, which was a terrible mistake, because it brought with it her lavender scent, as warm and familiar as ever. Memories, most of them happy and exciting, floated to the surface, but he squashed them and plastered a thin smile to his face before they could suck him under, a tsunami disguised as a gentle wave.

Harry's eyes flicked from Brandon to Natasha. If he picked up on the surprise, the anger, and, goddammit, the *lust* crawling beneath Brandon's skin and threatening to burst out, he didn't let on. With quick, efficient movements, Natasha unbuttoned her coat and shrugged out of it, letting it pool around her waist. Her red tank top cupped her ample breasts perfectly, leaving a subtle amount of cleavage on display. She ran her fingers through her chin-length dark blond hair and suddenly he was half-hard, watching her breasts strain for freedom beneath the red fabric. God, those tits. As if he'd ever forget how good they felt in his hands. In his mouth.

No. He couldn't let his mind go down that path. He needed to focus on other things. Like the fact that two years into their struggling marriage, she'd walked out on him without a backward glance. *That's* what he needed to be thinking about, not her glorious rack.

"Shall we?" asked Harry, leaning forward and flipping open what Brandon now realized was a mission dossier.

Bloody fucking hell.

Without waiting for an acknowledgment, Harry plowed ahead, spreading several pages and photographs across their sequestered table. "Last week, the United States Army Medical Research Institute of Infectious Diseases in Maryland was breached."

Natasha cut in. "We believe that Sergei Silayev, one of Europe's biggest arms dealers—"

"I know who Sergei Silayev is." Brandon's skin crackled with angry impatience.

She nodded and continued. "We're certain that Silayev's agents were responsible for the breach."

"What was stolen?" asked Brandon, his eyes narrowed as he studied the image of Silayev in front of him.

"Several vials of Marburg virus." Brandon's eyes met Natasha's as the magnitude of what she was telling him sunk in. One of the biggest arms dealers in Europe—if not the world—had stolen several vials of a highly potent and deadly biological weapon.

"Fuck me," muttered Brandon, finally allowing himself another sip of his Guinness. Something flashed in Natasha's gray eyes, a hot, searing spark, and she rubbed her thighs together, almost imperceptibly. Almost. "How did you lot cock-up so bad that you let one of Silayev's agents infiltrate an Army base?" He was deflecting, trying to cover his own arousal at seeing Natasha again. She didn't bat an eye, not allowing herself to be baited.

That was new.

"The chatter we've picked up indicates that the vials are here, in London. Silayev has just bought a house in Belgravia, and we believe he's holding the vials there until he can find a buyer," she said.

"Obviously, the Americans are keen to regain possession of the virus," said Harry, leaning forward and interlacing his fingers. "Which is why we're assisting the CIA on this mission."

"*You're* CIA?" Brandon turned in his seat, angling his shoulders toward Natasha. "You're not still at Aegis?"

In response, she pulled a CIA badge from the inside pocket of her trench, flashing it at him before tucking it away. "I haven't been at Aegis for years now."

"But you loved it there. Why did you leave?"

"I'm sorry, but that's classified." She tipped her lips up in a half smile. God, that half smile was maddening. It made him want to strangle her and kiss her, and damn the consequences of both. Instead, he smiled smoothly.

"Of course. Apologies." Brandon kept his voice deliberately flat. "Seeing as the vials are on British soil, and the mission falls under the MI5 umbrella, why doesn't the CIA leave it to us?" He glanced at Natasha. "No offense."

She smiled sweetly. "Because the CIA doesn't trust anyone, not even MI5. No offense."

The doors to the pub's kitchen swung open, and the heavy scent of deep fried foods wafted through the air. As a waitress rushed past carrying a tray laden with several orders of fish and chips, all conversation paused, an involuntary ceasefire.

Harry cleared his throat and lowered his voice. "Silayev is having a cocktail party tomorrow night and will be feeling out several potential buyers for the virus," said Harry. "Your mission is to infiltrate the party, retrieve the vials, and return them to the US Embassy. There are officials from the CDC on standby who will ensure the virus's safe transport to America."

"Harry, I have to ask …" Brandon shook his head and blew out a slow breath through his nostrils. "Why me? Given our …"

He gestured between himself and Natasha. "History. Wouldn't another agent be better suited to the job?"

Harry tented his fingers and studied Brandon, narrowing his eyes. "No. Given your skills, experience, and the cover necessary to infiltrate Silayev's party, it's got to be you. Additionally, you've never worked a mission involving him or any of his known associates before, so there's no chance of him making you for MI5."

Resigned, Brandon nodded, scanning the pages and photographs in front of him. He glanced at Natasha, who he knew was deep in thought, running her index finger along her bottom lip as she studied the dossier contents.

"Agent Clarke-Davies, I've secured you an invitation to the party tomorrow night." Harry slid a sealed envelope across the table to Brandon, who took it and slipped it into the inner pocket of his suit jacket. "You'll find your cover and all necessary information in that envelope. You know the drill." He turned his attention to Natasha and slid a matching envelope to her. "Agent Rowe will be working the party as a waitress; we've secured the cooperation of the catering company. Agent Rowe will secure the vials while you, Clarke-Davies, make sure Rowe is able to do so without any hindrance. We'll go over the finer points of the mission tomorrow. Questions?"

Brandon and Natasha looked at each other before shaking their heads. Harry stood and nodded once, his eyes darting back and forth between them. "Best of luck, agents." Shaking his head, he pushed open the door and set off down the sidewalk in the direction of the MI5 offices.

"So why did you leave Aegis?" Brandon asked.

"Why did you?" She threw the question back at him like a live grenade.

Why had he left Aegis, the private, international intelligence organization where he'd met Natasha almost eight years ago?

Because after their marriage had fallen apart and she'd left him, the shine of international espionage and adventure had lost its allure. Without his partner, his heart hadn't been in it anymore. Coming home to London and joining MI5 had seemed the best option at the time. But he bloody well wasn't going to tell her any of that.

So instead, he smiled, aiming for charming. "I'm sorry, but that's classified."

She laughed, her full lips pulling up into a genuine smile. She slid out of the booth, pulling her trench on as she went. "See you at headquarters tomorrow, C. D.," she said, tossing out a nickname he hadn't heard in years.

He found himself smiling as he watched her walk out of The Red Lion.

Bollocks.

Chapter Two

"NO, THE PLAN IS that *I* secure the vials while *you* look out for *me*. That's the mission, and we're not changing it!" Natasha spoke through clenched teeth, arms crossed, not caring that she was yelling at her ex-husband in the middle of MI5 headquarters.

"Listen, you lot already lost those vials of Marburg once. We can't risk another bout of incompetence." Brandon leveled his cool gaze at her, and she wanted to scream in frustration.

Why did he have to look as though he'd just stepped out of the pages of *GQ*? He looked so good that she could've cried at how unfair it was. Unfair that she had to work with him, and unfair he had to look like that while she did.

His chestnut hair was shorter than when she'd last seen him, with a hint of a wave that she knew turned into curls if he let it grow long enough. Piercing blue eyes looked at her, framed with thick, long lashes that most women would kill for. His nose had a bump in it that hadn't been there six years ago, indicating it had been broken at least once. He wore a simple white dress shirt that emphasized his broad, muscular physique. It was unbuttoned at the collar and tucked into gray dress pants. At six feet two inches, he was nearly a foot taller than her and a good seventy-five pounds heavier.

"So, what?" She jabbed her finger at the blueprint of Silayev's house spread before them on the illuminated table, focusing on her frustration. "You're going to sneak upstairs, crack the safe, and secure the vials while I'm *your* lookout? Ha! And let you take all the credit? Right. No fucking way, C. D."

"Is that what you're worried about? That I'll get all the glory?"

He braced his hands on the table and leaned toward her. "That would be a shame, wouldn't it?"

She opened her mouth to tell him exactly where he could shove his glory when he smiled, and it wasn't just any smile. No, it was the wolfish one that never failed to disintegrate her panties.

And he knew it. Her heart knocked against her ribs and her scalp prickled with the intoxicating mixture of lust, passion, and competitiveness that only Brandon could elicit, and she saw the flash of triumph in his eyes.

So much for not letting him get to her. Ever since she'd seen him in the pub yesterday and had nearly lost her lunch at the shock, she'd been fighting against the current of memories threatening to pull her under, trying desperately to exude cool indifference. But under that gaze, and with that smile, she was quickly melting into a puddle of nostalgia and hormones.

Her mind flashed back to the beginning of their relationship. They'd met on an assignment for Aegis, and their highly competitive natures had found them at each other's throats—and in each other's beds—before the assignment was over. They'd fallen hard and fast, the intensity of their feelings heightened by youth, by the danger around them, and by the exotic locations to which they'd traveled. Thanks to Brandon, she'd had orgasms on every continent except Antarctica.

God, the sex. She'd never been able to get enough of him, and in the years since, no man had come close to satisfying her the way Brandon had. She gave her head a small shake, sweeping away the memories like broken shards of glass.

"No," she said, leaning over the opposite side of the table and mirroring his posture, giving him a generous view of her cleavage. His gaze dipped. "I'm worried you'll fuck it up and make me look bad. Then I'll have to rescue your ass, and I don't have time for that. This time tomorrow, I'll be back at Langley."

Something flickered across his face that looked a hell of a lot like disappointment, but before she could be sure, it was gone. In an achingly familiar gesture, he raised a hand to his face, thumb under his chin, his index finger stroking the bridge of his nose.

He ran his tongue over his teeth, and in another familiar gesture, let his tongue linger on the slightly crooked eyetooth on the right side of his mouth. British dentistry jokes aside, it was his only imperfection.

Only visible one, anyway. The others only became apparent when one knew him on a deeper level.

The moodiness, the competitiveness, the cockiness. Granted, they'd been twenty-two, and if memory served, she hadn't been all rainbows and sunshine either. She'd like to think that now, at thirty, she'd matured somewhat.

"Fine. Yes. You're right. We'll stick to the plan." He rubbed a hand over the back of his neck, shooting her an apologetic smile. He crossed to her side and propped a hip against the table, facing her with his arms crossed. For several long seconds, he studied her, and then sighed. "It's not easy for me to trust you, Tash."

His words hit her with the force of a hurricane, almost knocking her over. She took a step away and folded her arms in front of her. "That's fair."

His brows knit together. "You're bloody right it is." He lowered his voice to a fierce whisper. "You just fucking *left*. I returned from that mission in Baghdad and you were *gone*."

"Let's not pretend we weren't making each other miserable, C. D."

His expression softened at the old nickname. "I wasn't miserable."

She snorted and rolled her eyes. "We fought constantly."

He leaned in close, bringing with him the warm scent of his woodsy aftershave. "We fucked constantly, too." Butterflies exploded in her stomach as heat curled over her thighs, and she fought the urge to rub them together. "It wasn't perfect, but it was *us*, Tash."

"It was dysfunctional."

Hurt flashed in his eyes, replaced quickly with anger. "So your solution was to walk without giving us the chance to fix it?"

She ducked her head, blood rushing to her cheeks. They'd hit a particularly rough patch, and she'd panicked. She'd run, giving in to her immature, selfish fears, and by the time she'd realized the magnitude of her mistake, it had been too late. She couldn't put the pin back in the grenade. She'd wrecked the best thing that had ever happened to her because she'd been too young to handle the complexity of marriage.

She could've tracked him down at any point over the past six years if she'd wanted, but she hadn't, too terrified he hated her guts for bailing. But it didn't seem like he hated her. And she wasn't sure what to make of that.

Harry cleared his throat as he approached, rubbing his hands together as though warming them. "All set for tonight then?"

Brandon pushed off the table and returned to his side, putting distance between them.

Not that she could blame him.

Natasha skimmed her hands down the front of the skintight, revealing black dress that all of the catering company's waitresses wore and sucked in a steadying breath. She smoothed her hair over her ears, further concealing the nearly invisible microearpiece in her right ear that linked her both to Brandon and to headquarters.

She hadn't initially understood why Harry had insisted on Brandon for this mission, but seeing him now, she understood perfectly. He'd assumed the identity of William Drummond, heir to a European banking fortune with several semi-illegal investments in his portfolio. Drummond was exactly the type Silayev's people would invite to a party like this: rich, connected, and crooked. She had to give MI5 credit—given the short notice, they'd done an excellent job of creating a deep and convincing cover for Brandon. Googling William Drummond brought up pictures, several news articles, a LinkedIn page, and an investment profile, all courtesy of MI5's Digital Intelligence team.

And now, chatting with guests, a tumbler of scotch in hand and wearing the hell out of a navy blue Hugo Boss suit, complete with light blue dress shirt and deep red silk tie, he looked perfect.

For the role.

Right.

She lifted the tray of champagne glasses from the counter and pushed through the kitchen's swinging door, her eyes scanning the open living and dining space currently filled with several dozen guests, all drinking champagne and feasting on toast points smothered in caviar. The decor of the large Wilton Street townhouse was opulent and over the top, with marble floors, intricate crown molding tracing across the ceiling, and lush, textured wallpaper in rich browns and blues hugging the walls. The entire place screamed wealth, power, and questionable taste.

She wove her way through the crowd, her eyes landing on the curved staircase by the kitchen that led to the second floor. Silayev's office and the safe within it were upstairs, and the next step in the mission was to get into his office undetected and start working on the safe. A guest's stray hand squeezed her ass in passing and she ground her teeth in disgust, suppressing a snarl.

"I saw that. What a cheeky bugger. I should break his hand." Brandon's voice came crisply through the earpiece, his accent having the same effect on her as always, sending sparks dancing across her skin.

She turned her head to the side as she spoke softly. "No. Focus, C. D." She smiled, covering the flash of irritation burning through her. Irritation at the creep who'd squeezed her ass and irritation at herself, because Brandon's words had tugged at something soft and warm right in the center of her chest. Something she had no right to feel, given the way she'd treated him.

"Hard to focus with you in that dress, love."

More sparks. "Suck it up. I need you on your A game. If I get shot, we're going to have a big problem."

"Bigger than what I've got in my—"

She turned her face to the wall, speaking in a whispered rush. "I swear to God, I'm going to rip you out of my ear."

"There was a time when you liked having me inside you." Instantly, her traitorous mind conjured up memories of just how much she'd liked it. How wild he'd driven her, how safe and treasured and whole he'd made her feel. When they hadn't been driving each other insane, that is.

She brushed by him, her bare arm grazing the soft wool-cashmere blend of his suit jacket. In a movement so small that everyone around them but her would've missed it, he dipped his head slightly as she passed and inhaled. His eyes closed briefly, and her stomach did a slow turn. Maybe if, after the mission, they snuck away, and didn't talk, and just ...

She shook her head. Talk about a spectacularly bad idea.

She smiled, her teeth clenched together with such force that if she didn't let up, she was likely to crack a molar. "Now isn't the time." She kept moving through the crowd and could feel his eyes on her ass as she strode away.

Through the earpiece, he laughed, his deep, rich voice sending a wave of heat rippling along her spine. Her stomach fluttered, and she swallowed thickly, fighting to regain her composure. He was unraveling her, probably on purpose. Probably as revenge for running scared and bailing out on their marriage.

She shook her head again, refusing to get sucked in to the lust simmering through her veins. She needed to get upstairs, crack the safe, and recover the virus so that she could get the hell out of here and away from Brandon before she did something incredibly stupid.

Again.

Chapter Three

NATASHA SLIPPED INTO THE kitchen and set down her now-empty tray, poking her head around the corner and glancing in the direction of the living room and the staircase to her immediate right.

"I'm heading up," she whispered, edging closer to the stairs, her gaze scanning every direction before she darted furtively up the stairs two at a time, not slowing her brisk pace until she reached the top. Finding the hallway dark and quiet, she headed straight for Silayev's office. It was locked; slipping her lock-picking tools from a garter under her dress, she made quick work of the simple pin and tumbler mechanism. Closing the door behind her with a quiet click, she crossed to the far side of the office and began her search for the safe, locating it in a low cabinet nestled into the wall. She pulled her phone out of her bra and started the process of hacking into the house's wireless network.

She snorted out a quiet laugh. "The network's not even encrypted."

Brandon chuckled in her ear. "What is this, amateur hour? I guess we can be grateful that he hasn't had a chance to put in all the upgrades yet."

She smiled, and then a pang of longing and loneliness slipped between her ribs like a knife. God, she'd missed him. She'd known that, but she hadn't realized just how much; seeing him again, arguing with him, flirting and laughing with him brought home the fact that without a doubt, she was still completely in love with Brandon Clarke-Davies.

The enormity of her mistake sat on her chest like a lead weight.

It was a mistake for which he'd likely never forgive her. Hell, she'd never forgive herself for leaving him the way she had.

Once she'd accessed the house's wireless network, she opened the CIA's customized safe cracking software on her phone. She tapped a series of numbers into the safe's electronic number pad, connecting it to the wireless network as well. With a swipe of her finger, the software connected to the safe, interfacing with it directly. The program began running through sequences of numbers at lightning speed.

For several tense minutes, there was nothing she could do but stay silent, let the program do its job, and listen to Brandon flirt with some Eurotrash socialite. When she excused herself to go powder her nose—probably with cocaine—Brandon checked in with her.

"How's it coming?"

"I'm still cracking the safe. All clear downstairs?"

"Maybe."

"Maybe? I don't like maybe." She stared at her phone's screen, willing the program to work faster, the prickling threat of sweat teasing along her hairline.

"Two blokes headed upstairs. I'm on it."

The safe emitted a series of beeps and popped open as the locking mechanism released. Triumph surging through her, she tucked her phone away and swung the small safe's door wide open.

"Hel-*lo*," she murmured to herself, pulling free both a small metal briefcase and a silver Walther PPK covered in garish scrollwork. She flipped open the case, verifying that it contained the vials. It did. Then, she checked the Walther's clip and found it loaded.

The office door swung open, cutting a swath of light across the darkened floor. Briefcase in one hand, gun in the other, she dove behind the heavy wood desk as the first bullet, muffled by a silencer, dug into the wood paneling to the left of the window, inches from where her head had been.

"C. D., I need you. I've got company."

Brandon's heart pounded furiously against his ribs. As soon as those men had gone upstairs, he'd excused himself from the party, made for the loo, and then charged up the stairs the second he was sure no one was watching. Natasha was unarmed. He couldn't let anything happen to her. Not that he'd let anything happen to a fellow agent, but this was different, somehow. The idea of something happening to Natasha sent him spiraling into a near panic, urged on by the sound of her laugh skimming along the surface of his brain, her lavender scent ghosting through his nostrils. Even now, after all these years, after the way she'd left, she had the ability to utterly and completely captivate him, even when he wanted to strangle her.

Bloody fucking hell. He was still in love with his ex-wife.

On silent feet, he approached the open door of the office. Two muffled shots reached his ears, and he broke into a sprint. Like Natasha, he was also unarmed—it hadn't been possible to sneak any weapons into the party. Two men stood just inside the room, advancing on the large desk. Swiftly, he grabbed the first assailant's arms from behind, slamming his hands against the doorframe and forcing him to drop the gun. Brandon moved in front of him and landed a hard right hook to his jaw, sending him sprawling backward. Brandon dove for the gun and recovered it as a shot whizzed by his ear, splintering into the wood paneling behind him. He rolled to his back, sat up, and squeezed the trigger. The bullet hit the first man square in the chest, and he slumped heavily to the floor.

Brandon pushed to his feet, the gun trained on the second man, whose own gun was aimed directly at Brandon.

"Drop your weapon," Brandon said, knowing he was going to have to kill him. He couldn't leave him alive and risk having both his identity and Natasha's exposed. Out of the corner of his eye, he saw her rise from behind the desk, a gun clutched in her hands. He kept his eyes on the man in front of him, not giving her away.

"Drop yours," sneered the man in a thick Russian accent.

Suddenly, Natasha was behind the man, the barrel of her gun pressed against the base of his skull. "You're outnumbered. Drop it."

"Fuck you," he spat, and spun, knocking Natasha away. Her gun flew from her hands, and the thug now had his gun trained on her. Without hesitating, Brandon fired two shots into the man's back, and Natasha scrambled out of the way before he fell.

"Did you get the vials?" he asked. Without a word, she dipped behind the desk and emerged with a small metal briefcase. He stuffed the gun into his waistband and closed the distance between them, his hands landing on her shoulders. "You're okay?"

She nodded. "Thanks to you."

He pulled her into his arms, unable to stop himself. She laid her head against his chest, and something deep within him settled, blood flowing like liquid gold through his veins. She pulled away and their eyes locked in the dim room, heat pulsing between them. He tucked a strand of hair behind her ear, letting his thumb trace along her cheekbone. She was so beautiful it almost hurt to look at her. Beautiful and smart and brave.

"You gonna go all James Bond on me and sweep me off my feet?"

Mentally, he added smart-ass to her list of attributes. Funnily enough, it also went in the pro column.

God, he'd never told her that, had he? No, he'd only given her grief for what he now realized were some of her best qualities.

He'd been a royal prick at times, but he'd been too young and stupid to realize the extent to which he'd pushed her away. Small wonder that she'd left when he could've done so much better by her.

"Let's get the hell out of here." He shoved the window open and scanned for guards, but the alleyway at the rear of the house was empty. He eased his feet out onto the narrow ledge and grabbed the drainpipe, climbing down quickly. Once he was safely on the ground, Natasha tossed the briefcase to him and then followed, her athletic body making quick, graceful work of the short descent. Without a word, he took her hand and they started to run, their feet slapping against the pavement as they wove their way toward St. Peter's in Eaton Square, where a car had been left for them.

The towering wrought-iron street lamps cast a warm glow

against the darkness, reflecting against the puddles dotting the sidewalk and street. Within minutes, they'd reached the black Fiat parked in a far corner of the church's car park.

Both Brandon and Natasha stepped up to the driver's side, and just as she yanked the door open, he pushed it closed again.

"What do you think you're doing?"

"I'm driving. I'm the better driver. I'd like to get to the Embassy before, oh, I don't know, tomorrow."

He laughed. "I don't think so, Top Gear. You'll drive on the wrong side and kill us. My country, my agency's car. I'm driving."

"I think—"

"Shut up and get in the fucking car, Natasha." He leaned his hands on the roof of the car, caging her in as he beat back the urge to kiss her until neither of them could think straight. Jesus Christ, the woman was infuriating. Sexy and smart and irritating as hell.

He fucking loved it.

She inhaled sharply and pulled her bottom lip between her teeth. "Fine. You're right. You drive."

Before he could fully process the miracle that was Natasha telling him he was *right,* headlights flashed as a car turned around the corner, and she scurried around to the passenger side. In what he felt was a generous compromise, he pulled the stolen gun from his waistband and handed it to her as he dropped into the driver's seat. She tucked the small briefcase containing the vials under the passenger seat.

He started the car, threw it in gear, and gunned it, heading toward Belgrave Place. The same headlights flashed again and then disappeared as the driver extinguished them. Brandon's stomach knotted, and he flexed his fingers around the leather steering wheel.

He floored it and took a sharp corner toward Belgrave Square Garden, and the sedan followed, tires squealing. "Shit," he hissed. "They're on us."

"Don't worry. I've got it." Twisting around in her seat, Natasha opened her window just enough so she could wedge her head and upper body out.

"What the bloody hell do you think you're doing?" If he hadn't been so intent on steering and keeping them in one piece, he would've reached over and hauled her back inside.

She ducked back in, frustration pulling at her features. "You saved us. Now I'm saving us. You really do want all the glory, don't you?"

"For fuck's sake. Not everything is a competition."

"Sorry, can't hear you. Too busy being awesome." She eased back out the window, the stolen gun clutched in her competent hands as she took aim at the black sedan pursuing them. Trying to avoid the main roads, Brandon swung around Hyde Park Corner, keeping the yawning darkness of Hyde Park to his left and avoiding the bright beacon of Buckingham Palace. Cutting his gaze to Natasha, he watched as she squeezed off several shots, pumping her fist in victory when the sound of squealing tires and then crunching metal pierced the night.

He tightened his grip on the steering wheel, the leather creaking beneath his hands. "Did you just—"

"Shoot the tires out in almost complete darkness?" She sent him an adorably cocky smile. "Sure did."

Something tugged painfully in his chest, and he fought the urge to curse. God, he was so angry with himself. He should hate this woman for what she'd done to him, but he couldn't. She might drive him mental, but, idiot that he was, he *liked* it. *Needed* it. In the six years they'd been apart, he'd dated plenty of women, and not a single one of them had challenged him, frustrated him, impressed him, and turned him on the way Natasha did without even trying.

The simple truth was, there was no one else for him except Natasha Rowe. Never had been, and never would be.

"Hey, you okay? You look upset." She laid a hand on his thigh and his knuckles went white on the steering wheel.

Now wasn't the time to process the confusing jumble of emotions churning through him, so he simply nodded and focused on getting them safely to the American embassy in Grosvenor Square.

Chapter Four

"IT'S FINE, C. D. I can get to my room on my own." Natasha shot Brandon a tired smile. After barely getting away from Silayev's men, they'd turned the briefcase in at the embassy and then headed over to MI5 headquarters for a lengthy debriefing. Brandon must've sensed her fatigue because he'd insisted on driving her to her hotel.

"I wasn't trying to be chivalrous. I need the loo."

"Oh. Okay."

The elevator doors slid open on the fourth floor, and she led him along the hallway, her limbs heavy. Her eyes stung and her throat thickened when she realized that the heaviness wasn't exhaustion, but sadness. Tomorrow, she was headed back to Langley. Home and out of Brandon's life.

He shut the door to the bathroom and, although she wanted nothing more than to flop on the bed, she paced to the window. She looked out onto the lights of Grosvenor Square, leaning her head against the cool glass as rain pattered softly against it.

Tired though she was, her brain spun at a hundred miles an hour as she wrestled with whether or not to say anything to Brandon. Whether or not to tell him how she felt about him, to tell him how sorry she was for leaving all those years ago. Would he even want to hear it, or was she simply looking to ease her own guilty conscience?

She turned as he stormed out of the bathroom, his chiseled features taut with a thrilling combination of anger and lust. "Why do you still have this?" His voice was a low growl.

With long strides, he ate up the distance between them, a slim gold ring clutched in his strong fingers.

"Did you go through my stuff?" Her voice rose, sharp with incredulity.

"Of course I did."

She laced her fingers together and twisted them, anxiety shooting through her and mingling with hope.

"Natasha." His voice was low, the three syllables of her name a warning that his restraint was fraying like worn rope. Excuses tumbled against each other in her brain, but she knew she owed him honesty. Owed *them* honesty.

"Because I couldn't bear to get rid of it."

"Why?" Something wild and desperate shone in his blue eyes, and she broke, unable to stop herself from being selfish and telling him the last thing he wanted to hear.

"Because I never stopped loving you. Because I regret leaving you with every fiber of my being."

"I see."

"I hurt you, Brandon."

He closed his eyes briefly. "Yes."

She licked her lips, and then spoke the words she owed him. "I'm so sorry. It was so …" She blew out a long breath. "It was so wrong for me to leave like that. I know that now. God, I'm so sorry for hurting you, C. D." Her heart pounded in her chest as she spoke.

He inhaled sharply and then extended the ring to her. "Put it on." It wasn't a request, but a command, and a hot thrill chased up her spine. With a trembling hand, she took the slim gold wedding band and slipped it onto her left ring finger. He took one final step toward her, backing her into the window. Her breasts pressed against his chest, and he looked at her, that wolfish smile she loved curving his lips.

With excruciating slowness, he raised his hand and traced his thumb over her cheekbone, her jaw, and then down to the hollow of her throat and over her collarbone. He dipped his head and buried his face in her neck, dragging his lips over the sensitive skin behind her ear. "Tell me why you left." He nipped at her earlobe, and she could feel herself melting. Only Brandon had ever had this effect on her.

"Because I thought it was the right thing to do. I thought we were making each other miserable, and I—" She sighed out a moan when he bit gently at the juncture where neck met shoulder.

"You what?" His hands skimmed over her waist, tracing up her back. He found the pull of her zipper and began easing it down.

"I didn't know how to fix it, and I thought you'd be better off without me. If you weren't peeling my dress off right now, I'd think you must hate me."

He let out a chuckle, the sound rumbling deliciously over her skin. "You drive me mental, but I could never hate you, Tash. I know things were hard between us. God, we were young. We didn't know what we were doing. You messed up, leaving like that, but I didn't know what I was doing either. I could've been better to you. We could've been better to each other." He pushed the straps of her dress off her shoulders and she wiggled out of it, letting the material pool at her feet.

She reached behind her and unhooked her bra, freeing her breasts.

"Sweet Christ."

She gasped when his strong hands cupped her ass and lifted her just as his mouth crashed into hers. There was nothing gentle, tender, or sweet in Brandon's kiss. It was the kiss of a man staking his claim: hard and hot and ravenous. His tongue stroked into her mouth, and she sighed against him, wanting to dissolve into him. She twined her legs around his hips and he tumbled them onto the bed, his weight solid and reassuring above her. He deepened his kiss as they worked as a team to undress him, his fingers pulling at his tie, undoing the buttons of his shirt, while she wrestled with the buckle of his belt.

"Bloody fucking bollocks," he swore, his mouth still against hers. He pulled back just as she freed his thick, hard cock from his pants.

"What?" She stroked him and he hissed out a breath, closing his eyes.

"I haven't a condom."

"So? I'm on the pill. Brandon, Jesus. I don't want to use a condom with you."

The wolfish smile reappeared and he pushed off the bed, shucked the rest of his clothing and then pulled her panties off, tossing them on the floor before crawling back on top of her. He notched the head of his cock at her entrance and rocked his hips, giving her only a taste of what she needed. He sucked a nipple into his mouth before raising his head to look at her.

"If we do this, if we try again, we have a lot of shit to work out. I need to know you're on board with that."

She nodded, swallowing around the lump in her throat. "I want to make it work with you. I promise to try harder, to be better. For better or for worse." Her voice shook and cracked on the last word.

"For better or for worse, Tash." His voice was hoarse, his eyes bright as he looked at her.

Happiness, relief, and hope filled her at the same time as Brandon eased himself all the way in, not stopping until he'd buried himself deep inside her. He slid his hands up and pushed her arms above her head, intertwining his fingers with hers. Over and over again, he filled her with slow, sensuous strokes that gradually gave way to harder, faster, deeper thrusts that all too soon had both of them crying out in bliss, sweating and shaking and panting.

As the sun rose over London and they lay sweaty and sated in each other's arms, she felt whole in a way she hadn't in years.

"I love you," she whispered, pressing a kiss over his heart, his chest hair crisp against her lips.

"I love you more," he whispered back, nuzzling into her hair.

"Are we going to turn this into a competition, too?" She propped up on one elbow, and he looked at her, one hand behind his head, the other sliding up her waist and to her breast. He looked so devastatingly sexy it took her breath away.

He shook his head. "No point. We've both already won."

She laughed and kissed him. Just this one time, she wasn't going to argue.

Tara Wyatt is a contemporary romance and romantic suspense author. Known for her humor and steamy love scenes, Tara's writing has won several awards, including the Librarian's Readers' Choice Award, the New England Readers' Choice Award, the Golden Quill, and the National Excellence in Romantic Fiction Award. A librarian by day and an author by night, Tara lives in Hamilton, Ontario, with the world's cutest dog and a husband who makes all of her heroes look like chumps.

Visit her online at http://www.tara-wyatt.com.

WHEN LIFE IMITATES ART

Marilyn Brant

I COULD TELL THEY weren't married by their voices. As the couple browsed through volumes on the second floor of Between the Pages, my favorite Chicago indie bookstore, a woman I decided to call "Cherry," after her bright-red fingernail polish, purred in response to her man—a tall, hunky guy wearing a black leather jacket.

I overheard the hunk in leather say, "I'm not going home without the book I need."

Her reply was kitten-like—playful but sharp. "Well, we'll find it for you. I'm not a woman who leaves without accomplishing her mission."

Ah, *defining* herself. She spoke a decibel too loud for the quiet section of the bookstore and used that irritating, overly solicitous, enthused tone reserved for people still trying to make a good impression. I guessed they'd been dating for three weeks. Okay, maybe four. But for anyone within a fifty-foot diameter, hearing more of their conversation was unavoidable.

"How about this one?" Cherry asked. "It's an hors d'oeuvres handbook."

"A Martha Stewart cookbook?" Hunk said slowly. "Well, um, that's a thought."

"Right!" she said, emboldened by his response, somehow missing the fact that he didn't even reach for the book.

After an awkward pause, he pointed to another title. "Hey, they have *Entertaining for Dummies*."

"That's funny," she said too quickly, her laugh sounding forced to my ears and tinged with relief at having managed to keep the conversation with him going. She reached over, fondled his leather jacket's collar and fluffed his hair, letting her fingertips play cat and mouse with his neck before sliding her shockingly red nails down his spine and bringing them to rest on the back pocket of his jeans. She announced her ownership of the man (and, apparently, all of his clothing) with a pointed stare in my direction.

I smothered a snicker and glanced down at my book.

Before their arrival that April night, I'd been lounging in a chair to their left. I was flipping through a huge volume of preschool "fun foods" and party ideas while surreptitiously taking notes for a short article I'd been commissioned to write for a parenting magazine. This was a solid text and, if I ever had a toddler in my life, I'd buy it for sure. With my single/no kids status, however, I tended to restrict my purchases to fiction.

The atmosphere upstairs in the Cooking & Crafts section was always casual and relaxing, though. I was in no rush to leave.

A moment later, the woman sauntered off to inspect books on a nearby table while the guy moved closer to my chair. There were other catchy party-planning titles displayed on a rotating shelf not more than three feet from me. Perhaps the book he was in search of was a present for someone unforgivably social, difficult to shop for, and/or really into complicated canapés?

I studied him carefully and scribbled a slew of mental notes while he was busy perusing the volumes.

A young professional—newly out in the world.

Preppy. Like he'd just walked off the set of one of those legal dramas on TV.

He couldn't have been more than twenty-five—about my age—and, beneath the black leather jacket, he was dressed in a layered cream shirt and pullover, fitted blue jeans, and dark loafers.

Attractive. No rings on his fingers, I couldn't help but notice.

I stole a longer look at his girlfriend, too. No rings either. Blond, fine-featured, and slim, she was clad in carelessly tight black pants, a red knit top, black boots, and was in possession of perfectly manicured, chip-free nails.

Add to that, she wore impeccable makeup and what had to be a pricey name-brand handbag (I'd be damned if I knew which designer) slung over her shoulder. She gave off an arrogant, entitled air, and my dislike was instantly cemented. I returned my gaze to the handsome dude in the black leather jacket, but when he glanced over at me, I buried my nose into my book.

I sensed him moving a few paces forward, though.

Searching.

Leaning in.

Taking another step or two nearer to me.

My left elbow, draped in part over the armrest, was closest to him and to the revolving shelf he was spinning in that slow, deliberate way. I was determined not to look up, but he was so close. His loafers were in my direct line of vision.

He inched even closer, his thigh brushing against my elbow. I just *knew* it was an intentional act. In that instant of epiphany, though, I lost my equilibrium. The big book I was holding wobbled. I grabbed at it, steadied it, but then dropped my pen, followed by several note cards and a couple of loose-leaf pages, which fluttered to the floor. I closed the book and bent to snatch my fallen items.

He immediately kneeled to help, but I was faster. Once I righted myself, I found his face at eye level with mine.

"Sorry," he mouthed, looking intense, uncomfortable, and *so incredibly hot*. Wow. I held my breath.

Our gazes locked for a second longer, and I noted with a writer's observation the way his light brown lashes appeared to disappear as they moved away from his eyelids. I struggled to think of an appropriate metaphor, but he angled his torso toward the bookshelf again and rose to full height before I could complete the thought.

The blonde, with the ever-present radar of somebody on perma-alert to potential threats, suddenly focused her attention on us. Ignoring me and addressing him, Cherry asked, "What are you doing?"

"Just looking at titles over here." He grasped a random volume, running his thumb along its spine.

With a shrill laugh that sounded like the scratch of a fingernail she said, "Oh, no, you're not. You just want to see what *she's* writing." Her eyes washed over me coldly, then she flipped her hair back and emitted another pseudo giggle.

I gazed directly at the guy, expecting some kind of reaction from him.

Expressionless at first, he caught my eye once more before turning away—his face reddening. Then, trailing behind her, I heard him protest, "No, I wasn't ..." And with that, they avoided me for the rest of my visit.

When I'd finished flipping through the book for inspiration and had jotted down the author's name and the title for reference, I returned the large volume to its shelf. I snagged one last glimpse of the couple, huddled in an aisle between two long stacks, before I walked out the door and into the spring night.

I thought that would be the end of it. After all, I lived in the heart of the city—an enormous, frenetic place. Any chance of running into Hunk and Cherry again in downtown Chicago would be unlikely at best.

The problem, though, was that I couldn't seem to forget them.

They haunted me like an unsolved mystery. Like a mental puzzle my brain had to unravel. I found myself wondering what was going to happen to them next. Were they falling deeper in love and on to a greater commitment? Or, was that day the pinnacle in their short relationship and had things already begun to break apart?

Over the next several weeks, whenever I would pass by Between the Pages, I would stop in, head to the second floor, and meander down the aisles in partial search for one or both of them. Not intending to speak to either of them, of course, even if our paths should meet. No. I just wanted to observe and try to determine what had transpired in their romantic saga. Like *Days of Our Lives*, only in 3-D. But I never encountered them on those visits.

Clearly, the days of *my* life were lacking in excitement.

I'd been working diligently as a part-time magazine freelancer, a part-time closet novelist, and a full-time neurotic for over four years. I was long convinced my chance of breaking into big-market fiction was minuscule, but I devoured how-to books on writing a bestseller and drank gallons of coffee while composing my first full-length novel, with cursory notes for a sequel.

I primarily paid the bills, however, by writing regularly for about seven different publications of varying status, exclusively nonfiction. It was a dry existence—research, write, edit, send—with very little whimsical fiction to entertain me on those nights when I lamented my lack of both fame and any kind of love life. I did have a few short stories published in obscure literary journals, but it had been months since I'd had the time or the energy to attempt writing another.

Suddenly, though, I was inspired to draft something totally different. Something light and … *romantic*. Pen, paper, and my own life intersected. Reality and fantasy converged on the page and within my mind.

The bookstore couple began to join me as I researched articles online or took the commuter train to conduct interviews in the suburbs.

They worked out alongside of me at the tiny gym in my apartment complex's basement.

They laughed and cried with me while watching the latest soap-opera intrigues.

They even ate next to me on my solitary park bench and returned with me throughout that May to my ant-infested studio apartment.

Before long, I knew everything about them.

Well, I *imagined* I knew, which—to a writer—was essentially the same thing.

Turned out, Hunk and Cherry had first met about six months before at a company basketball game. They were each cheering on players from the public defender's office where the guy (I named him "Neil") worked. He'd graduated from law school determined to be one of those good-guy underdogs. A man who toiled for humanity in a largely pro bono way, seeking justice for all. He'd been laboring as an underling at the office for nearly a year after finishing law school out East. He was from there—Ipswich, Massachusetts, specifically—and his family had made their money in banking and stock trade. He felt he was finally able to share his own good fortune by helping others.

Cherry (aka "Jessica"), well, she came from money, too, but it was of the alimony/trust-fund variety. Her mom had a habit of marrying wealthy older men and divorcing them before they could say "prenuptial agreement." It was a fifty-fifty asset split out in California, Jessica's home state, and her mom was on her fourth property acquisition there. No wonder the poor girl was so insecure. So weirdly possessive.

Jessica worked in sales at a cosmetic company, which was why her makeup always had to be perfect. Her best friend and colleague, Anita, was married to a guy named Bryan, another lawyer at Neil's office and a six-foot two guard on their firm's pickup basketball team. After several months of casually meeting up at various sporting and social functions, Neil heard through Bryan—who got the word via Anita—that Jessica had a crush on him. Neil, to be nice (and since she wasn't actually *horrible* looking), asked Jessica out. She, of course, nearly pole-vaulted at the invitation.

On their first date, Neil took her to dinner at an upscale Szechuan restaurant and then out to see a romantic comedy. He liked her, and Jessica worked hard to maintain appearances. A startlingly domineering streak and more than a hint of jealousy would find its way into her voice on occasion, but she did her best to minimize that and she scored a second date with him. That one culminated in a long kiss goodnight, which managed to erase—temporarily—the newly forming doubts from Neil's mind.

Then Neil was thrown a curve.

Bryan and Anita, wanting to promote the fledgling relationship, pressed him into service as a host. It started when they invited

Neil and Jessica to their house. Even though the event had been billed as casual, the meal was lavish, since Bryan took great delight in the culinary arts. A few years older than Neil and a few levels up in the office hierarchy, Bryan was well versed in the evening's wine selection. He made the crab and scallion appetizer dip and had grilled the filet to tender perfection—even offering a delectable mushroom sauce as an accompaniment.

Anita did her part as well with an impressive seven-layer fiesta salad, sage-seasoned wild rice, and a homemade apricot torte.

Neil was floored by this. He usually microwaved his food or had it delivered.

Protocol, of course, required reciprocation, so he masked his reluctance and invoked a sincere-sounding invitation to the other couple for the following Saturday night.

Nearly a week passed. Not yet frantic but feelings of worry escalating, Neil raced to change out of his work clothes, asked Jessica to meet him at the local bookstore, and together they spent the first hour of their Friday night in search of helpful information.

This was where I came in. Well, a character very much *like* me.

Neil bumped into me on purpose, and somewhat more dramatically than in the original scene, but instead of turning away when Jessica said, "You just want to see what *she's* writing," Neil replied spiritedly, "*Yes*. Maybe she's got the book we need."

I smiled, the epitome of warmth and graciousness, and said, "Perhaps another book will help you, but would you mind if I offered a suggestion?"

Neil agreed at once. Even Jessica, walking toward me with scorpion-like wariness, appeared politely attentive.

Upon hearing about the event they were planning, I drew upon my extensive background knowledge, obtained from so many years of information gathering, and recommended a book series that had full menus along with a coordinating selection of song choices to add the right musical atmosphere to the evening.

"My sister is married to a school principal," I told them. "She does a lot of entertaining and swears by these sets." This was true, by the way.

Well, of course they were grateful, even more so after I helped them find the menu/music sets on the shelf.

"So," Jessica said, not quite able to expel the snottiness from her voice, "how do you know so much? Do you, like, *work* here?"

"Oh, no. I'm a writer." The pride accompanying this announcement always made me stand up straighter. "And I spend a lot of time at this store … improving my mind through extensive reading." I doubted she'd catch the Jane Austen reference ("extensive reading" being one of Mr. Darcy's requirements of an accomplished woman), but I tossed it in there anyway. *Take that, you uncivil trollop.*

She narrowed her eyes at me.

Before she could speak again, Neil insisted on making formal introductions. He told me their names, and I told them mine, as well as a little bit about the article I was researching. "So you see, nothing I wrote down would have been of much interest to you, unless you were planning to have a group of three-year-olds at your dinner party."

Neil laughed at my joke and I grinned at him, certain that Jessica missed it since she was playing stupidly with the straps of her expensive handbag. He told me they were going to grab a late dinner and, while they were at it, select one of the recommended meal combinations to make the following night.

"Well, good luck," I replied, hoping to come across as encouraging. "I'm sure everything will turn out beautifully."

Jessica nodded, growing a fraction friendlier as she realized my departure was imminent. Neil, however, grasped my hand and said with genuineness and warmth, "Thank you, Lily, for your help! You rescued us from the complexity of Martha Stewart."

We both laughed at that and, then, said goodbye. Within moments, I was out the door, pleased with myself for being of assistance to someone so nice and—well, let's face it—so handsome.

Anyway, weeks went by and I was as busy as ever, bringing in a higher-than-usual income from my articles and making tremendous headway on my novel at last. On occasion, my mind wandered back to the evening I met Neil and Jessica. I wondered about them—*him* in particular. How had their Saturday dinner gone? I wished there would have been a way I could ask. Discover more. Or, better yet, run into him again. My love life was the only thing that had remained stagnant. Aside from some promising flirtations at the gym, which amounted to nothing, the only romantic overtures I experienced at all in recent weeks were in my imagination.

One rainy Wednesday, I was at Between the Pages—this time trying to dry off from the inside out with their strongest espresso. I wasn't actually depressed, because things were going pretty well in my life overall, but I'd managed to get into one of those reflective moods that turn melancholy if not immediately remedied. I needed a prescription in the form of some good escapist fiction.

I'd just read the first page of a Wisconsin author's debut romance with awe and envy—more or less equally mixed—when I caught a peripheral movement and looked up.

"Lily?" the voice asked. My ears registered its owner sooner than my eyesight.

"Oh, hi, Neil," I said, surprised, though not at all unpleasantly so. It was funny how you could forget certain details about people: his smile displayed two fabulous, but previously overlooked, dimples. His eyes were a piercing, Chris Hemsworth kind of blue. How had I missed that? What I said aloud, though, was simply, "How are you?"

"Good, good. Thought that was you over here. Working on another article?"

"No, not this time." I pointed to the books in front of us. "Just admiring the narrative styles of these authors."

"Hmm," he said, nodding as he cast his eyes along the rows of new titles. Then, he looked up at me. As before, I was startled by the intensity of his gaze. My mind went blank for a nanosecond before I remembered.

"Hey, how did the big dinner turn out?"

"Oh, yeah. Everything worked well, thanks to you." And he proceeded to tell me details about the menu they'd selected and the accompanying music. "Those sets were a great idea."

"I'm so glad," I said, sincerity gushing forth and overflowing.

But then Neil went silent, and I was left trying to figure a way out of the creeping awkwardness. "So, um, where's Jessica? Did she come with you tonight?" I swiveled from side to side, expecting her to materialize at any second.

"No, um … we haven't gotten together much these days. I haven't seen her at all, in fact, for a few weeks, so …" Neil shrugged but didn't look particularly despondent about the situation.

"Oh." I bobbed my head, struggling to appear calm, empathetic, understanding. Internally, I was hip hopping.

We moved on to other topics: the changeable summer weather, the state of world affairs and, in deference to our meeting place, good books we'd read recently. As I blathered on about some of my favorite romantic comedy authors, I could hear an odd, inflated tone hijack my voice and force it to rise to a delighted coo. Neil looked duly impressed with my monologue before embarking upon one of his own—featuring thriller writers and romantic suspense. I listened, attentive as a spellbound disciple.

All that remained now was the long-hoped-for setup for a future date.

Neil pointed to my espresso. "Hey, I love those, too. Did you get a double shot?"

"How did you know?"

He smiled. "That's the only way to do it. Decaf, herbal tea, and the like—those are for weenies."

I laughed and told him I agreed.

"Well, maybe we can grab a couple sometime soon," he said, "and, you know, just talk for a while."

"Yeah, I'd like that," I replied, beaming my best grin at him. Then, with pride at my casual assertiveness, I added, "I need to browse through some materials on promoting heart health this weekend. I was thinking of coming back maybe Sunday morning to check out their books, so if you want to join me—"

"Definitely!" Neil broke in. "What time were you thinking of getting here?"

"Maybe ten or ten thirty. I only need to do about a half hour of work."

"Why don't I drop by at about ten thirty then? If you still have some stuff to finish up, you can spend as much time as you need. There's always a lot to look at here. Then, whenever you're ready, we can take our espressos to go, stroll a bit if the day's clear, maybe even grab some lunch or something later …" He shot me one of his preppy lawyer grins. I was charmed.

We quickly exchanged cell numbers and then parted company with matching smiles and nearly matching fantasies of eternal love, which now seemed closer than ever.

And this was where my imagined tale concluded, complete with all the hopefulness and optimism that filled the heart of every romantic. That blissful, mystical time in a relationship's beginning, before anything could swoop down to erode the magic of infatuation. Only in soap operas, fairy tales, or love ballads by eighties hair bands could one find a rival to such a glorious moment. Oh, the sweet sensation!

I adored my little love story and called it "Browsing."

After several revisions and at least seventeen mocha frappuccinos, I submitted it to a regional magazine—*Midwest Fiction Forum: Stories for the Modern Genre Writer*—a journal that published monthly issues in print as well as weekly features online. They'd accepted a poem of mine about two years before, so I was positively inclined toward their publication. But what I liked best about them was this: their response time was a shockingly prompt three weeks or less.

I sweated out the days, always with that fluttery impatience just below my lungs whenever a new email would appear. Then one Monday, sometime in late June, I got a ping in my inbox. It was from the magazine … I crossed my fingers and clicked open the message.

An acceptance!

"Yes!" I exclaimed to no one but the ants in my otherwise-empty apartment. My story would not only be on the web, it would be included in one of the print issues, too.

After celebrating my good fortune alone with a dark Colombian roast/brandy concoction I mixed, I added this publishing acquisition to my short list of fiction credits. Cheerfully, I marked my calendar with an asterisk and the word "Browsing" next to the notes box for September.

In the weeks that followed, I continued to stop by my favorite bookstore with some frequency. Admittedly, thoughts of Neil and Jessica always accompanied me there, but I'd grown less hopeful of ever seeing either of them again as the summer progressed.

One time, shortly after my birthday in mid-July, I thought I spotted Jessica. I saw *someone*, anyway, who was a leggy blonde with an identical designer handbag. Could it have been a coincidence?

The woman was near the first floor information desk with her back to me, and I was on the escalator heading down. By the time I reached the ground level, whoever she was had vanished. But, since we'd never *actually* spoken, I supposed I wouldn't have known what to say if I'd met up with her face to face anyway. I was pretty sure she wouldn't have had a clue who I was.

My romantic short story came out in the September issue as scheduled, and I was pleased to see my name in print for something this lighthearted and creative. I pulled out my box of novel notes and began sifting through them at more regular intervals—gathering, organizing, refining ideas. I could feel my confidence in storytelling growing.

In early October, as Halloween approached, I was assigned an article on simple children's costumes for a citywide parenting publication. I went to my trusty bookstore on a Thursday night to peruse the shelves for costume ideas. I found myself drawn to my favorite lounge chair on the second floor.

I'd lifted four promising titles off the shelf and was scanning the table of contents page in the third book, when I noticed somebody stealthily taking a seat a couple of chairs to my right. I didn't look up immediately. I just registered that the invading individual was male, turned a handful of pages, and scribbled several notes on "baby bumblebee" trick-or-treat attire.

But I had *that* feeling—that inexplicable sensation that occurs whenever you first become aware that you're being watched. A weird *The Sixth Sense* kind of thing—minus the dead people.

Reasonably sure I could identify the source of the gaze, I glanced over at the man who'd come in a few minutes before.

In truth, I probably wouldn't have recognized him if it hadn't been for his loafers.

He was watching me intently—this guy I'd once named Neil—only he wasn't quite like my memory's image. Seeing him in person for just the second time in my life, I realized I'd glossed over some significant details in my recollection: the dark blond chin stubble, the moderately protruding ears, the serious set to his jaw, and the astuteness in his light blue eyes (although they *were* as blue as Chris Hemsworth's). The eyelashes were unchanged, but a more accurate picture of the other features was starting to come back to me. Dressed in a dark sport coat this time, rather than a black leather jacket, with tan slacks instead of jeans and a fat briefcase touching the toe of his right loafer, he regarded me with a steady, unsmiling expression.

Damn.

I looked away, expecting him to turn his attention elsewhere now that I had.

He didn't.

I took several yoga-style cleansing breaths—despite the fact that I never did yoga—and counted slowly to five before looking back at him. He was still staring, with a gravity that led me to mark the nearest exits if a quick escape would be required.

Crapola.

He couldn't know about the story, could he? Or be angry because of it, right? It was *fiction*, after all. I mean, I didn't even know his real name!

I was tempted to say something to him, but what? These fears had to be my overactive imagination working the late shift again.

Maybe he was just absentmindedly staring in my direction.

Maybe I looked like somebody he knew from Sunday school when he was ten.

Maybe this was his idea of flirtation, you know, smoldering like one of those television network vampires. (They do that.)

I'd nearly convinced myself of one of these scenarios—the

Sunday school one—when I saw the corners of his lips curl slightly upward.

At long last, he whispered, "So, you write for *Midwest Fiction Forum,* eh?" It was presented as a question, but I could tell from the undisguised sarcasm that he already knew the answer.

Oh, shit, shit, shit!

"Uh, w-well," I stuttered, "I've had a c-couple, um—*why?*"

He didn't reply. He got up from his chair two seats away and moved right next to me as I shot glances around the room in panic. I put the kiddie costume books on the floor and gripped my pen, dagger style, just in case.

Then he leaned in toward me. "I remember you," he whispered. My eyes widened while his crinkled at the corners. "You were the one here that day, weren't you? You lifted our conversation. Verbatim."

Oh, no. A psycho guy ... *who reads*. Short story and poetry journals, no less. Just my luck.

Then I thought, hey, if only I could escape the bookstore unscathed, this would make a wild story. Maybe even a novel. Consider the fun premise, the natural, built-in conflict. It had so much potential, but first I needed to slip away from the tall, hunky man with the dangerous glint in his very blue eyes.

"Um, look," I began, using my most placating tone. "It's just fiction, you know? I didn't mean to offend you or, or, *anyone*—but, it's—well, people are always asking writers where we get our ideas, and you can tell them it's in the 'random stuff' we encounter in real life but, a lot of times, no one believes us. You two were in a public location, talking kind of loud, and, and ... I mean, the things you both were saying made an interesting place for a story to start. So—" I ran fresh out of babbling steam right about then, but I forced myself to meet his gaze and hold my ground.

He snickered and sat back in his chair. I loosened my grip on the pen—a little.

"I should've known you'd be some writer. You had that shrewd, information-gathering look about you." He raised his eyebrows at me, and his gaze raked me over very deliberately before returning to my face. I felt myself turn pink.

"I must have reread the first conversation, especially your descriptions of us, and that sitcom-like elbow-bumping incident about fifteen times before I could believe it." He shook his head. "And you were hardly objective in your narrative. But, I guess," he said, wrinkling his nose, "it *was* a pretty bizarre night."

"Why?" I asked, careful to show both respect and interest. I needed more information for the psycho-bookworm story.

"Because my girlfriend and I broke up about ten minutes after you left."

"What? *Really?* The blonde?" Excellent. Crisis and several plot points already in place. Now I just needed more character details.

"Yeah. The blonde. *Jessica*, as you know her," he said, mocking me. "Her name's Kira, by the way, and *she's* the lawyer."

"Oops!" I covered my mouth with my palm, but I couldn't completely block out my surprise. "Well, so what happened?"

He inhaled and looked at me strangely. "Let's see—uh, *you*, actually—among other things. She was mad because I'd been talking to you, plus there were about three thousand major and minor infractions I'd committed that day ... and that month. She had sort of a jealous streak." He exhaled but continued looking at me strangely. "Long story."

Okay, I may have failed to guess Kira's name or real profession, but I'd totally nailed the jealous insecurity bit. I kept watching the guy standing in front of me, though, and was surprised to see the strange expression on his face morph into sadness, followed by hurt. Could he be missing Cherry, the fingernail-polish chick?

"Oh, I'm sorry," I began, figuring I could at least offer my condolences on the relationship's demise. "Are you all right? I have time, if you need to talk. I mean—I don't know what to say, but—"

"Don't *say* anything. Don't *imagine* anything. And, for mercy's sake, don't *write* anything." His acerbic tone punctuated every syllable like a stylus jabbing at something. He pointed at me for further emphasis, and his face took on the menacing cast of a disgruntled literary critic. "I'm *fine*."

He didn't look fine, but I merely squinted at him. After

forbidding me to do the only three things I felt remotely qualified for and/or capable of, I was left with few options.

Well, I also *thought* really hard. His problems with Cherry/Jessica/Kira weren't my fault, I reasoned. He needed to learn to make better relationship choices. He should be more like my character Neil.

Additionally, I wondered if crawling into a parallel literary reality of my own construction would disrupt the space-time continuum in both the real world and in the virtual one. I promised myself I'd check out Einstein's books on the first floor of the store later.

Meanwhile, the man in front of me tapped his chin with a curved index finger and pursed his lips, as if trying to hold back a cutting retort.

After a time he sighed and said, "I guess Kira was more of a snobby Caroline Bingley than a witty Elizabeth Bennet anyway."

I was a little awed by this statement. He spoke of Jane Austen's characters knowingly, as if he'd read *Pride and Prejudice* and understood all about faulty first impressions. Who *was* this guy?

"In any case, it turned out she wasn't my type." He shrugged, flicked at his fingernails with his thumb, and then ran his hand through his hair.

I was inexplicably tempted to fluff it the way his ex-girlfriend had once. I refrained.

"So, in addition to your charming tale, I read your byline, too," he continued. "Unless you write under a pseudonym, your real name is *not* Lily."

"Hm, well, yeah—that's correct. The byline is accurate, not the character name," I admitted. "But, who are *you*? I mean, who even reads *Midwest Fiction Forum*?" I waited and tried to project nonchalance although, by now, I was far from indifferent.

He glared at me when I asked this, his eyes awash with a series of emotions—none of them positive. "How *could* you?" he exploded. "Seriously. How could you name me 'Neil,' of all names?" Then he crossed his arms with very believable indignation. "When I think of Neil, I think: Diamond. Sedaka. Young. I am *not* some ancient, semi-musical has-been who—"

"You don't like Neil Diamond?"

"That's beside the point. Listen, I have a chunky Uncle Neil, who's really annoying. And my parents go to another Neil, their bald accountant, every year for their taxes. I do *not* look like a Neil!" He underscored this statement by banging his fist against the armrest.

"Okay. You're right, you're right. It—it was a hasty, ill-considered choice." I gripped my pen and noticed a few people staring at us from across the aisle in Travel & Vacation Guides. At the moment, I wanted to get away, too.

He studied my face carefully, then exhaled—a stream of hot air, no doubt. A beat later he thrust his hand out at me. I debated whether or not to shake it, but curiosity won out. It was a warm hand with a good grip and enough roughness to remind me that he was a man. A pretty strong man, actually. How did he get those calluses on his fingers? Weight lifting? Carpentry? Playing guitar? I debated the possibilities.

"I'm Art Cavendish—Artie to my friends—originally from St. Paul, Minnesota. Never been to Ipswich, Massachusetts, in my life, by the way, and I'm not *preppy*." His eyes flicked up to the ceiling and down to my face. "And if you use me as the basis for a character again—and I mean *ever*—I do not want some lame-ass name. Rick isn't bad. Something solid sounding like Steve or Brad is okay, but definitely not Neil, and none of those English names like Ian or Graham either. Or names with a *y* in the middle of them like Kyle or Daryl. Got it?"

"Uh, yeah. No problem," I said. "I'll remember your preferences."

Then he flashed a grin at me, the intensity breaking its hold. For a second, he looked almost normal.

"So, okay," Artie said. "I've read a fair number of thrillers and some romantic suspense like your character, who shall remain nameless, but I'm revisiting the classics at the moment. Ralph Waldo Emerson. Sinclair Lewis. Some Oscar Wilde. And I've been watching Fellini flicks. *8 ½* is my favorite."

He paused while I nodded my approval.

"I'm a set designer for a couple of small theaters in the city, and I've had an online subscription to *Midwest Fiction Forum* for about a year now. I do some scriptwriting, too." He gave me an arch look. "I'd gone to the bookstore that night trying to get ideas to flesh out a character—someone who might be one of those socialite, home-entertainment types—when I saw you. You sort of fit the profile, so I came closer. Thought I'd poke around, try to read what you were writing."

My jaw dropped open. Wide enough for a robin to fly in and nest awhile.

What?

He thought I was a Martha Stewart type? *Me?* The girl who lived in ratty jeans and old college sweatshirts? Whose idea of "holiday decorating" consisted of putting up a thin strip of icicle window clings? Who wouldn't know how to weave a dinner placemat or make a canapé if her life and future family tree depended on it?

"Are you kidding?" I sputtered.

"Yes," he said, not bothering to disguise his amusement. "I'm just messing with you. You deserve it." Then he collapsed even deeper into his comfy armchair, scanned my entire body from top to bottom like an MRI, before finally refocusing on my face, his lips twitching. "You're pretty cute when you're flustered."

I couldn't help it. I laughed, genuinely surprised for the first time in a long time. I'd misread this guy. I'd gotten his real character wrong when I'd assessed him before—or, at least, it was grossly incomplete. He had an edginess to him that I liked but, right this second, he seemed almost relaxed and personable, with an offbeat sense of humor and a quick wit I hadn't attributed to him in my story. I couldn't deny that all of those qualities were as attractive to me as his hunky appearance. Possibly more so.

I picked up one of my blank white note cards and waved it like a flag. "Truce?"

"Maybe," he said, but he was grinning. "So, were you really working on an article last spring?"

"Yeah." I pointed to the books on the floor and to my notes. "I'm doing it again tonight. Halloween costumes this time." Despite our less than auspicious beginning, my radar registered something flattering: he might just be interested in me.

"Ah," Artie replied with a nod, running his fingers through his light, wavy hair—a signature tic, perhaps? I didn't know him well enough to be sure. "Perhaps I should let you get back to your work. You must have a lot more to do." He motioned toward the door but stayed seated, waiting. Waiting for me … maybe?

"No, I'm done for tonight," I decided. "Wouldn't be able to work on more of this now anyway." I was conscious of eyeing him with interest, too, and of wanting to be utterly honest, even while I was flirting. "Having met you has put an end to my concentration for the day."

"Well, good. Glad I managed that at least." He laughed for a moment at my expense. "So, what are you gonna do instead?"

"I don't know." I looked toward the refreshment area. "Maybe get an espresso or a latté." Then, taking a chance—one that required more courage than I'd expected—I asked, "Want some?"

"Hell, no. Never touch that stuff." He brushed imaginary dust off the arm of the chair and granted me a dimply grin. "Caffeine makes me edgy."

"I see." I began collecting my belongings, trying not to look as dejected as I felt.

I capped my pen and stood to leave when Artie chuckled, low but challenging. He shook his head. A few nearby customers turned their attention to us, guessing something semi-dramatic might be afoot. I, however, had no idea what would happen. Even the many fictional scenarios I could imagine didn't give me relief in the moment. I wanted to know what this Art Cavendish guy would *truly* say next.

"No coffee, but I'm fond of tea—herbal, in fact," he explained, raising an eyebrow. Then, just in case I missed his intention, he pointed to the beverage counter.

Incredulous, I asked, "For real, or are you teasing me again?"

He nodded. "For real. Truth is stranger than fiction, you know." He grinned and motioned once more toward the café. "C'mon, we've got a second chance to write a new ending to our story. A more accurate one, I hope. Let's take it." He stood and stretched his palm out toward me.

As I took his hand, I squeezed and reveled in the actuality of the two of us connecting here and now, with the possibility of *for always*. It was a heady feeling. Then I said, "That's a pretty good line. You might see it again. In print."

He squeezed my hand in return. "I'd be disappointed if I didn't."

Marilyn Brant is a *New York Times* and *USA Today* best-selling author of contemporary women's fiction, romantic comedy, and mystery. In 2013, she was named Author of the Year by the Illinois Association of Teachers of English. She loves Sherlock Holmes, travel, music, chocolate, and all things Jane Austen. Her Austen-inspired debut novel, *According to Jane*, won RWA's prestigious Golden Heart® Award, and Buzzle.com named it one of the 100 Best Romance Novels of All Time. Marilyn's romantic women's fiction has been included in the Doubleday Book Club, Book-of-the-Month Club, Literary Guild, and Rhapsody Book Club. She's also written several romantic comedies, like *On Any Given Sundae*, as well as a coming-of-age mystery called *The Road to You*. Her latest releases are sexy contemporary romances in her Mirabelle Harbor series, set on the shores of Lake Michigan, near her home in the Chicago suburbs.

For updates, visit her website,
http://www.marilynbrant.com.

UNDER A BURNING SKY

Renee Luke

"WE NEED TO TALK."

With trembling hands, Mika Montrell tried to hold the edges of her towel in place around her body. Her throat went dry. She tried to swallow. Tried to breathe. Tears stung her eyes as the voice resounded in her mind. His unmistakable voice.

Jabbing at her phone, she listened to the voicemail again. "We need to talk." That's all. No number. No name. But she didn't need one. She knew exactly who it was.

Her husband.

She tried to hold in the tears. Tried to keep her knees from wobbling. To remain upright. Flung back to the devastation of the past, she failed. Clinging to her towel, she slid down the wall, collapsing on the floor.

She hadn't heard the phone ring from the shower. She hadn't been prepared when she listened to the voicemail.

Now, shaking so badly, she could hardly hold onto her cellphone, could hardly read the screen as she checked the number displayed. It wasn't one she recognized, but that didn't really surprise her. Either he'd gotten a new number since the last time they'd spoke, or he was using someone else's phone, thinking she wouldn't answer if she knew it was him.

He'd been right.

A tear fell. Another. "Fuck." Mika dabbed the edge of the soft terrycloth to her face. She'd cried enough tears. Enough damn tears. It'd been three years since she left her husband, and she'd thought she was over the emotion. Apparently not. A sob escaped. Her body shook, shoulders aching with sorrow and tension. Air burned in her lungs, but her heart raced.

Gathering herself, she pushed replay on her phone and put on the speaker so she could hear his voice fill the room. *We need to talk.* Again ... *We need to talk.* Again ... *We need to talk.* She played the message over and over. His voice, low and thick, still did things to her. Warmed her body. Stroked along her skin. Aroused her body as only he could. Reminded her of another time.

Destroyed, she felt sucker punched in the gut, but that was ridiculous. She knew this day would come. Had expected it to come sooner. She was consumed with an intense combination of wanting him to call, to hear his voice and comforting words, and needing him to stay away. She'd had to leave him. None if it was his fault. Had never been his fault.

It was all hers.

How could she look at him after the death of their son? How could she look him in the eye and not feel an overwhelming and suffocating amount of guilt? How could she look at her husband and not be reminded of the infant son who was his spitting image—a tiny DNA replica—who'd been stolen away by sudden infant death syndrome.

Everyone had assured and reassured her it wasn't her fault. That it had been nothing she'd done and nothing she could've done. The doctors had told her, the coroner, her husband. But despite logic, how could she not blame herself? *Why had she let him nap alone, and why hadn't she checked him sooner?* A mother is supposed to protect her child. She hadn't. And Rye Junior—RJ— was gone.

She'd left, too. Left her home, her husband, her friends, and family. For a while, she'd even thought she'd left her mind, slipping into deep and ugly depression. Not showering or eating. Rarely getting out of bed, except to work her online job enough to pay rent for her small apartment.

Closing her eyes, Mika tilted her head against the wall. The towel wrapping her damp hair fell to the floor. She'd sat on the floor so long listening to his voice that her hair began to air dry. It'd be full of knots and a pain in the ass to comb through. She pushed the curls from her face and listened one more time to the message. She just needed to hear his tone. A small moan escaped her lips as she remembered his calls after she'd first left. A dozen or more daily, begging her—pleading with her—to come home, telling her how much he loved her, how much he needed her.

She'd never returned a single one. Not even a single reply to a text. She'd shut him out of her life, wanting to rid herself of any reminder of her son. Many days, she hadn't been sure if she wanted to survive this, but if she did, closing him out had been her only way. Eventually, the calls slowed to a few a day, then a few a week, then a few a month. Now, it'd been nearly two years since she'd heard from him.

Mika sucked in a deep breath and tried to remember her husband during happier times. To remember how she loved him once—still—and how it felt to be loved by him. For so long, she'd only been able to remember the pain and horror on his beautiful face. How his light brown eyes had been tortured and twisted in loss and agony. She forced a memory of their wedding day. A memory of his smile—warm, welcoming. Engaging.

Drawing strength from the vision, she opened her eyes and returned the call.

It only rang once. "Mika?" His voice was deep, rough. The same languid drawl she'd adored whispered in her ear. A shiver danced across her skin.

Taking a moment, she replied. "Yeah, Rye, it's me."

Silence stretched. She could hear him breathing. Hear her pulse pounding in her ears. After what felt like forever, she heard him clear his throat.

"I wasn't sure if this was still your number."

"I was in the shower."

Her husband remained silent as heat burned on her cheeks, realizing she'd just told him something as intimate as being completely naked. Her nipples beaded up tight, but Mika rolled her eyes at herself and pulled the towel more firmly around her chest. Must have been the air conditioner on full blast. *Nothing else.* Definitely not hearing Rye's voice reverberate through her.

Swallowing the lump in her throat, she continued, "You said we needed to talk. It's been a long time, Rye. A long time … I figured I owed you at least a return call."

"Baby, you owe me a hell of a lot more than that." His tone was thick with emotion. There was pain, but it was the anger that sent a shiver along her spine. He sounded filled with rage, and yet he called her *baby* as tenderly he always had.

But he was right. *She owed him his son.* Guilt resurfaced with a vengeance. Mika used a corner of the towel to catch a stray tear. As much as she loved her husband—had always loved him—their future had died the same night as their son had.

"You're right," she whispered. If she spoke any louder, he'd hear her voice crack on a sob.

"Damn, baby." He mumbled some curse words. They were muffled, hardly audible, but she knew him well enough to know. "Mika, I didn't mean that the way it sounded."

She gulped. "Okay." She wanted to feel the anger she heard in his tone. Wanted to feel anything but loss. Instead, it was as if the three years had melted away and she was as raw as if she'd left him yesterday. "You said we need to talk?"

"Yeah. We do. But it should be in person. Can you meet me?"

She didn't want to. But it was time. *Past time.* She nodded, then rolled her eyes again knowing he couldn't see her. "I guess so. What did you have in mind?"

"That spot you liked on the corner of Truxel and Bell?"

"Fireside Café? All right. When?"

"An hour?"

Mika scoffed. "I'll need longer. My hair air dried." It'd take her a while to work out all the tangles and knots.

He chuckled, deep and husky. His low laughter was a soothing balm; it warmed and caressed little bits of her soul she'd forgotten existed.

"Leave it," he said, "I always loved your natural curls."

Mika closed her eyes as she inhaled and leaned her head against the wall, allowing the tension to ease from her shoulders. She smiled at his words. She'd heard them so many times, especially before bed, when he'd wind his fingers into her wild, tangled hair, and hold her in place while he kissed her. Made love to her. Fucked her. Heat churned low in her belly. It'd been a long time since her husband had made her smile.

"So an hour?"

His question shook her from her memories. She dreaded the inevitable conversation. She dreaded seeing him. But she couldn't wait to be near him either. She nodded as she spoke. "All right. Fireside Café in an hour."

"See you soon, baby."

See you soon, baby. Her hands were shaking again, his voice wrecking her. She took a few deep breaths and pushed herself from the floor. She was going to see her husband in an hour. Three years had been long enough.

Chapter Two

LEANING BACK IN THE too small metal patio chair, Rye tilted his face toward the afternoon sun. He tried to relax. Tried to slow the pulse drumming behind his temples. Taking a breath, he rolled his shoulders to ease the building tension, then scrubbed a hand up over his face and around his head. He had to get a grip. To find a way to contain his emotion. To settle his anger before it boiled over.

He'd been headed to the Fireside Café when he'd called his wife in the first place, knowing it'd been her favorite joint for a quick bite. Hoping, just as he'd done so many other times over the past few years, he'd catch her there. Force her into a conversation. He hadn't expected her to answer the call today and sure as fuck didn't expect her return call.

His heart raced. Every muscle in his body quivered with restraint and anticipation. "Shit," he muttered, glancing at his watch. She was already fifteen minutes late, and chances were she wouldn't show up at all. She'd been a ghost for nearly three years. She'd walked out the door and disappeared from his life as if she'd been a figment of his imagination. A combination of his sweetest dreams and most horrifying nightmares.

He growled, his frustration taking over. He'd been tortured for years not knowing if she was alive even, calling time and time again and getting nothing. No replies. No acknowledgments. Nothing. *Poof*, she'd been gone. Eventually, he'd given up hope and convinced himself he was over her.

But then today—today—she'd spoken to him, and all the old feelings rushed in. She'd said his name on the phone in her sweet, silken tone, and he was taken back to a decade ago when they'd first started dating, when everything was pure and real and filled with burning passion. Now the passion was contaminated with hurt and rage. But the love remained even though he'd convinced himself otherwise. Her voice, the crack of pain when she spoke, reminded him how deep the love had run.

Thirty-two minutes late. "Fuck this," he muttered, shoving the chair from the table. He'd waited too long to be stood up after she'd finally answered. As he was about to stand, he saw her. She stood on the sidewalk outside the small patio area of the café. Watching him.

Damn, she looked good. Thinner than he remembered, but her curves were still fine as hell, full and lush exactly where she should be. Her smooth skin looked a little paler; the delicious latté shade made his mouth water, assaulted by the recollection of how she tasted against his tongue.

Then he looked closer and saw the shimmer in her dark eyes. *Fuck*, she'd been crying. Something violent pulsed through his veins. He'd vowed to bring her laughter, not tears, but he'd failed. He gripped the metal arms of the chair to keep from breaking something.

She smiled a smile that didn't quite reach her eyes. A forced smile. She stepped in his direction, weaving her way through the small table settings to where he was sitting. "Hi," she whispered as she approached. She stood before him. She looked poised, but he saw how her body trembled, how she held onto an empty chair to steady herself.

"Hey, baby." He stood, moving around the table, and pulled out a chair so she could sit. Her honeyed scent mingled with the sunshine. Part of him wanted to grab her by the shoulders, shake her, and demand answers. Ask why the fuck she'd left him and where the fuck she'd been for the past three years. Rye gulped, fighting the conflicting desires to pull her into his arms and support her. To kiss away the sorrow, to murmur sweet nothings in her ear until she giggled with delight.

He stepped away, retreating back to his chair. Today wasn't about their vows. It was about closure.

"Sorry, I'm late." She touched her hair as she glanced away.

He grinned. She hadn't tried to wrangle it but had left it in wild curls. The way he'd always liked it best. "You're always late."

She flashed him an impish smile and shrugged one delicate shoulder. "True."

"You're so beautiful, Mika." The words came even when he didn't want them.

Her gaze settled on him. She smiled, but there was such sadness in the depths of her eyes. Her hands were on the table, and he had to fight the urge to reach over, take them in his own. To hold them as he always had, to comfort her. A lump of emotion tightened his throat, but he shoved it away. "Baby, you're still so beautiful." He cleared his throat. "You okay? You been all right?"

She licked her lips. "I guess." She worried a plump lip between her teeth. "It took a while, but I'm okay."

Rye looked to the side knowing damn well she hadn't meant to tease him. But his dick didn't give a shit. He'd been semi-hard since he'd seen her, and now she'd reminded him of the magic she could do with her mouth and he was rocked up hard. Throbbing. He shook his head and allowed her words to sink in. He didn't want to want her. Didn't want to feel sorry for her. He wanted the anger to resurface so he could send her on her way, to dismiss her from his life as she'd done to him.

Grabbing the bottle of ale, he took a good long drink and allowed the silence to descend around them. He took another drink, allowing the chilled liquid to cool his heated body.

"Where you been?"

She glanced down, and he could see her shoulders heave as she sucked in a deep breath. After a moment, she looked at him. "I got a small apartment, not much, really. Work from my computer like I did when I went on maternity lea—"

Rye studied his wife's face, the pain so unchecked and raw. All this time, he could have been offering her solace. He sure as hell needed it from her. But the fact that they hadn't had each other was entirely her fault. He'd done everything he could to be there for her even through his own sorrow. She'd shut him out. She was to blame.

A low moan escaped her lips, as if it was painful to continue, but she did anyway. "I don't go out much. Just keep to myself. Work. Read some." She shrugged.

There were a million questions he wanted to be answered, but at this point, they weren't really his business. Not anymore.

"Rye, you didn't call me here to chitchat. You said we needed to talk." Her voice dropped off to a whisper. "So what is it?"

A muscle ticked on his jaw. His shoulders ached with tension. "You're right, baby." Reaching into his back pocket, he withdrew the folded papers and smacked them onto the table. "I need you to sign these."

Her stare fixed on the papers on the table. "What are they?"

"Divorce papers."

He heard her low gasp, but she didn't look at him. She turned her face away, but he didn't miss the giant tear that streaked silently down her cheek.

"What did you expect, Mika? It's been three years. How long was I supposed to wait?"

"I don't know," she squeaked out. "I just wasn't ... wasn't expecting this."

"What were you expecting? Flowers? Candy?" The rage resurfaced. All the stress, the pain, the wondering, the fear, the anger, the hurt. It all came rushing back, shoving aside the strangled love.

She shook her head. The sun had begun to descend, and it shimmered golden in her curls. "No ... No ... I don't know." Her voice was low. Broken. He hated that he caused her pain, but shit, she deserved it.

"You did this to us, Mika. You destroyed us."

"I know." She sobbed.

"Why! Dammit, tell me why?" Oh yeah, the rage was controlling him now.

Her eyes glistened with tears, and she was trembling again. "I lost an infant son. I couldn't look at you and live with the guilt. It was my fault."

"You're wrong, baby. His death wasn't your fault, but you sure as hell killed us."

"I lost a baby," she whispered.

Rye stood so quickly the chair toppled over behind him. He slammed his hands against the tabletop. His beer tipped and spilled. "The fuck is wrong with you, Mika," he growled, "you think I don't know that? You think I wasn't there suffering, too? Nah, baby, I had it a thousand times worse." He leaned across the table, towering over her and looked her in the eye as he went on. "I lost a son, too, Mika, but I also lost my wife."

Mika wanted to close her eyes, to look away, to see anything but the depths of pain she saw in her husband's stare. She wanted to reach for him, wrap her hand around the back of his neck and drag him closer, to touch his lips with hers even if just one more time. She wanted to hold him to her breasts and allow him to cry out the agony she felt. Knew he felt, too.

He was right. Everything he said was right. His anger was justified. She had destroyed them because she hadn't known how to share the grief. She'd thought to carry the burden alone, but what she'd done—what she'd done to Rye—was anything but.

She'd done harm to this man. To this strong, stoic man. He'd honored all his vows and she hadn't. She'd walked away. No matter how bad it hurt, she knew he deserved his freedom from her. She'd made him hold on for three years. Time to let him go.

Leaning forward, she pulled the papers toward her. And then she closed her eyes, lifted her face to her husband, and kissed him. She needed one final taste to see her through a lifetime without him. His mouth tasted like ale and anger, but his full lips melted against hers. His mouth was gentle despite the violence he'd shown. As tender as he'd always been. She sucked his bottom lip into her mouth and touched her tongue to his skin.

He groaned into her. He didn't kiss her back, but he didn't pull away either. Just stood bent across the table and allowed her to taste him.

Slowly, she pulled away, ending the contact. His gray eyes were open and looking at her. The fury she'd seen before had defused into something else dark and smoldering.

Her entire body was trembling as she licked her lips as she

stood, bringing the divorce papers to her chest. "I'm sorry. I'll sign them. I'm so sorry." And then she turned and ran.

Mika rounded the tables and darted for the parking lot. Her pulse raged in her ears, and her heart was in her throat. Her stomach roiled, nausea prickling her skin. It'd been hard to leave him the first time, but something about running from her husband now felt even more final. More painful. Complete wreckage.

Her husband was behind her. She could hear his shoes thumping on the pavement. Hear his husky breathing. Feel his radiant heat. Reaching into her purse, she fumbled for her keys as she darted through parked cars toward hers, unwilling to slow down despite knowing he'd get to her before she got away. Her car was ahead, and her knees nearly wobbled with relief. The heel of her sandal landed on a pebble and she stumbled.

Large, strong hands grabbed her shoulders, yanking her back before she face-planted against the cement. The divorce papers floated to the ground. His grasp was unrelenting as he spun her body to face him, backing her up until she collided with her car, and there was no escape from Rye's massive body. Pressed between steel and iron hard muscle.

Squeezing her lids closed, she didn't want to look at her husband. Didn't want to see the hurt and anger in his eyes. Didn't want to be tempted by the lips she'd just kissed. A moan escaped, and she battled tears.

"You can't do this, Mika. Not again." His voice was harsh, angry. "You don't get to do this again."

She didn't open her eyes. "Do what?" The words squeaked out. She was shaking and wished like hell he wouldn't notice.

"Leave me."

Her lids popped open and, damn it to hell, she lost the fight with an unruly tear. *Oh, God, she'd caused the pain that tortured his features.* Her head swam, and she swayed. Sentiment rose in her throat, but she gulped it down. Forcing her gaze from his face, she saw the folded papers on the ground. The divorce papers.

Another damn tear. She licked her dry lips. "You're the one who wants a divorce."

He stepped aside, his hands falling to his sides, releasing her. She nearly crumpled, but she straightened her legs and steadied herself.

His shoulders were tense, his chest rising and falling as he growled out a few sharp breaths. Lifting a hand, he scrubbed his palm over his face, then over his head. "Shit." He glanced away and dragged in gulps of air before turning to her.

Mika shivered; his stare pierced her. A lonely cloud drifted in front of the sun, casting a shadow across her skin.

"What you expect me to do? Just keep waiting?"

"I'm not sure what I expected today, Rye." She glanced at the papers. "But it wasn't those."

"It's been three years. Three fucking years."

"I know. I know. I meant to call you. Meant to come back. I'd go to bed thinking I was going to call you in the morning but then wake up and life looked so bleak. The guilt and sorrow would return. The hurt. I'd tell myself I'd call you tomorrow." She swallowed. "Just ... just tomorrow never came."

"Tomorrow came—" he paused as he reached forward and wiped a tear from her cheek, "today."

Rye rubbed his fingers against his jeans, his wife's tears burning his skin. He'd have given anything to spare her. It was as hopeless today as it'd been when their son had left them. Divorce wasn't what he wanted, but what else was there?

He cleared his throat. "Look, baby, I am not trying to hurt you. We've had enough of that. But you don't want me in your life, and I'm ready to have one. A life. I need to move forward. I want a wife—"

"You're seeing someone?"

Dammit, he hated the way her voice cracked. He didn't want to answer, but this wasn't the time for lies. "I have. I've tried to date, Mika. I want a wife. A family. I will never forget RJ, but I need to move forward. For the past three years, I've been under the same soil he has."

Another tear slid along his wife's cheek. He tightened his fingers against his pants and let them fall. She was trembling, her eyes shimmering. He wanted to pull her to his chest and hold her. To let her cry. To heal. But despite what he wanted, Mika wasn't ready.

Turning, he bent and scooped the papers from the ground and handed them to her. "There isn't much else to say, baby. Sign the papers and let's get on with it."

She gripped the papers to her chest and nodded but didn't answer.

Every muscle in his body ached. His hands shook. His chest burned. Ending it with her was the last thing he wanted to do, but exactly what needed to be done. He took a breath and held it until it was a fire in his lungs. *They were done*. "I'll give you two weeks, Mika. If you don't sign them by then, I'll file for divorce without you."

It took every ounce of his strength, every fiber of his being revolting, but he turned from her and walked away.

Chapter Three

THE WEEK HAD BEEN overcast, but rainless. Not today. The clouds had broken and floated out of the Sacramento Valley, allowing the California sun to shine. Despite the briskness of the March air, his skin warmed under its glowing warmth. It dipped low in the sky.

Rye pulled the hoodie up over his head, casting his face into shadows to match his mood. He strode up the path, his body moving in pure muscle memory. He hadn't slept well, every dream swirling to the taste of Mika's lips. The sweetness of her mouth. It'd been a quick and unexpected kiss, but it tormented him. Haunted the nights.

The week had been hell. Every time his phone rang, his heart would stop, wondering if it was his wife calling to tell him she'd signed the divorce papers. He'd sought solace in running the trails along the river, on pushing himself physically to relieve his mind. It hadn't helped much. Fuck, not even a little bit.

Biting back a growl, he untwisted the cap of his water bottle and took a long swig as he rounded the bend, planning on watching the sunset from the knoll overlooking the river.

She was there.

It had been their spot. He shouldn't be surprised to see her there. But he was. Of all the times he'd been there, she'd never been. After she'd left him, he used to go there hoping to find her. Now, he'd gotten used to being there alone. It was *his* spot, and seeing his wife sitting there, her back against an oak tree, her shoulders slumped forward as she fiddled with something in her hands, he felt almost violated.

He choked on the swallow of water. They'd made love for the first time on a bed of clover here. Had probably conceived their son in the same spot. A breeze drifted past, the scent of the murky river along with something sweeter. Flowery. The alluring scent of his wife. He moved closer. She hadn't noticed him, her attention on the items in her hands.

He moved closer, glancing down to see what she fidgeted with. Folded white papers he assumed to be the divorce papers he'd asked her to sign. And her cellphone. His chest tightened.

"What are you doing here?" he demanded, breaching the distance between them, lack of sleep heightening anger and the odd sense of betrayal he felt by her being there.

"Oh!" She startled and scurried to her feet, keeping the oak tree behind her.

She wore a short summer dress that the breeze wrapped around her legs and a thin black sweater that slipped off one bare shoulder. Curls danced around her face, her gaze wide and defiant. She lifted her chin, and he nearly groaned when the pink tip of her tongue darted out to wet her lips.

"I was about to call you." She lifted her hand holding her cell.

"Why?"

Mika could feel her racing pulse drumming through her body. Her hands shook, but she squeezed her fingers so he wouldn't see. She'd planned on meeting up with him to give him the papers; she just hadn't expected it to be tonight. Hadn't expected it to be at their spot. She cleared her throat. "I signed the papers."

He stepped closer, the heat of his massive body encasing her, warming her as the sun had. She tried to read his face, but the hood of his sweatshirt shielded his eyes. She glanced to the bank on the other side of the river. The sun was low on the horizon now, reflecting gold and orange across the rippling water. Sunset burned across the sky.

"Is that what you want, Mika?" He moved closer. She wanted to touch him. To stroke his skin. To absorb his warmth. She retreated, pressing against the bark, but he was relentless. He stalked closer. "Is that what you want, baby? You left me; do you want to divorce me, too?"

She tried to answer, but no sound came out. She shook her head.

"Tell me," he demanded, grabbing the papers from her grasp, "why you signed them then."

Mika fought the need to look away. Despite how her hands shook, she reached up and shoved the hood from her husband's head. "For you. I signed them for you."

Not a moment had gone by when she hadn't been thinking about his words, his yearning for a wife and a family. From the day they met, it'd been a shared dream. A shared future. No matter how she tried to release Rye from her heart, she'd been unable to.

"For me?" He put one hand behind her against the tree as he leaned toward her. "What about for you? What do you want?"

It was a future she still wanted, too. "You." She touched his cheek, brushing her fingers across his sweat-damped skin. "I want you."

He growled as he closed the distance. His mouth came down on hers. His lips were soft, but demanding. He kissed her. Kissed her gently and with reverence. A brushing of lips with a tenderness that was her undoing. She opened her mouth to him. Deepened the contact. Welcomed him inside her.

She gasped as his mouth left hers, trailing soft and moist kisses across her face. He pressed his mouth to her closed eyelids. Stroked his lips across her cheek to the tender skin below her ear, swirled his tongue along her flesh.

Mika leaned her head against the tree, her curls tangling on the bark, her eyes drifting closed. Her heart raced, heat danced across her body, desire pooled low in her belly. She trembled.

He nipped her earlobe with his teeth, then soothed the sting with his tongue.

"Rye," she whispered, shivering.

"Yeah, baby?" He returned his lips to her mouth, nudging them apart with his tongue and gulping down any reply she meant to make. He nipped at her bottom lip, then pressed into her depths.

He tasted of sweat, of sunshine, of damp river air, of male, and oh so familiar. Her knees shook. Her inner thighs ached. She rejoiced as his mouth devoured hers, and she welcomed him inside. His tongue stroked against hers, explored and teased.

Slowly, he ended the kiss. "Say it again. Tell me what you want," he murmured against her lips.

"You," she replied.

He pushed away from her, his stare stormy and penetrating. "So we don't need these?" he asked, lifting the divorce papers.

She shook her head. "No."

He grinned and flung the papers toward the river. They caught on the breeze and scattered, flashing in the fading light like sparks against the flaming sunset. Hues of fire hugged the horizon, the sun dripping low in the western sky.

"We don't need those," Mika said, reaching for her husband. She grabbed his sweatshirt and tugged him forward. "But we need this."

Hell yeah, he needed this—her—like he needed to breathe. He closed the distance between them, needing to kiss her again. Needing to touch her, to drink in her sweet sighs and breathy moans, to claim her as his own. To make up for lost time. He touched her shoulder, shoving the sweater down her arm, exposing the creaminess of her lush skin. He kissed her there, filling his free hand with the fullness of her breast.

His body ached, his dick throbbing in the same demanding tempo as the pulse thundering behind his ears. The years slipped away, the tears gone, the hurt soothed; the past was yesterday. They were all that mattered. It was only the two of them under the burning sky.

Rye pushed the thin knit from her arm, his mouth following, his lips kissing and sampling her honeyed skin. She moaned, arching her back from the tree, filling his hand with the full swell of her body. He rolled her pebbled nipple between his thumb and finger until it hardened further. He pulled her dress away, exposing her dark nipple to the descending night and then covered it with his lips. He tugged it between his teeth and swirled his tongue around it until his wife was panting sweet breaths that had his body on fire.

She knew. She reached for him, pulling at the waistband of his basketball shorts, yanking the drawstring free, shoving them down his hips. Her playful fingers eased beneath his boxers and wrapped around his rocked up length. He damn near came into the palm of her soft hand.

"I need you," he mumbled, his voice low and husky. His mouth left her nipple and settled against her lips. She nodded and welcomed him, nibbling at his lower lip, sucking it into her mouth as she worked her fingers down his dick, then slowly back to the tip. She was a tease. A vixen. She knew exactly what he wanted. Exactly how to give it to him.

He pressed her against the tree. His hands were on her, smoothing down along her back, his fingers finding the edge of her dress. He pushed the cloth up, his hand settling on the curve of her ass. He moved his hand lower to her thigh, then lifted her leg into the air. Rye stepped into her, adjusting her so her foot wrapped around his waist. Her hand was trapped between them, but he didn't care. He thrust his hips forward, her hand working his length, her fingers smoothing down his sensitive ridge, then cupping his balls in her hand. He damn near exploded.

Reaching behind her, he moved his hand under her thigh and stroked her. Her lips were soaking. He pushed two fingers inside her tight body. "You're wet," he muttered against her mouth.

She moaned, her hips rotating into his hand as she rode down on his fingers. His dick bucked. He needed inside her. She must have known. She shoved his shorts down. Pushed his boxers away, freeing his hard-on.

"Please." Her leg tightened around him, pulling him closer.

He growled, fighting for control. Losing.

Pulling his fingers from her body, he grabbed his dick and touched his swollen head to her plump lips. She dripped arousal as she arched into him, rolling her hips. "Easy, baby." Her lips were gripping him, pulling him in. She was tight around him, honeyed velvet heat.

"Damn," he said through gritted teeth as he slammed into her, so deep her arousal seeped onto his balls. Her body quivered as she wrapped her arms around his neck. She held him close, releasing short raspy pants, her head rolled back. Her hair tangled on edges of tree bark.

He began to move. He had to. Long, slow strokes into her welcoming flesh. Rotating his hips, he eased out of her body until just his head remained between her slick, swollen lips. A deep thrust, all the way back in, until her mouth fell open and she cried out. Cried out his name.

He moved faster, thrusting into her even though he heard her sweater snagging against the rough edges of the bark. His wife moaned and moved with him, using her foot to pull him into her when he'd retreat. In and out, the tempo changing from fast, quick thrust to long and slow and languid and savoring. He kissed her neck. Stroked his tongue along her pulse point. Along her collarbone. Sucked the tender skin on her shoulder, leaving nips and marks.

The air cooled. The sun faded into purples as dusk overtook daytime. But he was hot, his body on fire, his skin burning.

"Rye …" his wife moaned, her body beginning to quake around him, her tight pussy pulsing and shivering against his erection. "Rye," she called out as she soaked him in honey. Called out his name as her body shook.

And that was all. She was everything. Her body gripped him. Closing his eyes, he roared as he let himself go, releasing into her. She held him, her hands soothing the straining muscles on the back of his neck, her body arching and accepting.

Come pulsed from his body. He was drained, but completely renewed. Rye held his wife's shaking body in his embrace, pressed between his chest and the oak tree. He was shaking with release, floating in pleasure. He closed his eyes and rested his forehead on her lush chest. Her breaths were sharp and short, but she held him tight as she gasped for air.

Every muscle in his body quivered, the tension finally released. Holding onto her thigh, he pulled her from the tree and spun them, collapsing into the grass and clover bed, settling her on top of him.

"I've always loved you," she whispered.

He grinned. "I'm glad."

She nipped his ear.

"I've been in love with you since the moment we met." He smacked her on the ass. "Nothing's changed, baby."

"I'm glad."

He felt her body go slack as she relaxed into his embrace. There was still so much that needed to be said, so much that needed to be talked about. But all he wanted to do now was hold her. To be enveloped by the love that had always been so strong between them. The rest could wait. They had a lifetime to make it right, and he meant to enjoy every moment.

The burning sun was gone now, set on the pain of their past. Holding his wife's limp body to his, he inhaled the sweet scent of her. He smiled. They were together again, and the sunset brought the promise of their second chance.

Renee Luke has been writing poems and stories since she first learned to write. After getting a box of Harlequins delivered by mistake, her love of romance novels blossomed from an obsession of reading into the desire to write her own stories of the heart. She writes keeping-it-real erotic romances featuring funky (sub) urban characters who get their groove-on and give up their hearts. She strives to write stories that both stimulate physically and satisfy emotionally. She's a believer in happily-ever-afters and definitely found her own, living in Northern California with her children and her real-life hero, her USMC husband.

JUST LOOKING

CiCi Coughlin

THERESE LEONARD STARED AT the spot where her breasts used to be. Back before the crazy began. Before Gary had left and the tests had come back positive and the seemingly interminable rounds of treatment had started. Back when she was just a pretty woman in love with a handsome, successful man.

She turned sideways to the mirror, lifting her right arm so she could stare at the unfamiliar profile of her upper torso, then prodded gently at one of the newly inflated pillows they'd tucked under her skin to replace the poisoned, traitorous flesh. Inflated. The exact opposite of her ego, which had barely survived the dual defection of her longtime boyfriend and her lifetime breasts. Or was that a triple defection, technically? One ass, two boobs?

She sighed and turned forward again, then gently cupped the foreign globes, testing their weight, marveling at their unnatural symmetry. Even the nipples looked real if she squinted a little. Not that anything about the process had been natural. Not the surgery that had changed her life or the treatments that had stolen her hair or the long series of appointments in which they'd blown up the implants a bit at a time, something like going to the orthodontist as a teen, though far more humiliating than having her wires adjusted. Surreal. That's what the whole thing was. Completely and utterly surreal. Except it had really happened. And it was really over, the intense part, anyway. She'd had her final post-surgery follow up this week and then hit Goodwill and her therapist to drop off the last of the crap Gary had left behind. It was time to start rebuilding her life again.

But was she ready to live? Live, live? Not just survive? Because she'd pretty well have to start over again. Her savings and 401K were gone along with the man she thought she'd spend her life with. The house she loved was about to go on the market. A surprising number of the people she'd once called friend had drifted away, too busy or too afraid to cope with the threat of mortality Therese now represented. Her body wasn't the only thing she barely recognized. She still had her job, at least, and she'd always loved that. Besides, she could hardly hang out in limbo until the magical five-year mark passed by. She'd missed too much already, wasting most of a decade with a man she'd always known didn't quite love her. Funny how obvious that fact seemed now—and how easy it was to face. Looking death in the eye had a way of clarifying one's vision, she supposed. Then there were the skipped girls' trips to Las Vegas and the Bahamas, adventures that would have interfered with her determination to pay off the house before they had kids. That foresight, at least, would come in handy once the house sold. They'd been almost there, after all. She supposed she could have bought Gary out. But, somehow, she didn't want to. She liked the idea of being debt free. Stuff free. Free.

She'd missed her fifteenth high school reunion for her final chemo treatment, but she didn't mind. It wasn't like there was a "most likely to be diagnosed with cancer the week after your boyfriend elopes with another woman" award for her to win. Besides, she'd quickly learned that no one knew what to say to a woman her age with breast cancer—not even the other young women with breast cancer. She couldn't imagine spending an entire evening with her old classmates, all of them wondering what was safe to ask. With the big C hovering silently in the background, no one wanted to talk about the other Cs: college, careers, and children.

They'd forget she'd had the first two and assume she'd never have the last one. They'd be unable to stop thinking about how it could be them. And how she might die. Just that short time ago, she didn't think she'd survive, either, though her odds were good. Now, she was pretty sure she would. Which made the question she'd posed to herself that much more significant. Given the number of women—and men—who didn't get the option, could she justify not giving her all to the rest of her life? Even if it wasn't the life she'd imagined.

Her phone alarm chirped a reminder to take her vitamins, and she blinked, surprised at how long she'd stood pondering her new contours. She needed to get a move on if she wanted to make it to the cancer center's weekly produce market before the best goodies had been snaffled. Her pulse skipped a beat, not at the thought of the farm fresh eggs she'd come to love, but at the sudden mental image of the farmer himself. Tall, broad-shouldered, and deeply tanned from working in the sun, J. P. Taylor had an easygoing manner that soothed her nerves, eyes that crinkled with his ready smile, and a range of knowledge that made her wonder about his past. Lately, she'd been wondering quite a lot. Dreaming occasionally, too. Then, last week, Nurse Turner had made that silly remark about how much he seemed to enjoy helping Therese choose her tomatoes, and now she couldn't stop remembering the way his strong, calloused hands gently squeezed the firm, ripe fruit. What would those doubtless skillful hands feel like on her body—on the breasts she hadn't yet gotten used to? Not much, according to the literature. But that didn't mean his touch would be any less arousing.

Her face flushed as red as her favorite heirlooms, and she shook her head, laughing at the sheer joy of rediscovering her libido. She paused, then slowly shook her head again, her eye distracted by the slight bounce of the short reddish curls that had grown in since her final treatment. She pulled one out to its full length. Three inches maybe? Not bad. She'd worn her hair straight, long, and blond for so many years that she'd almost expected it to come back that way. Her gaze strayed to the wig block on her dresser, and she fingered the high-quality synthetic golden strands as though touching them for the first time. Fake hair, fake rack, fake love. Was anything real in her world anymore?

Her eyelashes. Those were real again, finally, and pale as always. She reached for a tube of mascara, then stopped. Why? Why did she need to gunk on a heavy coat of God knows what? She'd fought for those lashes, dammit, sat through seemingly endless nausea, plowed through seemingly unendurable pain. It was about time she stopped taking things for granted. Her lashes, her hair, her body. Her relationships. She glanced at the wig again, then slowly opened the top dresser drawer to pull out the sparkly green barrette her goddaughter had given her for her birthday. She fluffed her curls, marveling at their softness, and then carefully clipped the barrette into place. Funny, but the emerald stones brought out her eyes almost as much as mascara ever had, and her natural hair color was far less orange than she'd recalled. Or maybe she was looking at herself with open eyes for the first time.

Time! She glanced at her phone again, then scurried into her closet to choose a skirt and blouse, sparing a thought for their looseness for the first time in a year. It might be time for new clothes, actually. To go with her new outlook on life. And maybe new bras. She'd fought for the breasts, too, after all.

Chapter Two

HOLY CROW, SHE WAS a redhead! J. P.'s eyes nearly popped from their sockets, and he blinked purposefully to keep from alarming those around him. The color wasn't surprising, really, given the deep green of her eyes and the creamy fairness of her skin. What shocked him was that she'd covered it up to begin with. Not that there had been anything to cover up for most of the time he'd known her, of course. She'd have been hiding bare scalp and then peach fuzz beneath the wig. God, that must have itched. He rubbed a grateful hand across his own dark hair. The growing-in stage was a bitch. His gaze lit on the pep of her curls again, so different from the smooth, controlled style he'd grown used to. So different from the blinding blondness that had covered her bent head the first day he'd seen her seven months earlier, when her hair was her own. Or not, apparently. Today was much, much better.

Her glance met his and she smiled, a genuine expression of pleasure that pushed the half-dazed glaze from her eyes. His face responded in kind, and he wondered if the grin stretching his mouth looked as silly as it felt. He didn't much care if it did. He'd been waiting for the day she came to life, hoping like hell it would happen for her and longing selfishly to be nearby when it did. Therese glowed every bit as lovely as he'd thought she would, and his heart leaped at the idea that a bit of her new sparkle had to do with seeing him. Something vaguely flirty in the way she held herself said it might. He winked without meaning to, then chuckled silently when she blushed and broke eye contact. She lifted a slender hand to her temple as though meaning to tuck her hair behind her ear. His heart froze as he waited to see how it would hit her, but after a short, startled exploration of the curls beneath her fingers, she laughed out loud and met his gaze again, crossing her eyes and poking the tip of her tongue from the corner of her mouth. Silly, apparently, was all the rage at the moment.

Not the only thing raging, he thought ruefully, shifting as his body tightened in response to her joy. He tried not to imagine kissing her rosy lips as she crossed the room, but it was harder than it had ever been, now that he didn't have to feel guilty about lusting after a sick woman. He tried not to stare at the gentle sway of her hips as she moved, but he was harder than he'd ever been, now that all of her was smiling. Once upon a time, barely there curls and nude eyelashes wouldn't have affected him so much. He was damned glad he'd gotten his perspective adjusted before she'd entered his field of vision.

"Hi."

Whoa. Even her voice had gained new life. Always pleasant, laughter now tinged even that single syllable. Always warm, it now invited him in. A rush of camaraderie and affection flooded his soul, filling him with a weird mix of horniness and hope.

"Hi." Oh geez, the unexpected emotion was thick on his tongue, and she wouldn't have any idea why. *Pull it together, J. P. You're going to freak her out.* He snagged his water bottle and sipped, hoping she'd think he had something stuck in his throat. Something besides his heart, which was doing its best to Grinch-grow its way out of his chest.

The whisper of an exasperated sigh tickled his eardrum, and he studiously avoided glancing to his left. He knew Aleshia Turner was there and didn't need to look at her to see her eye roll. She'd already given him what-for for obsessively checking the clock all morning and then refusing to admit that he was waiting for Therese to show up. Now he could practically feel her willing him to stop being an idiot, just as she used to will his body to accept the chemo.

"I have eggs," he blurted, then tried not to flinch at the disgusted squeak of the nurse's shoes as she walked away.

Therese, thank goodness, seemed less annoyed. Though puzzlement drew tiny lines across her brow, her luscious lips twitched in what looked like suspicious amusement. He took a deep breath and tried again.

"What I meant to say is that I saved a carton of eggs for you. Just in case you made it in. I was starting to worry."

"Really?" she asked, showing a dimple he'd never seen before.

His mouth and brain went dry again. "Yeah."

The dimple deepened. "Well, I did cut it pretty close to the wire." She glanced over her shoulder at the huge wall clock. "Wow. Really close to the wire. Sorry about that."

"No problem," he replied, drawing on every ounce of self-possession he had and pulling the eggs from the fridge. He slipped the carton into the turquoise market basket on her arm and smiled. "What else do you need today?"

The flare in her eyes nearly knocked him loopy again, but he managed to keep it together and help her choose green peppers, tomatoes, and an assortment of fresh herbs. Then they came to the squash, and he very nearly bolted across the table when she picked up a large, ripe zucchini, met his eye, and licked her lips. But before he could throw her to the floor and ravish her next to the check-in desk, she dropped the vegetable on the pile and started laughing as though she'd heard her first joke. A moment later, she wiped her eyes.

"I'm sorry," she said, merriment still dancing through her words, "I've no idea what's come over me today."

He knew, or thought he did. Remembered the euphoria as though it were only yesterday. "Last appointment?" he asked. "All clear?"

She nodded gleefully. "Just this week. Yesterday in fact. And I feel …"

"Like you just woke up from a very strange dream?"

"Kinda, yeah."

"Like you could fly?"

"Exactly."

"Like you never knew what it meant to be alive before?"

"Yes!" Her eyes glowed so brightly he thought they might zoom off to settle somewhere more appropriate, like maybe the night sky. Then she cocked her head, and her gaze turned penetrating. "Wait, how do you know?"

"Been there," he said, trying for a lightness of tone to offset the gravity of his confession.

She stared at him as though she'd never seen him before. Which, he supposed, she hadn't, not really. Sure, they'd met at the market nearly every week for months and the few words they'd exchanged at first had gradually grown to actual conversations. He'd emailed her a few recipes. She'd emailed him a few questions. He'd seen what he hoped were the seeds of interest in her eyes before, but he'd understood her preoccupation and been willing to wait until ... now, apparently. He was half afraid it was too soon, too early. But with the opening in front of him, he might as well take it. He'd learned not to take later for granted.

"Listen," he said, "would you want to get some coffee? The cafeteria here isn't bad, you know."

She peered at him so long he thought she'd refuse, then smiled. "I'd like that," she said. "But ..."

His heart sank. Well, hell.

"But can we go across the street to the coffee shop? I want to be normal today."

Oh hell yes they could. He'd go pretty much anywhere she asked him to at the moment. Instead, he nodded, took her money, and then slipped the zucchini into her basket. "I don't think I could sell this to anyone else," he said, hoping the innuendo wasn't too much. "Consider it a congratulatory gift."

Chapter Three

AS THEY CLAIMED THE coveted comfy chairs, hot drinks in hand, she realized she'd been thoughtless.

"I'm sorry," she said. "I didn't even ask if you needed to be somewhere else or if your produce would be okay. The hospital cafeteria would have been faster." But she hadn't wanted quick, she'd wanted time—time to ogle his work-hardened body while she explored the story behind the man. She only hoped he was as interested.

"I'm right where I want to be," he said, a low thrum of intensity underscoring the words.

Her toes curled, and relief crept across her shoulders. She was on a da-ate! Well, sorta. Close enough. Okay, so they were probably going to talk about *it*, but that was fine. She did want to get to know him better. When she'd left the house that morning, she'd been elated, flying high. She hadn't thought much past seeing him again and flirting a little. In fact, she'd worried a bit that he'd only been nice because he felt sorry for her, that she'd mistaken kindness for budding attraction. But the excitement in his face when she'd entered the center had pretty well wiped those fears away, and the way her heart skipped when she laid eyes on him told her she'd moved beyond physical attraction. Finding out about their shared experience added a depth to the possibilities between them that she hadn't anticipated, and she wanted to see where it could go. Always assuming they were on the same page. Why did she keep thinking that? Gary, of course. She'd have to talk to her therapist about that one next time. Just to reassure herself, she crossed her legs, letting the hem of her skirt inch up her thigh a bit. The gleam in his eye put her uncertainty to rest, and she settled more comfortably into her chair, anticipation and curiosity humming beneath her skin.

"I'm interested," he said, his tone half-teasing.

Oops, busted. A flush crept across her cheeks. "Ahem, yeah, well, you know."

"Yeah I do, actually," he laughed. "The first time a woman flirted with me after, I was convinced it was just pity. Totally blew it. That's why I figured we'd better get it out in the open. I'm interested. Very. You caught my attention the first time I saw you."

She thought back. "That would have been … early April? Shortly after my surgery. I bought grapes. You let me taste one."

"You remember that?"

"Sure I do. I thought it was really nice of you. I thought … you were really nice." She flushed again, suddenly embarrassed. She could still taste the sweet tang on her tongue. She hadn't seen him as anything other than a kind man at the time, and yet every time she'd bitten into a grape thereafter, she'd thought of him. She had a feeling it would always be that way, no matter what happened between them—or didn't. Lord, how weird her life had become.

He grinned as though he knew exactly what she was thinking, then seemed to hesitate. "Actually, that was the second time I saw you. The first time was a few weeks before. Friday, the thirteenth, to be exact."

Shock rippled through her, along with a weird sense of fate. "They confirmed my diagnosis that day. It was the first time I went to the center."

"I thought so. I saw you sitting in the lobby, and you had that look, the one we all get when we know for sure. You were so pretty, and I felt guilty for even thinking it because I knew what you were headed into. Well, I didn't, not really. There are so many types of cancer, so many stages. But whatever it was, I knew it would be tough."

Tears pricked at her eyes. How right he'd been about that. And, yet, it could have been so much worse. Her cancer was highly treatable, and she was young and had her family and friends to help her through. She'd seen the ones who had to go it alone, and the ones fighting terrifying odds. It could have been so much worse.

"I can't believe you were there on day one. I think of it in capitals, you know. Day One. But wait, why were you there on a Friday?"

"Five-year checkup."

"Oh wow! That's a huge milestone." *The* milestone, in fact.

"Yeah. I was so excited and then there you were, and I remembered exactly how lucky I was. I almost came and sat with you, but I didn't want to be weird." He laughed a little. "And I didn't want a husband or a boyfriend to come out of the bathroom and deck me."

Was that a question? She supposed so. And a reasonable one. "Yeah, the boyfriend was already gone by then."

He nodded. "That happens more than you'd think. My girlfriend made it through my first chemo appointment. A lot of others don't make it that long."

Horror flooded her brain and squeezed her heart. Here she'd been moping because Gary had run off with another woman, but at least he hadn't known she was sick. The timing had just been shitty. But his story …

"I'm so sorry!"

"Don't be. It was five years ago, and I have four sisters, so I was never alone—even when I wanted to be. Besides, Denise—my ex—never would have gone for my new lifestyle."

Lifestyle? Oh damn. Was he going to turn out to be a swinger or something? Because interested as she was, she was pretty sure she couldn't go for that either. Well, okay maybe once, but it certainly took anything more than sex and friendship off the table.

His laugh rang out, rich and delighted. "I wish you could see the expression on your face right now. You look like I might bust out a pack of sister wives and ask you to join in. I meant the organic farming and everything that goes with it."

"Oh! That!" Relief and chagrin curved her lips. "What were you before?"

"Ah, before." He leaned back, shaking his head as though embarrassed. "Kind of an ass, actually. Well, not an ass, exactly, but pretty proud of myself. I had a big-time sales job, raked in the bucks. Drove the biggest, most ostentatious SUV I could find, lived in a decked-out condo downtown. Thousand-dollar suits every day, hundred-dollar dinners every night. Ridiculous, in hindsight. It all seemed so important then, though. And then the cancer came and my priorities changed and when I started reading, I found out a lot of things I didn't like about our food system and, well, here I am."

"And Denise?"

"Ad exec. I heard she married since. Twice." He glanced over at Therese. "What about you?"

"Not so showy, but along the same lines. I was more about the perfect suburbanite life. Four bedrooms, three baths in a master-planned community, gas-guzzling vehicle, plans to be a stay-at-home mom for my future 2.2 kids." Her voice slipped a little on the last word, and she cleared her throat. Sharing was one thing, but it was too early in what one might loosely call their relationship for her to fall apart.

It didn't seem to faze him, though, and he didn't pull out the usual reminder about adoption as though she needed to think about alternative options before she'd had a chance to mourn her newly acquired infertility. He wrapped one of her curls around his finger and said, "I had chemo, too." When she nodded through the lump in her throat, he smiled gently. "Your hair is beautiful, by the way. I like the red."

She cleared her throat again. "Yeah, well, the blonde fit the image better. Or so I thought. Now, I'm just … I'm just done. I traded my beast for a hybrid months ago. I'm listing the house next week." Which was news to her, though she'd intended to do it sometime soon anyway. But as she heard the statement roll off her tongue, she knew it was true all the same. She was suddenly desperate to be rid of the trappings of her old life.

"You're moving?" he asked, taking a too-casual sip of his latté.

"Not far," she rushed to assure him. "I love my job, and I want to volunteer at the hospital and, well, since we're being open, I'm interested, too. In you, I mean. I've been thinking about one of those tiny houses that are all the rage right now. With a gazebo and a big garden. Maybe you could give me some pointers." She blushed furiously and took a long, slow drink of her cider. Surely that was an okay ask since they'd admitted mutual interest and all. When she glanced up, he was grinning from ear to ear.

"Seems like something I could do."

She fought the urge to dance in her seat and took another calm sip instead. "Good."

"In fact, why don't you come visit the farm sometime soon? We give public tours on Wednesdays, but I'd love to give you a private look at the place. Maybe make dinner for you? I'm a pretty good cook."

Therese's heart flipped over in her chest and chill bumps broke out along her arms. Once upon a time, a home-cooked dinner down on the farm would have seemed quaint at best. Just then, it sounded like the most romantic thing in the world. But the urge to play hadn't yet drained from her system, and she couldn't resist one more tease. She leaned over, giving him a glimpse of her revamped cleavage, and laid a hand on his knee.

"Are you inviting me to see your zucchini, Mr. Taylor?"

His eyes flashed sex and mischief. "Only if you want to look."

Chapter Four

HE COULD BARELY WRAP his head around the past couple of weeks, around the emails and the phone calls and the candlelit dinner they'd just finished. He couldn't believe she was standing there with him, their shoulders barely touching, watching night-owl water bugs dance across the surface of the pond. Somewhere nearby, a neighbor had a bonfire going. Someone else had Janis Joplin tuned high enough to send her whiskied strains shimmering through the half-light. He was so aware of the woman beside him it ached.

This was obviously the perfect moment to take her in his arms as he'd wanted to do for so long, to pull her to his chest like the hero she made him want to be, to kiss her like a man who'd gone mushy from the waist up and rigid with desire below. He wanted to kiss her, needed to kiss her, could barely control the hunger no food could sate. And yet here he stood, heart pounding and knees wobbling like a tenth grader at the homecoming dance. Like an idiot. Like someone who hadn't done far more difficult things in his lifetime. Except he wasn't sure anything he'd done before would turn out to be as important. It was early days yet, and anything could happen, but he just had this feeling about Therese, about their future. The last time he'd been so sure was the day he decided to start the farm. That had felt right, too.

He grabbed hold of his courage with both hands, reminded himself that he used to have balls, and said her name in a voice hoarse with everything building inside. She turned, a peaceful half smile on her face and answering need burning in her gaze. The desire very nearly took over, wiping out any possibility of the gentle, exploratory kiss he'd planned, and powering his body to move. He reached for her and, in one swift motion, crushed her to him as though he'd never let go and captured her lips in a kiss more passionate, more heated, than he knew he was capable of delivering. Maybe he hadn't been, before. Her curves gave against his hardness, but her body was as taut and wanting as his, and she met his fire flame for flame. She tangled her hands in his hair, tugging him ever closer as though she, too, had a lifelong hunger to satisfy. For long moments, pure, powerful lust swirled around them, stormy and desperate and laced with the kind of abandon most people could never understand. Tongues twined, hands roamed, and his brain buzzed so loudly it drowned out the waking pond frogs.

Then slowly, gradually, the physical intensity eased. Their bodies went loose and their muscles relaxed and their ravenous passion slipped into something more comfortable. His taste buds registered the sweet aftertaste of honeyed pound cake on her lips, his fingertips registered the softness of her sweater, and his heart registered the contentment soaking into his limbs. An unhurried diminuendo of tiny, breathless kisses eased them into reality, and she turned silently in his arms to face the pond again, serenity radiating from every line of her form.

He kissed the top of her head, counting every curly, soft blessing beneath his lips, and accepted that he was a goner. The farm had beckoned him from the moment he set foot on the land. But kissing Therese was coming home.

"I have scars, you know." Her voice was soft, barely audible above the crickets and the riot of his still-pounding heart.

He shook his head to clear the mist and kissed her head again. "What?"

"Scars. From the surgeries. I have them. I probably always will."

He nodded, then realized she couldn't see him. "I have them, too." His had been around longer, had far more time to fade, but that was okay. He still recalled when they were raw and ragged. He knew how to help them heal.

"I thought I should warn you," she said quietly. "For when we make love someday."

His pulse quickened, and he made a mental note to kiss every inch of all her scars when they reached that point. Then he took a deep breath, willing his voice to stay steady despite the heady combination of arousal and affection reverberating along his nerves.

"It won't matter," he said, his tone tender but firm. And it wouldn't. Because scars were powerful, a sign of determination. What mattered was that they were both going to live.

CiCi Coughlin is a storyteller, strategist, and chronic student—also a dog schmuck, Sinatra fan, and nacho connoisseur. She writes about the funny, sexy, quirky lives we all lead and loves experimenting with offbeat ideas. She pens everything from flash fiction and short stories to novellas and novels. Sometimes the heat level scorches; sometimes it simply simmers. Her twelve-book, high-heat series, *Boudoir de Deux*, is halfway finished and includes her award-winning novella *Tex-Mex Sex Hex*. As per usual, she has a plethora of other projects in the hopper.

CiCi, who lives south of Atlanta with the Staffy mix who rescued her, also writes mysteries, magic, and more as Maggie Marsh.

Find her at http://CiCiCoughlin.com and on Instagram @maggieshewrote or Twitter @maggieshewrote.

COVERT HEARTS

Ariella Moon

A PRICKLE SPIDER-WALKED DOWN my spine. I lowered my turkey sandwich and scanned the cliques scattered around the quad. Past the cheerleaders holding court in their thigh-high pleated skirts, past the skaters perched with their boards on top of the concrete retaining wall, beyond a trio of sophomore girls checking their cellphones, he drew my stare. Wind ruffled his hair as he leaned against the flagpole.

Our gazes collided like a six-foot swell crashing against the hull of a small boat. His lips parted; he straightened his lanky stance. I drew in a quick breath and averted my gaze. Where had he come from? *Vogue*? *Vanity Fair*? Maybe a castle in the United Kingdom was missing its ginger-haired prince.

First-day-at-a-new-high-school nerves trembled my hands as I stashed my half-eaten sandwich into its plastic cube and snapped the blue lid into place. *Be cool.* I finger-combed my hair. The sight of caramel brown tresses slipping through my fingers startled me. For a second I had forgotten the dye job, another layer in my disguise. If I didn't look like Sailor Saint James, and I didn't bear her name, then no one would hound me.

Sailor, why weren't you on the yacht with your father? Did he ask you to stay home because he planned to kill himself?

I wriggled on the boulder, searching for a more comfortable perch. A local pediatrician had donated the money for the wellness garden bordering the quad. The lavender, rosemary, and sage intermixed with the oversized rocks were supposed to lower student anxiety. Bees buzzed alarmingly close, a chaotic platoon of miniature drones. My throat constricted.

I should have sailed with him. Maybe I could have stopped ... whatever happened.

I rotated my cashmere-lined leather baseball cap so the brim shaded my eyes. Most of my trappings of wealth had been lost: my private school, our home and, of course, the yacht was collateral damage. My designer clothes hung untouched in the cramped closet in our small loft above a dying strip mall on the outskirts of town. Fashion editors and bloggers had praised my signature style—too distinctive now that I needed to blend in, not stand out. Only the baseball cap, seemingly ordinary but deceptively well designed and pricey, remained.

I risked another glance at the redhead. He had halved the distance between us. A rogue basketball escaped a nearby pickup game and bounced his way. He caught it, barely breaking stride.

"Over here!" a player shouted.

I expected the boy to send the ball bouncing back to the court. Instead, he lobbed a powerful chest pass.

"Dude! Join us," the player shouted.

The redhead inclined his head toward me. "Maybe tomorrow."

The other boy sized me up then pumped his arm at the ginger.

My plan to blend in imploded. The wretched boulder refused to crack open and swallow me whole. My adrenaline surged as the boy neared. Before I could formulate an escape, his shadow slanted across me. Hope and excitement gleamed in his eyes. "Sailor? Sailor Saint James?" His copper brows twitched.

My stomach free fell. *Crap.* I should have fled to the girls' bathroom while I had the chance. I cleared my throat. "You have me confused with someone else."

His pale sage eyes narrowed then he rubbed his lower lip. "May I join you?"

He knows. Panic rooted me. I pushed up the sleeves of my boy-shirt and vintage bomber jacket. Then, remembering my mini-sail-boat tattoo, I tugged them down. Good manners branded during Junior Cotillion fought with the word *flee* screaming inside my head. I gave him a one-shoulder shrug. "It's a free rock. Suit yourself."

Unexpected dimples emerged on either side of his perfect mouth. "Oh yeah," he said, grinning as if I had slipped up somehow and proven my true identity. He joined me on the wide boulder.

I hoped the cold granite froze his skinny butt.

"You don't remember me, do you?" he said.

"Sure I do. You're the guy who stared at me for forty minutes in first period Spanish." Remembering sent a blush storming across my cheeks. First day, first class, and he had me so distracted I nearly blew my chance to make a good impression on Señora Mendoza.

I tilted my chin up so I could stare at him from beneath my cap. Seeing him up close sparked an elusive memory that danced just beyond my reach. I bit my lip and shoved my lunch box into my messenger bag.

He stuck out his hand. "Nathan Sheehan, formerly of Three Oaks Elementary School."

My jaw dropped. I recovered, closed my mouth, and willed my features into a neutral mask. Hopefully, my jacket muffled my heartbeat's sudden spike. *Sheehan! This freckled fire god is the boy who sat behind me in fifth and sixth grade and tugged my hair?* Stunned, I shook his hand. The warmth and roughness of his skin sparked an unexpected flutter in my stomach. "I'm Haylee Birch."

Several emotions played across his face in rapid succession. His brows knitted together in confusion, then something sparked a flicker of triumph and validation in his eyes. My muscles tensed. Did he know Birch was my middle name and my mother's maiden name? Had my voice given me away? How many times had I whirled in my desk chair after a hair pull and snarled, "I hate you, Nate"? Never Nathan. Always Nate.

"Haylee, huh?"

"Yes." My ears burned. I withdrew my hand, but his energy still crackled across my palm. I smoothed my hands over my hair.

"Hmm." He shifted and his knee brushed against mine. Heat seeped through his black jeans. I inched away. He did a good job pretending he hadn't noticed.

"Can I trust you with a secret, Haylee?"

Good one. I crossed my arms over my torso, walling myself off. "I'm the queen of secrets."

"Okay, but promise you won't laugh."

"Promise." I prayed he'd say, "Wow, I'm such an idiot. I totally mistook you for the debutante daughter of a big shot developer."

He drew in a long breath, then released it through his nose. "At the end of sixth grade, my parents were convinced an earthquake was about to plummet California into the ocean."

I breathed in his scent, mandarin and spice with a hint of musk. "You're kidding."

"Would I lie about something so embarrassing?" he asked.

I would. I remembered his parents because of their bright copper hair. They had seemed down-to-earth, not flighty. Mrs. Sheehan—actually Doctor Sheehan, she had a PhD in psychology—had counseled veterans before she quit to raise Nate and his two brothers. Mr. Sheehan had been the carpenter for at least one of the Saint James planned community developments. He and Dad had greeted each other by name and shaken hands at the fifth-grade science fair. Funny. I didn't remember them speaking to each other at the sixth-grade fair.

I glanced about. "So divination wasn't their strong suit?"

"No." Nate's dimples reappeared, bracketing a sardonic smile. "It gets worse. They dragged me and my siblings to Indiana."

I pressed my lips together.

"Don't laugh. It sucked. The worst part was leaving my secret crush."

My brows arched. "Seriously? *That* was the worst part?"

"Don't hate on young love. A broken heart is a clinical malady."

His mock woe expression catapulted me back to fifth grade. *Don't be mad, Sailor. I removed a piece of seaweed from your hair. See?*

The little devil had dangled a length of fake kelp he had bought at the dollar store, complete with a realistic minnow hanging off the end. Irritation scrabbled against my memory vault. Nate had been in love with someone? I didn't remember him bothering any other girls. "She must have been quite special."

"She was … probably still is." His gaze roved my face. "But I think she hated me."

I smirked. "Maybe you mistook her for someone else."

"Very funny." Nate's stare rummaged my core. I blinked, and he dropped his gaze. "No, I knew exactly who she was." He picked at his thumbnail. "And what she was."

I shifted on the boulder. "What do you mean?"

He shook his head. "Totally out of my league."

"Ah."

"But I couldn't stop myself."

"What did you do? Trip her in the halls?"

"No!" Nate bumped his shoulder against mine. The breach zinged a charge along my arm that arrowed to my core. He fingered the zipper of his body-hugging hoodie jacket. "Give a guy some credit. I was much smoother than that."

Remembering the hair pulling, I had my doubts.

"I invited her to my house for my first boy-girl birthday party."

I flashed on his family's rambling two-story house. Dad had cajoled me into accepting Nate's invitation. *Sailor, you have to go! Even if you hate the guy, you'll love his house. It's a hidden gem. I bet you'll fill an entire sketchbook when you return.*

I had gone, determined to check out the old Victorian and then hide in a bathroom and text my parents to pick me up. Instead, I had been swept away by the house's lived-in charm and Mr. Sheehan's restoration: crown molding, wainscoting, and—in a side parlor that had been transformed into a small library—an intricate custom bookcase. Nate had discovered me tracing my fingertips over the sleek mahogany.

"Want to see something cool?"

My heart jumped at his sudden appearance. How had he ditched his other guests? Without waiting for my answer, Nate pressed on a side panel adorned with hand-carved mermaids. The panel popped open, revealing a pale sea-foam room, barely big enough to contain two gray beanbag chairs and a drum table. A mini-chandelier strung with sea glass hung from the ceiling. Splashes of colored light caught my eye as they danced across the superhero comic books strewn across the floor.

"Where is the light coming from?" I asked.

Nate clasped my wrist. "I'll show you." He drew me into the hobbit-sized room and pointed to a spot high on the exterior wall.

"Wow." Sunlight streamed through a circular stained glass window that depicted a golden-haired mermaid perched on a rock outcropping. In the turquoise sea surrounding her, three attentive dolphins stood upright in the water.

"Welcome to the inner sanctum of Mermaid Manor." Nate scooped a pencil from the table. "Come here." He situated me against the doorjamb. He smelled of barbecued hamburgers and boy. "Hold still."

"Why? What are you going to do?"

"You'll see."

I felt the pencil slide along the part in my hair then heard it scratch against the wood frame. When he finished, I eyed his handiwork.

Nate wrote my name and the year on the wall beside the mark. "There. Now you're an official member."

"Of what?"

"The mermaid club."

"Hand me the pencil." I made a flicking motion.

Nate passed it over. "Why? What are you going to do?"

I smirked. "You'll see." I drew a tiny sailboat next to my name and the date then slapped the pencil against Nate's palm.

His gaze slid from the sailboat to me. "I like it."

"Thank you. Dad promised I could have a sailboat tattoo when I turn sixteen."

"Cool." Nate assumed a somber expression at odds with his wild hair and mischief filled eyes. "Within these walls, you can only speak the truth."

I glanced past him. "And read comics."

His eyes glittered. "Well, yeah."

"Haylee?" Nate's voice brought me back to the present.

"Sorry. I was just thinking about what a smooth operator you must have been, luring your secret crush to your castle." I tried to picture the other girls who had been at the party, but all I could remember was the secret room and the sound of Nate's mother calling his name.

"I wasn't that smooth," Nate confessed. "I sat behind her in school. Her blonde surfer hair reminded me of a mermaid. I drove her crazy tugging on it." His eyebrows flicked up. "At least she noticed me."

My heart tightened like wire rope on a winch. I gathered up the ends of my dyed hair and dropped them behind my shoulders. Hopefully, Nate didn't notice my fingers trembling.

"Now you know my deep, dark secret. What's yours?"

A fresh blush fast-tracked up my throat and blazed toward my eyes. Blinking away tears, I collected my messenger bag and stood.

Nate scrambled to his feet and clasped my wrist. "Sail—Haylee, I'm sorry. I've been away for years. This is my first day back, and I saw you, and …" He released my wrist.

I clapped my hand over my mouth and fled.

I hate you, Nate.

Chapter Two

ALL NIGHT, OLD NEWSPAPER headlines had rippled through my nightmares like yellow and black contagion flags.

"Saint James Abandons Plan to Build 50 Luxury Homes."

"Tradesmen Hit Hard by Saint James Pullout."

The words remained imprinted on my mind while I made my way to my first period class. *Had our financial decline started four-and-a-half years ago?* My shoulders ached from being buffeted by the throng. I recoiled from the onslaught. Shoulders hunched, my torso angled sideways, I threaded through the pushing, cacophonous crowd. Were all public high schools like this, funneling hundreds of students into narrow hallways and stairwells? My old school resembled a low-key village. Right now, my friends would be sauntering across tamped earth paths as they headed toward clustered freestanding classrooms. "Hi, Sailor!" kids from all grades would call out. I'd wave and say, "Hey!"

Not here. And I'm not Sailor Saint James anymore. Well, technically I am, but only because Mom won't let me legally change my name. "Give it a year, Sailor, then see how you feel." She did agree to a temporary modification. Luckily, Mom and the principal had been sorority sisters in college. They must have taken a blood oath to aid each other because Ms. Miller got all the teachers to agree to call me Haylee Birch.

Finally crossing the threshold to Spanish, I checked my cellphone. My chest constricted. Still no texts from my so-called friends asking me where I had moved to or wishing me good luck. Maybe they had forgotten me. Or, maybe they believed the tabloid reports that Dad had been bankrupt and had deliberately sunk the yacht—and killed himself—so Mom and I would get the insurance money. Only the insurance company was holding up our claim pending their investigation. Standard procedure, we were told, when no body had been found and the payout would be in the millions. Meanwhile, the legal costs of fighting them were burying us deeper and deeper.

Dad would never have done that to us. Not on purpose. Never.

The school bell bellowed at about two hundred decibels. Startled, I dropped my phone. Nate, who had sidled up to me unnoticed, dove and caught it.

"Here you go." His long fingers grazed my skin as he handed me the phone. The contact fluttered my stomach. Nate Sheehan was a pest, I reminded myself. Yes, he had grown and thinned out. And yesterday after school, I might have fantasized about tracing the fine line of his jaw from his ear all the way to the soft flesh of his lips. But Nate could blow my cover any second. So, no way was I going there.

"Thanks." My fingers closed around the phone.

"My pleasure." Those pale sage eyes sucked me in. Students shuffled past us. Chairs scraped. Conversations died down. "About yesterday—"

"Please take your seat, Mr. Sheehan," Señora Mendoza commanded.

Nate grimaced. "*Sí, Señora.*" A strawberry blush bloomed across his freckles. He pivoted like a menswear model during Fashion Week and strode with haughty grace across the classroom.

"Work it!" a jerk-face in the row to my right catcalled. The plus-sized Goth girl seated behind the boy finger-flicked his head. "Ow!" He rubbed the spot as he swung about and glared at the Goth. Señora Mendoza rapped her yardstick against the linoleum floor. The boy startled and faced forward.

I slid into my seat and stowed my phone in my messenger bag. The thud of my textbook sounded overly loud as it slipped through my fingers and landed on my desk. My knees drew together. I countered my inclination to slump and hide behind my hair. "No matter what," my paternal grandmother often reminded me, "a Saint James does not acknowledge adversity or embarrassment. We ride above it." Well, maybe not Dad.

Throughout Spanish, I kept my gaze locked on Señora Mendoza or stared at my primer. My heels bounced as I discharged nervous energy through my toes.

Toward the end of class, Señora called on Nate. He shot me a sideways glance from across the room. My stomach looped. Then Nate answered her question in flawless Spanish. Señora's expression morphed from arched brow surprise to pleasure. The tension seeped out of my shoulders. *Well played, Nate.*

Five minutes before the bell, while Señora wrote tomorrow's assignment on the board, Goth girl pitched a folded note onto my desk. As I swept it into my jacket pocket, Señora whirled around and scanned the class. I avoided eye contact and copied the assignment in my notebook. The bell shrilled. I packed my messenger bag and surreptitiously read the note.

Lunch? Same spot as yesterday? Nate.

A montage of lunches with my friends at my old school cycled through my mind. A tsunami of hurt crashed over me, followed by a tidal wave of doubt. How will I make new friends when my Haylee persona is a lie? Maybe the alias had been a mistake. I had thought a fresh name would give me space, help me hide until the scandal passed. Instead, it paralyzed me.

Guilt twisted my insides. I couldn't go backward or forward. And the only person throwing me a lifeline was the boy who had driven me crazy in elementary school. How long could I maintain the fraud? I glanced at the students threading out the door. What would happen if word leaked? My insides twisted.

Nate sat sideways in his seat, making deliberate work of zipping up his backpack. He glanced up at me. My insides shivered. I broke eye contact and rose, hoisting my messenger bag against my chest like a battle shield. I half hoped Nate would rush up behind me and tug my hair. Instead, his wounded stare followed me out the door.

Later, when the lunch bell sounded at the end of English Three Honors, remorse surfed through me. Part of me longed to head for the boulder and see if Nate would show up. Maybe I should come clean. Apologize.

I decided to hide out in the library.

At a corner far from the librarian's watchful eye, I laid my messenger bag on the table and unpacked my dill pickle spear and peanut butter and boysenberry jam on rye. A quick check of my phone yielded a text from my mother, wishing me a great day. *You, too,* I texted back. It couldn't be fun for her meeting with lawyers and financial planners, sorting through the debris field left by Dad's death. I wondered if any of Mom's friends had stuck by her.

After Dad's accident, I had boycotted the reading of his will. It didn't matter what it said. I could tell by Mom's tight expression; the company was in trouble. *We* were in trouble. Mom had said, "I'll worry about the finances. You concentrate on school. Junior year is the make-or-break-it year for college."

Focus on school. Pretend the old me never existed. No more playing hooky with Dad when the winds and tide called to us. Time to get serious.

I blinked back the sudden tears and surge of anger.

I pushed my messenger bag aside. A small stack of magazines someone had left on the table tipped over the edge and dived onto the dusky blue carpet with a loud slap. *Great.* Kneeling, I skimmed the covers as I retrieved them. My pulse ricocheted. Someone had pulled the only three magazines containing photos of me. I double-checked the front covers and text. *Yes. Yes. And yes.* Holding the magazines to my chest, I scanned the library. Most students were in the cafeteria or the quad. But several, mostly loners and a few groups of two or three, had taken refuge in the library. None glanced my way.

I sank onto the hard wooden chair. Statistically, no way could this be random. I flipped open the top magazine to the five-page feature "Nouveau Riche Teens Practice Noblesse Oblige." The concept had been to feature wealthy teens volunteering for their favorite charity. I always wondered who had tipped them off about the First Saturday of the Month Club. I thought I had blended in—just another volunteer swinging a hammer or wielding a paintbrush.

"You must do it!" the editor on the phone cajoled. "Here's your

chance to inspire other teens—other girls! Think of how many more homes will be rehabbed; how many families you'll help."

I bit my lip and flipped the pages a second time. Pop star. Famous athlete's son ... and ... this time I saw it, the ragged edge where someone had torn out my photo.

My heart accelerated. I checked the next magazine. The bohemian fashion shoot at Joshua Tree National Park should be on page eighty-one. Seventy-nine. Eighty. Eighty-five. This time, the page tears were hardly visible. Sick fear drained the blood from my cheeks. My mind flashed to television shows where the police discovered an apartment where the stalker had plastered photos of his prey.

With dread rising like high tide, I reached for the last magazine. "Haylee?"

Startled, I whirled toward Nate's voice. He emerged from the floor-to-ceiling bookshelves, his hands raised like two stop signs. "I swear, I'm not stalking you. I thought you'd be in the quad." His copper brows knitted together. "You okay?"

My chest caved. "I'm fine." I placed the magazine on top of the others and pushed away the stack as though signaling a waiter to clear the table.

Nate angled his head as he studied the top cover. "'Tangerine: Fall's Hot New Hue.' Whoa. Totally not your color."

"Gee, thanks." I sniffed and drew the side of my forefingers across the thin skin beneath my lower eyelashes. "Good thing the issue is a year old." I eyed Nate. He acted innocent enough. But if he hadn't ferreted out the magazines, then who had? The flesh on my forearms bristled. My gaze swept the library. No overt paparazzi, tabloid spies, or stalkers. I kicked at the chair beside me in a quasi-invitation. "Sorry, I didn't answer your note."

"Hey. No problem." He averted his eyes, and his Adam's apple bobbed. "Well, bye." He pivoted toward the nonfiction section.

"Wait." I grabbed his hand. Nate stiffened. His fingers twitched indecisively. I released him. "I was in a bad space earlier." My chest corseted at the thought of my so-called friends.

"And now?"

My right shoulder lifted then fell in a shrug. "Still not great."

Nate's gaze drifted from my eyes, south to the magazines, then bounced north again. A long, slow whistle escaped his mouth. "Tell me his name. I know people. People who own baseball bats."

"I bet you do. Not." My lips curved upward. "Besides, 'his' name is Bailey, Sarah, and Cheyenne."

He pulled out the chair and sat. "You're having trouble with a trio of drag queens?"

"No." I swatted his arm. His triceps hardened beneath his hoodie jacket.

"Good." Nate grabbed half my sandwich and took an alligator bite. "Hey!"

He chewed for about twenty seconds, swallowed, then wiped his mouth with his hand. "You busy Saturday?"

"Yes, it's the first Saturday of the month."

He eyed my pickle. "What happens on the first Saturday—?"

The school bell drowned out the rest of his sentence. We scrambled to our feet. Five minutes to fight the throngs and push our way to class. I handed him the pickle, gathered up the rest of my stuff, and we hustled to the hall.

"Where are you headed?" Nate asked.

"Right. Pre-Calculus. You?"

"Left. Physics." He flicked his hair out of his eyes. "About Saturday—"

"Sorry!" A river of students swept me away. I glanced back once and caught sight of Nate's fire-god hair as he strode off. His head swiveled as if he sensed my gaze. His lips parted. Deep in my core, a tug connected us.

A purple backpack slammed my arm, knocking me into a cheerleader. "Watch where you're going!" she warned.

"Sorry." I hugged my messenger bag to my waist. I couldn't afford to antagonize anyone; at least not until I figured out who had stolen the magazine pictures, and why.

The headlines from my nightmares bobbed in my mind. Had Nate's father been one of the tradesmen burned by Dad's pullout of the Solstice Sunrise development?

My lunch curdled.

Chapter Three

NATE WAS ABSENT FOR three days. Three. Days. This shouldn't have been my first thought upon waking Saturday morning, but it floated to the surface, and I couldn't ignore it. Was he sick? Had his parents wigged out and returned to Indiana? Maybe he had transferred to the high school across town?

Throwing off the covers, I considered tracking down his phone number. My private high school had a student directory. Maybe public schools had them, too. Heading to the bathroom, I resolved to check my new student packet when I returned from the build out. Or rehab. I wasn't sure if we'd be building affordable housing or rehabbing an existing home. There had probably been an email I should have read.

The First Saturday of the Month Club met in the parking lot of the Presbyterian Church on Amador Avenue. I had dressed to work, layering an old hoodie over a blue and black plaid shirt I had bought at a discount store. I wore my oldest pair of jeans and paint-splattered low-tops. Normally, I'd sling on the leather tool belt Dad had given me. But I couldn't. Maybe next month I'd be ready.

By the time Mom dropped me off, ten of the twenty or so regulars were already grouped next to the two work vans. They stared at me over their plastic-lidded coffees, their expressions welcoming, but unsure. My steps faltered.

"Sailor?" Wendy, one of the middle-aged women broke from the group. "We didn't recognize you! What did you do to your hair?"

The pressure in my chest eased. "I'm incognito," I confessed.

Wendy wrapped her arm around my shoulders and steered me toward the others. "We've missed you the past few months."

"Thank you for the flowers and card." My voice caught. None of the volunteers knew the Saint James Family Charitable Trust paid for most of the building supplies. We had kept the grants anonymous so I would be treated like any other volunteer. The trust had been formed when we were multimillionaires, before the housing market crashed. Before, if the tabloids were to be believed, bankruptcy loomed.

"What about the charitable trust?" I asked Mom when she told me we'd have to sell our house. "Can't we use some of that money?"

Mom shook her head. "We can't touch it. Not for our personal use. We can only request grants for others in need. But that's huge, right?

"Project 114." Wendy gave my shoulders a final squeeze before releasing me. "Bless our anonymous sponsor!"

"Yes." My eyes watered. *It was huge.*

"It's good to have you back." Robert Ludlow, who everyone called Gramps, patted the top of my head. "Perfect timing, too. You're going to love the house we'll be rehabbing."

"Awesome." It had been a while since I had loved anything.

"This one is an interesting case," Wendy said. "A foreclosure that somehow slipped through the proverbial cracks. Several neighbors wrote asking us to help the new owners, a down-on-their-luck family."

Gramps checked his cellphone. "Time to roll, people. The advance team is on the site. The second van will grab the stragglers."

Someone slid open the door of the nearest van. I found a spot on the hard bench seat, buckled up, and closed my eyes. Nate's face flashed in my mind. My stomach looped.

The worst part was leaving my secret crush.

The corners of my lips ticked upward.

Chapter Four

"SAILOR, WE'RE HERE." A cool hand shook my shoulder.

"What?" I struggled up from the dream. Dad and I had been on a sailboat, but it wasn't our boat. The name *Solstice Sunrise* had been painted on the transom.

"Come see the house." Wendy pointed out the open van door.

My seatbelt unbuckled with a click. A cool breeze tinged with salt and low tide smells gusted into the van. *The sea.* Love and longing chased by grief and anxiety surfed through me.

Wendy's thrilled expression collapsed. "Oh, no! Sailor, I'm so sorry. Gramps should have warned you. I imagine you haven't been near the water since …"

"No. I haven't." The words came out strangled. "Don't worry. I'll be fine."

Wendy bit her lip. "Are you sure?"

"Of course." *A Saint James does not acknowledge kicked-in-the-heart pain.* Wendy moved aside, and I crawled out of the van. Seagulls cruising the cloudy September sky greeted me with their shrill squeals. My gaze dropped to the sandy path, half hidden by overgrown ice plants. *No. It can't be.*

"Do you know this house?" Gramps asked.

"Yes." I followed the trail to the rambling two-story Victorian. The cornflower paint with cream trim had flaked around the tri-windows facing the bay and near the front porch downspout. A riptide grabbed my insides. Screens had been torn from the first story windows and hurled into the ornamental grasses bordering the narrow lawn. Plywood covered three windows. Scanning to the right, I noticed the advance crew had left the front door open to the elements.

I barely registered the second van's arrival and the appreciative chatter of its occupants as they disgorged from the vehicle. My gaze swept the Victorian. "Where is she?"

"Who, dear?" Wendy asked.

"The mermaid."

Behind me, footsteps crunched across the sand that had blown onto the asphalt. The sound halted, and the familiar scent of mandarin, spice, and a hint of musk wafted over me. My heart quaked.

"You can't see her from this angle," Nate whispered in my ear. "We'll have to go inside."

I shifted, and my arm brushed his. Body heat escaped the thick fleece of his hoodie jacket. His complexion paled beneath his freckles, except for the fever blooming high on his cheeks. He squinted, as though the early sunlight hurt his eyes.

"You okay?" I asked.

He exhaled through his nose and copied my one-shoulder shrug—so no. We trudged up the path, side by side. I dropped behind when the ice plant forced us to walk single file.

Nate stopped at the edge of the lawn. "We lost the house during the recession," he confessed. "We moved to Indiana to live with my grandmother."

I pressed my fingertips to my brow as if I could stem the flow of unwanted thoughts. "This was my family's fault, wasn't it? Because Dad pulled out of Solstice Sunrise—" I clapped my hand over my mouth.

Wendy and Gramps caught up with us. "Everything all right here?" Gramps narrowed his eyes at Nate.

I lowered my hand. "It's okay, Gramps. Nate's an old friend."

Gramps crossed his arms over his chest and scrutinized us. Other volunteers began gathering up the broken window screens.

"Let's leave them to talk." Wendy nudged Gramps.

"See you inside," Gramps said.

"Yes, sir," Nate replied.

After they left, I said, "I'm so—"

Nate pressed his finger to my lips. "Too many people around."

My lips tingled. I glanced at the men setting up ladders and the group collecting the screens. "Okay."

Nate faced the house and squared his shoulders. "Let's see if the squatters found our secret room."

Our secret room. But I had only been there once. I slipped my arm through his. We mounted the white porch steps together. Nate paused and patted the railing before striding to the front door and crossing the threshold. In the foyer, his shoulders sagged as he exhaled a long breath. Thieves had stripped away the brass and etched glass wall sconces, leaving exposed wires. I blinked at the wall where the door to the library had been. "It's gone."

"No." Nate swiped his forearm across his eyes. "It's concealed. When you were here, the library door was open, so you didn't notice."

"Great. How many secret rooms are in this place?"

"Just two that I know of."

I blocked him with my hand. "Don't help me. I can do this." I studied the floor-to-ceiling wallpaper. The silver-blue damask contained a repeated cream floral design. I closed my eyes and filtered out the volunteers' voices, the sharp scent of wet paint as cans were opened, and the *thoo-ump, thoo-ump, thoo-ump* of a nail gun. *I am Haylee Birch, a member of the mermaid club. Show me the way in.*

Nothing.

I sensed Nate watching me. I pushed up my sleeves. "I am Sailor Saint James, a member of the mermaid club. Show me the way in."

A salty sea breeze gusted through the open front door. Opening my eyes, I noticed the library wall had once held two sconces, about two-and-a-half feet apart, while the opposing wall had only one. Stepping closer, I searched the wallpaper for a seam. Once I found it, I followed it to a discolored area the width of two fingers and pressed. The hidden door released with a satisfying click.

Nate beamed. "Good job."

"Thanks." I gripped the edge of the door with my fingertips and pulled it toward me. Mustiness assaulted my nose.

"Wait." Nate hunched so we were eye to eye. "I stole the photos. You walked into the library before I could shelve the magazines. I panicked and hid. I never meant for you to find them."

I stepped back. "Why steal my photos?"

"I did a computer search for Sailor Saint James. I was afraid you were in the Witness Protection Program or something. I found the magazine references."

"And you thought—"

"If I could find them, anyone could find them. You wanted to lie low. So I removed them."

I broke eye contact. "What else did your search reveal?"

Nate clasped my hand, sending tingles up my arm. "I'm so sorry about your father. I had no idea he'd ..."

"Thanks." I laced my fingers through his.

Nate squeezed my hand then angled his head toward the hidden room. "Ready?"

"Yes." I reached the bookcase first and pressed the side panel. It swung upon slowly, like a sail searching for the wind. Colored light dappled the beanbag chairs and faded floral rug. A thrill rushed my veins. "She's—"

"Still here." Nate pulled me into the secret chamber. I followed a shaft of light to the high circular window. A cobweb clung to the metal edge, and dust had collected on the bright glass, but the mermaid and dolphins had escaped the vandals.

"Amazing." My gaze dropped to the fine planes of Nate's face. His ears angled backward, reminding me somehow of an elf. "How did you find out about the First Saturday of the Month?"

His lips spread into a wicked grin. "*Noblesse Oblige.*"

"The magazine article?"

"Yeah, well, that and I know the family who bought the house at auction."

"Seriously? It would kill me to ready our old house for someone else."

Nate leaned against the doorjamb, his head far above the line bearing my name. "That's the sweet part. We bought it back."

My heart flipped. "You did?"

"Yep. Four years of relentless work. It took every cent we had. The whole family pitched in. Midwestern winters were a great motivator."

"Oh my gosh."

Nate tucked a stray lock of my hair behind my ear. "The winters weren't my only motivator."

Seagulls took wing inside me. "They weren't?"

Mermaid light danced between our feet.

Nate's voice grew husky. "Mind if I move to the desk behind you in Spanish?"

I shook my head. "I don't know. It depends. Did you pack your plastic kelp?"

His dimples surfaced. "Sorry. Kelp didn't make the cut."

"Then I won't be able to say, 'I hate you, Nate.'"

Nate slid his arms around my waist and drew me close. I pressed my ear to his chest and relaxed against the quick beat of his heart.

I love you, Nate.

Ariella Moon draws upon her experiences as a shaman to create magical young adult fiction. Her novels include The Two Realms trilogy, a medieval fantasy adventure, and The Teen Wytche saga, a series of sweet contemporary paranormal romances. Ariella spent her childhood searching for a magical wardrobe that would transport her to Narnia. Extreme math anxiety and taller students who mistook her for a leaning post marred her youth. Despite these horrors, she graduated summa cum laude from the University of California at Davis. She lives a nearly normal life doting on her extraordinary daughter, two shamelessly spoiled dogs, and a media-shy dragon.

ONE NIGHT
A STARK WORLD SHORT STORY

J. Kenner

BLAKE THORTON IS IN *the building!*

I stare at the text message, my skin suddenly clammy. My pulse kicking up into the danger zone. In the building? What the devil does that mean? The lobby? The coffee shop?

Dear God, is he coming all the way up to thirty-five?

I scramble for the keyboard, then open up my boss's calendar—but there's no Blake Thorton anywhere. Not that I really had to check. That particular name would have jumped out at me immediately. After all, seventeen months and twenty-three days is hardly long enough to forget someone. Even someone you spent only one night with.

One amazing night.

One amazing, unforgettable, perfect night.

And then I'd walked away—pushed out the door by a combination of ambition, stubbornness, and fear.

Line one rings, and I snatch it up, irritated that it's interrupted my memories. "Damien Stark's office."

"Did you get my text?" Sylvia's voice comes across the line

with crisp efficiency. She's a project manager in the real estate division of Stark International, and I'm a floater who one day wants to do what she does. We became friends when I worked her desk for three months while her assistant was out on maternity leave.

"It can't be him," I blurt, then cringe at the note of hysteria coloring my voice. "I mean, he lives in New York. And there must be hundreds of Blake Thortons in the world. Maybe thousands."

"He looks just like you described him. Sandy gold hair. Deep green eyes. And that boy can definitely fill out a suit. Not as well as Jackson, though," she adds, referring to her husband.

"Out of all the Blake Thortons in the world, I bet a lot of them are gorgeous." I'm being rational. Pragmatic. Because he can't really be here. In Los Angeles. In Stark Tower.

I can practically hear Sylvia rolling her eyes on the other end of the line. "He has the tattoo you told me about," she says, effectively cutting off all my hollow denials. "Right there on his wrist. I noticed it first thing. Peeking out from under the cuff of a very finely tailored white shirt, I might add."

My fingers itch with the memory of a snow-bound Chicago night. My body curled up naked against him in a room at the Hilton at O'Hare, where our New York to LA direct flight had been forced to land due to the storm. Me, gently tracing the lines of that tattoo. *A is A.* Him, telling me that we were meant to be together. That when the plane hit that first air pocket and I'd grabbed his hand as we'd plunged downward, I'd been grabbing onto destiny. "You know it's true, Penny. You can't argue against reality. *A is A*, after all."

I'd walked away, because I couldn't believe that lightning could strike us both so precisely, and I was terrified of risking my heart.

But he was right. Oh, dear God, he was right.

I take a deep breath and gather myself. "Fine," I say. "It's him. Why's he here? Is he on twenty-seven?" Of course he is. That's the real estate division. And Blake is a real estate developer with projects all over the world.

Not that he told me his full resume in our one night together, but in the months after, I may have Googled the man. Once or twice, anyway. Possibly five or fifteen times.

Maybe more. But really, who keeps track of those things?

My intercom buzzes, and I jump. "Hang on," I say as I reach for the phone to answer my boss.

"I'm squeezing in a lunch appointment," Damien Stark says. "Reschedule my one o'clock for two."

"Of course." I'm a model of efficiency. Not at all distracted by the memory of the man who'd played my body with such intimate perfection, that at one point I'm certain I'd actually touched heaven.

When he ends the call, I return to Syl.

"Are you okay?" she asks.

"Me? Of course. It's probably not even him. And it's not like I'll ever know for sure. I'm on thirty-five and he's on twenty-seven, and never the twain shall meet."

"I could suggest he go up there …"

"Cute," I say. "But don't you—"

"Hang on." Her voice rises, confused. "He's gone."

"Gone?"

"He was talking to Jackson in the conference room across from my office, and now it's empty. Do you want me to find out where he went?"

Yes. Yes, oh, please, yes.

"No. Seriously, Syl," I beg as the elevator dings, "don't say a word to him. Just walk away slowly. I don't—"

Across from my desk, the elevator doors open.

And standing right there—looking as delicious as I remember—is Blake Freaking Thorton.

Chapter Two

BLAKE THORTON.

He's standing right there next to Jackson Steele, and though Jackson is one of the finest looking men I've ever seen, I barely even notice him. I'm drawn to Blake like a magnet, and I can't look away.

Had Sylvia really said he had sandy gold hair? That doesn't even come close. It's wild and indescribable. Infinite variations of gold mixed with hits of darkness, like light against a smattering of clouds. He wears it short, but long enough for a woman to run her fingers through it and feel the heat. And his eyes aren't merely green—they're as tumultuous as the sky after a violent storm.

Blake Thorton is a force of nature, and at that moment, I want nothing more than to be caught in the tempest.

I realize I'm staring and tell myself to smile. That's my job, after all. "Mr. Steele," I say. "A pleasure to see you."

I glance toward Blake, but his expression is veiled, and I can't tell if he's indifferent or purposefully shutting me out.

I have absolutely no idea how to handle this situation. Should I greet him, too? Should I pretend I've never met him before? What is the etiquette for unexpectedly and out of context greeting the man with whom you shared the most passionate night of your life, then walked away, rejecting his offer to join him for a hedonistic week in a Hawaiian paradise?

I'm pondering that basic, philosophical question when Jackson takes the responsibility from me. "Good to see you, too, Penny. This is Blake Thorton. We're heading to lunch with Damien."

"Of course." I smile at Blake, but he only inclines his head.

I clear my throat. "Right. Just a moment." I pick up the phone, announce them, then push the button to open Mr. Stark's door.

They enter—and without a second look or word from Blake, the door swings shut behind them.

For a moment, I sit there, not sure if I'm relieved, disappointed, or simply stunned.

But honestly, if Blake isn't going to acknowledge me, then I'm not going to worry about him either. It's not as if I don't have better things to do. Correspondence to review, calls to make, calendars to update.

To prove my point, I turn my attention to my desk. But work doesn't come easy, and when Mr. Stark's door opens ten minutes later and the men file out, I'm still staring blindly at my desk calendar, wondering how to interpret the unfamiliar hieroglyphics that represent people and places and dates.

"Text me if anything urgent comes up," Mr. Stark says.

"Of course, sir." I glance at Jackson, who smiles at me, and then at Blake. He meets my eyes this time, but doesn't react at all. A slow burn of anger starts to grow in my belly. Maybe earlier I'd chalked up his silence to indifference or stoicism. But now I'm thinking he doesn't recognize me.

But how the hell is that possible after the night we shared?

I'd been on my way to Los Angeles when he and I were seated next to each other on that plane. I had a callback for a television pilot in Los Angeles, and I was moving across the country with the hope of getting that job and maybe, finally, establishing myself as an actress.

When I'd moved to New York after graduating at twenty-one, I'd given myself five years to pursue my passion of acting. Because even though I love being on the stage, I love eating more. I'd grown up with a single mom who spent her entire life in debt, worked a series of dead-end jobs she hated, and slept with a stream of men, each and every one the love of her life. At least until he left or she kicked him out.

I truly adore my mom, but the possibility of that kind of life terrified me. I wanted a job I loved. I wanted a bank account with money in it. And I wanted to be damn sure about a man before I unlocked my heart.

Since I love to act—and since I'm not only good at it, but pretty enough to get roles—I jumped in with both feet. Succeed on stage or in Hollywood and I could have passion and security in my work. But I'm realistic, too, and I wasn't going to spend twenty years chasing a dream that wasn't happening only to then realize that after so much time, I wasn't qualified for any other decent job.

Thus my five-year plan. Pursue acting with all my heart and soul. And if I hadn't nailed it by the time I was twenty-six, I'd quit and figure out exactly what I wanted to be when I grew up.

I'd been on a grand adventure that night, and the fact that Blake was my seatmate had seemed fated. We'd talked throughout the flight, but we hadn't touched until I'd grabbed his hand when the plane had hit that air pocket and seemed to fall from the sky.

That moment changed everything, and the awareness that had been bubbling under the surface of our casual conversation suddenly boiled over, turning into a hot, steamy, demanding need.

When the plane had been grounded, there'd been no question. No discussion. We'd gone to the airport hotel together, and I'd given myself to him, body and soul. I'd surrendered to his every whim, and I'd lost myself in the process.

And in the losing, I'd found part of myself, too.

That was a night I've remembered—and a morning after that I've regretted—for almost two years.

And now here he is again, standing right in front of my desk. And the son of a bitch doesn't even remember me?

I'm sorry, but that is seriously screwed up, and I'm tempted to say so, just so that I can get a rise out of him.

But that might piss off Mr. Stark, and I don't want to lose this job that not only pays well enough for me to afford a cute—albeit tiny—apartment in Venice Beach, but is also putting me through business school with an employee tuition program. I'm on the post-five-year part of my plan now, and I'm happy. I love working here, and I'm learning so much. And I'm excited about diving fully into the business world once I graduate. Plus, this life has the added perk of not requiring new headshots every few months.

So I stay quiet, my efficient smile plastered across my face as the men step onto the elevator. But I watch Blake, and the last thing I see as the doors shut, is the smallest hint of a smile on his face.

Unless, of course, I'm only seeing a shadow.

Chapter Three

MY PULSE POUNDS IN my ears, my heart beating so hard it feels like I've run a marathon.

I want to race after him and shake him. Why did he smile? Did he smile?

Does he remember me?

How can he not remember me?

Shit.

Obviously, I need to chill, and I grab my phone and my purse and log off the computer. I'm about to transfer his calls to the reception desk one floor down when the phone rings. "Mr. Stark's office."

"Mr. Thorton is on his way up," Mr. Stark says. "He's misplaced his phone, most likely in my office. Please help him find it."

"Of course," I say, understanding that "please help him find it" is code for "don't let this man I don't know poke around in my office alone."

I wait, numb, for the elevator to ding again, and even though I'm expecting it, the moment it does, I jump. I suck in air, mentally kick my own ass and stand behind my desk as he steps off, my hands flat against my sides so that he won't notice the way they're shaking.

"Mr. Stark called. I'm happy to help you look."

"I appreciate you taking the time." His bland tone pisses me off. He's playing with me—he has to be playing with me. Because if he's not, that means he really doesn't remember me.

I know it shouldn't matter. Blake Thorton is no longer in my life.

But it does. It really does.

Once we're inside the office, he goes to the seating area where Mr. Stark has a couple of leather chairs and a sofa separated by a coffee table. I lean against the wall near the door as he slips his hand between the couch cushions. I know I should be looking too, but I'm in a pissy mood.

"Did you find it?" I snap when I realize he's no longer fishing in the cushions. Instead, he's standing with his hands in his jacket pockets, his eyes on me. Now, his expression is no longer bland.

Now, it seems dangerous.

"I did." He pulls his hand from his pocket, revealing his phone, and for a moment I wonder if it's been there all along. "Sometimes you have the chance to get back the things you lost." There's a low, sensual quality to his voice that I recognize, that seems to vibrate through me like a low roll of thunder. He takes a step toward me. "I guess this time I got lucky."

He's mere inches from me, all his attention focused on my face. My cheeks flush, and I start to push away from the wall, but he moves in, caging me in his arms. I only have time to gasp before his mouth closes over mine.

I clench my hands into fists at my sides, fighting the urge to touch him. I don't know where this is leading, what game he is playing. But his hands are on the wall, not me, and I'm certainly not going to be the first to touch.

But even without soft caresses or frantic groping, this kiss is wild and hot and meltingly perfect. I imagine his palms stroking my skin, teasing my nipples, sliding between my legs. I want that.

So help me, I want all of that and more.

I'm on fire, on edge, my body hot with need and trembling with passion. I'm craving his touch, desperate for him to take this further, and so I cry out with disappointment when he denies me, instead gently breaking the kiss and pulling away to look at me with those storm-filled eyes.

"I didn't think you recognized me." My voice is raspy. "I thought you'd forgotten me."

"Forgotten you?" He moves in again, and the air between us crackles from the electricity we're generating. He strokes my cheek, and that erotic sensation steals my breath. "Baby, I remember everything. The way you clung to my hand so tightly, as if I had the power to take away all your hurt and fears. The way your mouth tasted of gin when I kissed you in the hotel bar. The way your lips parted when I traced a fingertip along the curve of your shoulder. The softness of your skin. The sweetness of your pussy."

I tremble as he eases closer, his breath tickling my ear as he continues. "I remember exactly how it felt to be inside you. To feel the rhythm of your heart and the heat of your skin. Most of all, I remember the way you cried my name when you came, and the way your body fit with mine when you curled up trembling and limp in my arms.

"Forgotten you?" he repeats, leaning back to once again meet my eyes. "No, Penny," he says as he traces his fingertip over my lips. "I haven't forgotten a thing."

I'm breathing hard, wildly turned on, and I think if he suggested it, I'd strip naked and fuck him right there in Mr. Stark's office.

Except he doesn't suggest it.

He doesn't suggest anything.

Instead, he pulls his finger away, then takes two steps back, putting distance between us. He pauses briefly, then exits the office. I follow, stumbling slightly as I try to adjust to this strange new reality.

Back in the reception area, he pushes the button to call the elevator. "I should get back to lunch."

"I—oh."

The doors open, and he gets on.

"Wait!" My voice sounds desperate, and I wish I could ask for a do-over. "Would you—I mean, maybe we could grab some dinner later?"

"Dinner?" he repeats as the doors start to close. "Baby, dinner is the last thing on my mind."

Chapter Four

THE REST OF THE day I'm too busy to think about Blake. And by the time I head to my car, all I can think is that it's Friday and I can sleep tomorrow.

Which means that when I pass the concrete beam that blocks the view of my car and see Blake, I am totally unprepared.

"You're here," I say stupidly.

He's leaning against my Chevy, looking like he just stepped out of the pages of a men's magazine. "I think you're right."

"Oh. Good." I frown. "About what?"

"Dinner."

"I thought you weren't interested."

"A man has to eat. I need my strength, after all."

"Do you?" A smile tugs at my lips. This is the Blake I remember.

"I certainly hope so. Have dinner with me, Penny. All you have to do is say yes."

"Yes," I say before I can talk myself out of it. Not that I would. The memory of that kiss in the office still lingers.

"Good. And just so we're clear, tonight you belong to me. All night, Penny. Completely and totally mine."

"I—wait. What?"

His eyes rake over me, his expression all power and control. "You heard me."

"That doesn't—"

"Is there someone else?"

"What? No," I say, then immediately fear I've revealed too much.

"Then I don't see any reason for you to hesitate. Unless you'd rather call the whole thing off." He's watching my face. There's humor in his eyes, but also a heat so intense that I'm surprised I don't melt into goo right there.

"Why?" My question is a whisper. A plea.

He steps closer, the air crackling and sizzling between us. "The last time we were together, you said no. This time, I'm not giving you a choice. I'm taking what I want, Pen, and under the circumstances, I think I'm being reasonable. My flight leaves for New York at noon. You're mine until the car service picks me up at nine."

He pulls me toward him until his lips are only millimeters from my cheek. "Those are my terms," he whispers. "Take them or leave them. The choice is yours."

His voice rumbles through me, igniting a bone-deep longing underscored by the frustration of unfulfilled desire. I want to beg for his touch. I want to slap his face. I've never reacted to a man like I do to Blake Thorton, and right then I'm not sure if I should lose myself in the fantasy or run to safety.

"Is this a seduction?" I whisper. "Or is it a punishment?"

He leans away, studying me, his expression a little impressed, a little surprised. Then he reaches out and cups my breast, making me gasp from the shock of his action as well as the electricity of his touch. Slowly, he rubs his thumb over my nipple, now hard under the lace of my bra. "What's the difference?" he asks, and the ache between my legs increases to a needy, desperate throbbing. "You'll come to dinner? You accept my terms?"

I can only nod. Words aren't in the cards right now.

He moves me gently to the side, then opens my car door for me. "In that case, sweetheart, I'll pick you up at eight."

Chapter Five

WHEN I GET HOME, there's a package from Blake on my door-mat. I have no idea how he got my address, but I'm running late, and I don't have time to give it much thought.

My apartment is tiny, but the price is right, and it's near the beach. And as far as I'm concerned, the only valid reasons to live in LA are to work in the entertainment business or to live by a beach.

I've turned my back on Hollywood, but I'm still in love with the ocean.

I strip off my clothes as I head to the birdcage-sized bathroom that features a shower so small I have to perform yoga to shave my legs, underarms, and other parts that I hope will get attention during the evening.

Once I'm out, I finger-comb my hair, letting it air dry while I do my makeup. My hair's my best feature—strawberry blond and wavy, and it complements the blue of my eyes.

I have a slim, athletic body, and I debate whether or not to own it and wear a silk tank with pencil slacks and heels, or if I should wear a low cut dress and enhance it with a padded bra and silicon inserts.

I'm still debating the point—dresses are sexier, but the effect can be lost if the guy gropes the fake boob—when I remember the package. I hurry to the futon where I'd left it, then untie the bow. The box opens easily, revealing another with a label from La Perla. I suck in air, then pull out the delicate bra and panty set.

Underneath that box is another bundle that turns out to be a turquoise wrap dress in the kind of soft, silky material that makes a woman feel luxurious.

A note is pinned to the dress:

Wear these. And heels, red if you have them.
Soon.
B

I smile, a little giddy. Blake knocked me off kilter today. His distance. That hard, unreadable look in his eyes. But considering the lingerie and the dress, I think it's safe to say that the night is looking very promising indeed.

I'm still debating which shoes to wear when he rings the bell. I don't have red, so my options are strappy black sandals or deep burgundy fuck-me pumps with heels so high a stripper would consider them impractical.

Naturally, I shove my feet into those, then try to hurry to the door. I fail, of course—I can't exactly sprint in these shoes—but the effect is that I seem casually in control. No need to rush. No hurry here.

I tell myself to own this calm and collected vibe, then open the door.

Immediately calm and collected is beaten down by hot and bothered. Did I say delicious earlier? That's woefully inadequate. He's wearing black jeans that hug muscular thighs, an untucked white tee with a V-neck that reveals a smattering of chest hair and a tailored suit jacket. His hair is slicked back, giving him a sexy movie star look, while his five o'clock shadow adds some bad boy appeal.

In other words, he's a walking, talking fantasy, and he's standing in my doorway looking like he wants to eat me alive, and all I can think is please, yes, please.

"You look great," I say, voicing the understatement of the year.

He says nothing, but he meets my eyes. Then his gaze dips lower and lower, leaving a potent trail of heat along my sensitive skin, as if his gaze is a physical touch, sliding in between the layers of this flimsy dress and making me wet.

He reaches the juncture of my thighs, and the sensation of

being examined with such erotic precision is enough to make my core clench and my breath release in a low, needy moan.

His inspection doesn't slow, but his lips curve just enough that I'm certain he's noticed my reaction. More, it excites him.

Finally, his eyes linger on my shoes. And when he very slowly lifts his head to meet my eyes again, I see both approval and desire. "Are you ready?" he asks, and I manage a nod.

Right then, I'm ready for anything.

Chapter Six

THE RESTAURANT IS THE kind where celebrities tend to gather. High end and trendy, where everyone watches everyone else, but pretends like they aren't looking.

I feel the eyes on us as we walk to the kind of booth that has a bench on one side and a table on the other. Blake guides me onto the bench, then slides in next to me. His hand rests gently on my thigh, and the touch discombobulates me so much that I miss the waiter's question.

"The lady will have a martini," Blake says. "Hendricks gin. Very dry. Extra olives. I'll take the same."

I glance at him, touched that he'd remembered my drink for all these months.

"I told you," he says answering my unspoken thought, "I remember everything." His fingers start to inch the soft material of my skirt up my leg. "Especially the feel of your skin," he murmurs. "The softness of it. The smooth sensuality."

I fight a whimper as his hand slides infinitesimally higher. "Please," I say, but I have no idea what it is I'm pleading for.

"I also remember how wet you get." His finger burns a red-hot path along my skin. "How sweet you taste."

He's reached the edge of my panties now, and I squirm, wanting him to continue yet desperate for him to stop.

"Hands on the table, baby. Close your eyes. I'm going to make you come."

His words ricochet through me, and my core clenches. I want release. I want to spin out of control. But not here. Not with all these people.

"Mine, baby," he presses. "That was the deal."

"No," I whisper, pulling my thighs together, trying to quell the ache. "Someone will see."

"Let them." He brushes a kiss over my ear, making me shiver. "They'll never know for sure."

Even with my legs so together, his fingertip finds my clit. I swallow a gasp, lost in the fire of sensation. The truth is, I do want to slide down deep into passion. I want his touch, his power. I want him to take me over the edge right here, right now. A secret that only we share, and the fact that we're in public makes it that much more exciting.

But not like this. Not like a reproach. Like a goddamn challenge.

I slide to the far side of the bench, trying to escape both Blake and my own traitorous desire.

"Is this what you're after?" My words, though harsh, are pitched low. "To break me? To make me lose control in the middle of a goddamn restaurant? Is that what you want?"

I expect him to deny it. To say nice words about the attraction between us. About wanting to touch me, needing to feel me.

Instead, he simply says, "Yes."

"You son of a bitch." I start to leave the booth. "Fuck that, and fuck you."

He grabs my arm. "Wait. Penny, I'm sorry. Please, just wait."

I hesitate. The truth is, I want what he is offering. Just not the way he's offering it.

"I'm listening."

He drags his fingers through his hair. "I was so goddamn frustrated when you walked away after Chicago. I'd played it all out in my head—the week in Hawaii, everything that came after. And then suddenly that dream—that possibility—was ripped out from under me."

"I—"

"Let me finish. I was pissed. Partly at myself for falling hard and fast. But mostly at you, for making me believe that something I knew in my gut was real, was just smoke and mirrors."

Tears prick my eyes. "But how could I know it was real that fast? How could you?"

"At first, I didn't. I thought I was a damned idiot. I missed you so much it was like a physical ache, but how could I miss something I never really had? Like you said, it was fast. Just one night. But the longing lingered, and I realized that it wasn't a question of time, but of quality. And we'd shared more—loved more—in those twenty hours than I ever had before."

I nod, my heart twisting in my chest. I understand completely. Hadn't I felt exactly the same from the moment I walked away?

He rubs a hand over his forehead. "So that's it," he says. "That's my apology. And yes, part of me wanted to punish, because when you walked away, you shattered something inside of me. But more than that, I want to know that even if it was just for a fleeting moment, once upon a time you were really, truly mine."

I am. I want to scream the words, but I can't. Not yet.

"Did you come to the office expecting to see me?"

He shakes his head. "No. I assumed you were still living in Los Angeles, but I didn't know where you were working." His mouth quirks up. "I almost looked you up, but I didn't want to see if you were in a relationship with somebody. Easier to just not know."

"I'm not," I whisper. "I haven't been."

He holds my eyes. "Me, neither."

For a moment, we just look at each other, but then I have to look away, overwhelmed by the pressure building inside me. I take a sip of water, but it does little to cool the heat that is now flooding through me.

"You didn't seem surprised to see me," I say, because right now talking seems safe.

"I was. I just excel at hiding my feelings. It's a useful skill in my business. Gives me the advantage in negotiations."

"Oh. Are we negotiating?"

He chuckles. "We already did. That's why you agreed to my terms."

"Because of your amazing business skills?"

"That," he says. "And because you want me as much as I want you."

"Blake—"

He shakes his head, silencing me. "I wanted tonight to color in the black and white lines of my memory. I wanted to have it so I could hold onto it and know—even if you would never admit it out loud—that whether or not you're with me, you still belong to me."

I swallow, his words touching my soul.

He smiles thinly, then lifts his hand to wipe away the words as he visibly gathers himself. "At any rate, that's what I was thinking." He sighs. "I'm sorry I came off as an ass." He starts to slide out of the booth. "Come on. I'll take you to your apartment."

"No," I blurt, the word forced out by that pressure in my chest. "I want to stay."

He tilts his head to one side, studying me. "Do you?" I hear the interest—and the hope—in his voice. "Why?"

"Because I hear the food is excellent." I lick my lips, then look hard at him. "But I understand the service is even better."

Chapter Seven

HE'S DRIVING ME ABSOLUTELY crazy.

His fingers have slipped under those expensive, delicate panties and are stroking and teasing me. His other hand is on the tabletop holding mine, as I squeeze tight, trying desperately not to react as I contemplate the martini glasses and smile at passing waiters and pretend as though Blake and I doing nothing more interesting than chatting.

In reality, I'm wet and lost and completely turned on. It's all I can do not to gyrate my hips in an effort to guide his movements. To get a little more pressure, a little more friction.

I'm more aroused than I can ever remember being, and the fact that I'm doing this in public only adds to the excitement. But that's only because of Blake. Because I know he won't push too far. Won't let either one of us turn an intimate moment into a spectacle by crying out or otherwise calling attention to ourselves.

And just when I think I'm going to finally explode, he pulls his hand free, leaving me to groan and whisper, "Dammit, Blake, *please.*"

He chuckles. "Not here, baby. My hotel. And when we get there, I'm going to fuck you so hard. I'm going to claim every inch of you, fully and completely. You think you want to come now? That's nothing. I'm going to make you come over and over until you beg me to stop. And then I'm going to take you there all over again."

I'm practically panting from his words, my sex throbbing, my nipples tight and hard. I take a sip of water, because my mouth is too dry to speak.

And then I do the only thing that makes sense. I raise my hand and signal the waiter to bring us our check.

Chapter Eight

I'M NAKED; MY WRISTS bound above my head with a luggage strap and Blake's hands on my hips holding me firmly in place as he performs a symphony on my body with his lips and tongue.

First, he teases my breasts, the tip of his tongue flicking over my nipples, one after the other before trailing kisses all the way to my belly button. He's leaving a column of fire, and though I try to squirm, he holds me fast.

With excruciating slowness, he maneuvers even lower, tracing the rim of my pubic bone with his tongue and then kissing along the soft skin at the juncture of each thigh. I tremble with each tiny sensation, longing for more, and at the same time not wanting this sweet torture to end.

Finally, slowly, his tongue laves my clit, and shockwaves rip through me, the precursors to what I know will be a blinding orgasm.

Not soon, though. Blake is taking his time. And only when I am balancing on the knife-edge for what must be the hundredth time does he finally push, releasing me to explode into a million pieces.

All the while he's holding me firm, unable to escape the onslaught of his attention. I can't shift. Can't lessen the sensation. And when I explode from the force of orgasm after orgasm, I have no choice but to be battered by a pleasure so profound it crosses the line to pain.

"Please," I beg as soon as my mind returns to my body. I'm limp and sated, but still I want more. I want him. "Please fuck me."

He doesn't disappoint, and when he thrusts inside me, every part of me is already so primed that when he climaxes, he takes me with him and I shatter once more, this time with his eyes on mine, and we get lost in the storm together.

After, he pulls me close, and I sigh, contented. I shut my eyes, just for a moment, only to find the sun streaming in when I open them again.

I sit up, confused, and then angry when I realize that we'd drifted off. We have so little time before he leaves, and I hate that we've wasted even a moment.

Beside me, Blake wakes, and I see the same realization play over his face. He tamps down the disappointment, then smiles at me. "I've missed you so much," he admits as he pushes himself up to lean against the headboard. "Please tell me it's not one-sided."

I sigh and scoot next to him. "There hasn't been a minute since I left that I haven't regretted not going with you to Hawaii after we finally landed in LA."

"But you had your audition, your five-year plan. You're working for Stark now, so I'm guessing you didn't get the pilot?"

"I got it. We shot three episodes, and I think it was some of my best work."

"Then ... what?"

"They shelved it." I say flatly. "And I quit the next day. I didn't bother waiting for my twenty-sixth birthday. There was no point. I realized I'd never be able to control anything so long as I stayed in acting. Too much of it was out of my hands and it made me crazy." I shrug. "Honestly, I don't miss it."

What I don't tell him is that the best moment of my life— meeting him—had also been unplanned and out of my control. I know it; I'm still not quite ready to face it.

"Anyway, I got the job at Stark International, partly because of their employee education program. I'm working toward my business degree."

"Do you enjoy it?"

"At first, I wasn't sure. I thought it might be an interim job while I figured out what I wanted. But I love it. And the odds are good I'll get a permanent job as a project manager once I graduate. In the meantime, I'm learning a ton."

I shrug again. "So that's me. Nothing earth-shattering. Not like you." I face him more directly. "You've been busy. Two major centers going up on opposite sides of the country. That's impressive."

"You've been keeping tabs on me."

My skin flushes. "Maybe."

"I like that." He draws his finger along my naked arm, making me shiver. "I like it a lot." He takes my hand, presses it to his mouth. "The world shifted for me when I saw you in Stark's office, Penny. I told you once we can't fight reality." He holds up his tattooed wrist. "We're meant to be together. As far as I'm concerned, that's a basic, core truth. I knew it the moment I met you, and I've only grown more sure with time."

I turn away, scared by how right his words feel. "Blake …"

The room phone rings, and he grabs it. I draw a breath, relieved by the interruption.

"Thank you," he says, then hangs up the phone with a scowl. "My car is here. Dammit, they were supposed to text a fifteen-minute warning." He glances at his cell, then looks at me. "Well, shit. I forgot to charge it. I was a little distracted last night."

I manage to wobbly smile. I know he has to rush to meet his plane, but I'm regretting the loss of those fifteen minutes.

"Why don't you come with me?" he asks once his duffel is packed and slung over his shoulder. "We can have the week we didn't take in Hawaii in New York. I'll take you to the opera, a bawdy Off-Broadway play. I'll make love to you on my balcony, and buy you a glass of wine at this little café near Columbus Circle."

Immediately my chest tightens. "Are you serious?"

"Baby, don't you see that I love you?"

"No—" I shake my head, my heart thudding in my chest. "You can't say that. Not yet. It's too fast."

This is what I was afraid of that first time. The impetuousness of going off book and running away with a stranger to Hawaii. The fear now that if I say I love you, I'm tempting the gods.

Love at first sight means that control is out of the equation. It means giving in to pure emotion. But how can that be real? God knows it was never real for my mom.

"Pen?"

"I can't." My voice is choked, and I realize that I'm crying. "I'm so sorry, but I can't."

For a moment I think he's going to argue. To try to convince me that, yes, of course, I can. But he nods sadly, then bends to kiss me. "All right," he says. "You know where Manhattan is if you change your mind." He cups my cheek. "Penny," he whispers. "I won't say I'm in love with you. Not if it scares you. But I will say that I could easily fall in love with you. And I think you could fall in love with me. Give us a chance, baby. Change your mind and come to New York."

And then he's gone, and I'm left standing in an empty hotel room, feeling more lonely than I ever have in my life.

I sit on the edge of the bed and let the tears flow, mourning the loss. Because the truth is, I want him here. I want him beside me whether it's in New York or here. It doesn't matter.

I just want Blake, now, and forever.

Forever?

For a moment that thought, so new and shiny, makes me freeze.

What's more, it doesn't terrify me.

I stand, my mind churning.

I'm thinking I want this to work. I'm thinking I need to try.

I'm thinking I need to call Human Resources.

Mostly, I'm thinking that I need to get my ass to the airport, and fast.

Chapter Nine

I'M GASPING AND OUT of breath when I finally reach the gate. The moment I'd arrived at the airport, I'd bought a coach ticket on the only United flight to New York that was scheduled to take off around noon. Now, I'm clutching the boarding pass tight in my hand. Everyone is staring at me, but I don't care. There's only one face I care about, and I don't see it. Dammit, I don't see him anywhere.

I turn a circle, surveying the crowd, but he's not there, and a well of panic swells inside me. He hadn't told me the airline; I'm only assuming it was United because that's what we flew when we got waylaid in Chicago. But what if he's on American? Or any of a zillion other airlines. For that matter, what if he's on a private jet? Or he's flying out of Burbank and he's not even in this airport?

I reach into my purse for my cellphone. I already texted twice from the taxi and got no response. Maybe he still hasn't charged his phone. Maybe he's ignoring me. I don't know, but I have to try.

I'm about to type out another groveling, plea for forgiveness, when I see him stepping out of a coffee shop across the corridor.

He hesitates, then looks right at me and starts walking toward me, as if I were emitting a homing beacon that only he can hear.

I see hope flash across his face before it's replaced by a neutral expression colored only by a hint of curiosity.

"Come to see me off?"

I shake my head, and for a moment, I can't seem to make my voice work. Instead, I thrust my boarding pass into his hand. He looks at it, and when he looks up, the hope has returned, along with a kind of boisterous joy that makes me feel light inside.

"What changed your mind?"

"I was scared," I admit. "Of change. Of taking a risk. Of everything." I draw a breath. "But then I remembered that it was you. And I know in my heart that you've got my back. I think I've know that from the first moment I grabbed your hand on that plane, and you held on." I smile, tears pooling in my eyes as I lift a shoulder in a shrug. "You take my fear away, Blake. You always have."

His smile is wide, boyish, and deliciously sexy. I smile too, then burst into laughter when he pulls me close, finally silencing me with a Hollywood-happy-ending kiss. Deep and melting, where the guy bends the girl back so far they are both defying gravity, both trusting the other not to fall.

We break apart, gasping and grinning, and he pulls me upright as all around us travelers start to applaud. My cheeks heat, but I grin, then take a little bow as Blake laughs beside me.

"What about your job?"

"I took a week's vacation."

I think I see disappointment flash in his eyes, but all he says is, "You'll stay with me."

"At least until I can find my own place," I say, then break into a broad smile. "I'm moving to New York, Blake."

"Oh, baby," he says, pulling me into his arms and holding me tight.

"And I'm going without a plan, totally out of control, and it feels great."

I don't mention that I have a couple of cushions—my job, for one, because the odds are good I can transfer to the New York office. And, of course, Blake himself is the biggest cushion of all.

I can see forever with him, I'm sure of it. But I'm not going to say that out loud. Not yet. For once in my life, I'm going to go with the current, without planning five steps ahead.

I'm going to trust what I feel, and I'm going to believe that what Blake and I have is real and forever.

Even so, for at least a little while, I'm staying in my own place. Once I find a place, anyway. Because Blake and I did everything backward. I want the dating, the nights spent at each other's apartments, the mornings meeting at a mutually convenient café.

I want all that first.

And then, yes, I want forever.

The first boarding call for our flight echoes through the terminal, and he glances at my ticket. "Coach?" he says.

"All I could get," I admit. "For that matter, all I could afford." My first-class ticket to LA had been a gift from my agent. "Smuggle a cookie to me, okay?"

"For you, anything. Although I think I can do better than that." He leaves me befuddled, then heads to the gate agent. I watch their negotiation, see the exchange of paper and my stomach leaps as I become more and more certain that he's negotiating a first-class seat for me.

Two minutes later, he's back.

"First class was full," he says. "Sorry."

"Oh." I never realized how physical an emotion disappointment is. I'm heavy from the weight of it. "That's okay. I've got a book. I'll be fine."

"So I traded my ticket with the lady who had the seat next to you."

I gape at him. "You downgraded? You're moving your seat from first class to coach?"

"Considering the company, I didn't consider it downward mobility at all."

"Wow," I tease, my grin wide with happiness. "This might be love." Only after I've said the words do I realize I've broken my own rule. My cheeks heat, and I start to call them back.

But I don't get the chance.

"Sweetheart," he says, with his eyes on me and his voice heavy with meaning. "I think it just might be."

A former attorney, J. Kenner (aka Julie Kenner) is the *New York Times, USA Today, Publishers Weekly, Wall Street Journal*, and number one international best-selling author of over seventy novels, novellas, and short stories in a variety of genres. A five-time RITA finalist, JK won the first RITA given in the category of erotic romance with her novel *Claim Me*, book two of her Stark trilogy.

Visit her website at http://www.jkenner.com to learn more and to connect with JK through social media!

THE JILT

Sharon Sobel

September 8, 1805

NOTHING CAN MATCH THE beauty of a late summer wedding, when the salt air carries the warmth of the sun-heated sea over the cooling landscape, holding off the inevitable darker days to follow. Everyone gathered in the ancient church at Cloverhill agreed this was so, though the lovely bride was scarcely more than a child, and more likely to be compared to the early buds of spring than the fading leaves of September. And yet, at sixteen, she had known her charming groom half her life, and the families had long hoped they would marry someday, for so well matched were they in temperament and intellectual pursuits and their passion for the marvels of the natural world.

"I am sure his horse threw a shoe, or something of that sort," whispered Mrs. Wharton, attempting to calm the bride and her younger sisters.

"Mother, Edward would then rely on his own shoes and walk from the peninsula," said Katharine. "It must be something else, for he is impossibly reliable."

She gazed upon the small bouquet she'd gathered that morning, confident in her groom. Edward was unfailingly steady, trustworthy, and strong. The bond between them was not created by lightning, but by a slow-building fire that grew in warmth and intensity over many years.

Nestled between the flowers were small fossil shells. Though the lilies would wilt by evening, the shells, ancient and enduring, would last forever.

She believed the same was true for their love.

"The guests are restless," said Mr. Wharton, emerging from the church. "Edward's family is not here either."

Katharine fingered one of the shells, a little snail Edward found years ago, telling her such a specimen was common in the far-off Caribbean, a place he might visit one day. He did not know how the little snail shell came to Cloverhill, but he knew where it was now destined. His smile as he said those words had a most extraordinary effect on her, for it felt like all the breath had left her body.

"Are you well, daughter?" her father asked.

Still caressing the shell, she glanced at her father. "There must be a reasonable explanation."

But when the explanation finally came, it seemed anything but reasonable.

As the Wharton family stood close together, circling their expectant bride, Edward's cousin approached them through the graveyard. Dressed in formal attire, as befitted a member of the wedding party, and one who would someday be the Earl of Penfield, he nevertheless looked wretched.

"He is not coming," he said.

"What is the meaning of this?" cried Mrs. Wharton.

"My cousin, Edward Danforth, eloped this very morning with Miss Delphina Rutherford and sends his most pained regrets to Miss Wharton." Denham winced as he handed a slim envelope to Katharine. "He asked me to deliver this note, with his prayer that you can somehow find the generosity in your heart to forgive him."

Mr. Wharton uttered an expletive his daughters never heard

before. And his wife screamed so loudly, congregants immediately rushed to the door of the church. The two little Wharton sisters sobbed.

But Katharine just stood, quite alone, trembling as a sapling in the brisk sea breeze. Her unusual bride's bouquet, representing everything she loved, slipped through her fingers to the slate path, suddenly hateful to her.

And so, as her wedding guests crowded about, wanting answers no one had, Katharine lifted her foot and ground the bouquet into the stone, feeling the shells crack beneath her white satin slippers.

Chapter Two

April 12, 1814

"WHAT IS THE NATURE of forgiveness, in a truly practical sense? We say we can forgive, but is it possible if one can never forget?" Katharine Wharton mused. She studied her three companions, wondering if anyone in Cloverhill still recalled the events of eight years before. Certainly, no one ever spoke of them. Nor did she, though scarcely a day passed without at least a fleeting thought of what might have been, of the joy that would have been hers and Edward's. Their life would have been a grand adventure sustained by their love; they would have had children and a home filled with treasures gathered on their travels. Even now, with hope long gone, the remembrance of that love remained. And because of that, she imagined that she forgave him.

The letter that had been thrust into her hand on the day she was to be married offered no explanations but revealed both frustration and anguish on the part of its writer. She did not know why he chose to leave her for another, but through the years and the losses she knew he endured, she somehow felt his pain as deeply as her own.

Katharine settled in her chair and sipped her tea. It had cooled even as her speech had become heated, but the sweet, strong taste of the brew remained invigorating. Over the rim of the teacup, she studied the faces of her friends, guessing Estella would be the first to speak.

"Act lively, my dears," she urged when no one responded. "Our tea is getting cold, and Mrs. Moon has gone to the village, leaving us to our own devices. Shall I pour you another cup, Estella?"

Estella Lakewood shook her head, perhaps distracted. She might remember. But, just as likely, she was formulating a philosophical argument, for she had the advantage of being educated along with her brothers when she was a child. Unlike Deirdre Clarke, Portia Watson, and Katharine herself, Estella was a true scholar.

But that was precisely the point of their weekly salons in the Octagon House. They each yearned to be scholars and philosophers, the bluestockings whom many of their acquaintances regarded with mild disdain. Estella was invited to join them when they were somewhat unsure of themselves, when they hoped she would raise the level of discourse. But, in fact, they each proved capable of reading, studying, and formulating opinions. Estella stayed on, often relinquishing her authority to the others. And the one who most frequently claimed it was Katharine.

Estella finally met her blue-eyed, questioning gaze.

"Is it possible to live a full life without regrets? Is there a single person who has not done the unforgivable?" Estella asked. "Excepting yourself, Katharine, for everyone knows you are a paragon."

Katharine blushed. "I am not, and I do not believe it is flattering to be thought so. To make an error is to be human."

"Then you have answered your own question," Deirdre pointed out. "If it is in our nature to err, then we must believe in forgiveness as well. If I spill my tea, then I should apologize and expect forgiveness. But if I …"

"Destroy someone's reputation?" Katharine suggested. "Break someone's heart?"

"Indeed," answered Estella. "That is another thing altogether."

No one said anything for several minutes. The April sunshine glimmered on the polished surfaces of their sanctuary. The Octagon House once served as a lighthouse on the Wharton estate, warning sailors of the approaching cliffs, but also leading smugglers to their shore. Katharine lived here now, separate from the rest of her family and free to do as she wished. It was her consolation for disappointed hopes.

"Even so, Estella," argued Portia, "think of the purpose of forgiveness. It is easy to dismiss a damp bit of carpet but magnanimous to dismiss a great indiscretion. To forgive such a thing would be an act of redemption."

Estella laughed. "'Tis a pity ladies are not permitted in the ministry, for we are quite compassionate."

"I am not certain I should be ranked among you," said Katharine, "for my thoughts on the subject are anything but noble."

She regretted bringing up the matter, for the Octagon Salon was intended to make her forget sadness, not revive the past. And yet she could never seem to avoid it, for her disappointment always remained on the edges of memory.

"I suspect such forgiveness might only lead to more pain," she said softly.

"But what if it leads to joy?" Deirdre asked. "Is that not possible?"

Katharine looked at her cold tea. "I would not know," she said at last, cursing herself for a lovelorn fool.

Chapter Three

SOME TIME LATER, KATHARINE leaned against the solid stone wall of the Octagon House, shutting her eyes as she lifted her face to the waning, afternoon sun. While her guests nurtured her intellect and her soul, the strange and ancient building was truly her source of strength. She sought refuge here eight years before, deciding to cut herself off from gossip and speculation and the cruel rumors she was somehow unfit to be Edward Danforth's wife. In truth, she wondered about it herself, for his defection was so sudden and so unexpected. Her mother, worried about the effect a jilted daughter would have on the marriage prospects for her younger sisters, seemed perfectly happy to have Katharine live close but apart from them, with several servants, on the edge of their estate. Joining the family for dinners and social events as she chose, Katharine did not quite live the life of a hermit, but remained as reclusive as she desired.

It was not a pitiable existence. In fact, Katharine quite enjoyed it.

By the time she was seventeen, she had read about the fashionable ladies' salons on the Continent and then sampled the goods on an extended journey to Italy. Choosing ladies with whom she would most enjoy conversation, she invited them to her own salon at the Octagon House, and the result was admirable. Distanced from the scope of London society, they were able to talk about the things that really mattered, and not just tiresome gossip about men and marriage.

"If you continue to stare at the sun, Miss Katharine, you'll go as blind as old Mrs. Rutherford's cat," said Mrs. Moon.

"I am sensible enough not to stare at the sun," said Katharine irritably, blinking. "And did Mrs. Rutherford not die in January? Not that I am interested in that family."

"Nor should you be," Mrs. Moon said sagely, "but that Elspeth Rutherford was a neighbor and had her hands full raising Delphina. She was a wild thing, poor girl."

Katharine frowned. "Do you think her poor because she died so young or because she did not live to become a countess? Surely, not even she could have guessed her husband would have ascended to the title, for he was far enough down the line."

"I think her poor because she was incapable of happiness and resented joy in others."

"That is rather pithy, Mrs. Moon. Perhaps you would like to join our Octagon Salon?"

"Hush," said Mrs. Moon. "I have other kettles of fish to fry."

"Like sharing gossip in town?"

"Perhaps," Mrs. Moon said slyly and narrowed her eyes. "I shall never forgive what Edward Danforth did to you; please do not doubt it. But I am not above hearing news of him."

"What have you heard?" asked Katharine, too quickly.

"Why, he is to return to Cloverhill in the next week. Mrs. Rutherford's cottage now belongs to his daughter, and he comes to inspect the child's inheritance."

Katharine felt physically ill, knowing she might face him again. It was foolish and cowardly of her, for eight long and painful years had passed. Her friends had done much to disabuse her of any embarrassment. She was no longer a girl and now lived a fruitful, stimulating life.

And yet, there it was.

"He is an earl now, and the Rutherford cottage would scarcely do service to his stable boy. He will have a look and be gone again before the dust is off his boots. I am sure we will not meet again, and we would not recognize each other if we did." Katharine again leaned against the stone wall, drawing strength from its heat and the very fact that it was hers alone, and Edward could not breach her sanctuary.

But, of course, he probably had no desire to breach her sanctuary or anything else.

"Of course you would recognize him, Miss." Mrs. Moon drew in a deep breath. "It is not for me to know what went on between you, but a love such as yours leaves an imprint on memory. You would know him the minute he walks into a room."

Katharine had no idea what wellspring of experience her housekeeper drew upon, but the thought was unsettling.

"You know a great deal on the subject," she said.

"There are some things we know not by experience but by good sense," Mrs. Moon said, thoughtfully. "Nor do I know about the nature of love by reading a book. I know it by reading you."

Chapter Four

EDWARD DANFORTH, THE EARL of Penfield, felt as if he'd never left the seaside community to which he now returned. The houses remained surrounded by sweet-smelling gardens, and the sea air, blowing briskly over Cloverhill's rocky peninsula, still brought with it the scent of adventure and excitement.

Here was where he spent his boyhood and where he became a man, in the long summer seasons during which his invalid mother sought a cure in the salty waters, and his father leased a modest estate for them. It was paradise to a young boy, who learned to swim alongside his older brother and fish with the local sailors.

But there were other distractions, which gradually became more interesting than fish. The community welcomed his family to Cloverdale, and while the ladies sat in the shade engaged in needlework and conversation, and the men gathered to enjoy a few games of cards, the children were often sent off to entertain themselves.

Edward was not sure when he realized Katharine Wharton was no longer a pesky little girl who showed him fossils she found along the shore and had become a beautiful woman. But it might have been the day he looked up from the pages of a book and noticed her eyes were the same color as the sea and her hair had loosened from its plaits. She returned his interested gaze and said he ought to close his mouth or a bird would fly in.

Instead, he leaned across the table and kissed her on her lips.

Their lives would always have been an adventure, through every joy and sorrow. This was nearly theirs, but for his own stupidity. He, who had already considered himself worldly and mature at twenty, acted impulsively, without a grain of good sense.

He hesitated a moment, thinking he'd walked too far, and then recognized the weathered cottage where Delphina once lived with her aunt. He had only entered it once, but what he did within changed his destiny. Now it was shuttered and the garden over-grown with wild roses, a trifling inheritance for the daughter of an earl.

He heard the white cat before he saw it and recalled there were always small creatures about the house. Perhaps the others ran off when the old lady died or were brought to new homes. When the cat raised her face and sniffed, he saw she was blind. And so perhaps she stayed where she was safe and, apparently, well fed.

Edward knew what it was to be blind, or, at least, unable to see what was apparent to others. He paid a bitter price for that and, even worse, made others suffer as well.

But he was back in Cloverhill, and the house was his. And he supposed the cat was his as well.

He sat on the stone wall, and the cat promptly jumped onto his lap, possibly the only resident of Cloverhill happy to greet him.

But he reminded himself that he was here for Pearl. And she was all that mattered.

Chapter Five

THE TUESDAY MEETING OF the Octagon Salon was not at all successful, having more the lethargic spirit of a summer afternoon than a fresh spring day. Deirdre seemed most concerned with her costume for an upcoming ball, and Estella hardly spoke at all. Portia and Katharine reflected briefly on the cool weather. In less than an hour's time, Deirdre ended their misery by announcing that she had some errands to accomplish, and Portia and Estella followed her down the steps.

Katharine thumbed some pages until her reverie was interrupted by the sound of footsteps. She looked around the room, wondering who had forgotten what.

"Miss Katharine," Mrs. Moon said breathlessly. "You have a visitor."

Edward Danforth stepped into the room, behind her.

She did not faint. Nor did she cry out or sob or throw something. She did not do any of the things she long imagined, including commenting on how the years had not been kind to him.

In fact, they had been very kind.

He had changed in eight years, but he was even more handsome and certainly more distinguished. The somewhat gangly boy she remembered, possessed of raw strength, had matured into a man to be reckoned with. But there was sadness in his eyes, a loss of exuberance in his manners.

"Katharine."

She ignored the catch in his voice, and did not answer at once.

"My lord," she said, ignoring his familiarity. "Welcome back to Cloverhill. But you must excuse me, for I am about to go out for the afternoon."

"Then may I join you on your outing, unless a gentleman is not welcome to do that?"

He sounded like the Edward she once knew, happy to follow her about, knowing she enjoyed his company. But he presumed too much.

"Not unless he wants to be a pest," she retorted. Mrs. Moon gasped.

But Edward smiled. "I should enjoy that very much,"

He followed her down the stairs and out the door. Katharine started toward town but thought better of it, realizing the rumor mill would be thrumming with the news of their reunion. Instead, she turned toward the steps to the beach, where no one but the gulls would see them.

As they walked along in silence, only once did she toy with the idea of pushing him over the cliff. Soon they were on the stone steps, carved into the chalky bedrock centuries ago, and now weathered by wind and rain. Katharine was a woman of many talents, but even she could not descend and think about Edward at the same time; it was too arduous a task.

The tide was out, leaving shells and debris in its wake. Jellyfish dried in the sun, and gulls scooped up fish and crabs, a decent meal for people or birds. Katharine found a few tarnished coins and the bleached jawbone of a fairly large fish.

"I see not much has changed in all these years," Edward said.

Her back stiffened as she reluctantly turned to face him. "You are mistaken, my lord. It is quite the opposite, for everything has changed for me. I am no longer someone you know, and I certainly do not wish to know you."

"Kitty ..." he began, and reached for her arm.

She pulled away.

"That child no longer exists. She abandoned that sweet name along with her naïve expectations." Katharine paused, waiting for an apology that did not come. "I am Miss Katharine Wharton now. It is not so stunning a transformation as to find oneself a peer, but it does reflect a certain amount of advancement."

"Miss Wharton," he said, bowing formally. "It is a pleasure to meet you, though I shall miss the Kitty who used to find fossils with me."

It was finally too much. The sluice gates opened with a torrent of words.

"You would not have missed her at all, if you behaved with any notion of honor on the day you were to marry her. You could have had baskets of fossils. Now, she can think of nothing that would give her more pleasure than to fling them at your head."

"I suppose I deserve that," he said.

"And you certainly could not have expected anything more, showing up in Cloverhill as if all could be forgotten," she retorted. "I somehow imagined I was prepared to forgive, but I am no longer certain of it."

"Is it not possible?"

Katherine was so angry, she could not articulate the words that came immediately to mind. Instead, she turned and walked away.

He deserved it. She could cut him up in small pieces and feed him to the gulls, and most people would think justice had been served. Why did he think he could return and expect any sort of forgiveness, let alone the possibility of winning her heart once more?

He watched her march up the beach, losing traction in the sand. But she held herself with much dignity, like a duchess. Or, perhaps, a countess. She would have been his countess.

But she deserved better. He had taken her heart and trampled it, believing himself obliged to another. He was only twenty when he'd run off with Delphina, a woman of wiles and a good deal more experience, but he still should have known better. He had been a fool and ruined two lives in the process.

But he would not leave Cloverhill until he explained himself, and the trap into which he fell eight years before. Only then could he have release and get on with the rest of his life. But perhaps Katharine would walk with him.

He could not let her go, not again.

He ran up the strand, the wind in his face, the sand shifting beneath his feet. Even though she had a lead, he was bigger and faster. "Katharine, please wait," he shouted, as he gained ground.

"I will never again wait for you, Edward."

"Please let me explain," he said, grasping her arm. He moved his fingers over the fabric of her dress and felt the delicate musculature beneath. The warmth of her skin sent a spark of keen awareness through his body, and he felt like a boy again, aching to kiss a beautiful woman for the first time.

"I … I can't let you go," he said hoarsely. The deprivation he had brought to them both was bad enough to reflect upon through the years, but devastating when confronting her in the flesh.

She pulled from him again.

"You already have let me go. There is no going back to what we were, my lord. Once something is done, there are no second chances."

She, who once danced on the sand and splashed him in the sea, was now a sensible woman with a mature wisdom. He did that to her.

"Of course there are second chances, Miss Wharton. If one gets onto a horse and slips off, one immediately gets on and tries again."

"We are not speaking of an accident, my lord, but a willful deed that harms another." She glanced up at the escarpment. "If one pushes another off the cliff, it is no accident, and punishment is merited."

"I have been punished," he said. "Not only in the choices I made, but in the tragic losses of several who were dear to me."

"That is certainly not my affair," she said, and turned from him, blinking into the salty spray off the sea.

This time, he did indeed let her go.

Chapter Six

THE OCTAGON LADIES PERSUADED Katharine that nothing would revive her spirits as much as attending the ball at Fairfields. Mrs. Wharton agreed and sent a lady's maid to the Octagon House, several ornate hair combs, and a parcel of dinner gowns from her sisters' closets.

While making a great show of resisting such attempts to bring her back into society, Katharine had to admit she rather enjoyed herself—and didn't look half bad. Indeed, she looked splendid in a gold gown overlaid with green sarsenet that set off the sun-touched tone of her skin.

"I should think a gold necklace would be quite the thing, miss," said the maid.

"So they might be, Nell. But I own but one necklace, and pearls will have to do for me."

"Oh, but pearls are splendid for …" the maid broke off when Katharine reached into a box. "But what is that?"

"That," said Katherine, "is a shell. I had it added to the strand when the pearls were restrung. It is a little talisman, a reminder of a happiness that once was mine."

Nell frowned. "I don't know about wearing shells, Miss."

"But I do. And what is a pearl but a fortunate gift from an unwitting little oyster? This little shell served a useful purpose, as it shall again this evening." Katharine caressed it thoughtfully as Nell secured the clasp.

"You seem distracted, Lord Penfield," said a pretty young woman.

"I apologize, Miss Watson. I am overly curious to see those I might recognize. Lady DuChamp seems to have invited everyone in the county to her ball."

"And you are now among our number," said Miss Watson. "I understand you have taken Bellevue."

Edward's attention returned to the lady at his side. "I have only made the arrangements this afternoon, Miss Watson. Is the news already about?"

"Of course. Do not doubt it." She smiled.

He should not, for this was a taste of what his life would be like in Cloverhill. He had given society much to digest over eight years, and once his daughter arrived he would be serving a veritable feast.

"Bellevue is lovely, though not very grand," she said, sounding disappointed.

"But then, I am not a very grand earl. It should suit me well. I shall only bring a few servants with me, who shall be sufficient for my daughter and myself."

"Your daughter? How charming."

"My daughter is a young lady of eight, as beautiful and willful as are most girls who are born with every advantage." Pearl was indeed that, and more. Whatever the circumstances of her birth, he was a besotted father. "I am bringing her to Cloverhill to play in the waves and to see the cottage that is now hers."

And then he saw Katharine enter the hall, her skin glowing in the candlelight and altogether too much of it on show.

It would have been so much easier if Edward's muscular frame had turned paunchy or if he had fallen on desperate times, and wore an old threadbare jacket with the sleeves let out. But he had grown into a very fine figure, and clearly was a man with deep pockets, none let out. Nearly every woman in the room gravitated into his sphere, and he managed to charm them all. No doubt, some now saw his defection as romantic, an escape from a youthful bit of puppy love, wildly passionate instead of boring and predictable.

Katharine's friends and family remained loyal to her. She saw Portia chat briefly with Edward and stare into his eyes, but guessed that was in service to finding out information. It was not long before her supposition was substantiated, for she soon heard the full report.

"I hope you are not engaged for the next dance?" asked Edward, suddenly appearing before her.

"I have no intention of dancing," she answered succinctly.

"Not to dance at a ball? Or not to dance with me?" he persisted. "It is very odd to attend a ball and not partake of the entertainment."

Katharine did not think him the person to take her to task on how to behave in public.

"Lord Penfield, it is not so much that I do not wish to partake of the entertainment. I simply do not wish to be the entertainment."

In an instant, his hand was on her arm, igniting a flame through her body that might have seared his flesh. She looked into his eyes, knowing he felt it and wanted it.

"The music begins, Miss Wharton. Please save me the awkwardness of finding another partner."

"You were not so ..." she began, and stopped. She knew perfectly well what she should say. He was not so concerned about her finding another partner eight years ago, when he left her standing at Cloverhill Church with her bouquet of flowers and shells. But somehow, the words mattered little now. He was not a stupid man, and knew perfectly well how he had harmed her.

"I was not so good a dancer, you were about to say?" he finished the sentence for her in his own way. Then he laughed out loud, guaranteeing they now had the attention of everyone in the room. Katharine was so warm she thought she'd burst into flames. "I was a dreadful dancer and must have trod on your poor toes until they bled. But you will find I am much improved."

He had. But then, so had she, for on those occasions when she chose to attend an assembly or a private ball, she had not wanted for partners.

"We are allowed to speak while dancing, I daresay," he murmured circling around her. "Your necklace reminds me that you were always fond of gifts from the sea."

"I have little to say to you," she said. But, in fact, she did. She wanted to know why he left her to start a life with another woman. She wanted to know if he had regrets. She wished to console him over the loss of his cousin and older brother. Indeed, she had a hundred things to say to him, including asking why he imagined he could suddenly reappear and act as if nothing had happened in eight long years. And because he did, she had a great desire to preserve some fragment of her own dignity and hold him in abeyance.

"A pity," he said, certainly unaware of her warring emotions. "For I shall be your neighbor through the summer. I only signed the papers to lease Bellevue this afternoon, but I am sure the news has already made its way to France. Or Eastbourne, at the very least."

And then, as light and lovely as the sun rising over a still sea, Katharine's sudden laughter filled his heart with hope.

Chapter Seven

IT WAS A START. Edward walked around the crumbling folly at Bellevue, pausing to admire the view of the vast sea. He might be a fool to return to Cloverhill and thus subject his daughter to speculation and disparaging comments. But he had a great desire to move on with his life, and hers, and dared to imagine their future entwined with Katharine's.

She had changed, and he admired her even more as a woman of twenty-four than as a girl of sixteen. Her promise of beauty had blossomed, and her inquisitiveness developed into a quick wit and intelligence. He guessed the society at the Octagon House did much to further her education, and he might learn a few things there.

But he ran ahead of himself, for she offered him nothing. And yet she danced with him and allowed him to hold her. She wore the little shell she once promised to carry in her bridal bouquet. He made her laugh.

And she had not married in all these years, though she might have had a long line of suitors circling the Octagon House. If she had, or even if the line had been short, she had accepted no one else.

"Lord Penfield is here," Mrs. Moon said, raising an eyebrow. "Again."

Katharine put aside her pen and scowled. "Please tell him I am not receiving this day."

But as she watched Mrs. Moon disappear down the spiral of the staircase, she realized Edward would not leave unless she pushed him out the door herself. So she ran after her housekeeper.

"I am busy today," Katharine said, as soon as she saw him at the bottom of the stairs.

"But I am most impatient to deliver this," he said. He set a package on a large table and pulled off string and paper to reveal an atlas of natural history. Without a word, he reverently opened the book. Mrs. Moon gave an exasperated sigh and left the room, but Katharine moved closer, her curiosity aroused.

"I will not be seduced, Edward," she said softly. "Though I am sorely tempted."

He looked up, smiling, and she was lost. "Then yield to temptation, my dear, and accept it. It is only a book."

It was not only a book.

And so, when his lips sought hers, she yielded completely, abandoning all thoughts of propriety or resentment. She only thought of him, achingly aware of everything about him. Her fingers roamed the landscape of his face, guided by sweet memory. But he was no longer her youthful lover, for he was more demanding and insistent. And she was now a woman and had learned a great deal in conversation at the Octagon Salon. She knew precisely what she wanted.

"I apologize, Katharine," he said, finally pulling away.

"It is only a kiss, Edward," she said hoarsely.

"I do not apologize for a kiss. I apologize for everything, for the great wrong I have done you, for being too cowardly to explain my actions. But I needed to protect someone else, and acted in haste." He paused. "My wife died seven months into our marriage."

"Delphina forced your hand." It was an explanation, if nothing more. Edward would not have had to marry unless he had relations with her while betrothed to another.

Edward pulled himself up, but the strength of the gesture was belied by the shadow that fell across his face.

"I married her willingly, Katharine, even as I left you most unwillingly. I can say no more."

"You have said enough. You loved her in a way you did not love me, for she was worldly, wise. I hope you had much joy with her."

"She was worldly," Edward agreed, as that truly explained it all. In any case, he offered nothing more.

Chapter Eight

SEVERAL WEEKS LATER, THE ladies of the Octagon Salon received invitations to a May Day ball at Bellevue, to be hosted by Edward's mother. As her friends chattered about what they would wear and who would attend, Katharine reflected that she scarcely remembered Mrs. Danforth. Though she had been present all those years ago in Cloverhill, she rarely socialized with anyone but a small circle of friends. That she would now host such an event marked either a change in her own sensibilities or an acceptance of the change in her son's position in society. She, who was not the widow of an earl, was now the mother of one.

"I have not been to Bellevue in many years," Estella mused. "It is an elegant house, if not a very grand one."

"Do you think many friends will arrive from town?" Deirdre asked, and they all looked at Katharine.

"I have no idea what Lord Penfield intends. You seem to know more than I about his business," said Katharine.

"I know his daughter arrived yesterday with his mother. Isabel Anders was walking along the road when their carriage slowed for her. Isabel said the little girl was quite unexpected," said Portia.

"Unexpected?" Katharine asked. "Lord Penfield told everyone he would bring her to Cloverhill. I believe he leased Bellevue for her pleasure."

"I suspect Isabel meant there was something unusual about the child herself," murmured Portia. "She did not offer anything beyond that."

"And, in any case, I rather think Lord Penfield leased Bellevue for his own pleasure," said Estella, while the others giggled.

Katharine sighed, unwilling to admit that possibility. Since Edward's return, she had not been herself. Utterly distracted from the business of her life, of salon discussions and reading and writing, she could think of little else but him. When she walked on the strand, she wondered if she would meet him there. When she heard the sound of hooves along the drive, she looked to her window, hoping to see him arrive. He was in every dream and waking thought.

"I cannot say. Certainly, I scarcely think about him at all."

"Well, my dear," said Estella. "You shall think about many things now, including what you shall wear, and how many times you will accept his invitation to dance. He intends to impress you, and you must at least give him the opportunity to right a great wrong."

Katharine was not sure she ought to give Edward any such opportunity, and yet she already forgave him. She knew the truth in that, for everything she learned in the past few weeks suggested he was a man not entirely in control of his actions eight years ago. Honor and concern for his child dictated he would not admit to making a mistake, but even now, she knew him well enough to sense his regret.

Her own honor proved something of a façade once she realized she still loved him. Though able to distract herself and find good company at the Octagon House, she had never met a man to match him—and likely never would. She loved him, and it was as painful a truth as his desertion of her at Cloverhill Church.

She walked along the edge of the cliff toward the chalk steps in the rock face, keeping her eyes averted, so she would not trip over a root or stone and find herself hurtling to the bottom. She guessed that the well-worn path she trod was not always so close to the edge but had become so through the ages, as rain and wind hammered away at the cliff. Someday, perhaps in her lifetime, there would be nothing left of it.

Something cried out from the direction of the stairs. It was a gull, perhaps, eagerly swooping on a crab. Or a small animal, fighting against the stiff wind.

Or a small girl, sitting on a step and sobbing.

Katharine rushed to the top of the stairway and called down as she started to descend. The girl looked up at her, surprised and still tearful. She was a lovely little thing, clutching a knitted shawl, her dark, curling hair blowing around her face. She had the complexion of Caribbean sailors who sometimes came to shore in Cloverhill and large eyes as dark as chocolate.

"Are you lost?" Katharine asked. "Are you a visitor in our neighborhood?"

She was much closer now and sat several steps above the girl. The child's clothes were very fine, and there was elegant embroidery on the shawl. Perhaps the child's father was not a sailor, but a pirate.

"I live here, and I am not lost. Not really, my lady." She knew her manners, though seemed a little shy. "I climbed up to pick some of the flowers and am scared to go down."

Indeed, she sat on a bunch of wilted flowers, mostly the clover from which the town derived its name. The stairs below her were as they always had been, steep and treacherous. Katharine remembered when she first came here as a young girl, and the prospect of looking down to the strand was terrifying.

"Do you wish to go up or down? I will help you. But is there no one waiting for you or watching where you have gone?"

"I think my father may be looking for me." The girl motioned below. "He is on the beach."

Katharine nodded grimly. "Then he must be going mad calling your name and looking out to the waves. He might not think to look up here. Come, let us find him together."

She caught the child's hand, and warmed it in her own. She pulled her up gently, until she was steady on her feet, and stepped around her. "I will go first, so if you stumble, you will only land on me and not the beach. I am Miss Wharton, by the by."

"My name is Pearl, my lady."

Katharine stopped abruptly and, startled, Pearl smiled reassuringly. And that expression was not only bright, but illuminating.

Delphina Rutherford had once been a pretty girl, who sought to trade on her looks for a chance to escape from Cloverhill. And now, it appeared she had returned.

Pearl looked like her mother in her fine features and wide eyes and nothing like the man who called her his daughter.

She continued to smile, looking over Katharine's shoulder, and waved gleefully.

With her thoughts coming thick and fast, Katharine followed the girl's gaze to see Edward on the strand, gazing anxiously up at them.

"She is mine, in every way that matters," Edward said, as they continued along the sandy beach, while Pearl dodged approaching waves. Mostly unsuccessfully.

"As she is yours, you ought to warn her to have a care for her dress, as the salt water will surely ruin it."

"I would buy her all the new dresses in the world to make her happy. And now I suspect nothing is more delightful to her than to play tag with the sea," he explained. "She reminds me of another girl I knew who did very much the same."

"I do not recall Delphina having the slightest interest in the water. Her pleasures were all on land," Katharine said, and blushed. It was indelicate of her even to suggest what Delphina did during the days and nights of her youth.

"I know all too well what amused my late wife, but I was not thinking of her. I was thinking of you."

"But I am not at all connected to your little girl, my lord. We have only just met."

"That is true, but it is a situation I should like to rectify. I hope that you might learn to care for her and teach her many things. She will not be easily accepted into our society and needs someone to give her confidence to hold her own among those who would have something to say about the color of her skin or the circumstances of her birth."

Katharine knew he was right, but was still not certain what he asked of her.

"Do you wish for her to join the ladies of the Octagon Salon? She is a bit young."

Edward rubbed his forehead, in a gesture of exasperation Katharine remembered well. He then said a word he would never have used in her presence then. But she was a woman now.

He stopped in his tracks, and water lapped up against his boots.

"Damn it. I want for you to be my wife."

"Damn it," Katharine repeated. "I have never received such a romantic proposal. You wish for me to be your wife so Pearl can have a mother?"

"No. I want you, as I have wanted you for all these years, and was too proud and stupid to come home and admit I ruined everything. I was taken for a fool by a woman who played on my inexperience, but I was not forced to do anything. I do not deserve to be forgiven, and you will surely never forget the events of eight years ago. I do not deserve you but neither am I complete without you." He went down on one knee and started to sink into the wet sand.

"Edward, please," Katharine began, and looked desperately around her. Pearl stopped her dance in the waves and stood watching them from a distance. Behind them, near the cliff wall, someone cheered.

"Marry me, Katharine. Give a fool a second chance, for you will always be his first and only love."

She said nothing, thinking of her grief and humiliation and all those lost years. But somehow, they were nothing now, if she could only spend the rest of her life with him.

He started to rise and was nearly knocked off his feet by the next wave. "You speak of romantic proposals. Have you received many of them?" he asked, sounding unsure of himself.

She could not continue to punish him. For all he deserved it, she loved him too much.

"I have only received two proposals in my life, and both from you. The first was in a spring garden, but nothing bloomed from it. Now here we are on a cool, windy day, wet with salt water and sprayed with sand. And yet I feel we have been set free on this beach, for it has brought us back to what we once were."

Edward regained his footing and stood before her. "I prefer to think of what will be," he said, and kissed her.

A member of Romance Writers of America for over twenty years, Sharon Sobel is the author of eight historical and two contemporary romance novels, as well as a series of Regency Christmas novellas. She has served as the Secretary and Chapter Liaison of RWA and has twice been president of the Beau Monde chapter. After earning a PhD in English Language and Literature from Brandeis University, she started her career as a professor of English and currently works at a Connecticut college, where she co-chaired the Connecticut Writers' Conference for five years. An eighteenth-century New England farmhouse, where Sharon and her husband raised their three children, has provided inspiration for either the period or the setting for all of her books.

FORTUNE'S TREASURE

Liliana Hart

LUCAS FORTUNE HAD BEEN in worse situations in his thirty-six years.

Heat baked the walls of the tiny cell, and he'd stripped off his shirt in hope of some relief, but there was none to be found. The sun blazed orange through the small rectangular window at the top of the west wall, and the iron bars cast interesting shadows on the foot of the rusted bed frame, amplifying the particles of dust that hung in the air. There was no mattress, so he'd used his torn cargo jacket as a buffer to keep himself from frying like bacon on top of the bed frame. It was better than sitting on the dirt floor with cockroaches the size of dinner plates.

He hadn't been there too long—maybe five or six hours. The bastards had sucker punched him into unconsciousness. There was a hazy memory of being jostled inside a crowded car trunk, and then he was in the cell, his jaw aching and his head pounding before fully regaining his senses. He'd realized soon enough that standing at the bars and yelling for someone to let him out was futile. There wasn't a sign of anyone—inside or outside—and he figured he needed to save his anger. He was a big believer in conserving his energy for the important things. And planting a fist in Damian Hunter's face had quickly moved up on his list of "important things."

Chinks of mortar were missing from the concrete blocks they'd used to build the jail. Or what he assumed had *once* been a jail. By the layers of dust and disrepair, it didn't look like anyone had stepped foot inside in quite some time. The only recent sign of occupancy was the shuffled footprints from the door to his cell and back again. He was surprised the iron bars still stood, but he'd shaken them, looking for weakness, and hadn't found any.

Sweat trickled down his spine and ran in rivulets from his temples into the scruff of beard he hadn't bothered to shave in a few days. Served him right for taking a vacation. All he'd wanted was a hammock, the sand and surf, a beautiful woman or two to keep him company, and if he was lucky, a little gold to line his pockets.

Lucas didn't have any tools to pick the lock of his cage or to chisel away the mortar on the outside wall. Damian's men had relieved him of the items he habitually carried—a Swiss Army knife, a small roll of dental floss, a compass, the emergency cash in his sock, a needle and thread, and the gold doubloon he'd gotten on his first find that he kept for good luck. The bastards had gone too far with that one.

He'd learned over the years that an opportunity for wealth and fame could come at any moment, but only to those who were prepared. Most treasure hunters lived by the same basic rules he did. Those who didn't … well … they didn't last long. It was a brutal and addictive lifestyle, and only the strongest survived. Damian Hunter wasn't the strongest or smartest or most talented treasure hunter, but he was the most cunning. And he was definitely the most ruthless.

Lucas perked up at the sound of muffled voices and footsteps coming in his direction, and he got up quickly, looking for something—anything—he could use as a weapon. To no avail—even the rusted iron bedframe was solid and too heavy to tear apart.

The voices quieted as they got closer and he settled himself on the bed, trying to look non-threatening and still weakened from the blow they gave him earlier. Not an easy accomplishment for a man who was six foot two in his bare feet and built like a brawler. His fists had gotten him out of more than one sticky situation. Learning to defend himself had been a priority once he'd realized hunting treasure left him with a target. The six-inch scar on his back from a knife was as much of a reminder of his first find as the gold doubloon now missing from his pocket.

He was a hell of a poker player, and that ability was the only thing that kept him seated and looking bored as two of Damian's men charged in, dragging another prisoner behind them. And dragging her was exactly what they had to do. She wasn't going to make it easy on them. He almost smiled at that. Miranda George had never made things easy. She was a hundred and twenty pounds of pure fire and prickly temper. And she'd once been all his.

"Let me go, you son of a bitch," she said between gritted teeth.

"We don't get paid enough for this bullshit," one of the men said. He had four distinct claw marks on the side of his face that oozed blood.

"Shut up, Ryan," the other man said. "I told you to knock her out. It's your own fault for not wanting to hit a woman."

"I didn't see you volunteering to do the job," Ryan spat. "You were the one going on about it being a shame to ruin a face like hers."

"That was before I realized what her mouth was like. Never in my life have I heard such a foul-mouthed banshee of a woman."

Lucas did grin at that. It sounded like Miranda hadn't changed much over the past couple of years.

Miranda hadn't seen him yet, and the hired guns had their hands full dealing with her. It would be the perfect time to spring into action. Miranda dug her feet in and went limp, making Ryan stumble. The other finally picked her up and tossed her over his shoulder like a sack of potatoes. He got an elbow in the head, and her tiny fists pounded at his kidneys hard enough that he'd probably be pissing blood for a few days, but he took the abuse stoically. Lucas knew instinctively he was the more dangerous of the two.

The old cell used a skeleton key of some kind, and Lucas figured they either didn't know where it was or didn't want to chance that he'd be able to pick the lock, so they'd wrapped a very modern and sturdy chain around the bars and fastened it with a padlock. Ryan fumbled with the keys and eventually got the padlock undone and the chain unwrapped. The cell door swung open with a rusty creak and the man holding Miranda tossed her into the cell.

She landed with an *ummph,* and the fall must've surprised her because she sat there looking stunned instead of hopping up to fight. Lucas had shifted his weight to attack the men as soon as the door opened, but Miranda was in the way, and he didn't want to take the chance of her getting hurt. They had the gate closed and the chains on and locked before he'd come up with another plan.

"How long is Damian going to leave us in here before he tells us what he wants?" Lucas asked. "I'm assuming he thinks he's got a lead on some treasure and actually needs people with skills to do the dirty work for him?"

He saw Miranda's body tense at the sound of his voice, but she didn't turn around to look at him. She just stared at the two men who stood on the other side of the bars.

"Or maybe he wants to see the two of you rot in a cell?" the one that wasn't Ryan said. "You've cost Mr. Hunter millions in lost acquisitions."

"You mean we found the treasure and wouldn't let him steal it from us like he'd planned?" Miranda asked, her voice saccharine sweet. "I'm sure all those museums are weeping at the thought of Hunter's lost millions. What's it feel like to work for a loser?"

"Shut up," Ryan said, his face going dark with a scowl. "You'll find out why you're here soon enough. Should've gagged you. Done nothing but yap the whole trip here." They turned and headed for the door. "Enjoy your night. I hear the rats start coming in as soon as the sun goes down." Their laughter trailed behind them as they disappeared.

"You're always bringing out the best in people," Lucas said after they left.

Miranda snorted out a laugh and stretched her muscles, rubbing at her sore backside. He shouldn't have watched. He'd always been partial to her backside—partial to all of her if he was honest.

His eyes skimmed over her, taking in the subtle differences

that two years had made. She'd been softer then. She'd always been in great shape. You had to be to get through some of the situations they'd found themselves in. But there'd still been a softness about her—not the lean, muscled wildcat that was standing in front of him ready to fight.

She'd cut her long red hair so it lay in choppy layers around her face, making her sea green eyes seem larger and more mysterious. He knew by looking at her that she'd been working when they'd taken her. Doctor Miranda George was a creature of habit. She wore thin cargo pants for a hot climate and the same hiking boots she'd had for as long as he'd known her. A red bandana hung from her pocket, and her nails were grimy from digging in the dirt. The navy tank top she wore had smudges of dirt on the front where she'd sometimes wipe her right hand if she wanted to touch an artifact. She could get more out of *feeling* an object than most people could get from looking at it through an X-ray. She had a gift.

The past two years had been miserable, though he'd tried his damnedest to forget her. In all honesty, he couldn't remember why they'd fought to begin with, but it was always a variation of the same argument. Only that time she'd had enough and packed her bags, saying she needed to be closer to the excavation site. She'd never come back. And he hadn't gone to find her.

Lucas lived for the rush, for the feel of diamonds as they trickled through his fingers or tarnished pieces of eight as they were pulled from a watery grave. He always wanted more, to push harder, to take more risks for the ultimate find. And for their cut of the profit to be larger. They had to make a living after all.

But he'd never understood how a woman with such a hard head could have such a soft heart. Miranda hunted for the thrill, just like he did, but she did it for the love of every little piece of history she held in her hand. In some ways, they should've balanced each other perfectly.

"I should've known the second they nabbed me that you'd be involved," Miranda said, walking a perimeter around the cell and looking for any weak points, just as he'd done. "Damian told you to watch your back two years ago."

"No, he told *us* that *we'd* better watch *our* backs," he argued. "If we hadn't thought to call in the news cameras so the find was on live TV, Damian would have shot us and left our bodies for shark food off the coast of Jamaica. We knew going in he was going to try to take the credit for finding the pirate treasure that disappeared when *Port Royal* sank. But it was you and me, babe. Like always."

"Yeah, like always," she said distractedly. "You blow your reward money already?"

He gritted his teeth through a smile. "Yeah, on fast cars and fancy women. Just like I want them."

"You always did have more ambition than sense, so I'm not surprised."

And there it was right there, he thought, the memories of that last fight rushing over him. She'd never believed that he'd loved her as much as he loved the hunt. As much as he loved the treasure, riches, or glory. He'd been damned tired of trying to convince her, so he'd let her walk. If she couldn't take his word for it and trust him, then there was no reason for her to stay.

Adrenaline and tempers had been running high after the *Port Royal* find, and the threat of Damian coming after them was always hanging over their heads. If they hadn't had national news coverage, they'd both be dead. But as it stood, Jamaica's government had allowed them the bounty for recovering not one, but two of the ships that had sunk with the island, and they'd allowed Miranda to continue with the excavation team. But even after they'd split, he knew Damian had been watching them both, biding his time.

Damian never did anything without a reason. He was a planner, and he was patient. If he'd gone to the trouble of kidnapping both of them, it was for a specific reason. He had a job only they could do.

"Yeah, well, I guess we should focus on getting the hell out of here, so I can return to living the high life," he said. "It'll be dark soon, and I have no desire to share this cell with the rats."

Lucas sulked at the reality of having preferred spending the night with her than pretending to escape from her.

Chapter Two

MIRANDA WOULD'VE RATHER BEEN anywhere else.

She wasn't ready to see Lucas. She hadn't prepared herself for it. He'd broken her heart and left her holding the pieces, and when she'd left after the *Port Royal* excavation, he'd shrugged his shoulders and told her to have fun. And then he'd hopped on a flight to Poland to search for Nazi gold as part of a treasure hunter show on The Travel Channel.

Ancient history. All that mattered now was getting out and getting away from him. She'd kept busy the past two years, and she'd just started feeling like she was almost whole again. Still cracked in places, but at least all the pieces were there.

"You were working when they got you?" he asked.

Looking at him hurt more than it should have, and she turned, searching for a way to escape. But she couldn't help but glance at him from the corner of her eye. He sat on a rusted bed frame, his arm propped on his knee and his body relaxed, though she knew he could spring into action unexpectedly. His dark blond hair was sun streaked and hung below his ears, and a couple of days of growth of beard shadowed his face.

By the looks of him, he'd been in the cell for a while. Rivulets of sweat trickled down the contours of his chest and abs. She'd dreamed of that body for two years. Woken in the middle of the night aching and sweaty and needing his touch so badly she could hardly stand it. The physical had never been the problem between them.

"Yeah, they found a mass grave off the coast of Florida. It dates to the seventeenth century, so they asked if I'd help catalog the find.

Looks like it was a massacre of Spaniards, and there might be more to Ponce de León and the Fountain of Youth than we thought."

"No way," he said. "You're barking up the wrong tree there. All the evidence we found indicated it's somewhere in Puerto Rico, not in Florida as everyone assumes."

She shrugged and stuck her finger through one of the holes in the mortar, scraping it with her nail to see how soft it was. It wasn't. It had petrified over the years.

"I guess we'll see. The sooner I can get out of here, the sooner I can get back. They grabbed me last night after dinner on the way to my tent. They must've tranqued me because the next thing I knew I was on a private plane with Tweedledee and Tweedledum and a hell of a headache. They shoved me in a car and took every back road they could find for the next three hours. I think they were trying to disorient me. Idiots."

"At least they let you ride in the back seat. I ended up in the trunk."

"For some reason, people always assume the worst of you," she said sarcastically.

"It's a blessing and a curse," he said soberly, and she wondered if there were some hidden meaning in the way he'd said it. "I don't suppose you know what Damian wants with us?"

"We're in a ghost town just outside of New London, Connecticut," she said. "Why do you think he has us here?"

The surprise on his face quickly turned to calculation. One thing Lucas was *not* was stupid. No one knew legend and lore of lost treasure like he did. It was why he was the best at what he did. He had the skills for the hunt, but he also had the brains for all the tedious research and fact-finding. Not bad for a guy who'd dropped out of college after his first semester. Some people weren't meant for classrooms, and Lucas Fortune was one of those people. Still, she'd learned more from him over the years than she had in most of her postgraduate work.

He closed his eyes and shook his head. "That idiot. Hunter thinks he's found the Thanksgiving Treasure. And he wants us to be the ones to sneak onto reservation land to retrieve it."

"Bingo," Miranda said, standing in front of him, hands on hips. "I overheard them talking in the car when they thought I was asleep. Apparently, Damian did his own half-assed research and came to the conclusion that the gold was buried on Pequot reservation land."

"Well, to give him the credit he deserves," Lucas said. "It was, at one time, buried on the Pequot reservation. But like always, Damian is late to the party unless he has someone else driving him there."

Miranda snorted out a laugh and then pressed her lips together to stifle it. The story of the Thanksgiving Treasure had always been one of her favorites. To think that most people in the United States thought they celebrated Thanksgiving because the settlers and Native Americans were at peace with one another and wanted to celebrate the occasion was laughable, when in reality, Thanksgiving was declared a holiday to celebrate the massacre of the Pequot tribe.

There had been one peaceful meal celebrated between the British settlers and Native Americans, and then the British thanked them by hauling them to England and enslaving them, then wiping out most of the tribe with smallpox. It was the Pequot tribe who'd refused to let the English onto their land once they returned to America for more, taking their resources and spreading their diseases. Then, on the day the Pequot tribe gathered to celebrate their harvest, known as *their* Thanksgiving day, the Puritans invaded and murdered more than seven hundred men, women, and children, so they could stake their claim to land that was never theirs to begin with.

Any survivors went into hiding or were taken into slavery, and the Puritans used the captives in their search for gold. The gold was eventually found and scheduled to be shipped to England aboard three different ships. But the gold disappeared from the camp before it reached the ships, and no sign of it was ever discovered. The Pequot slaves who had helped discover the gold were killed and Pequot were hunted and interrogated, but the gold was never found.

It had stayed hidden for hundreds of years, until fact became legend and the Pequot numbers dwindled down to nothing. It wasn't until Lucas Fortune had come along that the gold had been found again. She knew about his discovery but never approved of it.

The Pequot gold was only one of the things they'd argued about over the years. "Don't worry," she said. "I kept your secret. Besides, there's nothing left of that gold to find, is there?"

He smiled, but it didn't reach his eyes this time. "I'm amazed you stayed with me as long as you did with as little as you think of me."

"You were never one to correct my way of thinking, were you?"

"I shouldn't have to correct or explain anything. If you don't know the type of man I am after sharing my bed, my life, and my work for that long, then it's probably a good thing you moved on."

She was rendered speechless for a moment and took a second to take a deep breath. There was no use bringing up old news and starting the fight all over again. They needed to work together to get out of here. And they needed to figure out how to keep Damian off reservation land. He wasn't above killing anyone who got in his way if he thought he knew where the treasure was and couldn't get Lucas or her to do his bidding.

"Let's just get out of here," she said, changing the subject. "As long as Damian thinks that treasure is still up for grabs, anyone standing in his way is in danger."

"You really think I took their gold?" he asked, the anger in his voice unchecked. "You think I'm that heartless that I'd take a cut of the money that so many people died for?"

"People of all civilizations have died for gold for centuries. Why would your philosophy change?"

His laugh was filled with bitterness and hurt, and guilt crept along her skin and made her feel ill with the possibility she might have been wrong about him all this time. She'd known him better than anyone—at least she thought she had—but he'd always seemed so intent on the find. Not what happened to it afterward.

"I might not be a bleeding heart like you who'd give away everything we worked and sweated for, and hell, almost died for a couple of times. But I do have a moral compass. If you never recognized that it was your failing, not mine."

"If you hadn't been so intent on playing the tough macho guy and putting on a show, then maybe it would've been easier to see. You were never vulnerable in front of me. You never let me in. So I assumed the fortune hunter was who you really were. And you never let me believe anything else. All I needed to know was that I was more important than that gold doubloon you keep in your pocket."

"I'm not doing this again," he said, getting up off the bed frame and pacing around like a caged tiger. "I need to get out of here."

"Fine," she said. It was easier when emotion wasn't involved. "I'm assuming they confiscated your supplies?"

"That would be a correct assumption. They even took my belt. They're not nearly as dumb as some of Damian's other hired guns."

"Lucky us," she said. "But still dumb enough to think a woman isn't a threat. They didn't search me for weapons, and my cellphone has been in my pocket the whole time."

She unzipped the many pockets on her pants and laid everything on the bed frame. One thing she'd learned from him many years before was that the most unlikely tools could get you out of a jam. He grinned as she pulled out bobby pins and dental floss, a small coil of wire, her cellphone, which had no service, emergency cash and a credit card from her sock, a pen knife, a book of matches, a flashlight, Band-Aids and gauze pads, a detonation cord, and a blasting cap.

"That's my girl," he said, sifting through the supplies.

She didn't correct him, but she did take a step back.

"So we escape and then what?" she asked. "Damian will never leave us alone. Not until he has the treasure or he kills us. You've—" she started and then corrected herself. "*We've* always been a threat to him. But mostly you because you and Damian go back a lot farther than he and I do."

"You kicked him in the balls the last time we were all in the same room together," Lucas said. "Believe me, his vendetta is as much against you as it is me."

"He was rude," she said primly, remembering the moment with perfect clarity.

"Ha!" Lucas said. "That's an understatement. Okay, let's see what we can finagle."

He grabbed his shirt and pulled it over his head, and she thought it a shame he'd cover such perfection. She was angry with him, but she wasn't dead.

It took him all of two minutes to pick the padlock, and most of that time was spent trying to find the right angle once he got his hands through the bars.

"Well, that's something at least," he said, arranging the chains and padlock so it looked as if it were still locked. "Now we just have to wait and hope the rats don't eat us before we can escape."

"The closest town is about ten miles up the road," she said, biting her lip. She could deal with a lot of things, but the rats were giving her pause.

"Where's Damian in all this?" he asked. "He normally likes to get in my face as soon as possible because he knows he irritates the hell out of me."

"Only because you let him."

"Nah, I let him think I let him." He stopped and thought a second. "If that even makes sense. Whatever the case, I don't like that he hasn't made an appearance yet."

"I heard Ryan and Doyle mention that he was flying in from overseas. He's supposed to arrive around five."

"Doyle, huh?" Lucas said. "That's a stupid name." He looked at his watch. "It's half past five already."

"You've got something cooking in that brain of yours," she said. "You always tap your index finger when you're thinking. You do it when you're playing poker too."

He looked at her incredulously. "You must be kidding. I don't have any tells."

"If you say so," she said, shrugging. "But the better your hand is, the faster your finger taps."

"If you'd told me that five years ago, maybe you could have saved me a couple of thousand dollars in Mexico last month."

"If you want to save a couple of thousand dollars, then maybe you shouldn't gamble," she said, arching a brow.

"Doc, you've got to lighten up a bit. Learn to have a little fun."

"Since I've known you I've almost drowned, been shot at,

dangled from a cliff, fled from an active volcano, been pushed out of a helicopter, and been kidnapped. I'm not sure I could have more fun if I tried."

"Well, when you put it that way, I guess we have had some good adventures."

"Memorable for sure," she said, smiling.

And they'd made some amazing memories. There had been fun and excitement and passion. But there'd also been the quiet reassurance of love between two people who shared something unique and had mutual respect for each other's talents.

Maybe she had been the one who started to pull away. To see the faults in his personality, even though those same faults were things that had drawn her to him when they'd first met. Although she'd broached the topic, he'd never made it clear what he'd wanted for their future. Would it always be one hair-raising adventure after another? Would there ever be time to enjoy the things they'd worked for? To raise a family or leave a legacy? It hadn't seemed as if he'd been interested in planning for the future. She'd wanted a future with him, but not at the cost of their lives because the risk was as thrilling as the reward.

His arm brushed the side of her breast when he moved, and she gasped at the touch. He froze and stared at her, and the air became heavy with needs she'd hidden for two years. Blood rushed in her ears, and her heart thudded in her chest. And then she made the mistake of looking up at him—of seeing those dark chocolate eyes go black as want sizzled like electricity between them.

She put her hand flat against his chest, not sure if she was warning him to keep his distance or inviting him to move closer. But whatever the case, he moved toward her and she brought her other hand up to rest against his chest. She'd always been a tactile person, whether it be while examining precious artifacts or spending hours touching every ridge of muscle or scar on his body. Touch told a much better story than sight.

He moved in slowly, giving her time to react, but she didn't stop him. What they were doing was surely a mistake. His touch had always been addictive, but maybe the memories were better than the reality. Maybe she just needed to see if she'd been holding onto something that had never existed.

He didn't put his hands on her. Not yet. His lips hovered over hers, and the heat between them was palpable. Then he was kissing her, and old memories and thoughts of right or wrong vanished. This was the here and now, and it was better than anything she could've imagined.

His mouth slanted over hers—devoured—invaded—and her fingers curled into his chest as his tongue stroked against hers. It was then his arms slid around her, and his hands tightened at her hips.

Someone moaned, and she found herself moving closer, so there was no space left between them. Nothing else mattered at that moment but the feel of his hands and mouth on her. The desire was as strong as it had ever been—more so with the time they'd spent apart—and she didn't care that reality would soon set in. For this moment, she gave him everything she had and knew that he did the same. And if their circumstances had been different, she'd have let him take everything she was offering and more, and have no regrets, because she knew she'd never feel as whole as she did when they were joined.

It was Miranda who finally pulled apart. Their breaths were labored and their gazes intense as they held each other in a loose embrace. There was no need for words or explanations. That time would come.

"I've got an idea," Lucas finally said.

Chapter Three

LESS THAN AN HOUR later, they heard the slam of car doors and knew the moment of their escape had arrived.

"You ready?" Lucas whispered.

Miranda nodded, and they took their places. They'd left the door to the cell wide open and empty so Damian's crew would think them long gone, but they had a couple of surprises up their sleeves.

Doyle was the first to cross the threshold, just as Lucas had hoped, and he gave the guy a quick chop to the brachial plexus, sending him to his knees. Lucas grabbed him under the arm before he could face plant and tossed him into the cell as he heard the blasting cap detonate once Ryan came into the room. The blasting cap wasn't enough of an explosion to do serious damage, but it sure as hell disoriented Ryan enough that Miranda was able to toss Ryan in the cell with Doyle. She quickly checked both of them for weapons and came out with a couple of pistols.

"Was it there?" Lucas asked like a boy looking under the tree on Christmas morning.

"Was what there?" she taunted.

"My gold coin? They took it after sucker punching me in the alley behind the bar." He rubbed his jaw with a crooked scowl.

Her smile beamed as gold twinkled between her thumb and forefinger. It spun across the creep of dusk that faded through the small window. He snatched it in midair.

"Come on in, Damian," Lucas said. "We've been waiting for you."

"I can see that," Damian said, smiling a snake charmer's smile. He was always a politician. Always polite, even as he raked the knife across an opponent's throat. "I'm not sure what you're planning to accomplish here, Lucas, but you know as well as I do that I'll always be one step ahead of you."

"If that were true, you'd know I found the Thanksgiving Treasure more than ten years ago."

Damian laughed, but the smile didn't reach his eyes. "Now, there's no reason to lie. You and I both know if you'd found that treasure every media outlet in the world would've been alerted."

"You never did do research worth a shit," Lucas said, holding the gun on the other man. "Get into the cell." He reached inside Damian's suit jacket and pulled out the pistol he had holstered, like some modern-day mob boss.

"He's got a backup weapon too," Miranda said. "I can see the outline." She took the one from his waist and then patted his legs, taking one from an ankle holster as well.

Damian moved into the cell with the other two men, who were starting to stir, though they were both disoriented. Lucas closed the cell door and held it while Miranda chained and padlocked it again, then she broke one of the bobby pins she carried in the lock so they couldn't use the key once they escaped.

"You know you're making a huge mistake," Damian said, eyeing the rusted bed frame distastefully. "I was going to give you the opportunity to find the Thanksgiving Treasure on live television, and then you'd, of course, get a small portion of the find. Did I mention that I bought the little travel show you've been hosting? I think I'm going to have to fire you."

"Yeah, I've got to tell you I really don't care," Lucas said. "You'll run that show into the ground within a couple of months because you actually have to be a treasure hunter to keep people entertained. Your idea of being a treasure hunter is stealing what other people find."

Damian shrugged. "Semantics," he said. "But I have the name and the money to do exactly what I want to do, which is why you and the good doctor here are going to get that gold whether you want to or not. Your reputation will be in tatters by the time I'm through with you if you don't."

"We've been thinking of retiring anyway," Lucas said nonchalantly, though Damian's words bothered him more than he wanted them to. He'd worked hard to build a solid reputation as an explorer and treasure hunter, and a lot of his work came because of his experience. As had Miranda. She'd worked damned hard to be known as an expert in what was considered a man's field.

"Not to mention the fact," Lucas said, stepping back from the bars, "that even if the treasure were still available, I'd never help you take what rightfully belongs to the Pequot. Their tribe was essentially wiped out because of that gold. They deserve every bit of it and more."

"Give me a break," Damian laughed. "From one greedy son of a bitch to another. I've seen you on too many finds. You love the feel of fortune in your hands."

"Sure I do. But I also know when something greater is at work than stumbling across a mound of gold that's almost four-hundred-years old. Sometimes you do the right thing just because it's the right thing. Life doesn't always have to be a negotiation for the largest finder's fee."

"Those people have enough money," Damian spat, his anger finally beginning to show. "They're sitting on millions of dollars the government gave them out of pity. They didn't do anything for it."

"Except be murdered into near extinction," Lucas said.

"I would slit the throats of every last one of them if it meant getting my hands on that gold," Damian said.

"I know. Which is what makes us different. You would've killed Miranda and me after the *Port Royal* find, just to claim it as your own."

"In a heartbeat," he said, sneering. "People better than you have died on expeditions for me. Sometimes a sacrifice needs to be made for the greater good."

"The greater good meaning making you richer?" Miranda asked.

"We all have a claim to stake," Damian said. "And you and Fortune here are becoming more of a nuisance than a help for my cause. You can take it as a promise that your days are numbered."

"Interesting," Lucas said. "I'm sure the world would love to know that. And I'm sure the Pequot Nation would be very interested to hear that their lives are so expendable."

"Even better," Miranda said, "I'm sure the police would be interested in opening up any mysterious death cases involved during one of your expeditions."

Lucas pointed to the cellphone he'd rigged with dental floss in the corner of the ceiling and set to record. He climbed up and retrieved it and then handed it to Miranda.

"If you guys will excuse us, we've got plans tonight. We hope the rats don't give you too much trouble, but if I were you, I wouldn't go to sleep. They've been known to eat their young. I don't see why they'd pass up someone like you."

"Lucas, you bastard," Damian yelled as they headed out. "Let us out of here."

"I'm sure the police will be by … eventually," Miranda said, wiggling her fingers in a goodbye wave. "Nighty, night."

Epilogue

"I NEED TO TELL you something," Miranda said, several hours later. She nuzzled closer and ran her hand down his chest to rest on his taut abs. The sheets were tangled at the bottom of the bed, and their legs were entwined.

"If you keep moving your hand, I can't promise I'll be able to listen."

She smiled and dipped her hand lower, so her fingers danced around his hipbone, but she didn't go further. She could already see the effect of such a simple touch, and she needed Lucas to hear what she had to say.

After they'd left Damian and his men in the cell, they drove to the closest casino on the Pequot reservation. It was only right to surrender a copy of the recording with Damian's confession to the tribal police authorities.

"Think they'll believe what you have to say about Damian's plot to steal their treasure?" She questioned.

Lucas grinned. His eyes cast a thousand-yard stare that signaled to her his thoughts were far from the current conversation.

"Yeah, they're pretty familiar with me."

"Did they catch you taking their Thanksgiving Treasure or something?" she jeered.

"No, they helped me recover it and secure it on their reservation." His smile glowed.

"You old softie." She brushed her palm across his rigid forearm.

They'd ridden the rest of the way in silence, the adrenaline rush fading and the desire building between them. There'd been no question where they'd end up. The question was what would happen after.

"I owe you an apology," she said, and she felt his inhalation, as if he were going to speak. "No, let me say it," she continued. "We were good at a lot of things during our relationship, but communication wasn't one of them. We were both so busy trying to prove to the other how capable we were that we didn't leave a lot of room for the imperfections and mistakes. And if I'm honest, you were starting to scare me a little with the chances you were willing to take during that last dive at *Port Royal*. I thought we were both going to die, and I wondered if that was your endgame. To go out in a blaze of glory with your name in the history books as one of the greatest treasure hunters of all time. And if that was your goal, it didn't seem like it left much of a place for me or our future."

His fingers tightened on her arm briefly, but he stayed silent and she wondered if their window had passed. If they were only reconnecting for the night before moving onto the next job.

Several minutes passed before he finally spoke. "I think I scared myself there at the end. Do you know how intimidating you are? You've got all those degrees tacked onto the end of your name, and you have that natural born intuition that makes you a hell of a partner. We were great together, but I was always afraid that you'd see me fail and that I couldn't live up to the kind of man you deserved."

"Well, that's just ridiculous," she said, lifting her head so she could look him in the eyes. "I wouldn't have stayed with you if I hadn't wanted to be there. But what I wanted didn't seem to be the same thing you wanted."

His look was serious as he slid a piece of her hair behind her ear. "And what was it you wanted that I couldn't give you?"

"Not that you couldn't give me," she corrected. "But I wanted all of you. I wanted to know that what we had was it. That our future would be together, no matter what."

"You wanted marriage?"

"Not necessarily," she said. "But I wanted commitment. I needed the words. And I needed to know that our futures weren't going to be a shallow grave in some foreign country and that we'd leave our children as orphans for someone else to raise."

"You wanted children?" he asked, his face going pale.

Miranda shook her head and closed her eyes, wondering why she'd decided it was important to communicate at this moment.

"No, never mind," she said, resting her head against his arm again, her body stiff.

"No, Miranda," he said, putting a finger beneath her chin and lifting it so her eyes met his. "Don't stop now. I want to know. I never thought you wanted those things. You always seemed so focused on your career and the writing you were able to do after our finds. I never wanted to take that away from you. To make you feel like I'd try to keep you from your dreams because I wanted marriage and family."

Her body relaxed into his and they lay in silence for several minutes, each in deep thought.

"So where do we go from here?" she finally asked.

"I don't know," he said. "I'm on vacation. I don't suppose you need any help finding the Fountain of Youth?"

Miranda grinned and continued the exploration of his body with her hand, and then she rolled on top of him and looked into his eyes as he slid deep inside of her.

"I thought you told Damian you were ready to retire?" she teased.

"How about I semi-retire?"

"Semi-retire?" Her gaze flitted back and forth between his expression and what he was doing with his hands.

"You know, avoid the dangerous jobs. More of a consulting partner."

"As it turns out, I could use a good partner," she said.

He grabbed her hips and then rolled them, so he lay on top of her, and she gasped as he hit somewhere magical inside her.

"A good partner?" he said.

"Great," she gasped as he started to move. "I meant great partner."

"That's better," he said, silencing her moan with his mouth and riding them both to ecstasy. "Much better."

Liliana Hart is a *New York Times, USA Today,* and *Publishers Weekly* best-selling author of more than fifty titles. After starting her first novel her freshman year of college, she immediately became addicted to writing and knew she'd found what she was meant to do with her life. She has no idea why she majored in music. Liliana can almost always be found at her computer writing, working on various projects with her own real-life hero, spending time with her children, or traveling all over the world.

TWICE SHY

Damon Suede

"I DON'T THINK THE fetal pig was gonna have such a great life, hon." Jerome glanced at his battered watch. *Time to go.*

Keisha side-eyed him and shifted her backpack from right to left shoulder. She'd turned thirteen in October, so she knew everything now. "It's barbaric."

Kids streamed into Walton Academy around them. A couple nodded or waved, other black kids mostly. He knew that tuition and tradition put private schools out of reach for a lot of New Yorkers who weren't from rich, white families. Being a private school black kid made for some weird dissonance. He knew that from personal experience.

Knife-slim in her red coat, Keisha crossed her arms. "Mom wouldn't have made me cut up some pig." Now she was stalling for guilt and rewards. She was right, though. If her mother had been there, some savory bait would have been dangled to get their daughter into the building before homeroom started. They both knew it. Fetal pig or not.

But her mother had been gone for almost three years, sick for two before that.

Keisha glared at him.

Powerless, Jerome shook his head and frowned at the sidewalk.

Even from the grave, his wife had the last word. Olivia had always been better at negotiation.

"Then skip school, Keesh. You've got rehearsals anyway. Your call." His hands shook 'til he hid them in his pockets. "Fine by me." A lie and they both knew it.

She stilled, one eyebrow up. She didn't get many days off during the holidays. In general, October through December meant racing from Brooklyn Heights to school in the Village, then up to Lincoln Center so she could spend her downtime as a very acrobatic mouse in *The Nutcracker.*

"The fetal pig won't know the difference. You can always come to work with—"

She rolled her eyes at the idea of spending the day at the gym. "—me."

"Dad. You're *nasty.*" Just like that she was gone, floating through the crush at the door. When had she gotten so tall?

He blinked and called after her slim form, "I'll be here at three to run you to rehearsals." But she'd vanished through the doors.

The river of students began to thin out now, stragglers racing to beat the bell.

As he walked upstream, a glance at his watch told him he had time for the gym. He could make it to Wall Street to hit his back and legs before his first client. His life in four words: *medical school, personal trainer.* He wondered about that other life, the one where he'd returned to his residency and become a dermatologist, where his folks still respected him.

No point regretting. He knew better: second chances were sucker bait.

A chill wind picked up. *Snow tomorrow.* New York's weather had gone bananas these past few years: hurricanes and flash floods.

If Olivia hadn't died, he wouldn't have been standing there in front of Walton in the cold. If Olivia hadn't died, he'd have been home washing up the breakfast dishes while she ran to her agent's office. If Olivia hadn't died, his daughter would have laughed and high-fived him before she'd left the house to ace biology and dance the lead, instead of a mouse.

"Jug?" A deep voice called out to him, one he knew better than his own.

Jerome froze.

"Is that you?"

Sure enough, there he stood, seventeen years later and more handsome than ever, Wendell Stuart Farley, Wince to his friends, and Jerome's closest ally for most of the years that mattered. Pinked by the cold air and wearing a faded tee under a brown leather jacket. Same wavy hair that always needed a cut, same crooked grin, and square chin. Rough around the edges and squinting at the madhouse, same as ever. His partner in crime, once upon a while ago.

Jerome made himself smile in reply. A knot in his gut and tension rippled through him like a rock tossed into a pond. *Not today, Satan.*

Wince uncrossed his arms and took a hesitant step toward him, ignoring the kids surging toward the doors. He wasn't the same lanky boy he'd been. His chest stretched the faded shirt and laugh lines framed his eyes. Gray in the dirty blond now. He'd gotten as muscular as Jerome. *We're men now.* "Man, you look fucking *great.*"

Jerome nodded, numb. "Thanks. You, umm … You do too." He could feel himself overreacting like a freak. Right in public, in front of all these parents and kids. *Once burned.*

"Fifteen goddamn years." Wince didn't act awkward or hesitant.

Jerome nodded again, robotic. *Seventeen.* A rushing in his head. Time travel sucked, except he hadn't gone anywhere. He was right where Wince had left him. Thank Christ, Keisha was already inside facing her pig.

"Long time." Jerome smiled, but he knew it didn't reach his eyes. They hadn't seen each other since that night in the emergency room.

For one second, he imagined the road not taken. That the past seventeen years had been a weird hallucination. That he'd never given up medicine or fought his folks or gotten married or had a daughter. At the thought of Keisha, he paused; she was worth everything. Plenty of stupidity in his past, but his family was the one good thing. Coming up on three years since Olivia's funeral and he still missed her laugh and sass.

Wince gripped his arm casually, an old gesture. "You look good, man."

"Thanks." Jerome had always been vain about his skin, but some guilty part of him knew that Wince had a thing about his *darkness* and so, even at fifteen, he'd done everything in his power to amp what the Good Lord gave him. To this day, he baked in the sun whenever he could steal the time. His wife had made him lotion up so he wouldn't get ashy; on lighter skin it wasn't noticeable, but black as he was, it was part of his daily ritual.

Wince rocked forward and back on the balls of his feet, as if he might jump into the sky. "Great to see you, man. Wow. Fuck. I just moved back into the city last summer. I had no idea you still lived here. I had no idea you had *kids*."

"Just one." Jerome sighed. Of all places, this had to be where Wince snuck back into his life and screwed him up again. "Kid, singular."

"Same. For my sins." He put his fingers in his mouth and whistled. "Flip, c'mere. Come back." A nervous glance. "He hates being late." Wince must've gotten married, too. Only natural. It had been a long time.

"Dad, c'mon." Sure enough, a boy turned at the front door of the school and jogged right at them, slamming into Wince's leg. "I gotta *go*." A mini-Wince stood at his hip: jackass grin, dirty blond hair, even the same damn cowlick. All of nine years old. The boy looked up at Jerome warily, maybe at his size, maybe his blue-black skin, maybe sensing the panic Jerome was suppressing. "Hey."

"Flip, I want you to meet my friend." Wince ruffled the boy's shaggy gold hair. "This is Jerome."

"Hi." Flip gave a quick grin. "Hello." The homeroom bell rang somewhere inside, distant and mechanical. The last stragglers dashed past them for the door.

"You gotta go." Wince crouched in front of the boy. "What are we doing today?" He held up his hand.

High-five from his son. "Kicking ass, taking names." He even sounded like Wince at that age. The resemblance was truly freaky. Flip bolted inside while his dad waved behind him. *Parenthood.*

Wince had a kid, too. And a wife. And a life that went on beyond the emergency room at seventeen years old. Why not? They'd both grown up and lived their lives.

Of all the times he'd imagined this meeting, all the scenarios he'd cooked up and confrontations he'd scripted, this had to be the worst place and time possible.

Jerome wanted to flee. He already felt like an invader here; the last thing he needed was humiliation in front of his daughter's fancy school and all these nosy, white parents.

How on earth could Wince afford the tuition?

As it was, Olivia's insurance account had dwindled, and he'd started thinking about moving into a smaller place to keep Keisha going to school with her friends. She didn't mind being one of eleven black kids in a class of ninety. She didn't mind that they commuted two miles from Brooklyn or lived in comparative poverty when her friends spent spring break in Bermuda. She was proud and fearless, like her mother. He refused to go to his folks; he'd find a way.

"Here we are, huh? Respectable and everything. Twenty years later."

Jerome shrugged. *Seventeen, but who was counting?*

"Man." Wince smiled again. "I guess I coulda called. Later on, maybe."

Jerome scowled. *No.* "Calling would've been weird."

"Yeah. Yeah. It would. I still should've. Or written when it was safe. Your parents made it real clear." Another wary pause between them. "You look great, man. I swear you got blacker. And bigger, I think. You're so jacked." He thumped Jerome's shoulders and squeezed.

"I do. I'm a ..." Awkward. "I train people. At a gym. I'm a personal trainer."

"Oh." Doubly awkward. "I figured you'd be a doctor by now."

"I am. I was." Jerome studied the concrete. "Life got complicated."

Wince blinked at him. "Truth." He wasn't leaving.

He could almost hear Olivia urging him to *Talk to the man, Jerome.* "My parents had some problems when I was doing my residency, and I came home to help and I dunno … I never …"

Shrug, as if Wince wanted to put him at ease. "Well, you look amazing." He crossed his arms. "I need pointers. Hey, you wanna grab some coffee?"

Yes. Jerome shook his head, wondering what Mrs. Wince might be like, and then wishing he hadn't wondered. No reason to mention Olivia's passing. He wasn't hiding behind his wife's memory, was he? *Ugh.* "I'm gonna be late." *He has a kid.*

"Train?"

"The R."

"I'll walk you." Wince herded him toward the corner, not actually bumping into him but steering him with his presence the way he had since they were in high school. He even walked with the same loose, dorky shuffle. Time travel again. They could have been headed to the library or to the principal's office.

"Thanks." Uneasy, Jerome tried to get Wince back on track. He just needed to survive another five minutes, and they'd be done and over and nice to know you. "What about you?"

"Eesh." Wince grimaced at the winter clouds and hunched forward as he walked, like the memory was too heavy to carry. "Yeah. Well, after I got expelled … so, juvie for a stretch. You knew that. After the wreck. Then a little prison for flavor. Got out, ditched my folks, and knocked around. A lotta drugs, because … reasons. I dunno. It was there. A couple of shitty tattoos I don't remember getting. Then by accident, I fell into music. Bands, y'know."

"You were in a band?"

"No! Well, I was, but mainly as scenery. Downtown Clowns. Pretty boy pop punk. I pretended to play guitar mostly. They wanted someone to freak the crowd and set fire to their pubes. You know me: professional troublemaker. *That* I'm good for. Right?"

Jerome chuckled. "And you applied."

"Bullshit. I was recruited." Wince smiled, big and bright, like they were still kids sneaking out to drink on the roof of his apartment building.

Back in school, how many times had he asked Jerome, *What the hell am I good for?*

Me. You're good for me.

Wince faced him again and sighed. "Oh man. Fun gig. All that tail. Money eventually. Record label kept me out of court."

They reached the corner and started snaking across a wide-open farmer's market sprawled across a church plaza. In three minutes, he'd be safe. "I can't believe you were in a band. White boy rhythm and all."

"Hand to God. And then we found a real guitarist, and I sort of tagged along for kicks until our manager quit and I took over."

Jerome choke-laughed. "Wait, what? You managed something? A band?" No way in hell.

"You could call it that. It just sorta happened." Wince pushed his hand into his thick hair and scratched his scalp. "Made sure we got paid. Set up the venues. Fought with the label once we got signed. Kept the other guys clean-ish. Off hard stuff anyway. They figured I was crazy so they, I dunno, listened."

They snaked past stalls piled with bread and onions and fresh honey until they reached Union Square. "Never in a million years ..."

"I know, right? But after my folks, what did I care? Nothing scared me. Nothing grossed me out. Turns out I'm a perfect stiff for pop bands. Now the label sends me out to break new talent. I'm respectable, Jug."

"Jesus."

"Tell me." Wink. "But it pays great. How the hell else am I paying for private school in Manhattan?"

Right. "That's amazing. You finally figured out what you were good for."

You're good for me.

Wince smiled again, and for ten seconds they were boys sitting on a window ledge, a hundred feet above the city, sorting out their escape plan.

Jerome could see Union Square up ahead and the entrance to the R train. *Fright or flight, mofo.* He wanted to run away, and he wanted to let Wince kidnap him.

"Here's you." Wince paused at the top of the subway stairs. His dirty gold hair gleaming in the cold sunlight, his joker's grin teasing at the question that neither of them had the stones to ask.

Do you remember the two of us?

Jerome held out a shaky hand to shake.

Wince took it, but then pulled him into a quick hug, pressing their chests together for two impossible seconds. One breath, two breaths. And he still smelled great and felt better. And for two seconds, they were seventeen and anything was possible.

Once burned.

Wince muttered against his chest. "So great to see you, Jug." And then he was gone, walking away before Jerome could respond or wipe his eyes.

Downstairs, he stepped onto his train headed downtown. "Stand clear of the closing doors."

Chapter Two

HE DIDN'T SPEAK TO Wince again 'til the hospital a month later.

Jerome was helping teachers chaperone a field trip to Lincoln Center, mainly because his daughter had bullied Walton into visiting the theater. Ten a.m. on a Tuesday onstage at the Koch Theater. Trying to corral thirty kids, ages seven to fourteen, was no joke.

"No pushing."

"Jerome." A little boy voice about twenty feet away.

He looked up, and Wince's son was waving at him from a high wall gilded like marzipan. Flip was among the little ones. Wince hadn't tagged along, which should have been a relief but wasn't.

The older teachers were struggling. "Linda, get down please." A half hour in, the four other chaperons were already exhausted. "Linda? Don't push."

The stage manager led them through the orchestra pit and the dressing rooms, finally bringing them up onto the stage to show off the curtain and lights. He called instructions to the union guys up in the booth.

A few minutes later, Flip's voice again. "Jerome. Hey, J'rome!"

"Boys! Flip, no!"

Before he could turn to look, shocked shouts drowned out the boy. Then he heard screaming, and he made for the noisy knot of kids staring at the floor.

Flip lay at the base of the marzipan wall, stunned silent, his face gray, his arm at a wrong angle.

Jerome crouched. "Breathe, buddy. Take a breath. Flip?" He

didn't move him, but he laid a hand on his ulna. *Yep, broken.* "Keep your eyes on me now. You're okay, buddy. Huh? Just stay there."

Flip hiccupped and coughed but stayed still. "Hurts." He was going into shock.

"I bet it does. You're okay, though. Promise." Jerome ignored the fidgety, terrified third graders crowded around him.

The stage manager (*Jerry? Larry?*) was already in motion.

"His arm's broken. He needs a doctor. I'm a friend of the family." *Sorta.* Jerome looked up.

"Dad?" Keisha appeared from the wings in her mouse costume.

"A boy fell." He turned to the chaperones. "Someone needs to run him to an emergency room. Someone needs to call his dad. Wendell Farley." He wasn't a practicing doctor, but he knew what to do. Back to Flip's dilated eyes. "Flip? All good, buddy. We're okay." He took charge without meaning to.

And somehow an hour later, Jerome found himself in the Mount Sinai West emergency room waiting for Wince. Keisha had ditched her first-act mouse head and steered them through the maze backstage, holding the costume's tail in one fist. Wince's office must've made a call to the hospital because no one said diddly about him carrying in some white kid with a busted arm. Flip stayed relatively calm, all things considered. The break looked clean, and the resident on duty had set his arm quickly. Watching doctors work always made Jerome feel lazy and lucky at the same time. He'd hated his ER rotation.

Keisha hovered by the door, needing a task to calm her down. *Like her mom.* He gave her a twenty and sent her to the cafeteria.

"J'rome." Flip sounded groggy and hoarse on the gurney. "Is my dad here?"

"Not yet, buddy." Jerome flashed a smile he didn't feel and glanced at his daughter's retreat. "You're okay."

Flip tried to smile. His cast looked comically huge: a hard white flipper in a sling.

"It's like a big hard Band-Aid." Saying the word made him grin.

Growing up, Jerome couldn't ever figure out why bandages were *beige*. Why did all medical stuff come in that same neutral putty color? He didn't put it together until he was older than Flip. He said as much one day studying for a trig midterm: they weren't flesh-colored to *him*.

Wince had laughed until milk came out of his nose, then put his tan arm over Jerome's dark black. "Band-Aids are *mutt*-colored." Their skin slid together, feeling a little too good to be safe. "Oughtta call 'em Bland-Aids, f'sure. Bland-ages."

"What's that about?" Jerome had taken his arm away before the nerves got to him, "Brown Band-Aids. Black Band-Aids. Man, we'd make a fortune."

"I'm so in. Fuck the blands." Wince had laughed and shoved into him, unselfconscious and affectionate as a stray dog until Jerome stepped back because his best friend didn't understand.

"Flip?" Without warning Wince pushed through the ER curtain like a hurricane. "Oh buddy. You scared the … crap out of me." He turned. "Jug, thank you so much."

"I just stayed with him."

"That's not true and you know it." Wince looked about ready to faint. He hugged Flip, kissed his head, and then let go abruptly. "Is that—? Did I hurt you?"

"Nope. I'm cool." The boy glanced at Jerome, exhausted and brave, and shifted the cast. "Big hard Band-Aid."

Jerome nodded at them. "Brave."

Wince sat on the edge of the bed, eyes shining at his son. "Life saver. I mean it. You being there." He wiped his mouth shakily. "Thank you."

"Me? Wasn't a big deal."

"Bullshit." Wince frowned and glanced at his son. "Sorry, boss." He kissed Flip's head again and squeezed him.

Jerome held in a smile. "He's had a rocky day."

Flip sighed, quiet against his father's chest.

"Conked out." Wince peered at his son. "And I'm gonna freak the fuck out if I stick around here much longer. Whatsay we jam? Dinner maybe. I'm buying."

"Umm." *We?* "Keisha's in the cafeteria killing time. I uh … and I gotta run her over to rehearsal in a bit. Lemme text her."

"Oh." Wince's face slipped, a ripple of disappointment vanishing under a practiced smile. "I didn't mean anything."

"No. Maybe after or something? I didn't know how long it would take you." *Jeez.* Everything they said to each other meant all this other crazy shit. "Sorry."

Wince shook his head and squeezed his kid, voice raw. "Sorry, nothing. No way I coulda got there fast enough. I owe you, Jug."

"No, man. You know that." Jerome knew he knew.

"I remember."

First week freshman year in the cafeteria, Jerome had been pouring himself fruit punch from a plastic jug when kids behind him shoved him, and he stumbled forward. "Hey!" Punch sloshed onto the floor and his new Nikes.

He straightened just as Thad Plasky said, "Nigger!" hissing the word at him like an ugly prayer. *For real?* The jug clamped in his wet fingers.

The kids in line froze around them, rubbernecking. But before Jerome could do or say anything, Wince Farley, class criminal, had shouldered through the ring of bodies holding his empty lunch tray. "Wha'd you say to him, Plasky?" Everyone had already heard he was a pitiless psycho with junkie parents; a week in, kids were warning each other about him.

Thad squared his shoulders without turning to look, "I said *nig*—"

Whap!

Wince swung that tray and knocked Thad clean off his feet, like … his shoes actually came off the floor a second. Food everywhere and the room shouting. Pandemonium. Jerome froze holding the jug with dripping fingers. Thad collapsed into the counter and slid to the floor, nose crooked and the side of his face salmon pink.

Cafeteria mayhem and everyone pushed closer, hemming them in, egging them on. Whimpering through bloody snot bubbles, Thad scrabbled back from the class lunatic. Wince simply ignored him, turning to face Jerome. He hadn't even turned until that moment.

"Easy, Jug." He touched Jerome's arm, above the hand holding the punch.

When their eyes met, Jerome gave him a wary, grateful nod. Wince winked in reply and elbow bumped him. Instant friends, almost like they'd been looking for each other all this time.

Thanks, man.

Shared smiles, right before the gabbling teachers pushed through the mob.

No sweat.

Both Thad and Wince got suspended for three days, but Jerome had met his best friend. Fair trade. They were a perfect match.

First time they hung out, he discovered Wince loaded up on cafeteria food because it was the one meal he could count on. He attended Walton Academy under Prep for Prep, a charity program that paid for poor kids to go to private school in New York City. Tuition, books, everything, but you had to keep your nose clean, something Wince didn't do well. Jerome did it for him so he could survive.

Jerome's parents were wealthy, but Wince lived "at risk" in the Gompers Projects with absent addict parents and anger to spare. He'd grown up a great bullshitter who hit things hard and first, with no respect for authority. He got his nickname 'cause even the seniors flinched when he moved. Even now, even as a grown man with a kid of his own, he came at things like a groggy cage fighter.

"Jug." And that was Wince, seventeen years later like no time had passed, looking at him with bright eyes and a loose heart. "Thank you."

"You're so welcome." A real smile passed between them and knotted itself firmly. *Long time no see.*

An alarm beeped nearby, yanking Jerome into the present. The curtain skittered open.

"Dad?" Keisha stood over him with raised eyebrows. "Are we gonna go, like, ever?"

The quiet bubble around them melted, and they were sitting in an emergency room again looking at his impatient daughter.

"Soon." *Sheesh.*

She gestured at her fuzzy gray rig. "Wardrobe flippin' out."

"Sorry. Uhh, yeah. Sorry hon."

"Cool costume." Wince probably wanted to split, too.

Keisha twisted her braids into a thick coil and smoothed it over her collarbone. Her mother's gesture, her mother's bones. "Is he dead or what?" She eyed Flip.

Wince grinned. "Not yet. They did a brain transplant."

Keisha raised her eyebrows like that was a fine idea. "Dad, it's three and I'm still a mouse, mostly?"

To Wince. "S'my daughter. Keisha."

"I had a hunch." Wince's smile did that thing where it stopped joking and shone on her gently. He extended his hand. "Wince." They shook. "Farley."

"Nice to meet you." Keisha's brow creased. "Are you his friend?" Like he had only one. Well, back in the day, true enough.

"Jug and I went to Walton together, back when dinos roamed the earth." Wince's voice turned polite and got very sitcom-dad square. "Thanks for rescuing my kid."

She shrugged. "That was all my dad. I was putting on my mouse getup for the third graders." She turned and lowered her voice. "I'm gonna be late for rehearsal. Forty minutes?"

Wince squinted at Jerome.

"*Nutcracker*."

Keisha was having none of that. "We refer to it as *The Ball-buster*." Jerome grimaced. "She's dancing at Lincoln Center."

"That's so groovy. I never seen a ballet." Wince bobbed his head.

Keisha set the bait. "It's pretty dippy an' all. But I'm in two parts this year. Mice *and* Polichinelles." She glanced back with her mom's ruthless, elegant aim. "We can bring guests to the dress rehearsal, Mr. Farley. You should come."

What? Jerome tried to read her eyes.

Wince lit up at the invite. "Sure!"

Keisha approved. "He's cool." A peek at her dad.

Jerome shook his head. "You don't have to. Don't blackmail him. Not everyone likes Tchaikovsky."

"Butts in seats, yo. Dancers are athletes." She looked at Wince. "I think you should. Nuts will be cracked. Bring Flip. After his brain transplant heals." She motioned to Jerome, looked at her watch. "I gotta go."

"We'll be there." Wince nodded and stood.

Keisha didn't wait another second. *Like Olivia.* She hated being late, breaking the rules, disappointing anyone. Over her shoulder, she said, "Whole hospital smells like that stupid *pig.*"

Wince crossed his arms and raised his eyebrows. "Great kid."

"She is." Jerome stared after her. "So much like her mother."

"I'm glad."

"She was a soap actress. Her mom was …" And then he flat ran out of the words.

Wince watched him for a moment before he asked. "She died?"

Meaning Olivia. Meaning that whole other life and wife Wince had missed. Meaning Wince's forked path through exes and overdoses. Jerome nodded. Embarrassed at these feelings. Embarrassed to be embarrassed with Wince. Olivia would've made fun of him for not speaking up, not introducing her to his oldest friend with some panache. "Bone cancer."

Around them the hallway had emptied, a row of curtained areas to hide the people in pain from each other.

"Sucks. Sorry." Wince looked at the linoleum floor, fiddling with his watchband. "Flip's mom ditched us when he was three. She had … problems."

Jerome gave a tight frown. "You got burned, too."

"Not really. I got Flip. Fun job. Travel. Cool digs." He looked so tired. Beaten. "I made out great." He held up his fist.

Jerome did the same and bumped their knuckles together. "Sorry."

"For what? We both got burned doing what we loved. That's the deal. Live. Burn." He scooped Flip up, still fast asleep.

On the other side of the curtain, raised voices speaking Spanish as a gurney wheeled past.

"We okay to go, y'think?" Wince looked to Jerome. "I'd like to get this guy home."

Jerome scanned the room, plucking his bag and coat off the stool.

"I gave them everything, talked to the doc before I came in." Wince shifted his weight, itchy to flee.

Of course, Wince hated emergency rooms: How many times

had he watched his parents bleeding and screaming in these places? How many times had he had his stomach pumped and worse? And how much did Wince remember of the last night they saw each other? The only time they ever kissed, both drunk enough to pretend they hadn't. Wasted and wasting everything they had because they didn't know better, what mattered, what didn't.

Wince's teenaged voice in his head: *What am I good for, Jug? Me.*

And then kissing him, terrified and triumphant. So close to perfect, best friends for three years and they'd blown it in one horrible night, joyriding in the rain. Reckless and wrecked. The car Wince had stolen 'cause he knew how. The Lincoln they'd totaled. Blood in both their eyes from the dashboard. The taste of Wince and shit whiskey in his mouth while he confessed to cops and parents.

After that night, Jerome's parents forbade him to speak to his best friend, his only friend. Wince got expelled, vanished into juvie then worse. No goodbye, no contact. Jerome trudged back to his regularly scheduled life—prep school, undergrad, med school, wife—until that life vanished, too.

No one had died that night, but everything had ended in a white room just like this one; seventeen years burned-burned-burned to ash. Leaving them alone where they belonged.

Jerome trailed through the ER hanging a little behind father and son, afraid of making things worse. Up ahead, he could see Keisha's red coat by the exit, the mouse tail peeking out below.

Gotta go. Irrationally he caught himself wasting time, walking slowly. What if he never got to talk to Wince again like this? They had half an hour, and it was only seven blocks to Lincoln Center.

"What was Keisha's pig deal?" Wince glanced sideways at him. "Does *The Nutcracker* have pigs?"

Jerome chuckled and sighed. "Eighth-grade biology. Fetal pig dissection. I dunno." He slid his fingers together and crossed his arms. "Somehow dissecting this pig became a huge crisis."

"Well, her mom *died*," Wince spoke softly, but the words fell like a hammer.

Jerome'd never thought of that. "You think that's why?" They were almost to the door.

"I think she's a kid who's already had to hug death close, and that might make Porky Jr. a real drag." He sniffed and regarded his son gently. "When Flip's mom left, it took a year to be real to him, her bailing on us so easy. He still talks to her sometimes. Pretends. Y'know. Hurts to watch." His eyes did that thing where they softened without moving. Laugh lines. When had he gotten so grown up?

We're old, yo.

Maybe regret wasn't so bad. Maybe that was something you learned to live with. An inch at a time, like sliding into warm water over a fire until you could tolerate being boiled alive.

"Daddy." Flip's voice broke the spell. He squirmed against Wince's chest.

Wince blinked and looked down. "Oh lord. What now?" His warm tone made the words into an old joke.

The boy sighed. "Never mind." His cast was strapped against him like an oversized fiberglass fossil.

"Okay." Wince hefted him closer. "We're going home, mister." The automatic doors shushed open for them.

Keisha glowered at him through the glass, the mouse tail draped over her arm like a rubbery pink stole.

Before stepping out into the frosty air, Jerome wrapped his scarf around his neck and zipped his coat. "Keesh, we got ages still."

Keisha herded him toward the curb. "They're rehearsing Coffee with the new Russian couple. Chumakov and Petrachenko. I wanna watch. Legit."

Jerome laughed. "Okay. Okay. Legit."

She trotted to the crosswalk and glared at him to *hurry up already*. Wince smiled beside him. "Coffee?"

"The Arabian variation. *Nutcracker.*" Jeez. Not what he wanted to talk about at all. "The Coffee bit in Act Two, but she's too young." Jerome exhaled roughly. "Sorry, I hear about this stuff so much, I forget most people have no idea—"

"Doesn't matter. I get it. Good for her." Wince exhaled with a smile. "You're a great dad, better than yours was."

"Y'think?" His parents had been corporate lawyers: great with conflict, encouragement not so much.

Nod. "She's lucky."

"Well, she's not *old* enough to dance Coffee. Frankly, the music is too sexy. But mad beautiful. We spend a lot of time arguing about it." Jerome smiled. "Welcome to every dinner at my house."

Wink. "If you insist."

Somehow they'd stopped talking about ballet.

A hot hollow opened behind Jerome's heart. "Uh. Good." Smile. "You look happy, Jug. I'm really glad."

He glanced at his daughter cocking her confused frown at him. "She knows what she wants."

Wince dropped his gaze to his dozing son. "Lucky. A lot of people never know."

"That's not—" Jerome swallowed and tried again. "Wince."

Wince blinked. A shivery silence dragged between them like swords scraping blade to blade.

Jerome said, "I gotta go."

"I'll see you, okay? At the coffee-pig-mice thing. Ballet!" Wince grinned and winked at him, gorgeous and open as the sky.

They both chuckled, somehow calm standing there facing each other in the cold all these years later. His pulse thumped in his ears. If Jerome didn't feel happy, he at least didn't feel lost. *Regret never killed anyone.*

Olivia would have loved him. *Too.*

An awkward moment where they couldn't hug or shake or anything in farewell, so Jerome saluted and pointed at Flip. "Take care of him."

"What else am I good for?" Wince crossed the street to hail a cab. *Me. But we're bad for each other.*

Jerome caught up with his daughter distractedly. *What just happened?* He forgot to tug on his gloves 'til she did.

"I was right. He's cool." Keisha looked at him directly when he didn't reply. "Wince."

"I never said he wasn't." *But I implied it.* She didn't really understand because Wince's charm blinded people.

They doubled back up Columbus toward rehearsals.

She swiveled toward him and nodded in the cold. "Dad, I *totally* ship it."

He made an old man face. "What does that mean?" She couldn't possibly understand.

"Wince. It makes no sense, so it makes perfect sense. That you're friends." She tucked the tail tip in her pocket and took his arm.

"I haven't seen him in seventeen years, Keisha." A panicky edge to his voice made him sound like he was lying. "Give or take."

"What?" She narrowed her eyes at him. "So you *don't* like him?"

"I don't know him." He forced himself to speak more quietly. "Anymore."

Had he done something to give himself away? Had Wince noticed? What was she saying exactly?

"Dad. It's okay to like someone. He's nice to you." Keisha laughed at him and studied his face. "And you return the favor. I ship it." She squinted at something in the distance. "Did Mom like him? She must've." As if she'd read his mind a moment ago.

"She never met him."

"She would've though. A lot." A tight nod. "Why does he call you Jug?"

"A long, crazy story. Not for little people." A quick memory of Thad Plasky showing up to school with black eyes, chipped teeth, and his nose taped for a week. "Because that's what he calls me."

An approaching van made an illegal right. Jerome covered his embarrassment by turning to watch it barreling right through the crosswalk.

"So I was right." She pushed her hands into her coat, obviously proud of her mind-reading skills. "About Wince?"

The stage door buzzed and swung open. The security guard nodded at the desk.

"Maybe." He blinked and hugged her. "Even a stopped clock is right twice a day."

"Well, yeah." Keisha rolled her eyes. She stepped inside walking backward, laughing. "But only if you happen to be looking at exactly the right second." Only then she turned, dropping the tail.

Once burned …

Heading around to the Koch entrance, he made his way to the front of house in the dim theater and found a seat with the teachers and kids watching the empty stage.

"Places. Places, people," said a voice from overhead.

Chapter Three

THE DRESS REHEARSAL WAS not a date, but it sure as hell felt like one.

All November, Jerome had wrestled with himself, terrified he was overanalyzing but afraid of missing his chance, if one existed. *Impossible.* He kept hoping they'd bump into each other before or after school, but no deal. He saw Flip with a nanny a couple of afternoons, but no Wince. He found their number in the school directory, but it went undialed 'til Keisha called with her invitation.

Wince couldn't come 'til one. He'd see the second act, Keish's bit with Mother Ginger at least.

"He's been on a tour," she said. "He sounded weird. Tired."

"Weird how?"

"Dad, he's *your* friend."

By eleven a.m. Jerome was a mess. By the intermission, panic set in.

He'd slept like hell the past three nights. Distracted at the gym. Now he paced just inside the stage door, waiting for Wince and his son so they could run backstage before the second half got started. He forced his breath slower as if he were benching three hundred pounds.

If nothing else, they'd talk. *Right?*

"Sorry, Jug." Wince's hair was slicked back in a wavy helmet, parted no less, and he was wearing a suit. *Madman makes good.* He was out of breath and glazed with sweat in the cold air. "Sorry, I'm late."

Jerome whistled. "You look sharp." At least he'd put on khakis and a sweater. He saw a lot of rehearsals with dance moms. He never would've thought to wear a suit, but Wince looked like a million bucks. "I feel underdressed."

"You look great. You always look great."

He shifted his weight uneasily.

"Sorry I missed the first half." Since when did Wince sweat? "Label meeting. I tried to get away faster."

He waved away the worry. "First act is pretty much opening presents and fights."

"So I know this show's a holiday thing. Candy and fairies. And Arabian coffee?"

"Yep. Mice, sugar, princes, plums." He counted the nonsense on his fingers. He took a breath and asked, "Where's Flip?"

"Sitter." Quick blink.

Was he nervous too? A thin tendril of hope worked into Jerome's chest.

Wince said, "I gotta be honest: my kid wasn't interested in tights and nuts."

Jerome caught his eye then. "Unlike you?"

Wince snorted, which made him snort. A bright bloom of pleasure behind his ribs. He hadn't laughed, not inside-laughed, in a long time. Christmas coming and Olivia had been gone three years, the scar faded smooth by now. *Oh.* She hadn't been able to see Keisha in a *Nutcracker* since right after she got diagnosed. *All that time, where does it wind up?*

Wince studied his face and stance, getting a read the way only he could. "You okay?"

Jerome finally exhaled and held the backstage door open. "Sure. Yeah. Long story." Olivia had heard about Wince plenty, urged him to reach out for years. What would she think? Most likely, she would've grinned and kicked his ass and told him to *make a damn choice, Jerome.* Ten years of soap scripts had fed her unshakeable faith in happy reunions.

Wince blinked, but he didn't press. "Well, today it's just us."

"Old times." Jerome smiled at him.

"Speak for yourself." But sure enough, he smiled, still eager as a stray dog. He held up a bouquet of orange roses. "For Keisha."

"She'll love that; only, we can't go to the dressing rooms 'til after." Jerome put a hand at the small of Wince's muscular back and steered him past the rigging.

As they snaked toward the front of house, a few dancers eyed their progress cagily. Jerome nodded at the dance captain who'd been so patient about letting Keisha watch the Coffee rehearsals.

Wince clocked the ceiling and the cyclorama. "Gah. Some setup."

Jerome smiled. *Band manager.* "I forgot. You're in theaters all the time."

"Well, not this high end, but yeah. Same idea." As they neared the stage, Wince craned to check out the stored set pieces. He muttered conspiratorially. "So what'd I miss?"

Jerome kept his voice low as they cut through the wings. "First half, little girl gets a nutcracker that turns into a hot soldier. He fights mice and takes her to check out junk food." *Stop rushing.* "For real."

"But with tutus."

Jerome shrugged. "I guess. And dance belts: don't ask. S'pretty old school."

"Nostal-*gic.*" Wince's grin made the idea into a dirty joke.

"That's the word. So you're in time for Candyland." The ribbon of hope looped into a bow and squeezed his heart.

A heavy stage manager in black sweats corralled the *corps*, "In five. That's your five minutes." The stage lights pulsed bright then dark. The crew scurried for preset.

Jerome veered left behind black masking, almost to the edge of the actual stage. "Wait, Wince, c'mere."

"I don't wanna miss Keisha, man."

"Two secs." Jerome tugged him forward, holding his shoulders and standing behind him. "See?"

From where they stood, all 2,500 seats of the theater glittered at them in the dimmed house lights like a glass waiting for wine, but no one could see them. Not from before or behind. The swept stage gleamed under kaleidoscopic pastel lights, and the whole building seemed to hold its breath.

"Jesus," Wince whispered.

"Best view in the house."

Standing close, the warmth between them rose. Jerome's chest and Wince's back were an inch apart. His chin hovered over Wince's shoulder. The wings seemed unexpectedly quiet, and the sound of their breathing amplified.

Wince swayed against him, lightly, just resting his strong back against Jerome's torso, the bouquet held at his side brushing both their legs.

Neither spoke.

Slowly, warily, Jerome's hands rose like muscular shadows as Wince turned to face him like someone waking up from a dream. They stood pressed, breathing together in the wings.

The stage manager voice from out in the house. "Three minutes. Three minutes. Places, please." The stage turned mauve and peach then deep blue.

One breath together. Two.

"We should find our seats. C'mon." Wince looked terrified in his sharp suit. "Well, say something."

"That doesn't matter." Jerome raised his head in wonder. "I am a stopped clock." He took Wince's free hand and pressed it against his heart.

"A what?" Confused grin.

"Clock. I get to be right twice, even if I'm broken." The lights from onstage raked the wings, turning Wince violet and tangerine for a minute, then leaving them in brief darkness. "But only if my timing's right."

Wince stood very still, under the candy light. "It always was." His face crinkled in a smile, and his thumbs hooked Jerome's belt loops.

Jerome lowered his face.

Wince's eyes shone in the sudden dark, and without thinking, Jerome kissed him.

"J—" Wince may have been saying something, but the words vanished into their mouths and Jerome pulled him close; if he never had another chance, he wasn't going to waste this one.

Once burned, once burned. He opened his eyes. Not wanting to miss anything.

Wince pushed one thick arm around Jerome's ribs, holding their chests together as his mouth opened. He pulled away to tip his head and come back licking at Jerome's mouth under the lambent shafts of pink, amber, teal that swept over them.

Somewhere on the other side of the stage, the muted *kat-tump-a-bump* of toe shoes as dancers took their places for Act Two and the Land of Sweets. His hands were shaking, his legs too.

"Hey, fella. Easy." A quiet laugh from Wince and a rustle of roses. "Jug. Hey. Hey. Easy. I'm right here."

Jerome straightened, self-conscious and nervous about his daughter somewhere back here dressed to dance for Mother Ginger. "I wanted to, y'know. So much. And I didn't know if—" He snuck another kiss, quick, and then another. And then he stepped aside. "Sorry. I'm sorry."

"Don't be. I'm not." A nipping kiss pressed at the corner of Jerome's mouth like punctuation. "We're gonna have an accident, an incident. Look at me."

Jerome nodded. Wince beamed at him with easy, tested affection. And this time he *was* right, a stopped clock, a cracked nut.

Olivia spoke in his head, *You only get the chances you take.*

"There's no rush. We're okay, man. We're both grownups." He took Jerome's hand and gripped it, not letting go. "Well, you are."

Jerome squeezed back. He felt crazy and hopeful. What would they say to their kids? Would they go on dates? What would their friends say? His parents? Did he even care?

"Hey. Hey, Jug. Later." Wince tapped Jerome's forehead, as if he'd read his mind. "Leave it 'til later."

Jerome smiled. "Yes, sir. I'm good for it."

"I know you are." They made their way out to the orchestra, not saying any of the stuff they might've.

Wince paused at the end of the row to let him pass and then followed Jerome to their seats in the half-lights, bumping into him in all the right places. The director and the lighting team sat about twenty rows back with the board, deep in conversation. Dress rehearsals tended to be stop/start for hours, but just now, Jerome didn't mind sitting quietly for a bit.

As soon as they sat, Wince found his big hand in the dark and laced their fingers, black and tan.

Jerome grunted in pleasure. Wince grunted back.

"Fair warning, man. This may take a while. Plus dinner." He and Keisha usually celebrated after the dress with a massive pile of sushi.

"Cool. I'm in no kinda hurry."

Jerome smiled. *Maybe I'm good for you too.*

"What are your feelings about Christmas?"

"Uh, good?" Jerome shrugged. Was that an invitation? Before he could ask, the overture started up and the curtain rose on a confectionary castle eighty feet high.

"Jeez." Wince blinked happily at the sudden brightness.

For some reason sitting for any dress, seeing a show come to-gether, always made him so proud of his little girl, all that work and sweat and discipline that made her blaze onstage. Harsh joy spiraled up out of him like cinders lifted by a bonfire. He said a prayer for Olivia, another for their strong daughter, and a small one for himself. *Once burned.*

Wince turned and whispered in his ear, "What happens now?"

Jerome winked. "Whatever it is, it's worth waiting for."

Chuckle. Cellos and trumpets below and rustling from the dark wings.

Wince squeezed his fingers. "I missed you, Jug."

"Man." Jerome squeezed back and turned to look at his dark profile. "What took us so long?"

Wince kissed him again and whispered into his skin. "We were shy."

Damon Suede has lived all over: Houston, New York, London, Prague. Along the way, he's earned his crust as a model, a messenger, a promoter, a programmer, a sculptor, a singer, a stripper, a bookkeeper, a bartender, a techie, a teacher, a director ... but writing has ever been his bread and butter.

Damon is a proud member of the Romance Writers of America and serves on its Board of Directors. He also served as the 2013 president for the Rainbow Romance Writers, RWA's LGBT romance chapter.

Though new to gay romance, Damon has been writing for print, stage, and screen for two decades, which is both more and less glamorous than you might imagine. He's won some awards, but his blessings are more numerous: his amazing friends, his demented family, his beautiful husband, his loyal fans, and his silly, stern, seductive Muse who keeps whispering in his ear, year after year.

LOVE IS IN THE AIR

Rachel Hauck

Three days before New Year's Eve

SHE'D NEVER BEEN ONE to hide in a crowd, but today, she must.

A glimmer of recognition lit the eyes of some of the people waiting in the long customer service lines, their wilted, frustrated expressions softening to surprise. Or maybe disbelief.

Ducking into a crowded restaurant on Atlanta's C concourse, Ansley aimed for the only open seat at the bar. And even more luck! There was a power socket tucked against the wall. With her phone dead and a mountain of calls to make, she couldn't have asked for a more divine result.

"Pardon me." She angled her guitar case around the man sitting on the stool next to hers, tripping over his luggage and computer bag. "You might want to get those out of the way."

He glanced at her, his blue eyes bright and clear. "Not mine." The man gestured toward the packed in travelers, reaching for outlets, hailing one of the harried servers. "Take your pick."

"People should know better than to leave their stuff around—"

Truly, it wasn't that big of a deal. She was tired and hungry. Drained, just like her cellphone battery. But, then again, weren't they all?

"Sorry, they're mine." A dark suit reached for his bags, his brown eyes landing on Ansley. "Hey, aren't you—"

She waved him off with a mock laugh. "Ansley Moore? I get that all the time. Nope, but don't I wish. I just look a lot like her."

The man frowned. "Really? You sure you're not—"

"Would I be sitting here if I was?" She arched her eyebrow, pulling her best face. "*Please.*"

"Guess not." The suit grabbed his bags and backed away.

Good. Ansley fished her phone and power cord from her shoulder bag and plugged in. A harried server appeared, gave her the once over, but was too distracted to let her gaze linger. Her nametag read "Marie."

"The menu is right there." She pointed to the metal holder in front of Ansley. "What can I get you to start?"

"Diet Coke."

With that, Marie left, picking up checks and credit cards from the customers ready to leave, only to have others in the waiting holiday horde take their place.

"Pretty big mess." The man with the blue eyes, sun-bleached hair, and a soft tan on his cheeks pulled her attention from the menu—and out of hiding.

"The airlines will have to learn to back up their systems."

The man whistled. "Wouldn't want to be the man who has to answer for this."

"Or the woman."

"Especially not the woman." He grinned, winking—an action Ansley *felt.* A warm, spicy swirl.

She faced away, pretending to focus on her phone as the sensation faded. What was *that*? Ever since her boyfriend of three years, Hank, bugged out a year ago, deciding he didn't want to be in a relationship with an artist, she'd retreated from ideas of love and romance.

Though she believed one day she'd give love a second chance. Then came the stalker …

Ansley swerved around a little more, giving the man her back. Traveling alone, she needed to be wary. As soon as her phone charged up enough, she'd call Noël, her best friend and assistant, for an update.

Exhaling a load of stress, she glanced around. The airport was nuts. She'd tried to find the airline's Preferred Lounge when she arrived from LAX, but since she rarely traveled alone, she was lost. And the airline staff had no time for "Where's the Preferred Lounge?" when passengers were in long lines demanding an explanation and new flights.

So her growling stomach and need to charge her phone drove her to the nearest restaurant.

She didn't become a country sensation by waiting on others.

"Pardon me," a woman leaned around Mr. Blue Eyes, "aren't you—"

Ansley shook her head, offering a quick laugh. "Ansley Moore? No, I'm her doppelgänger." She sighed, grateful when the woman left without pressing.

"So, who's Ansley Moore?" Blue Eyes drank his Coke. From the glass. No straw.

She regarded him for a second. Was he serious or playing her? "A country singer. Pretty famous. The biggest contestant to ever come out of *An American Singer*."

He shrugged. "I don't watch television."

"Do you listen to the radio?"

"Some news or talk radio. Classical. Maybe '70s rock. Inspirational."

"Really?" Ansley's phone buzzed in her hand. Noël was calling. Her best friend. The future bride. "You look really young for being so old."

He laughed—a sound she liked—as he raised his glass for another drink.

"Hey, bride-to-be," she said. "Yeah, I'm fine. Just caught up in all the crazy … at a restaurant … charging my phone … hold on … the server is coming around." Ansley reached for the menu. Ah, she'd landed at a sushi place. "I'll have the tuna and a California roll."

"Ansley, why aren't you in the lounge?" Noël said.

"I was hungry, my phone was dead, so I headed for the nearest restaurant with a vacant stool."

"Why can't you ever remember to charge your phone?" There was an endearing rebuke in Noël's voice.

"Because I have you. Are you sure you want to leave me to get married?" Besides keeping Ansley's schedule, Noël was her clothing and makeup expert and all-around confidant. Especially when her reality show win shot her to stardom.

Then Noël met and fell in love with a pro surfer, Ty Houston, when she took over Ansley's vacation plans in Costa Rica last October. Ten short weeks later, they were getting married on New Year's Eve in Melbourne, Florida, Ansley and Noël's hometown.

"As much as I love you, I love Ty more. Ansley, isn't this what we always dreamed of when we were kids? To find the love of our life?"

"Yeah, I'm just mad you beat me to it."

"Just think, if you'd gone to Costa Rica instead of me ..."

Ansley had forgone the trip—sorely needed after a grueling twelve-week tour—to open for country legend Aubrey James.

"You're going to love Mindy." Ah, the new assistant. "She's even more organized than I am."

"But she's not my best friend since fifth grade."

"You don't need a best friend. You have me."

"Always." Though Ansley knew ... Ty was already taking her place.

"Tell you what, as my last act as your *assistant* ..." There was silence for a few moments. "The Preferred Lounge is by Gate 30 on concourse B, C, and D. Where are you?"

"C."

"Get to the lounge. I don't want my wedding to be eclipsed by your funeral."

She'd laugh if Noël's concern wasn't rooted in truth. Ansley cut a glance at Blue Eyes. He exuded confidence, giving her a sense of safety. "I'm fine. Hidden in a very crowded restaurant. Besides, I've ordered. I'll go as soon as I eat."

"Call me the moment you do. And Ansley, I know you've only met Ty a few times, but you're going to love him. I promise."

The tenderness in her best friend's voice watered Ansley's heart. She wanted to love him. She wanted to love someone like Noël loved Ty.

Saying goodbye, Ansley picked up her chopsticks as Blue Eyes was served another soda, his attention fixed on the TV above the bar. Football. Looked like a college bowl game.

"Where you headed?" He asked the question without looking over at her.

She hesitated, gripping her first sushi roll between the narrow sticks. "Florida."

But his attention was on the TV as one player tackled another. Ansley knew nothing about football. She'd devoted her teen and college years to her guitar, to music.

A fact her last two boyfriends never understood.

"Business or pleasure? This Florida trip?" So Blue Eyes heard her after all.

"My best friend is getting married." Ansley's phone lit up again with her manager, Jim Rubart's, face and number.

"You okay? Man, what a day to travel."

"I'm good. Safe. Listen, did you get my email about the rehearsal schedule?" She was about to record her second album, and she planned on doing it live, with her band. Old school.

"You're all set. Found a place for you to rehearse. I have some news, too. Joe Townsend wants to produce your next album."

"You're kidding. Joe Townsend?" The man who'd won every Grammy known to man.

"He saw you on the People's Music Awards last night. Said you stole the show with your performance. Your life is about to change *again*, Ansley. In a big, big way."

She cut a glance at Blue Eyes, then turned to the wall. The glint in his eye, the mold of his expression made her yearn, wanting something she'd never really had before. Not even with Hank. This stranger made her want what she felt and heard in Noël's voice.

But her career was her lover. She had no time for the hassle of romance. No room for longings of the heart.

She inhaled deeply. "But I planned to do a live album with Len Davis."

"Ansley, Joe Townsend. People would kill to have him producing. Listen, I got to run. Glad you're okay. We'll talk later."

With a sigh, Ansley swallowed the last of her Diet Coke, slung the strap of her bag over her head, grabbed her guitar and scooted past Blue Eyes without a backward glance.

"See you later, Ansley."

"See you—" She whirled around, her gaze meeting his. A slow grin lit his face.

She pressed her finger to her lips. "Shhh."

He nodded, returning his gaze to the football game. The longing from a moment ago twisted deeper.

Her path had just crossed with one of the good guys. Too bad it was only for a few moments in a crowded, crazy airport.

He watched her go, back straight, her guitar swinging from her hand. She was quickly swallowed up in the crowd, but the amber highlights in her brown hair lingered in his vision.

She was petite, determined, and pretty. Not beautiful. But pretty. In the way a man likes a woman to be pretty. Casual or decked out, pretty girls were always easy on the eye. On the soul.

But it was her lyrical voice that vibrated in his chest. Too bad they wouldn't ... Naw, man, don't even think about it.

You're better off alone.

Romance complicated life. Love hurt every bit as much as it healed.

Drew ordered another soda from the server and checked his watch. Three more hours before his flight. *If* they didn't cancel it. His trip from Hawaii started two days ago. Nice and smooth. Easy. Then he landed in San Francisco. What a madhouse. Twenty-four hours later, he boarded a flight to Melbourne by way of Atlanta.

In some sort of conciliation, the airline boosted him to first class for the hour flight, but until then …

Another weary traveler took Ansley's seat. Drew greeted him, then noticed Ansley had left her phone at the counter, charging.

"That yours, man?" The traveler said. "I need to plug in."

"Go ahead." Drew gathered Ansley's phone and plug. He'd take it to her, though he hated the idea of losing his bar seat. He had a perfect view of the game.

Living in Hawaii, he didn't connect much with stateside college ball. He missed the days of watching Big Ten play all day Saturday.

"Hey, you." Ansley tapped his shoulder. He peered up into her anxious hazel gaze, her high cheeks flushed. "Have you seen my phone?" She stooped looking around her stool and the counter where she sat. "I can't lose it. All of my new songs are—"

Drew held up her phone. "I was going to bring it to you."

"Thank you!" She snatched it from his hand, exhaled deeply, and reached into her bag. "You don't know what this means to me." She passed him a hundred dollar bill.

Drew recoiled. "What do you take me for? Go back to your lounge." He cut a glance at her. A mistake. Something in her hazel eyes made him yearn for more than a life of a bachelor.

The server set down his drink. He thanked her and turned the glass in his hands. He wasn't thirsty. He just needed something to do while he waited.

"Say … aren't you Ansley Moore?" A thirty-something woman dressed for business leaned through two men and a woman to fix her gaze on the singer. "I saw you on the music awards. You were—"

"No, no, just a resemblance." Ansley stepped closer to Drew.

"What? You're carrying a guitar case." The woman motioned to Ansley's instrument.

"That's my guitar." Drew slipped his hand around the handle, his skin touching hers. What's a white lie when rescuing a distressed damsel? "Drew Callahan, singer, songwriter, troubadour. For five hundred bucks and a good meal, I'll sing at your next party."

The woman gaped at him. She wasn't buying it. "I never heard of Drew Callahan."

"Man!" Drew smacked the counter with a glance at Ansley. "Some publicity agent you turned out to be."

"Well, some talent you turned out to be." A smile tugged the edge of her lips.

The woman started to ask another question, but someone from within the throng called her and she left with a final glance at Ansley, frowning, calculating if she'd been made a fool.

"Publicity agent?" Ansley reached for her guitar and the brush of her hand against his was soft, smooth.

"A no talent?" He curled his fingers into his palm. This stranger awakened a desire he'd rather leave sleeping.

She laughed. "Thank you. For saving me. I owe you."

"You're not going to give me another hundred bucks, are you?"

"No." She made a face. "I didn't mean to insult you. I just wanted to show my appreciation."

"The common way is to say, 'Thank you.'"

"I did that. Perhaps I can text you a download link to my last record?"

"Thanks, but I don't have a cellphone."

She grimaced, eyes wide with disbelief. "You don't have a cellphone? Look, if you don't like my music, just say so. I won't be offended."

"I'd love a copy. But I'm serious; I don't have a cell." He patted his hip pants pockets to prove his point. Sometimes he traveled with his business cards, but not this time. He'd left Hawaii so quickly he barely had time to pack. Baby brother and his impulsive decisions had him in emergency mode. Drew held up his arm, pointing to his watch. "This is the most technical thing I own."

Her smile, white and even, was sweet and inviting. "How do you communicate?"

"Land line. Old fashioned letters. And yes, email. Well, my assistant reads the emails."

She pinched his arm. "I just wanted to see if you were for real."

"It's a surprisingly simple and easy life. You should try it."

Ansley took one step back, still smiling, her movements smooth and flirty. "I wouldn't even know where to begin."

Yeah, well, he'd been *that* guy. The one with his phone against his ear, iPad in his hand, and a million details flowing through his brain.

But life had pulled the rug out from under him. He'd learned a lot in the past four years. Most of all, he'd never go back to the old, technologically driven Drew Callahan.

Not if his life depended on it. Which it did.

Chapter Two

NIGHT SETTLED OVER ATLANTA'S Hartsfield-Jackson Airport as Ansley took her seat in first class, putting on her Florida State ball cap, tugging it on low.

If she kept her head down, she'd minimize being recognized by boarding passengers.

An hour-and-ten-minute flight to Melbourne and she'd be home. Noël was supposed to pick her up this morning, but with all the delays, she was occupied with wedding prep.

So Mom would meet her.

Mom. She never approved of Ansley's choice. A singer? An entertainer? She wanted Ansley to be a nurse or a doctor. Because that's what *she'd* always dreamed of doing.

But in the quiet moments, when she wondered if Mom was right, Ansley felt God's pleasure in her choice.

"Guess we're seatmates."

Blue Eyes, a.k.a. Drew, dropped into the aisle seat. He carried nothing. No bag, no phone, no tablet. He glanced at her when he buckled in.

"Seriously, you don't even have a carry-on?" she said. "What kind of man are you?" In all of her travels, Ansley noted how burdened and bogged down passengers were with their carry-ons and their electronic accouterments.

He laughed, accepting a bottle of water from the flight attendant. "I checked my bag. Not that there was much to check. I like to travel light." Drew leaned toward her, motioning to the ball cap. "Nice touch. Why won't you tell anyone who you are?"

"Long story."

"Ah, okay, and we've only an hour flight."

She snorted a laugh. He was making her like him. Trust him.

Ansley leaned against the side of the plane, the world beyond the oval window dark with a moonless night, and studied him.

"I was stalked." Her words were quick, low, more to herself than Drew.

"Stalked?" He shifted in his seat, the fragrance of soap and cologne rising from his skin.

"A crazy fan. Followed me everywhere. Wanted to marry me." She raised her gaze to his.

He was listening. No one but Noël ever really listened to her. Her manager, her booking agent, her record label execs talked at her, through her, around her, about her, always trying to persuade her, yet never hearing her.

"That had to be scary."

She liked the cut of his jaw and the way his full lips held his next thought in check.

"Beyond ... He started out as an enthusiastic fan of *An American Singer* but fixated on me more and more with each episode."

"So you took to lying about your identity and wearing a ball cap."

"I traveled with a bodyguard for a year after he was arrested, but things settled, and this trip home didn't seem to require the usual entourage."

"Why not this trip?"

She grinned. "My best friend is getting married."

"Really? Must be the weekend for weddings. My bro—"

The flight attendant leaned in. "Miss Moore, can I get a quick picture?"

Ansley glanced at Drew. He nodded. *Go ahead.* Rising and stepping past him, she posed with the beaming woman.

"I love your music."

Thanking her, Ansley signed the back of her iPhone and returned to her seat.

"See, that wasn't so bad," Drew said.

"Enough about me." She adjusted her cap, raising it enough to scoop her hair from her face. "What about you? What does a man without a use for technology do for a living?"

"I have a little business. A-Hoi-Hou. A line of beach wear. Just getting started. Selling to the locals and tourist. But, um, if you're ever in Honolulu, come by the shop. I'll give you a discount." He offered his hand.

"Such generosity." Ansley slipped her hand into his, her eyes meeting his, his grip feeling perfect. "If I'm ever in Honolulu …"

Pulling her hand free, she settled in her seat and started to dream of Hawaii.

Drew stepped into the cool, dewy night outside baggage claim. His duffle bag came out first, so he waved goodbye to Ansley and headed out. Tempted to ask for her number, he restrained the impulse. Being engaged to a socialite taught him love and devotion were not enough for some women. How much more so with a rising country singer?

And he simply refused to put his heart through the ache.

Between the shadows, he caught sight of his brother, Tyler, leaning against a sporty rental car idling along the curb.

"You made it." Tyler gripped Drew in a bear hug.

"Barely. And I'm starved." Drew tossed his bag in the rear seat.

"Not to worry. Noël's dad is taking good care of us." Tyler slipped behind the wheel and steered toward the main road.

Drew cut a side glance, exhaling. Did he get into it now or wait until a decent meal took the edge off?

"You're going to love Noël, Drew."

"You realize I came to talk you out of this." Might as well get into it.

Ty chuckled, low, disbelieving. "You know, I'm grown up now. I know what I'm doing. I don't need my big brother looking out for me."

Five years younger, Tyler was the son of his mother's second husband. When the marriage went south, Drew made sure Tyler ate his breakfast, did his homework, and took his nightly bath.

"You just met this girl. On a surfing trip to Costa Rica. How can you pledge your life to someone you've only known for three months? Need I remind you about the *others*?" The ones Ty fell head-over-heels for. "You were engaged to—"

"I knew you'd bring up Amanda."

"And Kayleigh. And Jodi."

"I wasn't engaged to Kayleigh or Jodi. Look, I'm not the same guy. This with Noël? It's real. I know it." He smacked his chest. "I feel it."

"That's what you said about all of them." What Drew had said about Louise.

"I was eighteen with Amanda." Tyler sighed, hammering the steering wheel as he pulled up to a red light. The sign on Drew's left indicated they were heading up US 1.

"I'm just pointing out your track record."

"I'm sorry about what happened with you and Louise, but don't rain on my happiness."

"There's no rain. Just sound advice. Losing Louise, and my career, was the best thing that ever happened to me."

"Oh, really? So why are you hiding in Hawaii? When are you going to give love another chance?"

"I'm busy, building the business. But you … you're basing the next fifty-plus years of your life on a two-week dalliance in Costa Rica followed by three months of texting, FaceTime, and a couple of long weekends. There's been no testing of your relationship, of how you'll be together. You're not even out of giddy, butterflies stage."

"We've had plenty of reality checks." The light flashed green, and Tyler hit the gas.

"Okay, like what?" Drew powered down his window letting the wintery breeze of Florida's east coast cool his jet-lagged, hot skin, listening as Tyler rattled off a bunch of stupid "challenges" he and Noël had faced.

Like where to have the wedding. If he should wear a tux or not. If they should have a vanilla or chocolate cake.

Drew laughed, and even he heard the sardonic note. "Vanilla or chocolate cake? You think cake flavors are a test of your relationship?"

"Okay … we had a tough time deciding if we'd have joint or separate checking accounts."

Drew slapped his chest. "You're killing me."

"What? Money is the one thing couples fight over more than anything. We decided if we keep separate accounts, then we won't fight."

"Until you realize she spent three hundred dollars on a pair of shoes while you paid five hundred for the electric, water, and garbage bill."

"That's not fair, Drew. Don't make Noël out to be like Louise."

"My past doesn't change the truth, Ty. You're a dreamer, and this marriage is in haste. I aim to take you to Honolulu as a single man."

In the light of the dash, Drew caught the tense knot in his brother's jaw. "I'm not abandoning my fiancée three nights before our wedding."

"Then I can't be your best man." He threw down the gauntlet. It was harder to say than Drew imagined.

Tyler swore under his breath. "You beat all, man. My own brother …"

"I'm trying to save you from yourself."

"No, you're trying to save me from you. But you have us confused. It's my life, Drew. My choice. You can't always be bossing me around, playing the big brother. You haven't even *met* her yet."

"I'd love to meet her. Tell her exactly what I'm telling you." A sad dread twisted in his chest. The burn and burden of being both brother and parent. The fear of Ty's heart breaking like Drew's. He couldn't bear it. He couldn't.

Chapter Three

One day before New Year's Eve

ANSLEY RODE WITH HER mother to the hotel on the beach. She and Noël were staying in the honeymoon suite for Noël's last night as a single woman. Tomorrow night, Tyler would take Ansley's place.

"You slept well," Mom said, her reddish-brown hair whipping in the breeze. She'd insisted on dropping the top to her new convertible Mustang despite the cold late December morning. The woman who'd wanted Ansley to be a doctor recently started independently publishing sweet romance novels and apparently earned herself a new car.

And Dad had joined a golf club.

"Thanks for breakfast. It was good." Eggs, bacon, toast, a chilled Diet Coke. Mom carried it up to Ansley's room, the same one she'd slept in from eight to eighteen.

The home touches surprised her. She missed her family and the pieces of herself she lost while on the road.

Ten years ago, Ansley couldn't wait to leave. She bolted the day after she graduated from high school—a backpack trip through Europe with girlfriends, then off to Florida State to major in music—and never looked back.

She wanted to be a *star*. Away from the goody-goody life her parents espoused. But lately, she'd started to remember the sweet moments she had with Jesus and her guitar.

From her jean's pocket, her phone vibrated. Noël. Ansley answered with, "I'm about five minutes away."

"His brother ... he... he's trying to convince ... Tyler... too soon. He ... doesn't... know... me..." Noël's sobs echoed through to Ansley. "... not get married."

Ansley sat forward with a glance at her mother. "Noël, slow down. What are you saying?"

"His brother ..." Noël's sob echoed through Ansley. "Doesn't want us to get married. He said it's too soon ... we don't know each other well enough."

Who was this overreaching, evil brother? "Noël, we're almost there."

"What's going on?" Mom said, a side glance at Ansley.

"Tyler's brother is fighting the wedding. Told him it was too soon."

Mom clucked her tongue while Ansley promised to find the brother and give him a piece of her mind.

No one hurt her best friend.

Minutes later, Noël collapsed against Ansley as she crossed the honeymoon suite's threshold.

"Ans, what am I going to do? He's going to leave me. The love of my life ... What will I do without the love of my life?"

"Hush, hush, Ty is not going to leave you."

"We were fine ... doing great. So in love. So sure. Until his stupid brother showed up." Anger flashed over Noël's sorrow.

"What does Tyler want? What does he say?"

"H-he's thinking of ... postponing." Sadness rimmed her friend's blue eyes with red, tears welling and spilling over. "Going to Hawaii without me."

"Where's his room?" Ansley started for the door. Noël had been her rock when Ansley dropped out of Florida State to pursue music. She'd run interference with Ansley's parents, remind her of her dream when she faltered, and kept her life straight when she shot to stardom.

"What?" Noël dried her eyes. Blew her nose. "Are you going up there?"

"You bet."

"Ansley, now wait a minute." Mom, all sober and earth grounding.

"If he can be that manipulated by his brother, maybe Noël is dodging a bullet here."

"Or, maybe he needs to be reminded how amazing she is and why he fell in love with her in the first place."

"Mrs. Moore, do you think we should wait?" Now Noël was caving. "I asked my mom, but she's as upset as I am."

"I think you two have to work this out for yourselves."

"They're getting married." Ansley jerked open the door. "Noël, I wrote you and Tyler a wedding song and I'm singing it tomorrow night. Now, what room is he in?"

"Nine twenty-one."

Up the elevator and down the hall, Ansley rapped on Tyler's door, rehearsing a short speech, her heart thumping, as she waited for him to answer, the clank of dishes reverberating through the door.

When the door swung open, she launched her speech. "Listen, Tyler—"

But it wasn't Tyler on the other side, it was Drew Callahan from Honolulu, from Atlanta, from first class. A thick anticipation surged through her.

He leaned against the door in nothing but a pair of board shorts, his T-shirt fitted to his tan, muscled frame. His blue gaze bore through her until she felt every secret she possessed about to be exposed.

"Ansley Moore's doppelgänger. What a pleasant surprise."

"Wh-what are you doing here?" Her words tripped over her lips. Drew's presence set the edge of her heart on fire.

"I was about to ask you the same thing." He eyed her, still with that enticing gaze and stood aside for her to enter. "Want to come in?" He gestured to the open balcony doors. "The Atlantic is perfect this morning. Calm, blue, beautiful."

The word *beautiful* lingered on her.

"No, no, I can't. I'm on a mission." She backed away. "I must have the wrong room." Ansley glanced at the number on the door. 921. "I was looking for Tyler Houston."

He tipped his head, beckoning her to enter. "You're in the right place. He's my brother."

"*You're* Tyler's brother?"

He watched her as she entered, making her conscious of her movements, of her bare face, of her hair in a sloppy ponytail.

"He'd like to deny it from time to time, but yeah."

Drawing a deep breath, Ansley faced him. "Well, my best friend is a broken, scared, sobbing bride because of you." She tapped him on the chest.

His eyes widened. "Your wedding is *this* wedding?"

"Yes. And you're messing things up." She sat in the nearest chair, then shot to her feet again, hands on her hips, her jaw set. "You're really Tyler's brother? Where is he by the way?"

"Out running errands. Look, Ansley, I'm sorry for your friend, but Tyler has no business getting married to someone he's only known three months. Most of those long distance."

She regarded him for a second, trying to dislike him, trying to be angry. But compassion rimmed his eyes, and she knew he loved his brother.

"That's not your decision, Drew. It's theirs. Do you have a vendetta against happily ever after?"

"Ha! There is no such thing as happily ever after. My brother knows it. I know it. Our mom married four times trying to find that elusive land of happily ever after."

"Ah, I see. A cynic." She took a step toward him. "Did you know Noël's parents have been happily married for thirty-two years? My parents are going on thirty-five. Happy, lasting marriages do happen … despite the cynics and naysayers."

"Do you know Tyler has been engaged twice before?" He moved around the chair, his attention set on her. "He falls in love at the drop of a hat."

"I don't know about dropping hats, but what he has with Noël is real." Ansley stepped closer, into his space. A fragrant, clean space.

"How do you know?" He mirrored her step with his own. "How much time have you spent with them? And when were you last in love?"

"Besides not being any of your business, my love life has no bearing on theirs." She jutted out her chin and moved nearer. "But I know true love when I see it."

"Do you now? What is that, some sort of super power?"

"Maybe. Yeah, it is. It makes me a great country song writer." Ansley poked him in the chest again. His very *firm* chest. "Here's my question. What gives you the right to barge in here and demand Tyler abandon his fiancée? This is their wedding, their decision, their lives."

Drew snatched her hand, holding it tight, his body inches from hers. "I'm his brother. If I don't speak the truth to him, who will?"

"You should've spoken your piece before the wedding weekend."

"In a perfect world, yes." He released her. Her hand tingled where his had been. "But I didn't know about the ceremony until two days ago. He didn't tell me because he knew what I would say. What does that tell you, Ansley?"

"That he's a smart guy."

"You don't know what you're talking about. This … this whole wedding isn't about love, it's about … lust … or some fantasy."

"Oh, you're some sort of expert, are you?"

"Let's say I've had a few experiences."

"The kind that makes you bitter? Envious of other people? The kind that make you fly thousands of miles to break up a wedding? By the way, what kind of businessman doesn't have a cellphone?"

A red hue ran under his high cheeks. "You shouldn't talk about stuff of which you know nothing." He walked toward the door, his back straight and stiff, the edges of his hair curling at the top of his neck. "Have a good day, Ansley."

She paused in front of him as she exited the room, shaking her hand, trying to release the feel of his touch. Of the overwhelming sensation that with Drew Callahan, she'd be safe. "Stay out of their way, Drew."

"Sure, and you stay out of mine, Ansley."

He thought of *her* all day. He should be irritated, but the girl with the hazel eyes and determined soul drove him to distraction.

Heading to the beach for a run, he passed the rehearsal ball-room, pausing as a soft melody slipped around the open door, the singer's smooth, raspy voice capturing him.

"Sometimes you have to let go and trust your heart."

Peering around the door, he saw Ansley on stage with her guitar, eyes closed, singing as if she were the only troubadour in the universe.

He swallowed hard, quelling his pounding heart. Her melody, her posture, made him want to hold her, kiss her, and say things to her he'd not said to a woman in a long time—if ever.

When the last chord rang out, Drew slipped away. He didn't want to be moved. Or soften to love. He wanted his brother to come to his senses.

He'd spent the afternoon trying to reason with Tyler. But the more his brother talked, the more Drew felt his argument weakening.

By the time the sun was about to set, he'd been argued out and needed the run to clear his mind. He told Ty not to expect him at the rehearsal.

"You're just projecting your broken heart on me. I won't let you, Drew."

Ty's words reverberated through Drew as he ducked through the lobby for the beachside exit.

"I saw you. Listening."

He turned to see Ansley coming his way. "I wasn't necessarily hiding. Nice song by the way."

"I wrote it for Ty and Noël. Going to cut it on my next album. Maybe they'll have a hit song dedicated to their love."

"Or divorce." He pressed through the door onto the board-walk, stretching.

She followed, laughing. "Wow, you are cynical. What did *she* do to you? And rehearsal is that way." She pointed toward the door. "In the ballroom. And you're going to be there."

He snorted. "You're going to *bully* me into going? Send a henchman in to break my arm?"

She knocked on his forehead. "Why are all the pretty ones so clueless? Drew, he's getting married with or without you. You abandon him now, you'll create a wedge that will take forever to fix. But if you go in there as his best man, you'll be his hero. What if, God forbid, your dire prediction comes true and something does go wrong in their marriage? Don't you want to be the first one he calls? I don't know what happened to create this bitterness in you, but don't paint it all over your brother."

Her bold truth cut through his weakening resolve. Losing his relationship with Ty would kill him. "But they've only known each other a few months." Even to his ears, his argument sounded weak and tired. Joyless.

"So? They love each other. Is that so hard to believe, Callahan?"

He glanced toward the beach with a long exhale.

"Sometimes you have to let go and trust your heart."

"For ten years, I worked in San Francisco buying and selling businesses. Made my first million at twenty-eight. I slept with my cellphone in my hand. I had a drop-dead gorgeous fiancée, Louise. A socialite. Daughter of a hotel mogul. I had a staff of twenty and had the proverbial tiger by the tail. No, I *owned* the tiger. Then, four years ago, I had not one but two near heart attacks. Stress was literally killing me."

"Ah, I'm sorry. I guess that explains the anti-technology. But why the anti-love?"

"Wanting my brother to marry with his eyes wide open doesn't make me anti-love."

"But you are, aren't you?"

"I prefer cautious." He didn't like the way she read him, saw through to his core.

"What happened to Louise?"

"She left me at the altar while five hundred of our closest friends and family looked on. By left, I mean she flew to Bora Bora the night before with her maid of honor's brother. I heard they got married last year."

Ansley whistled low, soft and her quick touch on his arm sent a flame to his heart. "Okay, I get why you're cautious. But trust me, Noël would never do that to Ty."

"No one thought Louise would do such a thing to me. And

I'm not just concerned about Ty. Noël's getting in the ring with a guy who's tapped out once before."

"So maybe he knows his own heart and mind this time. Drew, your story doesn't change the fact that you need to be there tonight. And for the wedding. Be there for Ty. Your hurt doesn't give you a pass."

Drew regarded her for a long moment, his breath hot in his lungs. She disturbed him. Challenged him. Caught the kindling of his heart on fire. "Fine. You want me there?" He leaned into her, an idea forming. One that would get him out of this and away from her. "Then you have to go as my date."

She recoiled, just as he'd hoped. "Your date?"

"Yeah, my date." If she'd declined, he'd be free to skip the evening. Carry on with his plan to bring Ty to his senses. With his plan to never fall in love again. "Every best man needs a date, right? No date. No best man." When Ansley hesitated another second, he turned for the beach. "Just as I thought. All talk. No action. You call me anti-love, but I have a gut feeling you're not very high on the stuff either."

"Deal." The bold sound of her voice arrested him. "You're on. But I'm not agreeing to this scheme for you. This is for Noël and Ty."

"Same here." He slipped his hand into hers and for one Mississippi, two Mississippi, their hands remained locked, fueling the building fire in him.

He broke free and started inside, the melody of her song swirled around him.

"Sometimes you have to let go and trust your heart."

Be his date … the nerve of him. Drew Callahan walked a thin line. But she'd endure his stupid condition to get him to show up. Anything for Noël's happiness. Lord knows she'd pulled some odd favors for Ansley the past few years.

Ansley's surveyed the room, her pulse thick in her veins. Drew was late. Surely he'd not renege. Coward …

Then he appeared, wearing tan board shorts and a blue shirt that captured the hue in his eyes.

Ansley steadied herself, reaching for the nearest chair, biting back her smile, annoyed by the flutter in her middle.

"You came."

"I told you I would."

"Y-you look nice," she said, holding down her smile, glancing casually about the room, ignoring the way he made her want to lean against him.

"I had to press my shorts."

She peeked up at him. "You ironed for your brother? Finally a check in your pro column."

He made a face. "You're keeping a pro-con list?"

"Maybe."

His laugh came from a deep, free space in his chest, a sound and sensation she could not escape the rest of the night.

The rehearsal went quickly, and by the time everyone moved to the next ballroom for a catered dinner, the DJ was already playing music.

Rod Steward crooned "They Way You Look Tonight."

"I believe Rod's singing our song." Drew took her by the hand, led her to the dance floor, pulled her close, and moved them to the rhythm of the music.

"Thank you for coming," she said, keeping a stiff distance, trying not to let go. But everything about him beckoned. His fragrance, his teasing blue eyes, his tender tone. And maybe, just a little, the sculpted pump of his chest.

"You look beautiful."

"Don't … Drew." Ansley glanced away. "I'm not your real date. This is for show, for Noël and Tyler."

"I'm not pretending, Ansley." He wrapped her tighter, slipping his hand around her hip. When she breathed in, her senses were filled with his scent—like the sun and the sea. "I thought about what you said. Then I watched them tonight. I saw the way that Ty looks at Noël—and the way she looks back. The love that was in that room was palpable."

"They're lucky. We should be jealous of what they have."

"Or maybe glad we found it ourselves." He held her close, slipping his arm about her back, leaning his lips to her ear. "Come with me."

Drew led her to the beach, holding her hand as she slipped off her heels.

"What's going on, Drew?" The wind caught Ansley's nervous laugh. "Where's my friend, the cynical romantic?"

She clung to his arm as they passed into the shadows beyond the hotel's light, her feet sinking into the cool, damp sand.

"Maybe he's had a change of heart." He gripped her hand a little tighter. "What about you, Ansley? Love is good for others but not you?"

"No." She sighed, pulling her hand free to walk along the water's edge. "His name was Hank and, after three years, he decided he didn't want to be married to a country music artist."

"You were married?"

"Engaged."

"So we're both nursing broken hearts." He reached for her, wrapping her in his arms. "Ever think it was providence we met in a very crowded airport restaurant? That our seats were together on the plane?"

"That your brother was marrying my best friend?"

"Or maybe God crashed the airline's computer for us?"

"Wow …" She laughed with a shiver, the excitement of love seeping in. "That's an intimidating notion."

"What would you say if I found out I had some business in Nashville?"

"Drew, listen to what you're saying. Think—" The wind caught her hair as she stepped away from him.

"Now you sound like me. Skeptical and scared. I am listening. I *am* thinking. Let me take you to dinner. Don't say no, Ansley." He brushed her hair from her eyes and raised her chin. In the thin light drifting along the beach from bungalows and hotels, she saw love in his eyes. "Live the lyrics you wrote for Ty and Noël. Let go and trust your heart. I'm trusting mine."

When his lips touched hers, his passion was raw and real. Ansley roped her arms around his neck and let go.

Because love, no matter how new and tentative, truly conquered all fear.

When Drew pulled away, he tapped his forehead to hers. "I'm going to marry you, Ansley Moore. Mark my words."

"I might just let you, Drew Callahan," she said, her lips burning from the fire of his kiss. "I might just let you."

Rachel Hauck is an award-winning, *New York Times, USA Today*, and *Wall Street Journal* best-selling author. Her book *The Wedding Dress* was named Inspirational Novel of the Year by *RT BookReviews*. She is a double RITA finalist, a Christy and a Carol winner. A graduate of Ohio State University with a degree in Journalism, Rachel is a devoted Ohio State football fan. She lives in sunny central Florida with her husband and ornery cat.

THE FAMILY TREE

Brandi Willis Schreiber

I CAME TO SCOTLAND because I had nowhere else to look.

Standing in Edinburgh Airport, exhausted and alone, I clutched the piece of paper I hoped would give me what I needed. On it was a name and address: *Eleanor Brightwell, 267 Aubergine Way, Edinburgh*.

I'd found Eleanor a month ago. She worked for the National Records of Scotland, but more important, she was an expert in genealogy. I wrote her my story, and a few weeks later, I got a phone call.

"Come to Scotland," she offered, her accent so lush and unfamiliar it took me a moment to process the words. "There are plenty of records in Edinburgh, but they aren't digitized and will be impossible to access from Texas. You can even stay with me. Make the trip."

So I did. Out of leads, I took leave from my job for three months and booked a flight to Edinburgh. It was easy as a traveling nurse who had no place to return between assignments except a silent and empty house.

As deplaned travelers eddied around me, I shifted my travel bag to steady my shaking hands. Eleanor Brightwell was not on any limb of my family tree, but rather a bird that had alighted on a branch.

What if this was all for nothing? What if she was a bird that flew away?

Chapter Two

A FAMILY TREE IS a glorious set of blueprints. Like a plan for a home, it illustrates every detail and turn through the doorways that make up life until the present moment: Who was born. Who fell in love and had children. Who lived long, and who died young. The branches stretch out like rooms, each one housing a life and its story. When you flip through the pages, you should feel a sense of completeness, of place. *This is the house of my life*, a good family tree says. *This is where I belong.*

Only I didn't belong anywhere anymore.

Instead of a well-organized tree with branches telling every story, I had a diagram full of starts and stops, jagged and incomplete lines, some branches stretching into nothing at all.

But when I walked through Eleanor Brightwell's door that frigid February evening, I felt something I hadn't felt in a very long time: *home.*

Her walls were painted lemony yellow, and gilt-framed photos hung in a cluster near the entryway: a sepia wedding couple, a dark-haired family poised at the base of an ancient castle, a handsome young man in graduation regalia smiling with the sun behind him.

In the corner of the room, a log popped in a fireplace next to overstuffed floral chairs and couches, a spot where people obviously gathered. Indistinct jazz played from an unknown location and mixed with the sounds of clinking dishes and two teenagers—a boy and a girl—who shouted and chased each other around the room. Despite the cold outside, this sight warmed me, and I stood transfixed at the threshold, absorbing all the color, life, and energy of this Scottish family home.

"Children!" I jumped at the firm voice next to me. So mesmerized by the scene, I hadn't noticed the figure to my right. "Brian! Ansley! Please don't try to kill each other just yet. We have company." He turned to me, and I felt the open space of the room narrow.

The man was tall with a powerful build. He either worked labor or worked out, as evidenced by firm biceps under his navy tee. Thick black hair fell without direction across his forehead into his eyes, which were a hard-to-miss sapphire, as blue as the Texas sky before sunrise. Those eyes immediately reminded me of the past, and I felt a pain blossom in my chest.

"You came at a fine time. My wee brother and sister have decided to kill each other right before dinner, a usual occurrence in this zoo." The tenor of his voice and roll of *R*'s sent a current down my spine. He must have been a few years older than me, maybe thirty-seven or thirty-eight, because then he chuckled, and little furrows of laugh lines appeared around those penetrating eyes.

Oh, my.

He was altogether charming, and a rush of blood colored my cheeks.

He shuffled barefoot around me to shut the front door, and I realized a little girl was wrapped around his leg. Blue eyes, but these the shade of cornflower, popped beneath a knitted pink cap. She smiled at me, dimples puckering her cheeks. She must be his daughter, I thought, and my disappointment surprised me.

"Cairn!" the teenage girl yelled from across the room, yanking me from my thoughts. "The only reason this is a zoo is because your wee brother makes it his purpose in life to drive me nuts!" She started to taunt the boy again, but a movement from the doorway interrupted her.

"Brian. Ansley. For the love of everything holy, the two of you must get yourselves under control or I will make it *my* purpose in life to drive you nuts." The two teenagers deflated, and Eleanor Brightwell, a woman who had to be in her mid-fifties but seemed younger, wrapped her soft, sugar-scented arms around me.

"Bea, you made it!" Her smile was broad. With her large, blue eyes, feathery brown hair, and round cheeks, she reminded me a little of my mother. I absently rubbed my chest where the old pain flared again.

"Welcome to my home. You have met the twins, my two middle children, Brian and Ansley. The onset of hormones," she sighed. "My favorite part of motherhood. And this is my oldest son, Cairn." She gestured to the man now standing to my left, his hands on his hips, unfazed by the child still clutching him like a monkey. I smiled nervously, and he raised a dark eyebrow in return. "And this is my youngest daughter, Lizzie. Lizzie, say hello to our visitor."

"Hallo!" Lizzie chirped.

"Hello," I laughed. As I glanced from Lizzie to Cairn and then to the teenagers, Eleanor caught my questioning expression.

"We have a range of ages in this house, don't we? When I was sixteen, I never would have imagined how far apart I'd have my children." She shook her head as she smiled. "The twins came with the empty nest when he was away at university." Eleanor jabbed her thumb at Cairn. "And then this one," Eleanor swooped to tickle Lizzie, who exploded in a fit of shrill laughter, "we adopted two years ago."

"It seems like a lot of gifts to me," I said.

Eleanor's features gentled. "Yes. A lot of gifts. That's a wonderful way of putting it. Right, Lizzie?"

Lizzie grinned and released her brother's leg, and Eleanor pulled her into a little dance, humming and maneuvering her around the room toward the kitchen. Only when her back was turned did I realize no hair peeked from beneath the bright pink cap.

"Bea, while I finish up dinner, Cairn will get you settled."

I had almost forgotten the man next to me.

"Take your bags for you?" He held out a hand.

"Oh, yes," I said, passing them to him.

"Bea DuBois, is it?"

"Yes. Bea is short for Beatrice, but that's pretty old fashioned, so everyone calls me Bea."

Everyone did call me Bea. The pain in my chest sparked again like a match, and I rubbed the space above my heart.

"You okay?" The unfamiliar concern unsettled me.

"Yes, I'm fine. Thank you."

I certainly hoped I would be.

"So you are doing research on your family tree?" asked Max Brightwell. He'd come in late from work and went straight to his wife, whom he kissed on her eyes and lips, before sitting down to dinner. He had the same dark hair as the other Brightwell children, but his eyes sparkled with a hue of chocolate brown.

"Yes. There's only so much research I can do from the States, so I decided to make a trip here. Mrs. Brightwell—Eleanor—was incredibly kind to offer guidance and a place to stay. Thank you again."

"It's nothing." She smiled at me.

"And what exactly are you researching?" asked Cairn. He sat next to me, and I'd felt his gaze, intent and interested, all evening.

"Anyone who might be related to me," I said, not looking in his direction. It sounded so dire coming out of my mouth that I wondered if he thought I was desperate. I glanced at him, but his expression was calm and open, so I continued.

"My parents and husband died two years ago in an accident. I've been searching, but I don't have any other living relatives I can find in the States. I know my paternal great-great-grandfather emigrated from Edinburgh to the US in 1903. At least, that's what my father used to tell me. His parents died when he was young, and my mother was a foster child. They were both only children, so …" I fiddled with my napkin. "I don't know anything other than that."

The room had grown quiet. Max cleared his throat. "Cairn is a solicitor. He could help you with some public records, I bet."

"You're a lawyer?" I asked.

"Aye, I'm one of those."

"What kind of law do you practice?"

"Estates, wills, confirmations. I think in the States they call it probate."

"So civil matters."

Cairn raised an eyebrow. He was quite good at that. "My father is a lawyer," I explained. "Was. My father *was* a lawyer."

Cairn let the silence linger for only a moment. "Show me your family tree, and I'll help you figure out where to start."

After we cleared the dishes, I gave Cairn the single sheet of paper that held my entire family history. I'd traced it so many times that the lines had started to blur. Cairn slipped on a pair of wire glasses and studied it under the dining room light while I studied him. This broad man dwarfed my five-foot-three frame, even in boots, and despite a slightly crooked nose, he had a striking profile. He never pushed back the wave of dark hair from his forehead. Instead, he shifted his weight over the table and rested his chin in one hand. Still barefoot and in loose jeans, he was a mix of cool college boy and serious lawyer. Why wasn't this man married?

Cairn traced the lines of my diagram with long, lean fingers but lingered at the entries for my father, mother, and husband: *deceased 2015*. The bulb above his head seemed to grow brighter and made me feel naked in front of him. He removed his glasses, and fear he would discover my vulnerability washed over me.

"What are you going to do if you find a relative?" he asked in a low voice.

The question surprised me. I shook my head. "I don't know." The words felt heavier than I expected. What was I going to do? Hope for a connection? What if that person could care less I existed? What if that person didn't exist at all?

An old exhaustion overcame me. "I'm so tired," I said without thinking. "I think I need to sleep." I moved toward the stairs, but Cairn caught me. His hand wrapped entirely around my small forearm, and I flinched at the warmth that traveled up my arm.

"I have a meeting tomorrow, but I can help you after. Around four? I know where to start. Can you meet me at the General Register House?"

I couldn't free the words trapped in my mouth, so I nodded. He released me, and a chill peppered my skin. I'd forgotten how long it had been since someone had touched me. It was the coldest I'd ever felt.

Chapter Three

CAIRN WAS PACING THE stone steps of the old building when I arrived. Dressed in a sharp, three-piece suit cut to his frame, he alternated between checking his watch and shoving his hands into his pockets, which only accentuated the stretch of material across his very fine ass. When he saw me, he smiled. My pace, like my brain, slowed a little.

"How are you today?" That timbre rolled out like a lazy thunder.

"Well, thank you. I spent the day at the National Library hunting through some records. Hoped that would give us a head start. But I wasn't anticipating the rain." I looked up at the steely sky, which made a nest of my brown curls.

"Aye, it rains more here than in *Tex-sus*, I'm sure." He said the word with a Southern drawl, and I laughed at his teasing.

"Oh, is that how I sound, Mr. Scottish Solicitor?" I put my hand on my hip and pinched my face together, trying to mimic a stodgy lawyer. I knew I was ridiculous, but he laughed, a sound that carried us into the ancient building.

"Wow," was all I could say as we entered. The stoic and imposing space stretched beneath a soaring dome. I turned in a circle, taking it all in, until I realized Cairn was studying me. His expression conveyed something … *fiery*. I swallowed before asking, "How was your meeting?"

"Long. We're working on a tough confirmation right now for a rather well-known fellow whose affairs were not in good order when he died. It's been a bit of a mess, and there's a lot of pressure from the family to decide inheritances."

"The stuff of novels." I smiled. "Where people's entire lives hinge on their great expectations."

Amusement danced in his eyes. "Aye, something like that."

Cairn directed me up a flight of stairs and into a dark-paneled room with an ornate, cream-colored ceiling. Stacks of red, green, and brown ledgers were piled on a long wooden table.

"Census records." He gestured to a chair. "Everybody living in Edinburgh in the nineteenth century would have to be listed in one of these ledgers. If your great-great-grandfather was born here, then his name is somewhere in one of these books."

My mouth dropped open.

"I thought I'd give us a head start, too," he said.

Cairn and I spent several hours going over the archives. I was used to demanding work as a pediatric nurse, but I wondered if he had somewhere he needed to be. The building had closed, but somehow he'd gotten special permission for us to stay.

"I can keep researching, but do you need to go?"

Cairn scribbled on a yellow notepad at the end of the table. He wore his wire glasses but not his suit jacket and tie. Those he'd tossed over another chair. The top two buttons of his shirt were open, and he'd rolled his sleeves up his lovely, sculpted forearms. He studied me over his glasses, the same tone as his vest, and before my brain could process this vision, my stomach growled. Loudly. He set down his pen.

"No, but you do. Let's go eat."

As we walked to a nearby pub, a bitter wind forced me to shiver, and before I could protest, Cairn slipped his suit jacket over my shoulders. It was heavier than expected and smelled of earth and something verdant. A faint recollection drifted from the edge of my memory: roasting marshmallows with my husband on a camping trip in Colorado. There was a lot of coaxing, a pinewood fire, and smoky, vanilla sweetness on our lips as we made love under the stars.

When I was first widowed, every sight, smell, and sensation tormented the space between my mind and heart. After a while, the associations dimmed, but even on good days grief pulled me like a riptide to a dark place. I inhaled the scent of Cairn's jacket, fighting the onset of tears. I didn't know I'd closed my eyes until he grabbed my hand. His touch was electric and authoritative, a command I didn't yet understand.

"Let's stop here."

He pulled me off the sidewalk and through a narrow doorway. The pub was classic with dark wood, long tables, and a fireplace in a corner. Cairn seated us near the fire and caught me smiling. "Do you like it?"

"I do. It's exactly as I imagined a Scottish pub would be."

He raised an eyebrow, a gesture I came to expect now. "Sticky, dirty, and full of drunk men?"

I laughed and ran my hand across the worn table, which was, honestly, a little sticky. "No. I would say old, quaint, and full of character."

"Aye, that it is. More characters than you care to know, I can promise you that."

"Speaking of characters, it must be nice having such a big family. What's that like?"

"It's good. I spend a lot of time with them. I need to direct my brother in the ways of becoming a man." He winked. "I'm so much older than him that I don't want to miss being a brother. Ansley is a sassy teenager, so I've got to give her hell, you know. And then there's little Lizzie." His voice turned hollow. "She's sick. Leukemia. It's a bad deal."

Cairn traced a splintered corner of the table with his finger. "She's not responding to treatment anymore. She needs a transplant. Bone marrow. But none of us is a match. It's the beginning of the end, I think."

The gravity of his words hit me. I knew from my work that blood relatives only had a small chance of being a donor match. Seventy percent of people don't have a family match at all. And Lizzie was adopted.

"What about her birth family?"

"Out of the picture."

"And a bone marrow or blood registry? There's no match there?"

"Her doctors are on it, but so far … nothing." Cairn scrubbed his face and looked away.

A loss like this, of the best being taken while those who loved them watched, powerless, was brutal, I knew. "I'm sorry," was all I could say.

"Yeah, me too." Cairn said his next words with a cautious tone. "And your family? What were they like?"

"They were wonderful." When he didn't push, I felt a nudge from within to go on. "A drunk driver killed them two years ago. We were going out to dinner, and I was running late. I told them I would meet them there." His bright blue eyes focused on me with such sorrow that I shrugged. "It can't be undone. No matter what I do."

Cairn shifted closer to me and put his hand over mine, and I trembled, just once. Would I ever get used to this man touching me? At the thought, an ache bloomed in my belly, and my pulse quickened. Cairn's fingers drifted over my wrist.

"No, it can't," he said. "You can only go forward." His face hovered so near mine I could almost breathe in his words. He lifted one hand as if he might touch me but paused when I took a sharp inhale.

"Do you know that from experience?" It was too personal, I knew, but I needed the space.

"Yes, I do." He let his hand fall to the table. "We were young, knew each other from our primary days. Our families were good friends." Cairn leaned back and picked up the glass of ale that arrived. "But I was a dumb kid trying to take on the world. I wanted to be a big shot, so I made that my priority, and not her. So she found another guy to make her his priority. While we were still married, I might add. It was over really before it began."

"And you got to have the career you wanted?"

"Yes, but it came at a price. We aren't friends anymore, and neither are our families. My parents were disappointed. I felt really bad about that for a long time because they raised me better than that. I hurt her, and she, in turn, hurt me and all the honor went out of our marriage."

I nodded.

"But I won't make the same mistakes the second time around." He set the glass down with finality. "I learned that. I want the kind of marriage my parents have, with someone who wants the same things I do."

"And what is that?" I asked with trepidation.

"Family. Home. The things that really matter, for the rest of my life."

I swallowed and examined my own corner of the table. So did I.

This time, Cairn's hand made it to my face. He tilted up my chin.

"I know it's important to have family. I promise I'll do what I can to help you find yours."

In that moment, I'd almost forgotten that was what I was here for.

Chapter Four

CAIRN WAS AS GOOD as his word, and over the next week, we fell into a routine. During the day, I visited libraries and public offices. Cairn always joined me later, throwing his suit jacket over a chair and unbuttoning his shirt. When his glasses went on, I knew we were in it for the long haul. We would work for hours, only getting up to stretch or find coffee.

When my eyes were too tired to read, I would take a break and study him instead. That wave of raven hair always cascaded across his brow, but he never pushed it back. Many times I imagined myself touching that hair, touching that face. It became evident that I liked this man very much.

"I can't believe what you're doing for me," I stammered one night. "I mean, you don't even *know* me. Don't you have somewhere you need to *be*?"

Cairn examined me a beat over his glasses. "Nowhere but here."

After our research, I always walked to the Brightwell home, enjoying the graying streets at night, while Cairn walked in the opposite direction to his flat. One night a week later, however, we stayed out until almost midnight going over records and talking. As we stepped into the dark, I started in the direction of home, but Cairn grabbed my arm, pulling me to his side. The touch points sent tingles across my skin.

"It's too late to walk. Let me get you a taxi."

When it arrived, I started to say goodnight, but he surprised me by getting in. He pulled me next to him, flush against his side, and the feel of his warm body against me sent a jolt right to my core.

Cairn said nothing until we arrived at the Brightwell home, where he got out first and pulled me to him again with such intensity that I almost stumbled. His hands fell to my hips as he steadied me against the car, and he dipped his face close to mine.

"Please don't ever walk home alone on nights like this. If it's late, I will get you a taxi, and I will ride with you." His voice strained as he controlled the words. I felt his breath on my lips and caught the heady scent of his body beneath his unbuttoned shirt. I wanted to kiss the smooth plane of skin beneath his collarbone. My eyes flew to his, and without thinking, I licked my lips.

Oh, God. Cairn's eyes darkened with something I hadn't seen before. His hands, firm and heavy, still gripped my hips.

"Do you understand?"

Unable to speak, I nodded. But like a movie reel coming to its end, I watched the distance between our mouths close in slow motion until the taxi driver's voice stopped us centimeters apart.

"Mate, do you want to pay, or do you want to go?"

Cairn took a frustrated inhalation and released me. When I turned back, he was leaning against the car, his hands in his pockets, mouth parted ever so slightly, as if he intended to call after me.

I didn't sleep well after that.

As another week passed, the single thread linking me to family in Scotland unraveled. My great-great-grandfather was as real as sun and stone in the United States, but Cairn and I learned that in Scotland, he was a ghost. His past, like my future, seemed as intangible as the mist.

What I failed to learn about my family, however, I made up for with Cairn. He told me about his life in Edinburgh, his schooling at Glasgow, and what he loved and hated about his work. I learned that he didn't like pickles but had a thing for flavored mustards (I teased him plenty about that). He told me about being an only child until his parents had Brian and Ansley, and then still convinced there was more good to be done in the world, adopted Lizzie.

When he talked about Lizzie, his eyes clouded, and chinks appeared in his commanding façade. Over the past two weeks, her condition had deteriorated. The Brightwells tried to keep things at home cheerful, but her bubbly personality started to dull with her pain. It was unbearable to witness.

If I had known my family would die, I would have moved God, man, and mountain to stop it. Instead, waiting for them at the restaurant, watching the ice melt in my glass, I had gotten a phone call. I was told they were dead, and just like that, the life I had known evaporated.

Sometimes I wondered when Cairn would get the same phone call, and my heart broke.

I prayed for a different call to come.

Chapter Five

"TELL ME AGAIN ABOUT Texas," Ansley said. She sat next to me on the floral couch. Brian stretched across the floor, absorbed in a book. Cairn sat with his father by the fire and observed me as had become the norm. He hadn't tried to kiss me again, but a strong sexual current constantly swirled around us. It was difficult to ignore.

"Actually, I have a different story to tell."

"Did you get a break in your research?" Eleanor asked in a small and tired voice from one of the overstuffed chairs, where she rubbed tiny circles across a sleeping Lizzie's back.

"No." I studied the faces of those I'd come to love before pulling a folded paper from my pocket. "Something better." I spoke to Cairn.

"After you told me about Lizzie, I got tested. I'm a match." Something started to work in his eyes. Disbelief, maybe? And hope? And something else, something I hadn't seen in a long time.

Eleanor cocked her head, and Max let out a strangled sound. I kept my eyes on Cairn.

"I'm going to be her stem cell donor."

Eleanor started to cry.

The rest of the words rushed out. "I got good feedback on my results. I'm going to start the meds to stimulate my stem cell production on Monday. It won't take long for me to be, uh, ready for the procedure, and when my levels are good, I can donate."

By now Eleanor was weeping, as were Brian and Ansley. Lizzie woke and, upon seeing everyone else cry, burst into tears. Max pulled her into his lap.

I examined my notes, blurry through my own tears.

"Um—" I faltered. I glanced at Cairn again, who sat immobile with a hand over his mouth. Tears shimmered in his eyes, eyes filled with so much emotion I could barely breathe.

"This is going to work," I managed. "This is going to work. *I know it.*"

Cairn got up from his chair and went to his mother, who was now folded over Brian at her feet. He put a hand on her shoulder and leaned down to say something in her ear, his eyes fixed on me.

I rose to give the family privacy, but Ansley jumped up, wrapping her arms around me. I turned and hugged her as tightly as I could.

"I *knew* you came here for a reason," she squeaked in my ear, her wet cheeks pressed against mine. The same thought had crossed my mind many times since landing in Edinburgh. My hope of finding my own family had brought me to *this* family, who through some marvelous twist of fate needed me.

"I know," I said, pulling back and sweeping overgrown bangs from her eyes. "I'm so glad I can help her."

Confusion etched her face. "Not just for her. For him. He's always here with us, but no one is there for him." I turned to where she nodded and saw Cairn watching me with an intensity that sent white-hot heat through my body.

We stayed up late that night talking and making plans, and by two a.m., Cairn still hadn't left.

"Sweetheart, why don't you stay over?" Eleanor asked.

He instantly agreed. The thought of sleeping under the same roof as him made my body burn.

Eleanor and Max lingered at my bedroom door. They studied me with eyes red and swollen from crying. "You," Eleanor said as she tucked my hair behind my ear, "Are the very best gift."

"Aye, and we love you," Max added. As he leaned in for a gentle hug, I saw Cairn behind him. The entire night, he hadn't said a word to me, but the expression on his face confirmed what he felt.

My heart stopped. I didn't expect to be loved again, but this family loved me. And I hadn't expected to fall in love again, but I had fallen in love with this family. *And Cairn.* He changed everything. I backed into my room.

Ten minutes later, I heard a knock. Without waiting for an answer, Cairn walked in and shut the door behind him.

"What are you doing?" I pulled the sheet up over my thin nightgown.

Cairn's gaze raked over me, and without a word, he sat on the bed, positioning his arms around my body. Still clutching the sheet, I scooted back as far as I could. "Cairn?"

With one hand, he pulled the sheet away. I gasped as he wrapped his other hand around the back of my neck and drew me closer so that our foreheads touched.

"Bea, why are you doing this?" His voice was firm, but not cold.

"What?"

"Why are you doing this? I need to know. Why are you doing this for us?" His gaze traveled from my face down to my negligée and back. His question pissed me off more than his roving eyes.

"Why do you think?" I said, pushing him away from me. He sucked in a breath. "I'm doing it for your family! For that little girl so she'll have a chance to live! For your mother so she doesn't have to bury a child! I'm doing it for your father so he can read her stories and give her away on her wedding day …"

Something started to break in me, so I clutched at his shirt for strength.

"I'm doing it for your brother and sister so they can tell everyone what an awesome little sister they have." I pushed against his chest. "And I'm doing it for *you* because you are a good man who loves his family and has been kind and generous to a total fucking stranger who walked in off the street!"

At this, Cairn grabbed the back of my head and crashed his mouth to mine so fast I let out a cry. He wrapped his other hand around my waist and hauled me forward until I straddled him. And there, he held me in place and kissed me hard.

It was rough and needful. His lips worked mine until they

parted, and he thrust his tongue into my mouth, sending a shock directly between my legs. He tasted of vanilla and the faintest scotch, and this combined with his scent made me whimper. Keeping his hand behind my head, he plundered my mouth, tasting my lips and my tongue, and swallowing my breath until I was dizzy.

Pinned against him, I could do nothing except explore his body with my hands. His chest felt like a solid plate of muscle, and I trailed my hands up and down his back as much as I had sense to. He shifted, pressing me to him, and I felt his firmness through his jeans.

"Oh—" I gasped.

Cairn broke our kiss and lazed his mouth along my jawline to my ear, sending tiny tremors through my charged body.

"I have wanted to do that since the first night I met you."

"Good." The word took immense effort because of my pounding heart.

He chuckled and pulled away, cupping my face in his hands, and rubbed one thumb along my cheek. "Fuck," he exhaled. "Do you know how beautiful you are?" His fingers drifted over my lips, and I closed my eyes.

Cairn pressed his lips to mine again, this time with less urgency. He savored my mouth, licking and lapping and pulling until a groan I didn't recognize escaped from somewhere deep inside me. Cairn groaned, too, and moved his hand between my legs.

I quivered at his light touch over the lace of my panties, and he sucked in a breath.

"You're wet."

An ache began to build, and Cairn glided his hands up my body to my breasts. He kissed me while he teased one nipple through the silk, grazing and stroking before moving to the other. *God, I was getting so close.* I arched my body into his hands until he suddenly broke our kiss and pushed me to my back. He inched his hands up my torso, taking my nightie with them.

I was burning with need, but this was happening so fast.

"I can't—"

"I know," he said, his voice thick. "We won't." He paused and studied at me, those languid eyes heating to burning pools. "Yet."

Before I could say anything, he took my right nipple in his mouth and sucked hard, and I immediately bucked. He clamped one hand over my mouth to stifle me as I came, a storm of sensation, with Cairn at the center.

When the shocks subsided, he kissed my neck and then my chin, my mouth, my eyes, everywhere before pulling away.

"I have also wanted to do *that* since the first night I met you."

Euphoric, I burst into laughter, and he clamped his hand over my mouth again. "My parents are down the hall," he whispered, "and no matter how old you are, getting a girl off under your parents' roof is, I think, always disrespectful."

I pushed his hand from my mouth. "And yet, the good solicitor is doing it right here, and having fun while at it." I grinned. It had been so long since I'd felt this good.

"And having fun," he repeated, tracing my cheek with the back of two fingers. His gaze, as intent and interested as that first night, made me remember my nakedness. I tried to cover myself, but he caught my hands with his, linking his fingers in mine, and held them above my head.

"What is it?" I asked, uncertain.

"It's just that this is the first time I've seen you so happy."

I pursed my lips. *I am happy. With you. But it's more than just happiness …*

A blade of fear, the kind that alleged miracles weren't real, lanced my chest. I started to look away, but Cairn caught my chin.

"Bea, I have waited a long time for this, too. I'll go slowly with you, and wait until you're ready." He swept his lips to my ear. "But you will be ready, and when you are, I intend to make you happy for a very long time."

I was too stunned to understand what he meant.

Chapter Six

"WE NEED TO HAVE a party," Eleanor said at dinner a few weeks later. "On Friday. To celebrate everything that has happened since we met you, Bea."

The donation was working. My stem cells engrafted into Lizzie's bones, which were growing new, healthy marrow. I'd traded research days with hospital days and spent a lot of time conversing with her nurses and doctors. Everyone was filled with optimism for her recovery.

However, a chill had settled in me. My time in Scotland was almost over, and I'd gotten word about my next nursing assignment in the States.

I hadn't found my family, either, but I no longer cared. What was I going to do without this family? The old feelings of not belonging anywhere returned, but it was the thought of leaving Cairn that edged a cold into my bones.

"Are you going to leave, Bea?" asked Ansley. I sought Cairn's eyes across the table. Late nights at the hospital had darkened them, and he clenched his jaw. We didn't talk about the what-ifs. I was too afraid to broach the subject.

"Yes," I said at my plate. "I have to go back to my job."

"So it will be like a going-away party?" Ansley sounded worried. I glanced at Cairn again, who suddenly stood and walked into the kitchen, Eleanor close behind.

"Yes, I suppose so."

The restaurant Eleanor picked for the party was located along a side street Cairn and I had walked many times at night. Oval glass chandeliers spilled champagne-colored light through long windows, and vases of ivory roses—most early-bloomers from Eleanor's garden—dotted the old tables that were interspersed with flickering candles, silver glassware, and ferns.

Before we walked through the antique doors, Cairn pulled me aside and kissed me, the ardor and generosity behind it flooring me. Already fighting back tears I didn't want him to see, I hid my face in his neck.

"I have a surprise for you tonight. Don't leave my side," he said into my ear.

He would never understand how much I didn't want to.

Eleanor had invited all the Brightwell family and friends, so I didn't recognize many faces. This didn't stop the line of people who wanted to hug me or kiss me for what I'd done for Lizzie. An overwhelming, almost unbearable, love for these people filled my body.

After a while, Max held a glass high and clinked a knife to it. "Everybody, gather 'round, please," he said.

Cairn pulled me to his side, and I closed my eyes against his warmth. So much had happened in three months—so many unexpected and joyful things—but the best part was *this*. How was I going to live without it? The thought of my plane surging into the sky made me tense. Cairn sensed it and pulled me closer.

"We Brightwells have many things to celebrate tonight," Max said. "Friends. Family. Second chances. But above all this, love." He rested his gaze on Eleanor, who held her children. Max then shifted to me.

"A few months ago, my wife got an email from a girl far away. This girl was searching for a miracle of sorts. She was searching for her family." Cairn rested his cheek on top of my head, and my throat tightened.

"Now, as it turns out, we were searching for a miracle, too. And it came to us in you, dear Bea. Our Lizzie is in the hospital tonight, but she's still with us because of you." Max's voice broke, and my tears started to fall. "What is a family, Bea? What do you think it really is?"

My heart knew the answer. Had known it all along.

"A family is anyone who loves you."

This time, tears spilled down Max's cheeks. "Aye, dear girl, that's right. And we love you. That makes you *our* family." A sob escaped my mouth. For what we had lost to get here. For the love that had been waiting all along.

"But it's not me who needs to tell you that. Cairn, my son?"

I quickly wiped my tears as Cairn released me to retrieve a long tube wrapped in silver and ivory paper.

"For you," he said, his outstretched hand shaking.

"A going-away gift?" I asked, my voice breaking.

"More like a coming-home gift."

But I didn't hear him as I unwrapped the tube and pulled out a thick parchment scroll. When I unrolled it, I saw it was my family tree. A watercolor Scots pine, the national tree of Scotland, arched in the background, and over its branches silver lines linked the lineage I knew. Cairn had copied the entries from my worn page and made me a beautiful map of my family. I touched the paper and traced the names along the branches, as I had done over and over again with my original tree.

"I know we didn't find many answers," Cairn said. "Or your flesh and blood family, Bea. But it's my hope that you found something more. Because I know I have."

I stopped at my name, and everything that had spun in me for two years finally stilled.

More was here. A new branch connected my name to a whole family: *Max Brightwell. Eleanor Brightwell. Brian Brightwell. Ansley Brightwell. Lizzie Brightwell.*

And *Cairn Brightwell.*

A thick silver line linked my name to Cairn's, and on that line was a ring.

"Bea, look at me."

I couldn't stop the tears. Cairn cupped my face as he spoke.

"Oh, Bea. When you stepped into our house, I knew my life would change. I saw you, and I couldn't breathe. Here was this wee thing who came all this way alone to find her family. I was so impressed by your courage and your drive. I wanted to help you find what you deserve. But as I got to know you, other things impressed me, too. Your intelligence, your humor, your beauty. I fell in love with you. And then you did the unexpected." That low voice tripped with emotion. "You saved my sister."

His next words opened a new doorway to forever. "You've given us all a second chance with Lizzie, but you've given *me* a second chance with love. One I'm not going to waste."

He plucked the ring from the tree. Lowering himself, he took my hand in his.

"You are *my* miracle. You are *my* family. And I love you, Bea. Will you marry me and let me be *your* family?"

I knew at that moment that I wanted to be part of this story for the rest of my life.

"Yes," I cried. "Yes!" Cheers erupted around the room as Cairn pushed the ring on my finger. Before I could say another word, he wrapped his arms around me and lifted me into the air. He kissed me deeply, and I laughed when he finally released me.

"What's so funny?" he murmured.

"You told me that you would make me happy for a long time. I guess you'll have to start tonight." With joy, I touched that wave of dark hair.

"Yes?" he said, his eyes growing bright.

"*Aye*," I corrected. "And for the rest of our lives."

Brandi Willis Schreiber has imagined romance stories her entire life in her head but only recently started writing them down. A graduate of Texas Tech University, she has a master's degree in English literature and uses her love for nature, travel, poetry, and everything beautiful to fuel her fiction, which will always have a happy ending. Her work has appeared in *All Things Dickinson: An Encyclopedia of Emily Dickinson's World*, *The Texas Review*, *Red River Review*, and elsewhere. This is her first published romance short story, and for that she's over the moon. Brandi lives with her husband, rescue dog, and other wild creatures in her beloved West Texas.

Connect with her at http://www.brandiwillisschreiber.com, on Twitter (@bwschreiber), and on Facebook (authorbrandiwillisschreiber).

HOMECOMING

To: FordCampbell@MIT.edu
From: LGreene@realmail.com
Subject: Second Chance

Ford,

No, I have not changed my mind. This is it. My second chance. Finally, after four years of college, I'm returning to our little dinky hometown for two weeks. Moreover, during those two weeks, I fully plan on getting with Wesley Givens, former high school quarterback and my adolescent crush. Stop trying to talk me out of it.

— Lana

P.S. Don't forget to pick me up at the train station on Friday.

To: LGreene@realmail.com
From: FordCampbell@MIT.edu
Subject: Second Chances Suck

Lana-Banana,

And as I told you last week (plus every night since via text), this little plan of yours is flawed. However, you appear determined to follow through despite my warnings and multiple uses of emoji. Who can resist the smiling poo?

Despite my countless attempts to remove all memories of Wesley from your mind over the past four years—and I admit going to different colleges made the task harder—you seem set in your ways. For the last time, here's a list of reasons you shouldn't try this:

1. Wes Givens was a total douche-lord in high school. Must assume he wore some kind of invisible anti-douche shield when he was around you. Will consult various comic books about said garment.

2. You are so much better than Wesley Givens. You, my friend, are cool, fun, and kind. Three adjectives that could never be used to describe Wes the Less.

3. Wouldn't you rather spend these two weeks as a carefree, recently graduated, soon-to-be law student? You're about to move to Washington, DC. This makes you infinitely better than Wes-peaked-in-high-school-Givens.

Heed the advice of your oldest (and coolest—even if I wasn't cool in high school due to lack of high school footballing) friend. Avoid Wesley Givens.

P.S. Train station — Friday night — check.
P.P.S. I've missed you.

THE TRAIN HORN LETS out a loud welcome, and I step down the steps and onto the platform. My bags weigh a ton. Thank God my parents drove to Syracuse for my graduation and brought most of my stuff home with them. No way would I have been able to drag everything else through all the train changes and switches back to Pennsylvania.

"Lana-Banana."

I hear Ford's distinctive bellow as it mixes with the other noises of the train station. The chug of the engine as the train moves again, the voices of people reuniting, and the scraping of luggage wheels against the concrete.

I smile in spite of myself. Ford Campbell has been my best friend since the fourth grade. Ever since the day some kid was making fun of him in the cafeteria, and I decided to show my support in the only way a nine-year-old could. I made him a red-and-blue friendship bracelet. Then we were forever linked as best friends. A weird notion, I've always thought, since we are complete opposites. Apparently, the saying is true and opposites do attract because we've always been inseparable.

Well, until we went to different colleges. But I was only in upstate New York and Ford was in Boston. So, we still got to visit a couple of times a year. Besides, it's not like we live in the Dark Ages. We've texted on a daily basis for the past four years and Face-Timed like every other day.

Now that I think about it, he should totally be sick of me.

Only Ford never gets sick of me. That's one of his better qualities, I've always thought.

Bounding over to me with his signature lopsided grin, floppy brown hair, and light green eyes, I can't help but smile. Ford is the most positive, optimistic person I know.

He wraps me in a big, chest-crushing hug and I smile against his … *whoa*. When did Ford's chest become so hard and muscular? Pulling away, I give him a long onceover. His arms are a lot bigger than I remember, too. I think back to the last time we were together. I guess a lot can change in one whole school year.

"Are you ogling me, Banana?"

"Are you on steroids, Campbell? Or do you spend every waking second at the gym? Wouldn't that get in the way of your incessant comic book reading and crazy-boring computer programming?"

I tease him, but Ford is the smartest person I know. He left MIT with about a hundred job offers. After months of agonizing, he narrowed it down to two different positions. One is in San Francisco, and the other one is in Washington, DC. Guess which one I hope he takes?

"She comes off the train in rare form, everyone," he announces to the platform of dwindling pedestrians.

I roll my eyes because I'm honestly not sure what else to do besides openly stare at my suddenly kinda-hot best friend. "Ha. Ha. Ha. You are so hilarious. Why don't you stop being such a goober and help me with these bags."

"I thought your parents were up a couple of weeks ago to help you with your stuff," he says as he grabs my two heavier bags as if they weigh no more than a paperback book.

"They were." I look over at him as we walk through the door that will take us to the tiny parking lot. The Cherrydale train station is less of a station and more of a platform attached to a parking lot with one tiny vending machine that has been out of order more years than I've been in college.

"Coulda fooled me," he says and points toward his car. "Bet they were bummed they couldn't be here when you got home."

"Totes," I say and climb into the front seat. "But they had that wedding for my dad's boss's daughter. They're making a whole weekend out of it."

Ford laughs and puts the car into drive. As we make our way from the train station and through our super small central Pennsylvania town, I do my usual inventory of the area, noting what's changed (not much) and what's new (also, not much).

Letting out a sigh, I lean my head against the headrest. I don't think I can ever live in this small town again. Washington, DC, will definitely be a welcomed adjustment. I still can't believe I'll be starting Georgetown Law in two short weeks. *Ahhhh*.

"Tired?" Ford asks.

"Nah. Just feeling … introspective," I decide.

"Well, if that's all." He makes a turn onto my parents' street. "I happened to hear of a party that one certain redhead might like to attend tonight."

I turn said red-haired head in his direction. "Someone in this town is having a party?"

"Ran into Sam this morning. Some girl who was a year younger than us is returning to college next week, so she's throwing a sort of alumni homecoming and end-of-summer party tonight. Should be some people from our year, too."

My heart starts beating fast. "Really?"

I watch Ford roll his eyes. "Yes, really. Seriously, Lan? Is this whole hook-up-with-Wes-Givens plan still green-lit?"

"Yes! Of course. This could be the last time I ever see him."

"Not really. Just come home for the holidays and stop by the gas station."

My turn to roll my eyes as Ford pulls his car into my driveway. "Wes doesn't work at the gas station." What a cliché if he did. The talented high-school quarterback pumping gas and cleaning windshields.

"No, but he works for his dad's insurance company here in town. Nothing glamorous about it."

"Shut up. Stop ruining this moment for me." I get out of the car. Ford has already grabbed my bags and is heading to the porch.

"I wouldn't dream of ruining the perfect night of cheap keg beer and high school dreams for you."

"You're so dramatic. Quit whining and go take a shower. We have some partying to do tonight." I stick the key in the front lock but quickly turn around and wrap my arms around Ford. "Thanks for picking me up."

I feel him relax against me. I also can't help but notice that he smells amazing. When did he start wearing whatever scent this is?

He offers up his grin. "Pick you up at eight."

Chapter Two

AFTER A MUCH-NEEDED LONG shower, my day of travel is washed away, my hair is shiny, and my skin is nice and clear. I throw on a pair of tight leggings and a baby blue tank top, accessorizing with both a long and short necklace and tiny star earrings that Ford gave me for my birthday last year.

As I make my way around my childhood bedroom, I can't stop thinking about Ford. We didn't get to see each other as much this year as usual. We had the same spring break but Ford went to Puerto Rico with some friends. Instead of spending Christmas at home like usual, my family went to Arizona to visit my grandparents. I missed him.

We've known each other for so long. No one knows me better than Ford Campbell.

On cue, I hear his car horn. Looking out my bedroom window, he spots me and waves and I wave back. I stop for a spritz of perfume before I dash down the stairs and yank the door open.

I pull up short to see that Ford has exited the car and is standing on my front porch with his hands in his pockets. "Ready?" he asks. "You smell good," he adds.

"Just some perfume," I say. Then I take him in.

Ford looks like … totally Ford. He's wearing jeans, a button-down plaid shirt over a—what else—vintage *Star Wars* tee. Only, there is something else. Something … sexier. *OMG.* Did I just think my best friend looked sexy?

"Why is your face getting red?" he asks.

"No reason. Let's go." I slam the door shut, grab his hand, and quickly head for his car.

It only takes us five minutes to drive to the party. I remember the girl who's throwing it even though Ford is clueless. Shocker. Still, as we walk around the house taking in all the kids of varying ages from high school to recent college grads, neither of us is really comfortable.

"Who are all these people?"

Ford shrugs. "Hell if I know." Like me, he looks around the room. "I think I saw Scott and JT over there. Other than that, I feel like we're party crashing."

"Want to go see if we know anyone outside?"

"Sure."

We make our way through the kitchen, stopping to snag a couple of Jell-O shots, and then out the door onto the deck.

"Oh look," I say pointing. There is a white gazebo in the backyard, all bedazzled in twinkly lights. "Come on."

"Are you going to make me act out *Twilight* again?" he asks.

I shove him. "Shut up. That was one freaking time. And that waterfall we came across while hiking reminded me of Forks." Sticking a finger in his face, I huff. "Besides, I know you read that book."

"Didn't need to." He chuckles. "You practically recited it for me on a daily basis."

I do a little turn in the gazebo. "How could I not? Romance and werewolves and vampires …"

"Speaking of things that suck." Ford hops up on the railing. "I didn't catch Wes Givens inside."

I bite my lip. "Maybe he won't show up."

"And maybe he'll go to something else interesting that's happening in town. Oh, wait. That's right. Nothing else ever goes on in this town."

I laugh. "True."

"So your lover boy will be here."

Sighing, I let my shoulders rise and drop. "I don't get why you don't like Wes or my plan to hook up with him now. Do you want me to live with regret for the rest of my life?"

"You got close that one night."

Prom, senior year. How could I ever forget? We'd both gone to the dance with different people, but at the after party we almost hooked up.

"I'm just glad I kept you from hooking up with him senior year," he says under his breath.

I whirl around to face him. It's clear from Ford's expression that he hadn't meant to say that out loud.

"What did you say?" I ask, although I'm sure I heard him correctly.

"Lana," he begins. But then he stops, puts his hands in the air. "It was you. The night of prom."

I cast my mind back. I can still see the lavender dress I'd worn, still smell the lily in my corsage. Wes and I had been talking for a long time out on the deck of the house as we drank some delectable Boone's Farm. I'd shivered, and he'd asked if I wanted to go upstairs with him where it was warm.

We'd made our way to one of the bedrooms. But before anything had happened, Wes slipped out to go to the bathroom. When he'd come back, he said he'd changed his mind. He didn't want to do anything with me. That had been that. Embarrassing and confusing.

Now, four years later, I'm learning that Ford may have had something to do with us not getting together.

"Ford, you better start talking now." I feel my blood starting to boil.

He gives me this look where he makes his green eyes go all big and remorseful. It usually makes me give in to him. Tonight might be the exception.

"Now," I say.

His shoulders collapse, and he lets out this long sigh. "My date was in the bathroom and I ... I kinda told Wes not to hook up with you."

"Why?"

"Because he's not a good guy, Lana. He never was."

"You know how I felt about him. How much that night would have meant to me ..."

"He was a bully. He made kids' lives miserable. For fun. Because he was bored."

He takes my shoulders, and I try to shake his grip, but he holds firm. "All these years, Ford. Why didn't you tell me?"

"Because I pretty much expected, and wanted to avoid, the reaction I'm getting right now."

"You ruined everything."

"I saved you." He steps closer.

"You were jealous of Wes."

"Yeah, Lana, I was jealous of him. I still am. Wanna know why?" Do I? "Yes."

"Because he has your attention."

"Well, at the moment you have it, you crazy person." I flick him on the chest.

"I am crazy. Crazy to have hoped ..."

"Hoped for what?" I ask. I'm confused but at the same time the hair on my arms is standing up at full attention. Ford's eyes are boring into mine, imploring me to pay attention.

"Hoped that you wanted what I wanted. I mean, that you would come to want what I want."

"What are you even talking about? What do you want?"

He takes a deep breath, like he's about to go under water. Then he leans toward me. "This."

Ford presses his lips against mine, and I'm so shocked that I feel my eyes go wide and a small sound escapes my mouth. As it does, my lips soften and open and Ford frames my face with his hands.

OMG, my BFF is kissing me. But the really crazy thing is, I start to kiss him back. Even as I allow him to run his lips over mine, my heart starts beating harder, and my stomach does a little flip-flop.

Holy hell. Ford is a good kisser. A *great* kisser.

So good that I find my arms acting independently of my brain. They reach up and wind around his shoulders, my hands clasping behind his neck. I lean back and Ford takes the opportunity to place kisses along my neck. I shudder because, oh man, that's a super sensitive spot.

Then he's running his lips up and down, and I move my hands to his shirt, pulling him closer.

"Yes," I utter in a husky voice.

Ford's hands moved to my waist, circling my hips and tracing circles just under the hem of my tank top. Lazy fingers slide up my skin, making me shiver as they pass over a rather ticklish spot. They stop when they reach my bra, a moment of hesitation.

But I want more, so I shift to the right and meet his lips once more. I push my tongue into his mouth, hoping he understands that this is an invitation for his hands to pick up where they left off. I taste the cherry Jell-O from the shot.

I know we're outside at a party. In the background, I can hear the music blasting through the house. Someone is yelling "chug" at the top of his lungs, and a car horn is blasting out on the street.

I don't care though because this feels so amazing. I know we'd been fighting, but if you put a gun to my head, I wouldn't be able to tell you what we were fighting over.

Finally, Ford takes the hint, and his fingers begin to move under my top again. They brush over my lacy bra, passing over my sensitive nipples. I push into him even as I continue to draw him toward me by clutching his shirt.

Then his hands fall to my waist, and he plants one last kiss on my lips.

When we pull apart, there's a long moment that passes between us. I search his eyes, hoping, praying I won't see any regret. Even though I really can't believe I've just made out with my oldest, closest friend, I can't deny that it felt amazing.

Then Ford's face breaks out into his usual grin, and I relax in his arms.

"Well," I say.

"Well." He brushes a hair from my face. "That's something we've never done before. I mean, we've both kissed other people."

"But never each other." I realize I've been grasping his shirt while we made out and smooth the fabric. Then I look up and meet his serious gaze. "Are you okay?" I ask tentatively.

"After that? Oh yeah."

I lightly punch him. A line forms on his forehead. I know it well. It's his thinking line.

"Banana, I want to say—"

But he's interrupted when a couple of drunk people stumble into the backyard. Oblivious, they immediately start playing beer pong on a long table already set up on the patio.

Ford and I untangle ourselves. I wonder what he was going to say. But the moment—this unexpected, yet totally perfect moment—has ended. I throw my best death stare in the direction of the beer pongers, and Ford laughs. Then he grabs my hand and interlocks our fingers. My breath catches. I've held hands with Ford before. But never like this. With our fingers intertwining like this, it's more than a simple gesture. This is the hand holding of a couple.

Are Ford and I going to become a couple? Are we one already? Would I even want that? Does he?

Questions flood my mind, and I glance over to see that Ford's thinking line has returned as well.

"Come on," he says. "Let's grab some drinks."

Alcohol to calm my uber-frayed nerves? Yes, please. "Sounds good."

I follow him into the house, but we're stopped by Kacey, a friend from high school. Ford snatches his hand from mine in record time, and I can't help but feel disappointed.

"Lana, hi." Unaware of the fact that I can't think of anything except for the way Ford's lips felt against mine, Kacey wraps me in a big hug. "So good to see you. Hi, Ford," she offers.

"Why don't you guys catch up," Ford says, stepping even further from me. "I'll grab us those drinks. Kacey, you want something?"

She holds up her red Solo cup. "All good, thanks."

As Kacey catches me up on her plans for the fall, my eyes follow Ford as he heads toward the kitchen. What just happened? Maybe I'm imagining something, but it seems like he didn't want anyone to see us holding hands. Weird.

I tune back to Kacey. "So I'm going to have to go shopping for new clothes. I mean, it's my first real grown up job. Not an internship. Actual paycheck." She wiggles her eyebrows. "Do you need some stuff for law school?"

"Oh, I don't know. Probably." In truth, I haven't thought about it. I've been too busy obsessing over the possibility of seeing

Wes. Then Ford and I kissed, and any thoughts of law school were so far away they might as well be on a different planet.

"Why don't we plan a shopping trip while you're in town?" I'm about to agree when Kacey lets out a huff. "Look who showed up."

I turn my head in the direction she's staring, and I can feel my mouth fall open. Wesley Givens has just walked in the front door. He high-fives some guys by the door, and his eyes are sweeping the room as he walks further into the house.

He looks so similar to the Wes I remember from four years ago. He's even wearing the same Cherrydale High Football tee. Well, hopefully, it's an updated version at least.

But he has the same dark blond hair in the same short haircut. Still tall and big, but maybe with a little less muscle.

Even as I'm ogling him, he turns in my direction. He takes in me and Kacey and slowly heads in our direction.

"Hey," he says with a quick flick of his chin in our general direction. "Haven't seen either of you in a while."

"Yeah, because we both went away to college," Kacey says. I continue to practice my mime impression.

"Don't be all holier-than-thou. I went to college, too. Football scholarship. Remember?"

"Yeah, well we both stayed in college and actually graduated."

I look over at Kacey. Whoa. She's going for the jugular. If I remember correctly, she and Wes never really got along back in the day. Still, ouch.

Wes seems unperturbed, though.

Kacey rolls her eyes and nudges my shoulder. "I'm gonna go say hi to some people. You okay, Lana?"

"Yeah, of course." Then she's gone, and Wes and I are alone. For the first time in four years.

"Hey," he says with another head nod.

"Hi."

Crickets. All this time spent obsessing over seeing Wes Givens again, and I never thought about what to say. Great, Lana, I chastise myself.

"So you in town for a while?" he asks.

"Just for two weeks. I graduated in May, but I was working at a Syracuse law firm until a couple of days ago. Thought I would come to town before I move to DC for law school." It might be the light, but seems like Wes's eyes are glazed over.

"Cool."

"Yeah, it'll be great. So you're still around here?"

"So?" His eyes flick to mine.

"Nothing, just making conversation."

Whoa, defensive much? I cast my mind back to high school and even junior high before that. Did Wes and I ever have an actual conversation? Because we are barely having one now.

He starts saying something about football and preseason games and I tune out. My eyes search out the room for Ford, but I don't spot him. As Wes rambles on and on about tackles and tight ends, I can't help but remember going to Friday night games with Ford. We used to have the best time.

And we always ended up at the diner after. I ordered mozzarella sticks and Ford would get cheesecake.

I wonder if he remembers that. Again, I look around for him as Wes babbles on. Where is he?

Then, the next thing I know, Wes reaches out and snags my hand. Interesting that his touch doesn't feel anything like when Ford held my hand. I don't feel butterflies in my stomach. In fact, the only thing I do feel is Wes's sweaty hand. Gross.

"Let's go somewhere and catch up," he says and then takes off. Yanking my hand, I stumble before catching up to his pace.

"Where are we going?"

"I just want to talk. Come on, let's go upstairs."

I realize pretty quickly that I don't want to go upstairs. Yet at the same time, I'm curious. How could I not be? This is the guy I've been waiting to go upstairs with for the past four years. Plus those years in high school.

I should be thrilled. However, I find myself wondering what's taking Ford so long with the drinks. I turn my head just as Wes and I start walking up the stairs. I see Ford coming out of the kitchen, two cups in hand.

He spots me and looks up to take Wes in. Then his smile fades. I pull on Wes's hand and try to stop him. But he doesn't notice.

"Come on, Lana," he says as I watch Ford put the drinks down and head toward the door.

Chapter Three

"YOU SEEM DISTRACTED."

Busted. We're in what appears to be a little girl's room. From the massive amounts of pink and ruffles and *Frozen* paraphernalia, I have to assume a very girly girl. Wes is lounging on the bed, holding a teddy bear.

"Sorry. I was texting my friend. He gave me a ride here, and I think he may have left."

"Don't worry, baby. I can drive you home."

"Thanks." My fingers quickly tap out a message to Ford, and I hit send. "I hope Ford is okay."

Wes stops playing with the teddy bear and looks up. "Ford Campbell?"

I nod.

He drops the bear on the bed. "Are you guys still friends?"

"Yeah. We've been friends forever."

A moan escapes his lips. "Right, forgot about that. Listen, it was just a dumb bet."

I tilt my head and narrow my eyes. "What are you talking about?"

"That night. You know."

I shake my head.

"Prom," Wes says as he waves a flippant hand in the air and shrugs. "The bet I made to get you in bed." He holds his hands up in front of his chest. "I mean, I didn't film *every* girl I hooked up with."

It's as if the sound of brakes roar in my head. My mouth falls open, and I quickly close it.

"Ford threatened to turn me into the police. I don't know how he found out about it. Probably used his geeky little computer to hack into my personal thoughts or something."

"Yeah, computers don't work that way," I mumble. I push away from Wes and pace to the window as I gather my thoughts.

With the info I know already, I start making a list in my head. Wes had made a bet about sleeping with me. He thought about filming it, too? Ford somehow knew about it. Ford got Wes to leave me alone.

"That was like ten years ago, though, Lana."

I turn to face Wes. "It was four years ago."

"Huh. Feels like more."

I walk over to him and jut a finger in his general direction. "Let me get this straight. You had some kind of bet to hook up with me, and to prove you succeeded, you were going to film it?"

"Yeah, you know. Just a good-natured bet."

"You're disgusting."

What is wrong with him, I wonder.

"What's the big deal? You were like in love with me."

Yes, I was. And for the first time, that little fact makes me feel like vomiting. My cheeks burn, and I gulp a big breath.

I take a good, long look at Wesley Givens. In the back of my mind, I hear all of the things Ford said about him earlier. I remember how dismissive Kacey was with him. Am I the only one who didn't see how awful he is?

"You're right; I *was* in love with you." At my statement, his eyes light up, and his face contorts into a cocky expression.

"But you know what word is super important in that sentence?" I continue. "*Was*. I was a lot of things in high school. But the great thing about me is that I grew up. Maybe one day you'll be able to say the same thing about yourself."

I feel empowered. I feel strong.

"So does this mean we're not going to hook up?"

I don't even respond as I head for the door. I came to Cherrydale for a second chance. And I know just where to get it.

Chapter Four

I MAKE MY WAY through the now-raging party, dodging sweaty dancers and binge-drinking minors until I find Kacey in the kitchen. I ask her to give me a ride to Ford's house.

"Sure, no problem." Then she steps back and takes me in, a knowing smile blossoming on her face. "Are you and Ford Campbell finally going to get together?"

I let out a nervous laugh because I have no idea what's about to happen. All I know for sure is that there is no one in the world I want to see more than Ford. "Um ..."

Kacey pulls her car keys out of her purse. "Didn't mean to pry. Come on." She starts walking toward the front of the house and I follow. "I know it's none of my business, but Ford was in love with you all through high school. When I saw you guys tonight, I assumed you'd finally gotten together. Then you went upstairs with Wes."

I groan as we get into her car. "Big mistake." We start the drive toward Ford's, and I turn to face Kacey. "Ford was in love with me in high school?"

Kacey shifts in her seat at a stop sign. "You didn't know?"

I shake my head, dumbfounded.

"Seriously?" she asks as she pulls to a stop in front of Ford's house.

"I had no idea. I mean, I kinda got clued in tonight."

Kacey's eyebrow shoots up. "What happened tonight?"

I laugh as I push the door open. "Something I'm going to go finish right now. Thanks for the ride. Call you soon."

I run to the front door and knock lightly. No one answers, but I see Ford's car in the driveway. I try the door and luckily it's unlocked.

As familiar in this house as I am in my own, I walk through the foyer, across the living room and around to the back where Ford's room is. Peeking my head through the half-open doorway, I see that Ford is sitting in his usual place—in front of his computer. Only, I notice the computer's not on, and he's staring out the window. His hands are on his lap, curled into fists.

Those hands had been roaming under my shirt not so long ago. I tremble just thinking about it. Thinking about everything I've learned tonight.

Ford, my best friend in the whole world, has been protecting me for a very long time. And all of these years while I've been running toward one guy, the right one has been waiting in the background.

How could I have been so blind?

I take a step into the room, and the old floorboards give out a little creak. Ford's head whips around. A brief smile crosses his face. But it's replaced by a determined frown and furrowed brows.

"What are you doing here?" he asks.

"I ..." What? What am I supposed to say right now? I don't have to think too long though because Ford speaks up again.

"Shouldn't you be making out with Wes somewhere and reliving his glory days? Maybe looking through the yearbook at all of his pictures."

I let out a sigh and walk toward him. Back in high school, I often had to get his attention from his computer by jumping up and plopping my ass on his desk. I try the same thing now.

The corner of his mouth twitches.

"Ready to listen or do you want to pout some more?"

His only reply is the raise of his left eyebrow.

"I don't want to hook up with Wes. Or look at his yearbook pictures."

"Since when?"

"Since I realized what a jerk he is. Since I forced myself to accept that you were right and he's always been a jerk. Since he told me about what you did the night of prom. Since you kissed me."

"Lana," he begins.

"I prefer being called Banana thank you very much."

Finally, I get the grin. The famous Ford Campbell grin. My stomach takes a little dive because I'm seeing this familiar smile through such different eyes.

"How'd you find out about prom?" he asks.

"I think the question should be, why didn't you tell me about it?"

"I don't like when your feelings are hurt. I had overheard Wes and a bunch of the jocks in the bathroom during prom. They were making bets on all of the girls. Your name came up, and I knew how much you liked him."

He runs a hand through his slightly too-long hair. "Listen, Lan, I can accept you dating someone other than me. That's not what this is about. But if you're going to be with someone else, I want it to be someone amazing. Because you don't deserve any less than spectacular."

In his eyes, I see an earnestness that takes my breath away. He means every word he's saying.

"Why?"

"Because I've liked you for a long time."

I reach for his hand but stop when I realize he's holding something. Turning his fist over and prying his fingers apart, I see that he has the red-and-blue friendship bracelet I made him a million years ago.

I freeze. Then my eyes flick up to meet his gaze.

"You kept this," I say.

"It's the first thing you ever gave me," he says as if this is the most obvious thing in the world.

My heart melts. Like actually dissolves inside my chest into a puddle of sparkly goo.

"Well, it won't be the last."

"It definitely won't," he says mysteriously.

I tilt my head in question.

"I accepted the job in DC. Looks like we're moving to the same city, Banana."

With that, I lean over and press my lips to his. Softly. I came home for a second chance and looks like I got one.

We continue to kiss for a long time, until finally we pull apart.

"What?" Ford cocks his head even as his hands continue to roam along my skin.

"This is one hell of a homecoming."

Grinning, we go right back to enjoying our second chance. The first chance of many more to come.

Award-winning romance author Kerri Carpenter writes contemporary romances that are sweet, sexy, and sparkly. When she's not writing, Kerri enjoys reading, cooking, watching movies, taking Zumba classes, rooting for Pittsburgh sports teams, and anything sparkly. Kerri lives in Northern Virginia with her adorable (and mischievous) rescued poodle mix, Harry.

Visit Kerri at her website (http://kerricarpenter.com),
on Facebook (www.facebook.com/authorkerri),
Twitter (@authorKerri), or Instagram (@authorkerri),
or subscribe to her newsletter (http://bit.ly/2fXHVEA).

JAKE'S DJINN

Alyssa Day

Second chances you never knew you wanted …

JAKE CARDINAL WOKE UP with a massive hangover, an empty whiskey bottle, and a genie sitting on his windowsill. He groped for the glass of water that wasn't on his bedside table, shoved the whiskey bottle out of his bed, and closed his eyes against the blinding glare of the gorgeous genie in all her purple-haired, pink-sequined glory.

And then he groaned. "Not *again*."

"You're not my fantasy man, either, Cupcake," she told him. "So get your ass out of bed and make your damn wishes, and then I can get on with my life."

"Coffee. I need coffee to deal with this," he mumbled into his pillow. "Also? Never going on a family vacation again."

"The coffee. Is that your first wish?"

He heard the glee in her voice and decided to thwart her, just because he could. And it had been kind of fun, the last time. Not "hot, naked woman in Tahiti" fun, but … intriguing.

Intriguing was enough to propel him to roll over and shoot

her a look. "No, that's not a wish, Princess. It's a *need*. Like, for example, your need to periodically pop in and ruin my life."

She glanced out the window. "Feels like you're doing a fine job of that all by yourself. Is this ... a log cabin? What happened to the penthouse suite?"

She'd said "log cabin" in the same tone of voice that most people would use to say "rotting corpse." Or, in his case, today, "morning breath."

"Hold that thought. I've got to brush my teeth." He sat up and groaned again when something inside his skull started playing the bongos. "I'm going to kill my cousin-in-law."

He rolled off the bed, stood, and headed for the bathroom. Behind him, he heard her start laughing.

"Nice ass, wizard. But maybe next time you can put your pants on first."

"So don't look."

"Is that a wish?"

"Ha. Not a chance."

"Barbarian," she grumbled.

Jake filled a cup of water, tossed back a couple of Tylenol, and brushed his teeth until death breath was only a distant memory. Sadly, the bloodshot eyes looked like they might hang around a while.

He pulled on his shorts and opened the door, half hoping that she'd be gone.

Half hoping that she'd still be sitting on his windowsill.

She was in the kitchen, instead. "Coffee?"

"Is it magic?"

"No, it's Folger's," she drawled. "That's all you had in this nasty little kitchen."

She was holding the fridge door open, bending down, which gave him a really terrific view of her really terrific ass. Damn, but she was beautiful.

"Look, Ruby—"

In one smooth move, she straightened and tossed a carton of milk at him. "It's not Ruby this time. Smell that and see if it's fresh."

He sniffed, recoiled, and recapped the carton before tossing it in the trash can. "Two points. We could go out to breakfast … Amethyst?"

"Not Amethyst. But—" She went completely still for a second, not blinking, not even breathing. She had the bluest eyes he'd ever seen. Dreaming, drowning, summer-sky-just-after-a-rain blue. He almost forgot to breathe.

"Are you asking me to go to breakfast with you?"

"Yep. And no, it's not a wish, before you ask." Jake took the deep breath his lungs were begging for and blew it out. "We need to get this wish thing out of the way. Tell me your real name, already."

"Why?" Suspicion curled her sensual lips and soured her tone. "I know all about wizards and witches and the power of a name."

"Then you know about the power of domicile. I could command you to give me your name."

Her laughter was like a peal of silvery bells, with the crash of thundering surf underneath. Delicate beauty and imperious power, combined. It suited her.

It *was* her.

The short, spiky, purple hair? Not so much.

She sneered at him. "*You* could command *me* to do nothing."

He flicked a tiny spell at her, and she disappeared. Just vanished before his spell was even halfway across the room. The target gone, the magic fizzled and swirled its way out of the window, into the rosy light of sunrise over the lake.

And then she materialized in front of him and punched him in the face.

Chapter Two

Beware wizards in log cabins …

DONYA FALLING STAR SHERAZELLE wasn't so much angry as she was confused, and maybe a little bit worried, but she wasn't going to let the human see it. She shook out her hand and made a mental note: No more punching—at least not when the man had a jaw like iron, to match the hard-muscled body that fascinated her so much.

Not that she'd admit that, even to herself. But washboard abs and bite-able asses aside, she was worried because this had never happened before: In three thousand years, she'd never been compelled to grant wishes to the same person twice. Sure, the guy who'd rubbed the lamp didn't qualify, but why hadn't the wishes bounced to somebody who hadn't already had their chance?

Nothing about this made sense.

"You hit me!" He rubbed his jaw, but he was grinning. Damn, but he had a sexy-as-sin wicked smile. She just bet that women lined up to jump in his bed, and they were probably pretty happy once they got there. Jake Cardinal, of the famous—some said *infamous*—Cardinal Witches, was a little over six feet of hard-bodied man. He had muscles like a gladiator—and she'd known a few. Luckily, Jake smelled better.

She flashed to the other side of the counter, just in case he tried for retaliation. Also, she needed ice for her knuckles. Because, *ouch.*

"You deserved it, Cupcake. Okay, wishes. What have you got? Let's get this over with." She tapped her fingernails on the counter and tried not to look into his fascinating amber eyes. "You only get three, no wishing for more wishes, no love spells, wishing for anything pervy loses you everything, blah blah blah. You know the drill from last time."

He shoved his tawny golden hair out of his face. He really was unfairly beautiful. Unfair to mortal women, gay men, and horny Djinn.

"Yeah. Speaking of that, I'm a scholar of all things magic. Maybe the best damn magic scholar on the planet, not to be immodest. I've got books and scrolls and even a few computer programs written by the best programmer nerds in their mothers' basements across the country. All of them tell me that you can never receive wishes from the same genie twice. What's up? Did you miss me?"

He was smiling, but Donya could see the flash of sincere interest in his eyes.

"Yes," she drawled, examining her fingernails before yawning. "I missed you. Desperately."

He put his hands on the counter and leaned over it toward her, which gave her a close-up view of the corded muscles in his tanned forearms.

And the trail of silky hair that led into the shorts hanging perilously low on his hips.

She shivered, in spite of herself, and of course, he noticed.

"Like what you see, Princess?"

"Actually, I'm cold. But, hey, seeing a drunk loser in a smelly wooden cabin totally does it for me, too," she said with a straight face and flat voice.

"Ouch. Would you believe me if I told you that you've managed to find me on the only two times I've been drunk in years?" He started to prowl around the corner toward her—a golden-eyed jungle cat stalking his prey.

Except she'd never been prey. Not even when they'd caught her and cursed her to eternity as a slave. Captured, yes. Prey, never. And those who'd trapped her were long dead, which was its own form of revenge.

She held her hand up, palm out, and he stopped where he was. "You asked me about the wishes finding you twice."

"Coffee … Jade?" He poured another cup of coffee and held up the pot.

She shook her head, but had to fight to keep from smiling at his attempts to guess her name. "Not Jade."

"So, Not-Jade. The wishes? And what *is* your name this time, Genie?"

"I'm not a genie; I'm a Djinn. No music, no Major Nelson, no Disney. Stupid American popular culture," she grumbled, flinging open cupboard doors to look for food. "Really? Fruit Loops and Captain Crunch? Aren't you a little old for this?"

He winced. "Great. First, a hangover, then the beautiful woman in my house punches me and calls me old. I think I'm going back to bed."

"And no milk, only beer. That's just nasty. What about—" She blinked when his words caught up to her thoughts. "Beautiful?"

Great. Now he was sucking up to her to get more wishes. Humans. Except, last time …

He drank his coffee, put the mug on the table, and raised an eyebrow. "Like you don't know it. Although, honestly, the sequins are a bit much. I like the purple hair, but the combination makes you look like an ice skater crossed with a drag queen."

She bared her teeth at him and then took her coffee out to the deck. A single thought and her coffee was flavored with sugar, cream, and cinnamon, just how she liked it. Another twinkle of thought, and the rough wooden deck chairs transformed into cushioned chaises.

"Ahhhh." She sank into her chair and looked out at the beauty of the sunrise over the lake. The birds were waking up, too, and one of them landed lightly on the arm of her chair and twittered at her. It might even be worth staying in a log cabin for a few days to wake up to this.

"Good morning, Sir Robin." A twirling movement of her finger, and bread crumbs appeared in midair, scattering on the deck railing for the bird and his friends. But her mind was only half on her magic.

"Drag queen. Jerk," she grumbled.

"I heard that." He was suddenly right behind her, though she hadn't heard him approach. Jake Cardinal made her nervous; not that she'd let him see it. There was a frisson of awareness—a sharp edge in the air between them—that had only intensified since the first time they'd met. They'd spent the entire night dueling with quips and jests, and she'd fallen asleep on the couch, only to wake at sunrise in his arms.

She'd disappeared before he'd woken and regretted it ever since.

"Vegas, right?" He sat on the other chair, leaned back, and closed his eyes against the light.

The idea that he might not even remember exactly where they'd met—when she'd carried the memory with her for more than two years—stung her pride and might even have hurt her feelings, if she admitted to any feelings. She shrugged, putting on a mask of indifference. "Who can remember?"

Jake opened one eye and grinned at her. "I can remember, and I was drunker than I've ever been in my life. You're not exactly forgettable, sweet thing."

She refused to tell him she felt the same way about him. Stupid human. His ego was already big enough, no doubt. Instead, she drank more coffee and looked out over the water.

"Three wishes, huh? What did I wish for last time?"

"A giant tattoo of a pinup girl that covered your entire back," she told him, rolling her eyes.

He laughed. "Well, I know I don't have that, so what happened?"

"Your *second* wish."

This time he laughed out loud, and his laugh was deep and rich and delicious, just as she'd remembered it so many times, alone in her solitude. She suddenly wanted to curl up in his lap and bite his neck.

Oops. No biting the humans. It was one of her cardinal (*Ha!* See how she did that?) rules.

He stretched and, truly, his body was a work of art. She suddenly wished she were a sculptor instead of a Djinn.

"What about the third?"

Donya shook off her wistful, lustful thoughts, drained her

mug, and flicked the cup into the air to send it floating to the kitchen sink. "A bottle of whiskey. How can you not remember any of this, when you remember me, and that I called myself Ruby?"

His smile faded, and his eyes darkened to a gleam of emerald fire. "Because all I remember is you," he said roughly. "I've been remembering you and nothing but you for two years, five months, and three weeks. I remember your laugh, and how beautiful you are, and that you smell like jasmine. I remember your intelligence and your stories about ancient cities. I remember that you fell asleep next to me and didn't wake up when I wrapped my arms around you. I remember that I woke up wishing you were there with me in my bed."

She caught her breath. "I—"

He put his mug down and stood. "Remembering anything as insignificant as wishes didn't matter to me one damn bit."

She stood, captivated by the power of his words, the emotion in his voice, and the truth in his gaze. "But—"

"Your *name*," he insisted, with a touch of Power in his voice.

"Donya Falling Star Sherazelle," she whispered, before she could strengthen her defenses against his magic. Now he'd have power over her.

Now she was in serious danger.

A slow, dangerous smile crossed his face, and fear pounded a rhythm in her heartbeat. She raised her chin and glared at him. "I warn you—"

"Donya Falling Star Sherazelle, my first and only wish is that you will now and forever be free of the curse of the Djinn."

Lightning sizzled a blinding strike on the surface of the lake in front of them, thunder crashed and destroyed the dawn's silence, and suddenly she was—for the first time in three thousand years—free.

Free.

And then she fainted.

Chapter Three

Not even Irish ...

JAKE DROPPED TO HIS knees on the wooden deck and managed to catch his Djinn before she hit the ground. The last thing she needed was to start off her new life with a concussion. At least he'd known that she'd retain her magic, so she wouldn't be helpless—

Wait.

His Djinn?

When did that brain fart happen, that he'd even think about claiming her?

She was a *Djinn*, and she'd been one for a really long time, so the last thing she'd want is to be caught up in a relationship with a human, let alone a human who also happened to be a wizard. He'd wanted her and missed her and dreamed about her for too damn long.

Sure, his head told him to forget her, but his arms tightened around her, and he caught himself inhaling a deep jasmine-scented breath. She was warm and soft and curvy in his arms, turning his memories into his present reality, and he didn't want to let her go. Dumbass realization to have after he surrendered his wishes.

He could have wished for an evening of holding her again— just holding her couldn't violate the "no perviness" rule, right?

He sighed. He was losing his freaking mind. Right there on the porch of a rented cabin, during the Cardinal family vacation that he'd been blackmailed into attending.

At least he'd put his foot down when Astrid, his borderline nutcase sixteen-year-old cousin, had tried to move into his spare room with her four suitcases, two computers, and a little pug dog named Ninja. She would be staying in the cabin three doors down with her sister and their crazy grandmother when they all arrived tomorrow afternoon.

Granny. Now *there* was a story.

Donya stirred in his arms and then opened her enormous blue eyes.

"Hey, there. You left me for a minute." He smiled at her because he couldn't help it. She was just so damn beautiful and felt so good in his arms.

She started to speak, but then swallowed, hard. "Free? Just like that? You didn't even use your other two wishes first?"

"I didn't want anything as much as I wanted you to be free of that lamp. Did a bit of research on that, too."

She sat up and then quickly stood and backed away from him. He tried not to feel the sting of that, and instead of reacting he headed indoors.

"How about we go get that breakfast?"

"Is that a ..." Her voice trailed off, and he realized that it would probably take a long time for her to stop expecting wishes. To stop seeing every person she encountered as a greedy jerk who wanted more and more and more.

Hell, he wanted more and more, himself. More time with her. More of a chance to get to know her.

Less of the sequins, though, if he had to be honest.

Speaking of which ... "Do you want to borrow a flannel shirt? As much as the pink sequins and lace fit in when we were in Vegas, you're going to catch a lot of attention at a diner next to a fishing lake in Ohio."

He glanced at her and froze. She stood completely still; her face lifted to the golden early morning sunlight, her arms held out to her sides—palms up—as if she were welcoming the dawn. She was a goddess, inviting all to worship her, and his magic yearned toward her like a hound called to heel by his mistress.

And suddenly he was a freaking poet.

Damn hangover.

He was going to *kill* his cousin Rose's husband.

As if called by the thought, Alejandro pushed open the front door and ambled in. "Hey, Rose wants to know if you want to go to breakfast with ... oh, I'm sorry, my friend, I did not realize you had company. Hello, beautiful lady."

"Forget how to knock?" Jake bit off the words as he took a step toward Alejandro. The man might be a *married* FBI Paranormal Ops agent, but Jake knew at least ten ways to choke the life out of him.

For the hangover *and* for the way he was looking at Donya.

"Aren't you going to introduce us?" Alejandro asked.

"No. Get out. I blame you for this hangover." He stalked over to the door and held it open. "Out. Now."

Alejandro ignored him. The jackass.

"That's very rude, Jake," Donya said, in that sultry voice of hers. "I'd love to meet Mr. Tall, Dark, and Delicious."

"Right. Don't be rude, Jake," Alejandro said, moving out of arm's reach.

"That's it. You have to die. I know I have some arsenic around here," Jake told him.

"Maybe behind the Fruit Loops," Donya said dryly.

Jake shot her a look. "You're not helping ... oh. *Oh.*"

She didn't have purple hair or pink sequins now. Her hair hung in rich dark waves to the middle of her back. Her dress was the color of sunshine and hugged her rounded curves in a way that made him suddenly, desperately jealous—of fabric. He almost swallowed his tongue.

Then he noticed Alejandro and his dumb grin, and he figured he didn't have any choice but to introduce them before he kicked his cousin-in-law's ass.

"Donya, this is the rotten apple of the family tree, my cousin Rose's husband, Alejandro, the former vampire hunter and current P-Ops not-so-special agent."

"Alejandro Vasquez, and I am delighted to meet you. Are you

Jake's special friend?" He shot a smart-ass glance at Jake, who was suddenly thinking of how easy it would be to stage a fatal fishing boat accident. "I wish you'd tell me—"

"I am Donya Sherazelle, and wish me no wishes, vampire hunter, for I am free now. I will give you nothing," she said, and her voice was ice.

Suddenly, Jake felt a lot happier.

Alejandro's mouth fell open. "I didn't—I wasn't—I was just going to crack a stupid joke about giving me tips on how to get Jake to act civilized."

Donya blushed. Jake didn't know genies—Djinn—could blush. He also didn't know that watching a Djinn blush would give him a raging hard-on, so he moved closer to the counter for cover and thought about cold showers.

"My apologies, Alejandro Vasquez. It is nice to meet you. I might be oversensitive to anything that sounds like *wish* for a while." She didn't offer to shake Alejandro's hand, though, which cheered Jake up enormously.

"So, introductions made, get out. And never bring your rot-gut tequila into my life again," he told Alejandro. "I think my head exploded once or twice last night."

Alejandro shrugged. "Not my problem if you're too weak to handle your liquor," he said slyly. "Or your women."

The door slammed open, and Jake's favorite cousin Rose, who looked to be about fifteen months pregnant and was all golden hair, glowing skin, and belly, swept the room with her gaze and then focused in on her husband. "Did I hear you say something about 'your women' to my cousin? Please tell me you didn't pull such a B.S. macho line out of your butt and say those words in front of our guest."

Jake whistled. "Somebody's in *trou-ble*," he sang out.

"You shut up," Rose said, pointing at him. "You kept my husband out until four o'clock this morning, and when he did return, he was singing an Irish drinking song and calling me his sweet *macushla*."

"It's a fine Irish term of endearment," Alejandro protested. "I love you, and you are my darling. So—"

"You're not Irish. You're from *Guatemala*." Rose rolled her eyes.
"But—"

"Shut up, both of you. Our guest will think we have the manners of a great bunch of carnivorous leprechauns." Rose walked, slowly and heavily, over toward Donya, who rushed to greet her.

"Please sit and rest. When is the child due?"

"Two weeks, even though it feels like he or she is coming any minute."

"He or she? Would you like to know the baby's gender?" Donya's eyes sparkled.

What was it about women and babies? Even Djinn women, apparently.

"No, but thank you. With an entire family of witches, it has been harder to keep this surprise than it was to rescue Alejandro's partner from the basilisks." Rose smiled at her husband, and the sheer weight of the love in that smile hit Jake in the chest.

Not that he begrudged Rose her happiness. She deserved it more than anybody he knew, and Alejandro wasn't a bad guy, after all. The man would protect Rose and their baby with his life; they'd all seen that when their cousin Lily had nearly died.

It's just that Jake would have liked to feel that kind of soul-deep happiness for himself. His gaze went, almost involuntarily, to Donya. Maybe if …

No.

Time to quit chasing dreams.

"I'm Rose, by the way, and I apologize for the men in my family. They're idiots."

"Donya, and I think they're kind of cute, actually." The Djinn—*former* Djinn—flashed a smile at Jake, and his heart stuttered in his chest. But, *cute*?

Hell, no.

He scowled. "Panda bears are cute. Kittens are cute. I'd prefer hot. Or sexy, or—"

"Moronic?" Alejandro interrupted, an evil glint in his eye. "A lightweight? Sad? Lonely?"

"Stop. Right. Now," Rose said, glaring at both of them, but

then her eyes widened, her mouth rounded to a perfect *O*, and she looked down.

Which made everybody *else* look down.

At the puddle of water on the floor in the spot directly between her legs.

Everybody started talking at once. Loudly.

"Is that—"

"Do you—"

"Can I—"

Rose whistled, also loudly, and the piercing noise silenced the room.

"Stop babbling and get my bag, right now. We have to go to the hospital. I think," she said, breathing hard and clutching her belly.

Donya grabbed Rose's arm. "Jake, Alejandro, get over here."

Alejandro stood there, staring at his wife. "What—what's happening?"

"I'm having our baby, *macushla*," Rose bit off. Then she arched her back and groaned, long and low; an almost-feral sound.

Jake, on his way across the room, froze. "Now?"

"*Now*, Cupcake," Donya said, her face lit up with glee. "This being human is a lot more exciting than I'd expected."

Chapter Four

Six hours is a long time ...

"HOW COULD SHE CHANGE her mind and refuse to go to the hospital? What could possibly be taking so long?"

Donya watched Jake—with a shirt on now, sadly—pace across the deck of the cabin, and then she sighed.

"Why can't they just transport themselves here?"

"They're garden witches. Their only magic mode of transport is by minivan," he said, rolling his eyes.

"If I could carry them here, I would, Jake, but my powers don't extend that far. Still, your family is on the way, and it has only been a few hours—"

"Six," he flung at her, eyes wild and hair standing up in every direction from all the times he'd shoved his hands through it. "Six hours. How can it take six hours to get one tiny baby out?"

"Well, it's coming out of an opening the size of a—"

"Gak! No! Don't talk to me about openings, or dilation or—" Here, he looked around furtively and then lowered his voice. "Or cervixes."

She laughed. "I think it might be cervices."

"Who cares? I don't want to hear about either of them!" He flung himself in the deck chair, and then jumped up. "They're in my bedroom, and I feel helpless out here. I should be boiling water."

"Why?"

"I don't know. That's what they do in movies!"

"Okay ..." Donya didn't even know she was going to do it

until she did: she wrapped her arms around his waist from behind and hugged him. "You really love her, don't you?"

He stood perfectly still, as if he'd surprised a wild creature coming up to him. If she thought about it, she had to admit that he sort of had. She'd been wild and untamed for so long, nothing to anyone but a conduit to their greedy desires and often dark and depraved wishes. But this man—this foolish man who'd freed her without a thought for himself, who was terrified for the family he loved—this man made her feel safe.

And that scared the hell out of her.

She let him go and stepped away. "I'm going to make some more food."

"I think we're good," Jake said dryly, glancing in at the table, heaped with all the food she'd conjured up an hour ago. "You're a great cook, by the way."

She laughed. "I tried cooking, once. I don't see the point of it. Why go to all the trouble when magic is so much easier? I don't wash dishes, either."

Rose suddenly cried out, loudly enough that they both stiffened.

"Is she in trouble? Do I need to get help?" Jake smashed his fist against the railing. "I feel so damned helpless."

"She knows I can get her to the hospital in the space of a thought," Donya said soothingly. "She wants to do this naturally. She's a garden witch, Jake. You know that. She would hate to be stuck in an antiseptic hospital."

He took a deep breath. "I know. I know. Talk to me. Distract me."

Donya closed her eyes and wished herself into a sweater and a pair of jeans. The late afternoon lake air was getting chilly. "Shall I tell you about the wishes?"

A flicker of interest crossed his face and, for the first time in hours, he quit pacing. "Yes. Tell me about how and why I got a second chance, when that's against the rules."

She pulled her legs up and hugged her knees, thinking of the best way to tell it. A story shaped over millennia wasn't easy to share.

"It wasn't about you," she finally admitted, because beginning at the beginning was impossible. "It was about Alejandro."

"What?" He pulled his chair around to face hers, and dropped into it. Stared at her with those lovely golden eyes. "What are you talking about?"

"He had the lamp. I'm not sure where he got it, but he was showing it to Rose last night, and he rubbed it in jest, and thus summoned me." She shrugged. "The same way it always happens. Do you remember the fake 'genie lamp' you won that night in Vegas?"

The astonishment on his face amused her, but it also reassured her that he hadn't somehow been part of a scheme to seek more wishes, or to subvert her magic to his own purposes. Although, he'd proven that wasn't the case, hadn't he?

He'd set her free.

Goosebumps shivered up her arms. *Free*. Why was she still here? She had the whole world to roam, and she never, ever had to answer to anyone ever again. Why in the name of all the gods and goddesses was she still here, in this awful little cabin?

Jake took her hand, and the shock of connection answered her question. There was something here, something she wanted. Maybe, just maybe, something she needed.

"But if Alejandro rubbed the lamp, why did you come to me?"

She looked at their joined hands and wondered why it was suddenly hard to breathe. "The magic wouldn't work for him; he has perfect PH balance."

Jake's eyes widened. "His alkaline/acidity levels are balanced? What does that have to do with anything?"

She laughed and took a deep breath of fresh lake air. "No. He is Perfectly Happy. He has no need for wishes; the magic doesn't work on him."

Rose's voice suddenly rang out through the open window to the bedroom. "If I wanted you to remind me how to breathe, I'd *ask* you. Go shoot some vampires or something."

Alejandro's quiet response, reassuring and soothing, must have worked, because Rose let him stay in the room. Jake and Donya locked gazes, and then both of them had to fight back the laughter.

"Anyway," he finally said, when the danger of a stressed-out garden witch hearing them laugh while she was in labor had passed. "That doesn't seem fair. Happy people deserve wishes, too, right?"

Donya's smile faded. "But they don't deserve the dark twists of Djinn magic. Have you never heard the expression 'no good wish goes unpunished'?"

"Deed."

"What?" He was still holding her hand, and it confused her thinking.

She ... liked it.

"We say, no good *deed* goes unpunished. For you, it's wish?"

Because she liked it so well, she forced herself to pull her hand away from his, and then she stood and walked over to the railing. "For me, it was always about the wish. If a man wished to be surrounded by gold, the magic took him literally and encased his body in molten metal, so he died screaming. If a woman wished to be beloved of all, love turned to obsession and her lovers killed her from jealousy. Alejandro is perfectly happy with his Rose, so he deserved none of that."

Jake walked up behind her and put his hands on the railing on either side of her, surrounding her with his strong arms and the tantalizing scent of his body. "But I deserved it? Twice, even?"

She shuddered at the thought of the magic backlash harming him. "No. Which is why you came to no harm. You weren't selfish, greedy, or destructive. You were funny, and kind, and you didn't try to manipulate or capture me."

"And this time?"

"This time the magic bounced to you, as the nearest person to it who wasn't perfectly happy," she said quietly, daring to lean back and rest her head against the hardness of his chest. "But you weren't greedy this time, either. This time, you set me free."

He rested his cheek on her head and wrapped his strong arms around her. "It was the right thing to do. You should never be anything but free; wild creature that you are."

She turned in his embrace and looked into his golden eyes, feeling her heartbeat speed up and then settle into a matching rhythm with his. "And now I always will be, Jake Cardinal."

"May I have a wish after all?" His voice was husky; silken smooth and whiskey rough all at once.

"Name it first," she whispered.

"I wish you would kiss me."

She raised her hands to touch the sides of his face. "Oh, Jake. This wish I gladly grant."

She kissed him, first gently and then with a hint of the longing he'd ignited in her. She kissed him, and he pulled her into a breath-stealing embrace.

He kissed her back, and she caught fire.

Their magic exploded between them and sang out in a symphony of desire and heat and passion. She couldn't breathe, couldn't think, couldn't resist him.

Never wanted to resist him.

When they finally had to break apart, just long enough to breathe, she found herself clutching his shoulders so she wouldn't fall. Her legs were trembling.

Her entire body was trembling.

Jake inhaled a deep breath, and then a fierce smile of purely masculine joy lit up his face. "How many wishes did you say I could have? Because I'd like to request that same thing, over and over and over."

She wanted the same thing, she tried to tell him, but she couldn't force the words past the tightness in her throat. She wanted to kiss him, forever. Didn't she? She *did*.

Except …

She'd never been free. Could she—would she—truly give that up to the first man who'd kissed her as a free woman?

"Jake, I—"

The indignant wail of a newborn babe interrupted her. Jake shouted out a wordless cry of happiness and relief, lifted her into his arms, and twirled her around.

"Rose's daughter is born, and she's healthy," Donya told him, smiling.

"It's a baby! I mean, a daughter? A girl? We have to go see her," Jake said, and his joy was so bright she almost needed to shield her eyes.

He grabbed her hand. "Let's go see her. Them. And then we can talk and wish and anything else we want to do, for as long as we want to do it."

"You go ahead," she told him. "I'm right behind you."

And then she smiled like her heart wasn't cracking in two.

He took a step, then whirled around and kissed her again. "Hurry!"

Donya laughed. "I'm coming, I'm coming. Get in there already."

When Jake turned around, she was gone.

Chapter Five

Exactly one year later ...

JAKE TOUCHED A FINGER to the edge of the lamp that his cousin had given him the year before at the lake, when all of their lives had changed. Rose and Alejandro had a beautiful baby girl, and the entire family had gotten together today for Bryony's first birthday.

He shuddered. Nobody had needed to see Granny making out with the guy she'd met at Senior Yoga, though. There wasn't enough eyeball bleach in the world for that.

He opened a beer, the strongest thing he drank these days, and tried not to think about how his life had changed that day. The day he'd fallen in love with a Djinn.

The day she'd left him.

His family was trying—hard—to set him up with a nice witch. They'd even brought a pretty and smart woman who taught at the local Magic Munchkins preschool to the party. She'd been sweet and kind and funny.

But she hadn't been Donya.

A cool wind swept through his house, and he knew the windows weren't open.

"I see you kept my lamp," she said, and he forgot how to breathe, all over again.

He turned around, slowly. Just in case he was dreaming; he didn't want to move too fast and wake himself up.

But she was there. Wearing a red dress and a hopeful expression.

"Hello, Donya. Was freedom everything you'd hoped for?" He could hear his voice trembling, and so could she, because she started toward him before he got all the words out.

"It was glorious and wonderful. I had many amazing adventures, and I saw the world on my own terms," she said, her smile tentative but growing as she walked into his open arms.

He almost didn't dare to hope, but he asked, anyway, because she was here, and because he could do nothing else. "Are you here to grant my wish?"

She tilted her face up to look into his eyes. "Actually, Jake, I'm hoping you'll grant mine."

"All of your wishes," he said, already kissing her. "Always."

So the wizard fell in love with the Djinn, and they lived happily and magically ever after. But their families? That was, as they say, a whole 'nuther story ...

Alyssa Day is the *New York Times* and *USA Today* bestselling author of more than thirty-four books, including the Warriors of Poseidon and Cardinal Witches paranormal romance series and the Tiger's Eye Mysteries paranormal mystery series. Her many awards include Romance Writers of America's prestigious RITA award for outstanding romance fiction, and the RT Reviewer's Choice Award for Best Paranormal Romance novel of 2012. Her books have been translated into a zillion languages, but she's still holding out for Klingon.

You can find her at http://alyssaday.com or on Facebook and Twitter talking about her future pug ranch.

ABOUT RWA

ROMANCE WRITERS OF AMERICA®:
The Voice of Romance Writers

ROMANCE WRITERS OF AMERICA® (RWA) is a nonprofit association whose mission is to advance the professional interests of career-focused romance writers through networking and advocacy. Founded in 1980, RWA has grown to one of the largest writers associations in the world. RWA represents more than 10,000 members who live in more than 30 countries. RWA provides programs and services to support the efforts of its members to earn a living from their writing endeavors.

If you are interested in becoming a part of this diverse and growing community, visit www.rwa.org for more information.

Like RWA on Facebook:
www.facebook.com/romancewriters

Follow RWA on Twitter:
@romancewriters

Made in the USA
San Bernardino, CA
23 March 2018